Mafia Sinner

The Mancinelli Brotherhood

Sabine Barclay

0 9 8 7 6 5 4 3 2 1

Published by Oliver Heber Books

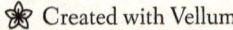 Created with Vellum

Salvation doesn't always come from above.
Happy reading,
Sabine

Subscribe to Sabine's Newsletter

Subscribe to Sabine's bimonthly newsletter to receive exclusive insider perks.

Have you read *The Syndicate Wars*? This FREE origin story novella is available to all new subscribers to Sabine's monthly newsletter.

The Mancinelli Brotherhood

Mafia Heir

Mafia Sinner

Mafia Beauty (6.27.23)

Mafia Angel (8.22.23)

Mafia Redeemer (10.17.23)

Mafia Star (12.12.23)

Do you also enjoy steamy Historical Romance? Discover Sabine's books written as Celeste Barclay.

Chapter One

Carmine

"This place is supposed to be amazing. Like award-winning amazing. I can't wait to try the lemon cupcakes. And I hear they have the most incredible Italian wedding cookies."

The type that is dipped in a creamy glaze with sprinkles. I shake my head.

"Don't let Auntie Carlotta hear you say that. She'll never forgive you. Then again, say it loudly. I'll take your share."

My cousin Maria rolls her eyes and elbows me in the ribs as I hold the door open for her and her best friend, Veronica. We've just arrived at a specialty bakery near Maria's place in Manhattan. Froofy is how I would describe it. It looks like a Hallmark movie vomited in here. But who am I to turn down a cupcake? I've already spent my requisite two hours at the gym this morning, so the calories don't count, right? I almost roll my eyes to match Maria. I think that's one of the most asinine jokes I've ever heard.

As my gaze sweeps the place for any threats to Maria, and I

suppose Veronica too, I spy the most delectable ass bent over to unpack a box. The things I would do while tapping that ass. Fuck. I haven't had this visceral a reaction since I was like sixteen. But I can't help it. I almost need to adjust myself. I turn my attention to a window display.

"Good morning. Welcome to *Morso Migliore*." Best Bite.

She's Italian. Like from Italy. I can tell from her accent. I shift my focus to her and stop dead. My hand self-consciously moves to the slight bump on the bridge of my nose. I glance down at Maria and catch her wicked grin. Fucking hell. She knew. She did this on purpose.

I look back at Serafina Carosi and have an even stronger reaction to the front of her than the back. Curvaceous. Voluptuous. Rubenesque. Fucking hot as holy fucking hell on the fucking hottest day in August. And her expression tells me she still thinks she's looking at shit on her shoe when she focuses on me. My heart's racing now that the initial shock's worn off.

"*Ciao, Maria. È passato molto tempo.*" Hello, Maria. It's been a long time.

Her greeting is sincere when she smiles at my cousin. Then she looks at me, then my best friend, and back to me. Her lip practically curls when she recognizes Gabriele. From how he moves to stand farther down the counter, as though he's looking at the pastries, I can tell he feels the Arctic wind too.

"Carmine, Gabriele."

"*Salve, Serafina.*" Hello, Serafina.

My greeting hangs in the air as I approach the counter. A magnet draws me to her when it should repel me. It's because we're such opposites. My north pole—my tongue—would love to meet her south pole—her pussy. I nearly shake my head to clear my mind of my ridiculously inappropriate daydream.

I'm close enough to see her translucent gray eyes with the green flecks take on a wary hardness. Her hair is much shorter than it was ten years ago. But it's still the same rich honey brown that it was then and when we were twelve. She was adorable as a kid. She was hot when she was in her late teens. And she's fucking gorgeous now that we're twenty-eight. I find my tongue again since it's not where I want to put it.

"*È passato molto tempo.*" It's been a long time.

"*Sì. Solo un decennio.*" Yes. Only a decade.

She says that as though it hasn't been nearly long enough.

Veronica—God, how I dislike the woman, but Maria adores her—brushes against me as she comes to stand beside me. Oh, hell no. One fucking drunken hook-up when we were eighteen, and she still thinks she can lay claim to me when she senses any competition. Ten years ago. The same time I last saw Serafina. It was at Uncle Salvatore and Aunt Sylvia's wedding. It was also the night Uncle Salvatore, the Mafia don of New York City, and her father, Piero Carosi, the *Mala del Brenta* of Venice don, announced my betrothal to Serafina. It shocked the shit out of both of us. We knew there'd been talk since we were children, but we had no idea both grandfathers signed documents.

Vicenzu—of course it would fucking mean victorious because the man refused to be anything else—Mancinelli arranged the marriage with Serafina's maternal grandfather, Fantino Catalano. They were both dons of their respective *Cosa Nostra* branches. My grandfather ruled New York with two iron fists. Fantino wasn't any better in Sicily. Our marriage was supposed to be the next generation's connection to the old country. Uncle Salvatore married Aunt Sylvia as the tie between the current leaders' generation. Those old men have come back from the dead to keep a tight clutch on everyone in their respective families. Fuck my life.

"Mmm. Which one are you getting, Carmine?"

Veronica's attempt at purring pulls me back to the present.

She sounds like a magpie being murdered when she speaks normally, but she sounds like the poor little rich girl she is when she attempts to sound seductive. Retch.

"Do you still like red velvet the best?"

Serafina cocks her head to the side and smiles serenely. Fuck my life again. She doesn't want me, but she doesn't want Veronica throwing in her face something that doesn't exist.

"Yes, please."

"Aren't you going to ask what I want, Carmine?"

"No."

Let me be very clear to everyone that Veronica and I are *not* a "thing." I step away and go back to the window display I looked at when we arrived. I take in the perfectly planned aesthetic, and I can appreciate the wisdom of the arrangement. They definitely did it to entice impulse shoppers. I'd have one of everything if I could.

I glance back, and Maria, Veronica, and Serafina are chatting. My gaze meets Serafina's before she looks back at Veronica. Maria laughs at something, and Veronica's voice carries to me. Of course, it does. She has no concept of inside voices. She's a veritable foghorn when she's drunk. God, I dislike her.

"Carmine just came back from Sicily a couple months ago. He spent four months in the beautiful Mediterranean, escaping the humidity here. I would have loved such a long getaway. I was only there for three weeks."

I grit my teeth. It was no vacation. It was forced hard labor. Punishment.

The woman doesn't know when to stop.

"I didn't know you were there, Veronica. I was too busy working on the vineyard."

That makes Serafina's eyebrows shoot up. Is it my dismissive tone or the fact that she believes I don't work? Most people don't. Before my exile to Sicily for four months, I had the shit lackey jobs for Uncle Salvatore. But now that I'm back in his good graces—mostly—I've assumed my rightful position as a *capo*.

Serafina assesses me before she turns away and moves to the dessert case that has the cupcakes. She pulls out two lemon ones: one for Maria and one for Gabriele. She gets a boring yellow cake one for Veronica. She hands them out, leaving me waiting. Finally, she pulls out a red velvet for me. Maria and Veronica are sitting at a little table, and Gabriele's back to guarding the door. I wander over and take the dessert from Serafina.

Fina.

I always thought that was a more unique nickname than Sera. But her friends and family call her Sera. I wonder how she would react if I called her Fina.

"*Grazie.*" Thank you.

"*Prego.*" You're welcome. She hesitates, then looks past me at my cousin and her friend before we continue in Italian. "My guess is Maria, or her friend, suggested this place."

"Maria. She heard you'd won awards, so she wanted to check it out." I take a bite and relish every moment. Holy crap. "This is amazing."

She grins.

"Hence the name." It really is the best bite. Except, I almost choke on the second one when Fina speaks again. "It's nice to see the two of you are still a couple after all these years. Are you married?"

I look down at the cupcake. One bite is all I got before my appetite went to shit.

"Serafina, we are not married. I'm not married. She and I were never a couple. One regrettable night when we were all still teenagers. I had no clue what was going to happen when she and I came back into the ballroom. You wouldn't let me apologize, but I never, ever meant to humiliate you. I never would have left with her—with any woman—if I'd known Uncle Salvatore and your dad were going to make that announcement. I know everyone knew what I'd just done. I'm so sorry."

Before four months ago, I'm uncertain if I would have said any of that. I would have felt it all, but I was too much of a smug bastard to admit my faults, let alone apologize for them in public. I didn't even do private apologies well. But I turned over a new leaf in Sicily.

"Thank you."

"That was long overdue. I didn't know you were in New York."

Her brow furrows. "I figured—" She shrugs.

"What did you figure?"

"That you knew and avoided me."

"I didn't."

"I saw you do it, Carmine."

"When?"

"At Lorenzo's club about three years ago. You had two women on your arm, and one sitting on your lap."

Could this get any worse? I shouldn't ask that. It only tempts fate.

"I never saw you at Lorenzo's club or any other. I wouldn't have snubbed you."

I would have run for the hills.

"You looked right at me, then turned away and kissed the woman to your left."

"Fina, I honestly never saw you."

Except I probably would have done what I did, anyway. Her nostrils flare, and I realize what I called her. I take a steadying breath, waiting for her to correct me. But she remains silent. The longer she just looks at me, the more impatient I grow to escape. The longer I remain silent, the more disdainful her gaze grows. Then resentment bubbles up from the bowels of my belly. She's looking down on me for my playboy ways, but I bet she had a boyfriend since that fucktastrophe of a night.

"Have you been in the States long?"

She nearly flinches. Guilt.

"Nine years."

"Did you come here for college?"

She hesitates.

"Yes."

A half-truth. My life depends upon me detecting lies, white lies, and every other form of untruth. I read people and adjust my attitude accordingly. Part of it is because I was a manipulative child and adult. Part of it is because it's kept anyone from killing me.

"What else brought you here?" I'll keep prodding until I'm satisfied.

"A guy."

I cock an eyebrow. Me?

"But we broke up three years ago."

"You were together for six years? Were you married?"

"No. That was why we broke up. I wouldn't say yes."

Her eyes bore into me, and I feel completely exposed. Did she refuse because she thought she was going to marry me? Fucking-a. She broke up with the guy three years ago. That's when she saw me man-whoring. I was nowhere near as promiscuous as I led people to believe, but neither did I become a monk.

I want—need—to know more.

"Are you married now?"

"No. Have you been?"

"No."

Her lips twitch in a smirk. Apparently, that doesn't surprise her now that she knows Veronica and I aren't together. I look down at my half-eaten cupcake. I'm not letting this go to waste. I take another bite, and I'm back in Heaven.

"Would you like to take some for the others?"

The others. That would be my cousins Luca, Marco, and Lorenzo. They're Maria's older brothers. And Matteo, Marco's best friend and their honorary brother.

"I'm certain they would appreciate it. Could I have a fifth, please? Luca's married."

"He is?"

"You didn't know?"

"My invitation must have gotten lost in the mail."

"I thought you declined. Fina, I saw the final invite list. You and your parents were on there. They attended."

It was a big deal. I know Luca and Olivia would have rather eloped than dealt with the fanfare that wasn't really for them but for show. As the underboss, our Uncle Salvatore's heir, people expected a celebration. It was a show of wealth and power. A reminder to the city's elite that we are as strong as we've ever been. A chance to rub it in the face of the other syndicates.

"I didn't know."

"Would you have attended?"

For some reason, her answer is important to me. Too important. Would she have avoided me intentionally by not attending? Or would she have snubbed me the way she believed I had her?

"When was it?"

"Early March."

Her eyes widen. It's the end of March now, so they're still very much in their honeymoon bubble, having just gotten back from their Caribbean vacation.

"My parents asked me to visit my grandmother in Venice. She's nearly ninety and likely to outlive us all. But they said she wasn't doing well, so I wanted to be sure I saw her one last time. The woman walks two miles each way to the market every day of the week. They didn't want me there."

Were they trying to avoid a scene? Were they trying to keep us out of the same room as a priest? Once our grandfathers died, my uncle and her father "forgot" about the agreement, but as far as I know, no one dissolved the arrangement. The connection through his wife, my aunt Sylvia, satisfied Uncle Salvatore. She's Serafina's aunt by blood and mine by marriage. Maybe I can wave the white flag.

"It would have been nice to see you there. Maybe you'll save me a dance at the next event."

She's done packaging the cupcakes and hands me the box. She responds with a jerky nod before she forces a smile. Our couple of moments of headway don't last nearly as long as the minutes of awkwardness. Blessedly, Maria comes back over.

"Serafina, I'm going to bring my sister. She's going to love this place."

I wonder if I can be either of my cousins' bodyguards that day. No woman in my family goes anywhere without a member of our immediate family as one of her security detail. Our family is too infamous and recognizable. We trust other men to guard us and our properties, but we only trust each other to protect our daughters, mothers, sisters, wives, and female cousins.

"Sister?"

Maria smiles at Fina's confusion. "Yeah. Luca got married. I don't know how she puts up with him, but they adore each other. Soulmates for sure."

I watch Fina, and her eyes dart to mine. Does she believe in soulmates? I didn't ask if she was dating anyone. Has she found hers? I definitely haven't found mine. I haven't been on a date or hooked up with a woman since before Sicily. It's not been a dry spell. I've had offers. Hell, Veronica would strip here if I told her I'd fuck her. It just hasn't interested me. I haven't been to my BDSM club either. My left hand works as well as my right when the mood strikes.

"It was nice seeing you all again. I look forward to meeting your sister."

Maria turns the same mischievous smile on Gabriele and me as she's had since birth.

"Give me the box, Carmine. I don't trust you and Gabriele not to devour these before we get to Uncle Sal's. You'll hide the box and say you left them here."

Gabriele looks duly insulted as he crosses his arms. He's the biggest of us all, and his muscles flex under his suit. Most women have to wipe the drool from their mouths, but Fina looks disinterested. She's still watching me as Gabriele responds.

"We will not."

"Gabe, that's what you did the last time Auntie Carlotta baked cookies. The rest of us only knew you and Carmine ate them all because Matteo mentioned them."

Gabriele and I shrug at the same time. We've been best friends since we were ten. Inseparable most of the time. Our mannerisms are so attuned that people frequently ask if we're fraternal twins. We're not. We're distant cousins several times removed. Gabriele flashes the ladies a smile.

"I'm still a growing boy."

Maria snorts. "Yeah, out not up. Auntie Paola's been feeding you way too much."

My mom is like Gabriele's surrogate mom now that his parents have moved back to Palermo. Auntie Carlotta isn't really anyone's aunt, but she's Maria's mother's best friend.

She's also Matteo's mom. She and her husband, Domenico, have been in our lives since our conceptions, so it was natural as children to call them auntie and uncle. Nothing's changed. My mom is Maria's dad's younger sister. Our uncle Salvatore is their older brother. Our family tree has more branches than a Christmas tree.

"It was nice seeing you again, Maria. Veronica." Definitely not as friendly toward Veronica as she is to Maria. Serafina waves and smiles at Gabriele. "Goodbye, Carmine."

It sounds so final.

"Goodbye, Fina."

I look back when we get to the door, but she's already back to unpacking the box she abandoned earlier. And I'm back to lusting after the most glorious, upturned ass I've ever seen. Will it be my left hand or my right hand tonight?

Chapter Two

Fina

I shouldn't care that Carmine Mancinelli just left my store. But I do. Holy fucking hell on the fucking hottest day in August. He's even hotter than he was when we were eighteen. He still had a boyish charm to him back then. Now he's all man. All six-foot-something of him. He has muscles upon muscles. I couldn't see any under his suit, but you can just tell. He looks like he could be a pro athlete, maybe a bodybuilder. He was hot when I spotted him at Lorenzo's club a few years ago. But he was sitting, and I was too embarrassed to look back again.

His apology surprised me today. I didn't know he knew the words I'm sorry. He didn't when we were twelve, and he pushed me under a wave that spun me like a rag in a washing machine. I scraped my arms and knees on the sand as I fought to right myself and find the surface. I can see the slight crookedness of his nose from when I punched him and broke it.

He'd come to Sicily with Gabriele and spent the summer with his best friend's family. They're close friends with my mom's family, who we were visiting. He'd seemed nice until he teased me about being the runt since I was so short back then. Gabriele warned him it wasn't a good idea to taunt me. I had a reputation for a temper as fiery as an eighty-year-old Sicilian woman. I've tamed it over the years.

But it threatened to come out at *Zio* Salvatore and *Zia* Sylvia's wedding when he walked back into the ballroom, adjusting his bow tie and tux jacket. Veronica was smoothing back her hair and still needed to fix her gown's neckline. They returned just as *Zio* Salvatore was calling out to him to join us and my dad on the stage. I have never been so mortified in my life. Once my temper calmed, I cried the entire flight back to Venice.

Then I saw him at the nightclub with those women. I'd heard about his reputation plenty of times. I'd seen him in some tabloids and gossip rags that called him a playboy. I thought of him as a gigolo. It's not like I've pined for him or curbed my dating life because of a deal no one's discussed in ten years. But it was just a reminder that he would never settle down with one woman, never commit to being a proper husband. He was all the things I'd read about him.

But the Carmine who walked into my store is completely different. He seemed—humble. Even reserved. He was still wearing a designer, custom-tailored suit, but he didn't appear flashy. None of the pictures ever showed him looking like a *guido*, but he likes nice things, and he doesn't mind showing them off. Most often, those nice things are women built like Barbies on his arms.

"Sera?"

"*Si.*"

My assistant manager, Rosella, is working beside me. Since she speaks Italian fluently, we continue in it.

"Who was that?"

"Some people I knew from childhood. I haven't seen them in years."

"Those guys were gorgeous. Like hotter than any model."

That describes all the men in the Mancinelli family. Gabriele is a Scotto, but he may as well be a Mancinelli. He's like an extra nephew or cousin. Rosella continues to stare at the door. I knew she could see them from the kitchen, but she was up to her elbows in batter. I'm glad for that. She's sweet as can be and nosey as fuck.

"Do you think either of them is single?"

I don't know, but I've seen Gabriele in the same photos as Carmine. He's as notorious as his best friend and my supposed betrothed. Take me back to the Middle Ages. Betrothed. I loved my *nonno*, but most of his ideas on family were prehistoric. Carmine's grandfather wasn't much better. I wonder how Carmine's parents are. Paola got pregnant at nineteen, and her father forced her to marry Carmine's father, Cesare Ciccone. He was a nice enough guy the few times I've met him, and Paola is hilarious. But no couple has ever been more poorly matched.

That's why it shocked everyone when *Zio* Salvatore and my dad made the announcement. It nearly knocked me over when I found out our grandfathers made the agreement that summer I broke Carmine's nose. Nobody bothered to mention it to either of us for six years. I'd sensed Carmine's resentment toward his cousins during the wedding ceremony, and he avoided them at the reception. But the moment we stepped off that dais, bitterness poured off him like a waterfall after the spring thaw. I kept my distance. He sulked the rest of the night. In all fairness, so did I.

"I heard that guy's name was Carmine. Is that the same one you're—"

"Yes, but it's never going to happen. If our families intended to enforce that, it would have happened years ago."

"Then you wouldn't mind if I talked to him if he comes back?"

I don't like that idea at all. Why do I mind? Fuck if I know.

How did I get myself roped into this?

I don't want to attend an Easter dinner party. Who even has one of those? Brunch. That's what you do for Easter. You sit through a bells and smells Mass—which I don't mind; when I do church, I like to do church, which means incense and the whole nine yards—then you go out to brunch with your family. Or if you really want to be old-school Italian, you go to your *nonna's* house for brunch. But I don't have a *nonno* or *nonna* in New York. I don't have any of them. My grandmother in Venice passed away a week after Carmine came into my shop, so I went back to Venice less than a month after my last visit.

It's been nearly a month since he ordered his red velvet cupcake—or rather I gave it to him because I remembered they're his favorite. I don't know why or how I did. I've thought of him way too many times since that day.

"Are you ready, Sera?"

Gio is my guard tonight. I nod before he opens the front door. I hang back, as is protocol. He scans the surrounding area, then he escorts me to the town car. The privacy glass is up, so I don't see him slide into the front passenger seat. David is driving and will be my other guard. A tiny part of me wished that moving to the U.S. would free me from having two shadows everywhere I go, but the rest of me knew it was a useless dream. I pull out my phone and tap my sister's contact.

ME

How many people are supposed to be at this thing?

JULIANA

No clue. I hope it doesn't run that late. I'm exhausted. I wore new shoes today. Big mistake.

My sister works on the New York Stock Exchange floor. She's one of those people you see on TV waving papers over her head and calling out bids and prices. She loves it. The noise gives me an instant headache. I always wait for her outside if I meet her for lunch.

Do you know who's going to be there?

The Mancinellis and everyone else. Who do you expect?

The Mancinellis are a given but I thought maybe Mama or Papa told you about anyone else.

It's the Mancinellis who are hosting this shindig at the Waldorf. Supposedly, we're celebrating Jesus's resurrection. Maybe we are, but mostly, we'll be celebrating how rich they are. Apparently, New York needs a monthly reminder since it's been six weeks since Luca and Olivia's wedding reception that I didn't attend.

Do you think HE'S going to be there?

I assume so. He's a Mancinelli and the don's nephew.

Carmine. Dark haired, dark blue-eyed Roman god. I

17

haven't been able to stop thinking about how good he looked that day. I can still smell his cologne as though he were standing right in front of me again. My thoughts have vacillated from resentment to annoyance to baying at the moon lust. I'm not dating anyone, and I haven't been to the BDSM club I belong to recently because I'm opening a second location in Harlem.

I've been too exhausted to think about finding someone to scene with, and I'm not interested in dating. I don't do randos at the club. There are four guys I've known since I joined when I became single. If none of them are available, then I'm a voyeur and get myself off. I'm certain my list of partners is nowhere near as long as Carmine's. There's that resentment again.

I sigh as I close my eyes. I'd rather crawl into bed with my rabbit than make nice with people I don't know well. At least my vibrator guarantees the night will have a happy ending. If I'm awake enough when I get home...

My phone vibrates, and I look down to see it's a message from Maria. She and her new sister-in-law, Olivia, came by the shop today. I suspect Maria knew I own the bakery, and that's why she brought Carmine the last time. Today, it was Matteo and Marco. Luca was at some meeting. The guys talked to my security detail while she and I exchanged numbers.

MARIA

You're coming tonight right? Aunt Sylvia just told me you were.

ME

Yeah. I'm on my way. I'm meeting my parents sister and brother in law.

I don't think I'm anywhere near as close to my brother-in-law as Olivia is with her in-laws. Ernesto is all right, but he's boring as fuck. He is every stereotype of an accountant. But he loves my sister more than anything, and she returns those sentiments. That's all that matters to me.

> Find me when you get here. I just arrived. I'm flying solo tonight since Roni isn't welcome at these events anymore and there's no one else I can bring.

Roni? Oh, Veronica. What did she do to get herself blackballed? Fuck a Mancinelli minutes before his practically-an-engagement-announcement is made? Seeing her again shouldn't annoy me so much, but it brings back all the humiliation from that night. Back then, it tempted me to find his friend Gianni who'd flirted with me earlier that night. I considered a revenge fuck. I would have made sure Carmine knew his friend banged me, too. But Juliana guessed what I planned and glued herself to me.

> That's a shame.

> It's not like it's easy for us to bring dates to these things. Well me at least. Do you have a boyfriend or husband? I never thought to ask but I didn't see any rings.

Even if I had rings, I wouldn't wear them to work. Hands in batter and dough all day aren't conducive to hand jewelry.

> Single as the day is long. Too busy with work.

> I get that. And it's not like we have easy families to explain.

I found out today that Maria's a radiology resident. Olivia just became the main marketing rep for Luca's various car rental businesses and gas stations. That last bit shocked me. I would assume the gas stations launder money, so I didn't think Luca would have her work anywhere near them. Then again, she knows what the family she married into is. Maybe it's smart to have her make them look legit.

> No it isn't. The only men we can bring are men I'm not interested in.

There's a long—long—pause before she responds. I almost think she ended the conversation.

> Would you mind if I moved the seating cards so we can sit together? Otherwise I'm in a sea of testosterone. Olivia will sit next to Luca who'll sit next to Uncle Sal. If you'd rather sit next to your family, I totally get it.

> I'd like that. My parents aren't in town for long but I can visit with them this week.

> Awesome. Thanks.

> See you in a few.

I slip my phone back into my purse and close my eyes for the rest of the drive back into Manhattan. My parents waited until the last minute to tell me about this, forcing me to go home to change. I stopped by the bakery to check on a shipment that arrived after I left yesterday. I went there straight from church. If I'd known I was going to be in Manhattan for the evening, I would have saved myself time and brought a fancier change of clothes. My mom claims the invitation came after I left the church, but my family and the Mancinellis were still there. I didn't see Carmine during the service.

The privacy glass rolls down, and David cants his head to talk to me while driving.

"Ms. Carosi, the street is extra crowded today. Something's blocking traffic up ahead. We can't tell what it is. I'd feel more comfortable taking you to a side entrance."

"All right."

We pull to a stop, and Gio gets out to open my door. I spot Carmine immediately. He rushes forward and opens the hotel door before the doorman can.

"Fina, come with me."

Gio looks skeptical for a moment when I glance up at him, but I step closer to Carmine. Gio's arm drops away, and Carmine rests his hand at my lower back. I haven't touched him since we were twelve. Blessedly, it's not like we had to seal our betrothal with a kiss or anything. We didn't even have to hold hands. It shocks me how the moment his hand rests on my lower back, I calm.

"Carmine, what's happening?"

"The Colombians."

I glance back over my shoulder. "The Cartel? What are they doing?"

"We're not sure, but Lorenzo and Matteo recognized some of their men working in the street crew. Why are they doing sewer work on Easter Sunday? It's suspicious, and that makes us nervous when our entire family is here. And yours."

He tacks that on at the end. Clearly, an afterthought, but his hand presses heavier against my back. He guides me into the sectioned off ballroom, and I spot my parents.

"My mom and dad are over there. Thanks for walking me in."

"You're welcome. It was nice seeing you again."

Did I just hear something in his voice? Do I just want to, so I'm making things up? I don't know, and I don't have time to figure it out. He steps away, and Gio walks with me to where my parents are standing at a table. My mom smiles before looking down at the table.

"We don't see your place card, Sera. I know I told Sylvia you would join us."

"Perhaps she got confused with Luca's reception, since they thought I was coming to that."

I can't believe I just blurted that out. I've kept that to myself since I found out. With *Nonna* dying recently, I didn't think it was a good time to sound petulant about missing a party. But it just slipped out.

"Maria texted me on the way here. She asked me to sit with her since the only other woman her age is Olivia, and she'll be sitting at the other end of the table with Luca."

I kiss my parents on each of their cheeks, then do the same with Juliana and Ernesto. I sweep my gaze around the room. There's a long rectangular table for the Mancinellis—there's like twenty something of them—and ten circular tables for their guests. Just how many people are they having over for dinner? I look toward the doorway and almost take a step back. It's the Kutsenkos. I haven't seen the leader of the Russian bratva since *Zio* Salvatore and *Zia* Sylvia's wedding.

A moment later, my gaze darts to where Carmine now stands with his relatives. The Diazes just entered. If the Colombians are causing problems outside, then what the hell are they doing here? Enrique Diaz, the *jefe*, is aging well. His hair is salt-and-pepper, and there are laugh lines around his eyes and mouth. His dark features contrast with the two Andreyevs, who he's talking to. The Russian brothers have blonde hair and piercing blue eyes.

I notice Pablo, Enrique's nephew, walks beside his uncle. He's equivalent to Luca as Enrique's heir. Three more men walk in, and they look remarkably alike. I recognize Pablo's parents, who talk to the woman on the *pakhan's* arm. The *pakhan* is the Russian equivalent of a don. The rest of the bratva moves to the table almost across the room from the Diazes. I don't know any of them, but I remember them all from *Zio* Salvatore and *Zia* Sylvia's wedding. All of them make memorable impressions.

"I'm going to say hi to the Mancinellis. Maria is waving me over."

What I really want is to go back to Carmine and ask him if we're safe now that the Diazes arrived.

"Have fun."

Only Juliana and Ernesto look like they mean it when they speak together. My parents don't approve. I don't know why not, but I don't care right now. I make my way across the room, having to stop for the three Colombian brothers to cross my path. But they freeze and gesture for me to go ahead. I smile and nod. I make my way across the ballroom, leaving my parents scowling at my back. Gio is stationed near one door, and David is at another. When I get to the Mancinelli table, Maria greets me, then offers me a kiss on each cheek as we embrace loosely.

"Hi."

I turn and exchange the same greeting with Olivia. "Hi, ladies. It's nice to see you again."

Maria grins as she looks down her family's table. "I'm so glad you came. Otherwise, I might spend my night keeping Pia and Natalia occupied."

Maria points to two little girls who wave at us. They're *Zio* Salvatore's and *Zia* Sylvia's little girls. They're six and eight. I adore them, but once you wind them up, there's no turning them off. As the various syndicate families find their tables, Maria gives me a rundown, warning me the most about the O'Rourkes.

"Stay away from them, Serafina. They're the most

dangerous of all our enemies for the women and children. The bratva are the only ones you can absolutely trust will never harm you. They're likely to save you."

Maria looks at me, and her eyes widen. She glances over at *Zia* Sylvia then me. My mom is *Zia* Sylvia's older sister by eight years. They had a younger sister who was closer to *Zia* Sylvia's age, but a rival Mafia in Sicily killed her. She got separated from her guards and ran. She passed at least two or three families who would have understood, but they also never would have sheltered her. The men caught her, raped her, and murdered her. She was pregnant. Maria bites her bottom lip.

"I'm sorry. I didn't put that very sensitively. Honestly, I forgot how we're related."

"It's in a roundabout way. I don't know how we'd describe it, so I get it."

Carmine steps behind us, and I find myself breathing easier. I recognize that cologne again, and it fills my senses. It's not overpowering at all. It's the fact that there's only a hint that makes it intriguing. I want to brush my nose against his neck and sniff.

"Maria, don't go anywhere without one of us." Carmine looks at me, and I can tell he wants to say something. He notches up his chin and stares at me. "Don't go anywhere either unless you're with your dad or brother-in-law."

My left eye narrows. I'll have to cross half the room just to get to them. I guess, according to his rules, I'm not going anywhere. I nod and turn away. So much for him turning over a new leaf. Same insensitive and inconsiderate ass. Maria shifts to speak to Matteo.

"Fina—"

"Why do you insist upon calling me that?"

He stares dumbly for a moment, then shrugs. "I don't know. I just do."

"You've got some *huevos* to give me a nickname when you don't care what happens to me."

"If I didn't care, I wouldn't have advised you to not go anywhere alone."

"You told me not to go anywhere without my dad or brother-in-law, but I'd have to cross most of the ballroom alone to get to them. By your reasoning, I can't go anywhere. Or I'm SOL and have to take the risk."

"Fina—"

I glower at him, but he only pauses for a breath.

"You aren't part of my family. I didn't feel comfortable insisting someone from my family escort you. I thought it was too presumptuous to suggest it. I didn't mean to insult you or imply we wouldn't help. I was trying to be considerate."

"Oh."

Come on, brain. Think of something more to say. I'm drawing a blank, so I settle for a nod and a smile. I see him relax, so I suppose that's enough. I notice Matteo appears annoyed as he shakes his head. He's in the middle of saying something when Maria turns back to me, dismissing Matteo. The man looks ready to throttle his best friend's sister. She looks back over her shoulder.

"Thanks for the suggestion, Matteo. I'll take it under advisement."

The politest of fuck-offs. I look up at Carmine, and he appears baffled by the exchange. He looks at the chair I'm standing next to. It has a place card for Maria. The one to the right has Lorenzo's name on it. There's a blank one to the left. The next one down has Carmine's name. He looks past me to his cousin.

"Maria? I thought I was supposed to sit on the other side of you."

"I moved you down to make room for Serafina. I asked her to keep me company during dinner."

She reaches out and turns the place card around. It has my name on it. Did she do that on purpose? I thought I might sit across from her since I didn't see a name on it. I spotted Lorenzo's and Carmine's.

"I got distracted with Pia and Natalia when I moved this over. Sorry."

Lorenzo walks over as everyone moves to their seats. He pulls out Maria's chair, and Carmine does the same for me.

"*Grazie.*"

"*Prego. Gradisce del vino?*" Would you like some wine?

"*Sì, per favore.*" Yes, please.

He's generous with his pour. Did he ask because good manners insist he offers the woman next to him a drink? Does he not want to be stuck offering me more? He pours himself a glass that's not quite so full. Does he think I'm a lush?

"I don't care for this one that much, but Lorenzo and Maria love it. Savor what you have before they each polish off a bottle. You might not get another glass without losing a finger or two."

He switches back to English, and I miss the Italian. That makes me wonder why he spoke it just now and at the bakery.

"Why don't you and your family speak Sicilian?"

"We do frequently, but not every single person in our family grew up speaking it, and many of the men we have grew up with Italian living in New York, even though their families are originally Sicilian. Italian makes it easier for everyone."

"That makes sense. I don't use my Sicilian much anymore, so it's pretty weak. I appreciate everyone speaking Italian."

"Can you follow along if other people are speaking Sicilian?"

"Yes. I just don't have the same vocabulary as I did as a kid."

Sicilian has words that come from Arabic, French, Catalan, Spanish, and Greek. It's a reflection of its location and role in history. I wish I still spoke it as fluently as I did when I was a kid, but I grew up in Venice. I only spent my summers and some holidays in Sicily. My family there also spoke Italian, so I didn't even use it much then. Carmine offers me an understanding smile before he explains.

"I get stuck sometimes too, and I speak it pretty regularly with my dad's side of the family. Fortunately, now that—"

He cuts himself off and looks away. He takes a sip of wine and thanks the waiter as the first course arrives. Once we both have our food, I press him.

"Fortunately, what?"

"It wasn't a kind thought. Never mind."

"Now I'm completely curious."

He looks at me before glancing down the table. His parents are sitting across from Massimo and Nicoletta, Maria's parents.

"Fortunately, now that my *nonno* is dead, no one gives me shit for not speaking Sicilian as well as I do Italian."

He keeps his voice quiet, so it doesn't carry. But the resentment oozes from every word. I'm not sure which grandfather he's referring to.

"Vicenzu?"

"He didn't care if I spoke at all. No, I meant my other grandfather. My father's father."

Nothing about his tone makes me think he wants to talk about this. I take the hint. But I don't know what else to say. Luckily, he holds up his end of the conversation.

"You said you came here in part for college. Where did you go to school?"

"Princeton."

I know that shocks him. I wonder if he thinks I dropped out

or something. I bet he expected me to name some no-name culinary school.

"Did you study business or some kind of chemistry?"

"Chemistry?"

"Isn't that what baking is? Mixing ingredients to make physical and chemical changes?"

"Well, yes. But no. I didn't study Chemistry. I studied business. How about you?"

"Stanford for structural engineering."

I didn't expect that. Nothing about the boy I knew or the young man I had to stand beside screamed that level of intelligence.

"No, my parents nor Uncle Sal did not buy my way in."

"I never asked if they did."

"You were thinking it, Fina. It was clear as day. You're shocked I could be that smart."

Fuck. Why does he have to read my mind?

"No. Studious. I didn't take you for being studious. I didn't doubt your intelligence."

As I think about it, I realize I haven't given him much fair consideration. We were kids on vacation when we met the first time. I thought he was mean. When we saw each other at the wedding reception, I thought he was a royal *stronzo*—asshole. It was easy to label him as an idiot in my head, but I don't really know much about him. He doesn't strike me as dumb now. Just the opposite.

"What made you go all the way across the country?"

He takes another sip of wine, and now he appears completely shut off. He doesn't look at me as he cuts a bite of salad.

"It was a good place to go where no one knew me."

What does that mean? It sounds like more than just no one knowing he's a Mafia don's nephew. But I don't have time to press because the next course arrives. Carmine's leg bumps mine, so I pull away. His arm nudges mine. I don't think I'm in his personal space, but he's also a lot broader than me. When I move again, his leg presses against me. His hand drops beneath the table to rest on my knee for only a moment, then it's gone. What does this mean? I thought he wasn't interested since he's been talking to Gabriele for most of this course. I keep my focus on getting the food in my mouth and not missing my aim, since I'm taken aback.

"Fina, you didn't have much of the antipasti. Do you not like the gnocchi either?"

If he wasn't looking at me, how did he notice what I did or didn't eat?

"I didn't dislike the antipasti. I just don't eat meals this big anymore. I'm saving room for each course. I heard Lorenzo say that this is a full seven courses. I'll never make it through to *dolce* if I eat everything placed in front of me. Not all of us still have the metabolism of a nineteen-year-old."

I tilt my head and look at him sideways. His expression confuses me. There's a hunger in his eyes that I'm unprepared for. His gaze sweeps over me before he leans to whisper in my ear.

"The last time I saw you was when we were eighteen. Neither of us looks the same, but you're more beautiful than when we were teenagers."

I've always been hourglass shaped, but I've filled out since before college. I usually feel like my best days are behind me. Not because I'm old or aging badly, but I'm not as slender. I work out, eat well, and don't have more than a sample of my work. I've just settled into what I think my body was always going to become. I look like my dad's side of my family, not my mom's. I'm not runway ready like *Zia* Sylvia and Mama.

"Thank you."

I expect him to sit up, but he doesn't. He continues to whisper to me, and I get nervous that we'll draw people's attention. I look to my family's table, and they're all watching us.

"Maybe you'll just have to work up an appetite before our next meal."

Next? It's been years since we've seen each other, and we're indirectly related. Now he thinks we'll be having family dinners?

"I didn't know you had these large gatherings often."

"We don't, and it's ridiculous to do it on Easter. But it was a great excuse, I suppose."

Now I'm confused. I turn to look at him directly.

"Fina, I meant dinner with me."

"With you? I must have missed the invitation."

His heated gaze sweeps over me again. "I would make it a standing one."

"Why?"

Despite facing each other, he leans toward me again, and this is the quietest he's spoken so far. "Because I'd have you for dessert."

I don't think he means have me *over* for dessert. "And what if I'm full before we get to that course?"

My eyes sweep over him, pausing for a moment on his dick. I can see the bulge that the tablecloth only partly covers. Did it just grow?

"What would you like to fill you up?"

Are we really doing this?

"Some say tongue is a delicacy, but if it's done right, I could have it every day."

We have to pause our conversation as servers clear our plates and bring the next course. Two lamb chops sit before me, and I can't help but think the meaty portions look like two balls sitting in front of me. The bones pressed together could be the cock that goes along with them.

"I see we've finally come to a dish you're hungry for."

His hand rests on my thigh, but he tries to pull it away a second later. I snap my knees together, trapping his hand. His fingers press into my flesh, and he pulls my leg closer to his. I have to let him go, so he can eat, but neither of us moves our leg.

Of course, this would be the moment Maria remembers I'm sitting next to her. She and I chat through the sorbet, the next dish of the *secondi* course and *insalata*. The *formaggi e frutta*, or cheese and fruit, arrives. The figs once more make me think of a man's balls sitting on my plate. Obviously, far smaller than real ones. But now I can't stop thinking about them and what Carmine's might look like. I pop a date into my mouth, enjoying the sweetness along with the crunch from the almond in the center.

I eat the rest of the fruit on my plate because I like it but also, so I don't feel guilty for how much more I enjoy the cheese. I fight my frown when dessert arrives. It's a *cannolo* and two *zeppoles*, fried dough balls in powdered sugar. The custard center is leaking from mine, and it appears runny. Why does almost every dish remind me of a cock and balls?

"Next time, I'll suggest Aunt Sylvia orders the dessert from you, Fina. I'm already disappointed."

"Maybe they'll taste better than they look."

They don't. I choke on my sip of water when the back of Carmine's hand brushes mine as I set the glass down. It's what he says next that nearly makes me spit it out.

"If I fed you dessert balls, they'd be far firmer and much more filling."

"When I'm alone, I like to lick the powdered sugar off them first. Would you mind if I licked yours first?"

It's Carmine's turn to splutter. He clears his throat and

adjusts his tie. We sit quietly as *Zio* Salvatore gives a brief speech to thank everyone for attending, then music begins. Carmine sticks his hand out to me, and I stare at it for a moment.

"Carmine, people will talk. They're going to think we're following through on the betrothal."

"We'll never do anything you don't want, but I'd like to have a dance with you."

Our eyes meet, and I know he means way more than marriage. Heat surges through me as I place my hand in his. Other couples are moving to the dance floor, and we find a place among them. His arm slides around my waist, his little finger resting on the top of my ass. He draws me close as though to make room for other people.

"What do you want tonight, *piccolina?*"

Chapter Three

Carmine

What the hell possessed me to flirt with Fina during the meal? Something came over me, so I tested the water by bumping my leg against hers. She moved to be polite. I think she did the same when our arms brushed, but she didn't recoil either time. It was more like she worried she intruded upon my personal space. When I put my hand on her leg the first time, she didn't push it away or tell me to stop. I almost came in my trousers when I did it the second time, and she trapped my hand there. That's when I decided the flirting might continue, but the games were done.

"Carmine, I don't know how to answer that."

I keep my voice low, so no one else but Fina hears me. "Do you want my hand between your legs again?"

I feel her suck in a breath before she turns her head to look in my eyes. I'm dead serious.

"Yes."

She is too.

"Do you want my fingers in you?"

"Among other things."

"Fina, I'm flirting with you, but I'm not joking." My tone shifts and becomes harder, more commanding. I'm testing her because I like my sex rough and kinky. I'll do vanilla for her, but I'd prefer not to. Her tone softens, and I fear this time I truly will come.

"Same, Carmine."

I wait for her to say something more. I'm giving her a chance to tell me what else she wants or to change her mind. She remains silent.

"I'm not fucking you in some restroom, Fina. It's my bed or yours. But if you agree to this, it's for an entire night."

An entire night. As in the singular. For now. I don't think once will ever be enough. I watch her press her lips between her teeth, and she appears to be having second thoughts.

"*Piccolina*, that's what I want. But if that isn't what you want, I won't push you. I think we'd enjoy it, but I won't hold it against you if our flirting just went further than you're comfortable with."

"Why would you want me?"

I didn't expect that question.

"Because you're witty and intelligent."

"Oh. Thank you."

That doesn't seem to be the answer she hoped for. I pull her closer until our bodies touch. I know she can feel my arousal, and the longer her tits are touching my chest and her pussy brushes against my cock, the harder I'm getting. I'll embarrass us both—for a second time—if I don't calm this hard on.

"Because I've wanted to bend you forward and fuck you since I saw your ass. Then I want to turn you around just before you come, so I can enjoy seeing and touching all of you."

Her cheeks pinken, but she prefers that explanation more than knowing I like her personality. That seems counterintuitive to her nature. I tested her limits again, and she surprises me yet again. I worried I'd insult her by being so blunt, but I see her eyes darkening with the same lust I feel. She leans in to whisper against my ear.

"Carmine, I don't think you're into vanilla either."

Either? Fuck me. I'm ready to carry her out of this ballroom over my shoulder. How the hell do we get out of here without making a scene? I'm ready to reserve a room here and start the fun.

"*Piccolina*, you have no idea."

"Then give me an idea."

"I want you tied to my bed with a plug in your ass and nipple clamps I can tug to make you scream every time I thrust into your tight little cunt."

Now I'm saying things for the shock factor, but she doesn't recoil.

"And if I wanted you to wear a cock ring to make what you just said last longer?"

Fuck if that doesn't shock the shit out of me.

"That might be a good idea because I think I might come embarrassingly fast once I'm inside you."

"My mouth or my pussy?"

"Holy fucking hell on the fucking hottest day in August, Fina."

"Well?"

"Both."

Now I'm the one doubting this. Is she teasing me, and I'm going to make a fool out of myself when she walks away?

"*Piccolina*—"

"Why do you keep calling me that? Why little girl? And I say that too. The hottest fucking day in August thing. Small world. You still haven't given me a good reason for calling me Fina."

"Because everyone else calls you Sera."

"So?"

How do I explain that it's purely possessive and territorial? That I want something with her that no one else can have. Apparently, we already have an unusual saying we share. I want more that's just ours.

"Do you dislike it? Do you want me to stop calling you that?"

"No." She's quick to answer, and she seems to surprise herself. I'm past testing the water. I'm up to my neck and praying I don't drown.

"You like it because only I call you that."

She just gazes into my eyes, and I know I'm right. She doesn't have to say anything. The song ends, and some people move off the dance floor, but we continue to move together. We are definitely drawing attention. We should return to our seats and make it look like our one dance was just a courtesy. But Maria is back at our table, and she doesn't need to hear a word of this.

"Why do you call me *piccolina*?"

"Partly because I see the same feistiness and boldness as when we were kids, but you are no child. You are an alluring woman. But you're also smaller than me. That's why it came to me the first time."

"You make it sound like there's another reason tonight."

"Because I hated seeing you with only one guard coming into the hotel. Getting to you might be the most urgent thing I've felt in years. I don't know what the fuck the Diazes are up to, but I still don't feel comfortable with you being anywhere unprotected. I wanted to take care of you the moment I saw you, make sure you were all right. That's why I thought of you as *piccolina*."

"We know now that we both like it kinky, but I'm not a little, Carmine. Not at all. That's fine for other people, but I'm not into age play. I'm twenty-eight. I feel forty sometimes. But I feel nothing less than my real age."

"I'm not a Daddy Dom, but I am dominant."

"I can tell."

"Are you a sub?"

She hesitates, then looks around. As though someone hearing her answer now would be worse than anything someone might have heard up 'til now.

"I am not a sub in so far as I don't want to enter that kind of relationship. I like to be an equal."

"You prefer a fluid power exchange."

"No. I'm not interested in being any kind of Domme, even if it's only for a few minutes. I mean I prefer a say in each thing I do with a partner. I don't want things done to me, but with me. Does that make sense?"

It does. But I don't think that's all of it. "Would you agree to the things I said I wanted to do *to* you if I were doing it *with* you?"

"Yes."

She doesn't want to surrender control. Maybe she's afraid to. Maybe she hasn't found a partner she trusts enough to let go. I want to be that man. I need to be. And that scares the shit out of me. I'm not sure I'm worthy of that, but fucking hell if I don't want to be.

"Do you want this tonight, Fina?"

"Are you backing out?"

"Not at all. Are you calling my bluff?"

"Yes."

"Then we need to agree to where. Your place, my place, or here."

She glances up at the ceiling, then toward the door. "You know I have bodyguards. Anywhere I go, they will come. If you come to my house, they will know."

I knew that already, but it puts a damper on things when she says it aloud. "Will they report to your father?"

"Since it's you, maybe. I can tell them not to, but I can't guarantee they'll listen."

"Would your father agree to letting me escort you home?"

"I honestly don't know. I know you saw how my parents watched us during the meal. They're watching us right now. I don't think they like us together."

"I can't blame them. Fina, I'm certain you and your family know my reputation. It's one that I'm finally mature enough to realize was completely shortsighted and foolish to create. I've done some shit lately that I'm not proud of. If I could do it all again differently, I wouldn't hesitate to change course."

"What are you saying? What happened?"

"Anyone you talk to will say I'm a spoiled idiot who does Uncle Salvatore's shit jobs that are too low for anyone else. Or they will call me a manipulative motherfucker. I was the latter, which meant I didn't mind people believing the former."

I'm hardly excited to delve into my misbegotten ways, but I feel compelled to be honest with her upfront. If she finds out, she'll think I hid it from her. And I don't want her to feel humiliated and duped when she learns about it and can't respect me.

"What do you mean? I've seen the articles in the gossip columns."

"I know. I'm no virgin, Fina. You know that as well as anyone. But I cultivated the image that I care about little but having fun and banging hot chicks. I had some fun, but I looked at a lot of it as work. I didn't have sex with most of those women. It was for appearances. When I went out, the end of the night came, and I'd already introduced them to my men. If the women were interested in any of the guys, they did what they wanted. Or I came up with excuses to bow out. I didn't fuck half the women the gossip rags suggested I did."

"Why all the subterfuge, Carmine?"

"That's complicated, and something I will explain to you honestly. But not here. If you don't like what you're hearing and don't want this to go any further until you know the truth, I'll tell you before anything happens tonight. If you'd rather nothing happen and hear about this another time, then I'll accept that."

"You're scaring me."

Well, shit.

"That's not what I want. But you may not respect me at all by the time I'm done. You may think even less of me if that's possible. I don't want you to regret being with me or feel disgusted with yourself that you were."

"Carmine, you are not making this better for yourself. Is this one of those ways you backed out of things? Did you flirt with me just to make a fool of me?"

She tries to pull away, and I let her. I steer her toward the bar, but I stop us before we get to the line. We stand near a wall.

"No, to either of those. I'm not proud of the man I was. I spent four months surviving the consequences of my choices and realizing that I had little self-respect left despite how superior I'd once felt. The things I've done aren't a secret, even if my reasons were. Anyone you talk to in my family, or any other syndicate can tell you what I've done. Even if no one else found out if we slept together, you would know. I never want you to be ashamed."

"Nothing about you since you came into the bakery seems

like the boy or young man I knew. It doesn't match any of the things I've seen in the papers. Are you telling me all of it was manipulation?"

"I was a jerk to you as a kid because I've felt like shit about myself my entire life. I couldn't be nice to anyone but Gabriele because I was too resentful. I was a self-centered and lusty teenager the last time we met. I didn't care about respecting the event or Uncle Salvatore, so I thumbed my nose at it. Now—I don't like myself very much, but I'd like other people to respect me."

This shit got heavy fast. I can't believe I just told her any of that. I admitted some of this to Luca a while ago, but I have told no one else. Gabriele knows because he's been my best friend despite who I became and what I dragged him into. I don't know anyone more forgiving and loyal than Gabriele.

"Carmine, I don't want to end this conversation, but people are watching us, including my family and *Zio* Salvatore. I also don't want to say no to what we talked about before. How do we do this?"

"If you left and had your guards bring you back here, what would happen?"

"They might tell my father I came back, but I wouldn't let them know who I'm meeting."

"Would that be unusual?"

"I don't fuck strangers or have random hook-ups, Carmine." She sounds duly insulted.

"I meant, do your guards usually report what you do to your father?"

"No. But everyone's seen us together. They'll probably guess."

"And if your dad did find out?"

"I'll point out he doesn't have much of a leg to stand on. If he doesn't like it, then he can get around to dissolving the betrothal. But either way, he's sworn since that day that I get to decide who I'm with. He regretted it when he saw—" She shifts uncomfortably.

"When he saw how miserable it made you."

"Yes."

"Uncle Salvatore said the same thing to me in private. He didn't want me to ruin our families' ties, but he also promised not to force the issue. He would support me if I wanted out, even if your family wanted to go through with it."

"What happens if you tell me things I don't like, and I want to leave?"

"Then you leave. Either your men take you home, or I will. If you don't like either of those ideas, two of my men will. But I don't like that last choice. I don't really like your men taking you either. I'd feel better if I saw you safely back to your place, but I know your father trusts the men assigned to you. I can accept that." *Because I may have to.*

"Why do you want it to be you?"

I lock eyes with her. "Because no one will ever do more or try harder to protect you than I will."

She looks ready to say something, but she holds back. She glances around before returning her gaze to mine.

"I believe you. I'm scared I'm a fool to after how ominous you make your impending confession sound. But I feel safer with you than I ever have with anyone else. When the Diazes walked in, I needed to get back to your side. I don't know why because Gio was there. I was already near my dad and Ernesto. I can't explain it, but there was this urgency. Even though I didn't go to you, just being closer made me feel better. Why is that?"

"I don't know, *piccolina*. But I've never meant anything more than what I just said. Nothing will stop me from protecting you." I see her sigh, and her shoulders relax. "I'm going to walk you over to your family and greet them properly. Then I'm going to say goodnight to you before I say goodnight to my family. Everyone will see me leave alone. I will arrange for a room then text you the number. Double back once you leave and come directly up to the room."

"How long should I wait before I leave?"

"At least half an hour."

"You're just going to sit up there alone?"

"It'll save your reputation and keep you from having to answer questions you don't want to hear."

"Carmine, this sucks. I don't want to play these games. I want…"

She trails off and looks down at her feet. I wish I could tuck my finger under her chin and lift it until she's looking at me again. I want to be transfixed by her luminous gray eyes with the green flecks.

"What do you want, little girl?"

"You." She whispers it, but she's adamant. "I want to dance again, so you're holding me."

"I want the same. Let's go see your parents, so this doesn't drag on for forever. I want you back in my arms, Fina. This might have started as flirtation, but it's something different now."

"I know. I don't understand it, though."

"Neither do I. But I'm glad you feel it too." She nods. "Smile, little one. I don't want anyone to think I made you sad."

"You didn't. It's this situation. I'm glad we're talking. I'm glad you're giving me the opportunity to change my opinion. Or at least form it without speculation."

"What's your number, so I can text you?" She rattles it off, and I repeat it to myself several times before I nod. "Come on."

We cross the ballroom, skirting the dance floor. Allegra and Piero don't appear happy to see me, but Juliana and Ernesto are polite. I know Ernesto because he once held a similar position in his family as Lorenzo. He was *Mala del Brenta's* accountant. I knew Juliana moved here, so I've seen Ernesto since he came with her. I never asked about Fina, and he volunteered nothing. He's mostly severed his ties with Mafia life, starting fresh in America. But once in a while, he handles money exchanging hands between the *Mala del Brenta* and us.

"*Buonasera, signori Carosi. Ciao, Juliana, Ernesto.*" Good evening, Mr. and Mrs. Carosi. Hello, Juliana, Ernesto.

Piero barely acknowledges me, but Allegra smiles and responds. "Carmine."

I suppose that's better than *stronzo*—asshole—or *scopatore* —fucker. I'm fairly certain those are what Piero would like to call me. Juliana definitely has the warmest reaction to me. She casts her sister a speculative expression while Ernesto is his usual reserved self. We continue in Italian.

"Hi, Carmine. It's nice to see you again. How're you?"

"I'm well. You?" I keep it short.

"Really well. Did Sera tell you we're expecting our first baby?"

I force my eyes not to dip to Fina's belly as my imagination immediately jumps to Fina being pregnant with our first child. That may be one of the most disturbing thoughts of my life. I've practically double bagged it since the first time I had sex to make sure that never happened.

"Congratulations. Do you know what you're having?"

"Not yet." Ernesto wraps his arm around his wife and smiles. It's the most excited I've ever seen the man. But Juliana's and Ernesto's smiles drop when Allegra snaps at them.

"We do not find out in this family. If God meant us to know, then He'd tell us Himself."

I don't think she believes the second part. She wants to make her point, but the happiness dims from both Juliana's and

Ernesto's eyes. I feel badly since I didn't mean to open that can of worms.

"Please let us know your due date. My cousins and I would love to get something for the baby."

Piero finally speaks up, and I wish he hadn't. "I thought you would have learned not to speak on Luca's or any of your cousins' behalf."

Oh, hell. I wonder just how much Piero knows. From the way he's glowering at me, I'd say too much. It's time for me to make my exit.

"Serafina, it was nice to see you again. Mr. and Mrs. Carosi, Juliana, Ernesto, thank you for spending Easter with my family. I hope you all have a good night."

I switched to English, and I don't notice until Fina looks at me oddly. Or is it because I used her full name? She appears confused and unsure how she feels about what I said.

"Goodnight, Carmine."

Only Fina's voice is clear. Everyone else mumbles their farewell. I don't linger but go straight to my family's table. I find Gabriele and jerk my head to the side. He's the only one I'll confide in. But I need to check one thing first.

"What's the deal outside? What are the Diazes up to?"

"Turns out it's legit. There was a sewer line rupture."

"And the crew just happened to be Enrique's men? I smell shit."

"Your puns blow. But yes, it was just a false alarm. I'm certain he arranged for that particular crew since he and his family are here. He wants the extra guns, so it was convenient."

"If you say so."

"What's going on with you tonight? Plenty of people were watching you."

"I'm staying here tonight. Fina is coming back. If anyone

asks, tell them I went home with a headache." Right now, that isn't far from the truth.

"Car, this is *not* a good idea. It's going to blow up in your face. There's no way her guards won't tell her father that she came back to meet you."

"I told her the same thing. She still wants to come back."

"Considering the last time her parents saw you in the same room as their daughter, you'd just come back from banging a one-night stand, I don't think this is wise."

"Fina is *not* a woman who is a one-night anything."

"You are asking to get yourself castrated. If not by Piero, then by Uncle Salvatore. This is going to piss him off. He's kept your head off the chopping block with the Carosis. Now you're putting your neck right in front of them."

"Gabe, I'm going to tell her everything tonight. If she wants to stay after that, then maybe there's something to this. If she bolts, then I know."

"Everything?"

"Yes. All of it."

Gabriele stares at me. I know he still disagrees, but I also know he'll support me. "Just be careful, Car. She's not a one-night stand kind of woman, but she is the kind who could break your heart."

Wiser words have never been spoken. I head to the front desk, glancing over my shoulder to see who's watching because someone is bound to be. I spy Javier Diaz, and I want to groan. I just need to get a room key and go up alone before he disappears to tell only half the story.

"Mr. Mancinelli, would you like your usual suite?"

"No." I answer so quickly that the man's eyebrows shoot up to his receding hairline. "Something equivalent, but not that one, please."

I am not meeting Fina somewhere I've been with anyone

else. In the past, I arrived with whomever I brought, or they were already here and came upstairs with me. This is the first time I'm leaving a key for someone. I suddenly feel even skeezier than I have in the past. That would probably be because I never cared about any of this—my reputation, my partner's reputation, my family's opinion—before. Now I want to be extremely cautious. When the man comes back with the keycards, I hand one back.

"My girlfriend is meeting me. She will ask for this by room number. That is how you will know she should get it." I haven't referred to anyone as my girlfriend since high school. It rolled off my tongue and hangs in the air around my ears. I like it.

"Yes, Mr. Mancinelli."

I don't want Fina having to ask for me or giving her name. Plus, hopefully, with a key card, her guards won't insist upon sweeping the room. I head up to the suite and do exactly what her guards would. I pull my gun at the door and ease it open. I doubt the man at the front desk would call anyone to tell them I'm alone, but I can never be too cautious. Once I'm satisfied, I lock the door and tap her number into my phone.

ME

Room 33109. Tell the front desk that number. They'll give you the key. No names piccolina.

I wait twenty-five minutes, and I'm trying not to go out of my mind wondering if she's going to ditch me.

FINA

Just got in the car. Going to tell them to turn back. I'll knock four times so you know it's me before I use the key.

> Do you want me in there? Will your guards insist on sweeping the room? I can wait down the hall until they leave.

> No. I can convince them not to sweep the room. But they will stay outside the door.

> Are you all right with that?

There's a long silence again. It's unnerving.

> They know I'm not a virgin.

What the hell am I supposed to read into that? Because there must be something.

> Use the key card. I'll stay out of sight.

> I'm walking back in.

I try not to get too nervous or too excited. I feel like a teenager again, and it's disconcerting as hell. I wait near the door. The moment I hear the four knocks, I pull my gun again and move behind the door. It opens, and Fina steps through. I watch her gaze sweep the suite before I push the door shut. I'm quick to cover her mouth before she screams when she spots my gun.

"Shh, *piccolina*."

I remove my hand, but she turns terrified eyes to me.

"Please don't kill me, Carmine."

Chapter Four

Fina

My heart races as I stare at Carmine's gun. I shift my gaze to him as I plead for my life. I see the flash of hurt in his eyes as he holsters his weapon.

"Fina, I can't believe you felt like you needed to say that to me."

"What am I supposed to think when I walk into a hotel suite with you hiding behind a door with a gun drawn?"

"That I'm protecting you from anyone who might force their way in behind you."

That makes me pause. That's sound reasoning, and if I hadn't been so shocked, I might have thought of that myself. "I'm sorry. It startled me."

"I know, *piccolina*. Come inside."

I listen to him turn the lock as I move farther into the suite. It's lovely, but I've always thought the suites at the Waldorf Astoria are over-the-top. The ostentation feels gaudy to me, but

I can recognize the luxury. Just because it isn't my taste doesn't mean I can't appreciate Carmine spoiling me with a night here.

"Did you have any trouble?"

"No. I almost ran into my parents, though. I spotted them as I came back in, so I bolted for the restroom. Gio and David already knew what's going on. I explained in the car."

"And they accepted your explanation?"

"Yes. I don't go to hotels and meet random guys, Carmine. Nor am I usually secretive if I am meeting up with someone. But they know I've had more than one boyfriend since moving to America, and they know I haven't been a nun in between."

Carmine's arm slides around my waist, pulls me against his hard body, and walks me backward until I bump into the wall. His mouth descends to mine before he devours me. This kiss is possessive and threatens to consume me. His hand fists my hair and holds my head in place, unwilling to let me go. I can't move anything except my arms, so my hands roam over every part I can reach. He pushes his thigh between mine, and I can feel his cock pressed against my hip as my pussy rubs against his unyielding thigh.

I try to take control of the kiss, but he nips at my lip. I give in, and he redoubles his efforts. I cling to him, unable to believe how different this first kiss is from any other first kiss—any other kiss period. I don't want to stop, but he finally pulls away.

"Fina, we still need to talk."

"Do we really?"

"Yes, *piccolina*. If, after what you hear, you want to leave, I won't stop you. I shouldn't have distracted us."

"Why did you?"

"Because I hate knowing you have a past as much as I regret having one at all, let alone one you know about."

I think for a moment, and I know I feel the same way. Both that I wish I didn't have a past, and that I wish I didn't know about his. He kisses along my jaw and along my neck up to my ear.

"Come sit with me, Fina."

I close my eyes and sigh. I don't want to talk. The only thing I want to hear are his groans as I make him come. But he backs up and takes my hand before guiding me to the sofa. He sits and pulls me onto his lap. I kick off my shoes and pull my feet up. I get a whiff of his cologne again, and I want to lick him. I nuzzle my nose against his neck, and I hear that first groan.

"Fina, what do you know about my parents?"

I draw back and look up at him. There's hesitation and even shame in his gaze. "They got married when your mom got pregnant with you at nineteen."

"Sort of. My mom thought she was protecting me by insisting that they not marry until after I was born. It ensured I got the Mancinelli name. She never contested my father's paternity and agreed to his name on the birth certificate. But my grandfathers never forgave *me* for my mother's decision. As though I told her what to do from the womb. As though it were my fault I was a *bastardo*."

Wow.

"My mother's father swore my father got her pregnant to force her to marry him for her inheritance. My father's father— Mario-Andrea Ciccone—insisted I wasn't my dad's child, then he claimed she trapped my father to make him and my grandfather the Mancinellis' bitches. Everyone of that generation knew the story of my birth, and they sided with one grandfather or the other, but they all looked down at me for being illegitimate. Funnily enough, the only people who never made me feel shitty about being a bastard were my cousins, and I've treated them the shittiest of all."

I cup his cheek and turn it toward me. I gaze into his blue

eyes and wonder who he inherited them from since, from what I remember, both his parents have brown eyes. But he looks enough like his father for no one to question his paternity, even if he favors his mother's side of the family too.

"My maternal grandfather, Vicenzu, was second generation Sicilian American. My maternal grandmother, Lucretia, was born and raised in Sicily. All of my dad's family was third generation, so *Nonno* Vicenzu didn't consider them Italian enough to be part of the Mancinelli family, even if only tangentially related. He made that known all the time and blamed them for why I didn't speak enough Sicilian. Never mind that he only spoke to me in Italian."

There is *so much* pain in his voice as he relives this. I'm tempted to stop him, reassure him he doesn't need to tell me any of this. But I think it's cathartic. I don't think he's told anyone outside his family who knows, anyway.

"My cousins never made me feel inferior, but I did. I was jealous a moment ago when you said you've had boyfriends and others. I know that feeling because I've felt it way too many times. Except, this time, it didn't create anger. It made me want to prove I'm better. That isn't how I've reacted in the past. Just the opposite. If everyone thought I was a shit stain, then why try to convince them otherwise? Why not just accept it and be what they expect, since they'd never believe I was anything else?"

I picture him as a little boy. One not much younger than when we met. It breaks my heart because it isn't a stretch of my imagination to envision it.

"The summer we met, I was such an asshole to you because I was so jealous. I saw you with Juliana and how much fun you had together. I saw how your grandparents loved you and enjoyed your visit. My aunts and uncles love me, even though I've been a constant disappointment. But at twelve, it felt like no one but my parents loved me. I have never doubted that, but they fought all the time. It often eclipsed knowing they cared about me. I lashed out. I deserved the broken nose."

"No. They should have punished me for that instead of you getting in trouble. I had a horrible temper. I wasn't prone to temper tantrums or anything, but I was quick to anger. I don't know why." I think about that for a moment, and that isn't true. "I take that back. People compared me to Juliana a lot. My sister couldn't be more awesome, and she was always my best friend. But I was never like her. I wasn't pretty like her. I wasn't—"

"Wait. What do you mean you weren't pretty? Yes, you were. You were an adorable kid. People always said so. It's part of why I was so jealous. I was awkward at twelve. You were like a doll."

"Hardly. I was pudgy."

"That is *not* how I saw you."

"You called me a runt."

"Because you were shorter than the rest of us who were twelve. You were a lot smaller than me in build, too. I was gangly, but my shoulders had already broadened from being a swimmer."

"I didn't feel small. Plus, Juliana could sing, and she was artistic along with smart and hard working."

"You were those things, too."

"I can't sing, and my artistic side comes out through my baking. I can't draw a straight line with a ruler. I haven't wanted to admit it before because it makes me feel guilty, but I was jealous of Jules. That's often what sparked my temper. When I didn't feel good enough. It was all my perception, too. I knew even then that my parents didn't love her more or think she was better. Jules never acted like she was better. It was the way people would gush about her."

"Then you just weren't around when they gushed about you. I wanted a family who spoke as highly about me as they did you."

"I'd say it was funny how off our impressions were, but it's really just sad."

"Fina, I wasn't wrong. I know what I overheard, and I know what they said right in front of me. It made me resent Luca and the others. They weren't Uncle Sal's kids, so it's not like we knew back then that Luca would be the underboss. But their parents were married well before Luca came along. I figured if everyone assumed the worst of me because of my birth, what was the point in trying to prove them wrong? What was the point in trying my best to only fail? Why be anything but what they expected, which was nothing important?"

My heart aches as he speaks. He's said the same thing more than once, so it's obvious it weighs heavily on him. I wonder how many times people said those comments in passing, and no one realized how a young Carmine would interpret them. I wonder how many they said purposely to cut him down. I'm afraid more of them were intentional than not.

"Since no one expected anything of me, I decided it meant I could do what I wanted. When Gabriele moved to America when we were ten and spoke no English, kids picked on him. He was also way taller than everyone else, but he was a nice and really considerate kid. He wasn't what any of us men have grown into. Neither of us fit in, so we fit together. But he wasn't part of the don's family. I was. I was the black sheep, so I lived up to the reputation they'd already given me. I pretended not to care about anything or anyone except Gabriele and Maria. I did what I wanted, and people left me alone. I got in trouble to say fuck you to both my grandfathers. People called it attention seeking. I didn't care if I got their attention. I wanted to flick them off and cuss them out, but that wasn't an option. So, I made them look bad because they couldn't control me."

This makes a lot of sense. I definitely don't think he's told anyone, except for maybe Gabriele, any of this.

"As we got older, Uncle Sal didn't trust me, and I didn't care. It meant I could keep doing what I wanted, which was manipulating the shit out of people, including him. I liked the power it gave me when I could maneuver people into doing what I wanted without them realizing it. I would mention things in passing a few times until they took root. I would make sure I was coincidentally in places to hear what was going on when no one intended on including me. I took the shit jobs because it meant I actually had more contact with people in the neighborhoods. I did things on the sly for them that made them like me more than my cousins, who only showed up when there was trouble. I got information they couldn't, and I would drop breadcrumbs that Luca and Uncle Sal followed. I've never wanted to be the underboss or the don. But I loved knowing I influenced them, and they didn't even realize it. It felt vindicating and vindictive."

If he could lead *Zio* Salvatore and Luca around and they didn't notice, nor did anyone else, then he is a master manipulator.

"Fina, I'm telling you all of this, knowing you might fear I'll do the same thing to you. That I'm telling you to manipulate you. I'm not. I can understand why you wouldn't believe that either. I'm telling you because I want you to know the truth about me. If our families ever force us together, I want you to know the man you're getting. I'd rather you not be blindsided, even if you are ashamed to be with me."

"Carmine, no one is going to force us together."

"Because your father doesn't want a shitbag marrying into the family."

"Because he did what his father-in-law insisted to keep the peace until the man died."

"Sure. Either way, I'm not proud of my past. If anyone finds out you came here tonight, my past will drag you down."

"You make it sound like you haven't gotten to the worst of it."

"I haven't. Veronica mentioned I was in Sicily for four months. She didn't mention I was there as punishment. Uncle Sal sent Luca, Gabriele, and me to work on a vineyard owned by a man who owed Uncle Sal a favor. The man made us work twelve and fourteen-hour days sometimes. Ten at a minimum. He would refuse us food and water if he believed we weren't working hard enough. He routinely had his other men surround us and beat us. He took a shovel blade to Luca's back when he didn't pick enough grapes. Luca already had his arm in a sling from the punishment Uncle Sal doled out."

"*Zio* Sal beat Luca?"

"All three of us. Fina, we deserved it. We fucked up, and I was the cause. You saw the Kutsenkos tonight, right?"

"Yeah."

"Did you see the really thin woman with Niko? She looks like a model, but she's a waif."

"Yeah. She could be one."

"Her name is Anastasia. Right around the time Niko and Anastasia got together, the Kutsenkos put a hit on several of our men. They were friends and family. Uncle Massimo pushed Luca to prove himself and strike back hard. It was my idea to target Anastasia. I didn't mean it to go as far as it did. We were supposed to take her to one of Luca's rental properties in the Bronx and scare her. The Kutsenkos were supposed to understand that we'll take from them if they take from us. But they shot up the house to rescue Anastasia. She got hurt when one of our guys pushed her out the door. She fell down the porch steps and got injured badly enough to need surgery."

Part of me wants to say I can't believe he'd do something like that. But after how he's described himself, I can see it. "You planned it, didn't you?"

"Yes."

"Anastasia looked okay tonight."

"She made a full recovery, but that was the least of the trouble we caused. When Uncle Massimo pushed Luca to prove himself, I put a bug in his ear that he should make a move on the Chicago *Cosa Nostra* and flex some muscle. Luca thought marrying Cecelia Rizzo would strengthen our hold on everything between the Atlantic and the Mississippi. It would have, so he tried to arrange a marriage. The Chicago don wanted him to prove himself, too. I told him to make the don think we could bring the Ivankov bratva to their knees, so I asked around with the Chicago bratva. I wanted to know what a half-Russian woman involved with Niko was worth. Word somehow got back to a Moscow bratva that has a personal vendetta against the Kutsenkos. When Niko and Anastasia went on vacation to Greece, men from Moscow kidnapped her just after they got engaged. I don't know everything that happened, but we're all certain she killed at least one man. She must have done something else because she terrifies Uncle Sal. He will not cross her. I don't think he knows specifics, but he senses something about her. She's not violent by nature, but I think she's capable of some dark shit to protect her family."

I sit quietly as I listen. If Carmine is making his confession right now, it makes me wonder if I should make mine too. He appears so remorseful, even disgusted with himself, that I don't know if sharing something from my past would make it better or worse. But he's confiding in me. This isn't tit-for-tat. But I want him to understand I appreciate him being candid.

"Carmine, Anastasia isn't the only woman who'll defend her family."

"I know that. I'm certain women in our families would too."

"No. I should have said Anastasia isn't the only woman who *has* defended her family."

He watches me. When he says nothing, I take that as a hint for me to continue.

"When *Zia* Sophia died six years ago, I was in Sicily. It was the last time I was there before my two trips last month."

"Two trips?"

"Yeah. My *nonna* died two weeks after I saw you. It was a good thing I went to visit her when I did, even if my parents hadn't thought she was dying. But I'm trying to tell you something I did, Carmine. I don't know what you'll think of me once you find out."

"What happened, *piccolina*?" He sounds like he's ready to come to my defense. As though he has someone to find on my behalf.

"Like I said, six years ago, I was in Sicily when *Zia* Sophia died. I overheard who did it. Not just which family, but the men who did it. I heard *Zio* Alfredo planning to retaliate. I knew the murderers were brothers, and they owned a restaurant and a café. I slipped out one night and ditched my guards. I went to the restaurant and let myself into the kitchen. I didn't have the bakery yet, but I'd spent my life cooking and baking. I recognized the appliances, so I made it look like a gas leak. I torched the place. I hid in a building across the street until the brothers came. I was in the second-floor stairwell and had a clear line of sight to them. I put a bullet in the back of each of their heads. I went back to *Nonna* and *Nonno's* house and fell straight back to sleep. Two days later, I was at a nightclub and recognized the men's uncle."

"Their uncle was the don."

"'Was' is the operative word. Fucking filthy bastard. He didn't know me. He hit on me. I knew exactly who he was and that he'd ordered the hit on *Zia* Sophia. I ditched my guards again and led him to the back part of the dancefloor. Men aren't the only ones who go nowhere without a knife."

I reach for my purse, which I'd dropped on the sofa as we walked around it to sit. I pull it over to me and click it open. I pull out a stiletto dagger. I hand it to Carmine, and he just looks at it. I take back what looks like a hair pin and press a little button. The blade shoots out the bottom.

"Fina, what the hell? What the fuck did you do?"

"This went into his spine at the base of his skull. He was dead before he let go of me."

I yelp as he flips us around, so I'm on my back, and he's hovering over me. The dagger hair clip lands on the coffee table. He's staring at me and breathing heavily. He rears back and easily turns me onto my belly. Then my skirt is over my back, and his hand lands on my ass. He's not gentle either. It's a sound spanking. This isn't kinky foreplay. This is a punishment. It shocks me, but once I get all the pieces in line in my head, I don't fight him. Instead, it's cathartic.

"You will count each one, Fina." His hand smacks me, and the sting shoots straight to my pussy.

"One." His hand lands on my right ass cheek, then my left. "Two, three."

"No. Two." He smacks my left cheek, then my right.

"Three." He alternates back and forth until I think I can barely stand it anymore. "Ten."

My ass is on fire by the time he stops. Tears stream down my cheeks. I kicked my feet over and over, and it took all my willpower not to reach back and try to cover my ass. He lifts me into his arms and sits back down with me on his lap again.

"Fina, so many things could have gone wrong with all of

that. But to be in arm's reach of him and attempt that... You would have died if you'd failed. You would have died if any of his men caught you. How could you be so reckless?"

"They killed my aunt and my unborn cousin."

"Women don't get involved."

I snort.

"Women have been getting involved since the beginning of time. Women make far better assassins."

"You are not making a strong case, little girl. If you don't want a far harsher spanking, I would stop if I were you." We look at each other in silence. Then he softens his tone. "You needed that spanking, didn't you? You've felt guilty about that for years. Maybe not about killing those men but putting your-self in danger. You needed that punishment to clear your conscience."

I don't like him understanding me that well. I try to pull away, but he holds me close.

"Don't retreat from me, Fina. You've heard my confession, and you made yours. You can't confess and not expect penance. Mine would be you running away."

I'm slow to nod, but I do. He kisses my forehead and tucks me back against his chest. He strokes my back, and I truly feel forgiven for something that I've carried with me for years but have justified over and over. I feel no remorse for killing those men. Evil as that might make me. But in our world, that was fair and right. It was justice. I regret the danger I put myself in and how that would have hurt my family if something happened to me. My heart and mind feel lighter.

"Carmine, I told you this because I knew you'd understand. I didn't realize the weight it's been until now. I regret risking my life for the sake of my family. But to be clear, I do not repent for killing those men."

"I know, and I don't expect you to. But I will punish you any and every time you endanger yourself, Fina."

"You speak as though you'll have a say in the future."

We stare at each other again. Just before his lips brush mine, he whispers. "We both know I will."

Chapter Five

Carmine

My tongue swipes across Fina's lips, and she opens for me. My tongue slides into her mouth, and I move slowly. It takes all my willpower not to thrust my tongue into her just like I want to thrust my cock into her pussy. She moans and sucks, nearly breaking my resolve. As she sits on my lap, I glide my hand up the outside of her thigh until I can cup her luscious ass. She's wearing a thong, so I had an unrestricted view while I spanked her. I thought I wanted to do dirty things to her before. Now I crave every depraved and erotic scenario I can imagine. I press my fingers into her tender flesh, and she yelps. I only tighten my hold. She moves restlessly against me.

"Do naughty little girls deserve rewards after punishments?"

"Carmine, please. I know you saw how wet I am for you."

"I did."

My fingers press beneath her thong and slide down to her pussy. She's soaked. She moans as I continue to draw my fingertips along her swollen pussy lips, but I don't enter her. I tease her over and over until she whimpers.

"What do you need, *piccolina?*"

"You know what I want."

"I didn't ask what you wanted. I asked what you needed. Tell me, *piccolina.*"

"You."

"To do what?"

"Anything. Carmine, please. I—"

"What? You said you wanted to be a partner, an equal. Tell me what you need me to do."

"I don't know!" She clings to me, then she's scrambling to pull my tie loose and push off my suit coat. I capture her hands in one of mine as I pull my tie undone.

"If you don't know, then I will tell you." I stand with her in my arms and carry her into the bedroom. "Strip."

She stares at me for a moment before she reaches back for her zipper. She tugs it down, then slides the dress down her shoulders, letting it drop until it pools around her feet. She unfastens her bra, and that falls to the floor next. I grab the front of her thong and yank, making her take one, then two steps toward me.

"Never wear panties around me again, Fina. I will shred them." I tear the lacy strip of fabric from her. She stares at me in disbelief before glancing down at the discarded scrap. "Put your arms out."

She obeys immediately. She might not be a sub or a little, but she's being submissive to me. I take my tie and bind her wrists in front of her.

"Climb on the bed, Fina... Put your arms over your head... Arch your back for me...Good girl."

She follows each direction as I strip off my suit coat, which she'd tried to get off me, but I'd resisted. I give the commands

64

and decide how we're fucking for the first time. I unbutton my shirt and place it on top of my suit coat at the foot of the bed. I unfasten and withdraw my belt as I kick off my shoes. I reach down and yank off my socks, shoving them into my shoes. I place my gun on the bedside table, but Fina isn't fazed. Then I prowl closer. I trail my fingertips over her left nipple, making her shiver. I circle it until it tightens into a nub I can pinch then twist. I lean forward and kiss along her neck until I reach her ear.

"What's your safe word?"

She hesitates. I wonder for a moment if she doesn't know the term. Then I realize she's thinking of one. Does that mean she's coming up with something she's never used before?

"Fondant."

I pause. "As in the frosting?"

"Yes. It looks great, but it tastes disgusting. It's overrated."

I chuckle, then return my attention to her nipple. I twist again, and her back arches off the bed. "Say your safe word the moment anything becomes too painful, or you don't like it, or it makes you uncomfortable."

"I'm not going to say it, Carmine. I want this."

"But we are getting to know each other. If I take the pain from pleasurable to hurting you, I will be royally pissed, Serafina. I will punish you for that. I never want to harm you."

"Don't call me that. I don't like it."

"Serafina?"

"Yes. You did it in front of my parents, and I get why. But you don't call me that anymore. It feels like you're scolding me. I'm not a little."

"I only wanted you to know that I'm serious."

"I know. I can tell from your tone."

I cup her face in both hands and gentle my voice. "*Piccolina*, I only want to bring you pleasure. I'm a lot stronger than you, and I'm worried I'll inadvertently hurt you. I don't know your limits yet. Please don't take something just because you think it's what I want. I wouldn't forgive myself for harming you."

"May I sit up?"

"Of course. You don't have to ask."

"Yes, I do. Or rather, I want to." She shifts until she's upright, then she moves again to kneel in front of me. Her bound hands rest on the waistband of my pants, just below my belly button. "Carmine, my only hard limits are birching or caning and shaming."

"Has someone called you a slut or a whore before, Fina?"

"Shh, Carmine. You don't have to be ready to defend me all the time. No one's hurt me. I just don't like it."

I've used those words and others before while doing scenes at my club. I've used them with women who weren't into the same amount of kink as I enjoy, but thought it was hot. "I can't imagine saying those things to you. I don't have the heart to do it. I only want praise kink between us. Is that all right with you?"

"Yes. In the past—" She stops herself, and neither of us wants reminders of what we did with other people, but it must have been important if she brought it up.

"You can tell me anything, Fina."

"In the past, my only limits were the caning and birching. But I don't want to hear you call me those things."

"I want to spank you with more than my hand, but I never want to leave marks that'll last for days. I don't want to see you bruised because I can't stand the thought of marring you like that. Welts from a belt would be hot, but that's as far as I'd take it. Would that be all right?"

"Carmine, is there really going to be more than tonight?"

"Yes." I witness her entire body relax. She sits down on her heels, but I lift her until her legs come around my waist. I sit on the bed with her on my lap. "We both know this isn't a booty call. This isn't a one-night stand. Neither of us is going to be satisfied with just once."

"Then make it all night."

"Don't you worry about that. You aren't sleeping until at least noon. But you know what I mean."

"I do. But I'm scared you'll change your mind. I don't want to want this so much. It's scary. A few hours ago, I thought I'd be in bed alone, falling asleep to my TV on a timer. Now I'm naked while you're still half dressed."

I cup her ass and pull her closer. She rocks on my aching cock. "You can feel how hard you make me. I'm going to make you come on my fingers and my tongue. Then I'm going to fuck you over and over until all you can think about is me being inside you every time you move tomorrow. I'm going to make you crave me the way I crave you. You're going to need me buried inside you just so your mind will be quiet. And I'm going to give you everything you need, Fina. Every time you need it."

"Are you always this possessive?"

"Never."

"Why me?"

"Because you're mine."

We stare at each other, both shocked by the vehemence in my words. But I don't like the nervousness when she responds.

"Will you ever be mine?"

"I have been since the moment I saw you in your bakery. Fina, I haven't been with anyone since before I went to Sicily." She swallows and nods. "Fina?"

"I was with someone last week. I—I—Carmine, I said your name when I came. I was so mortified and confused. But I wanted you, and I didn't think I could ever have you. I was thinking of you the entire time."

"What happened?"

"It ruined the moment. I got off, but he didn't. I didn't even feel bad."

I want to rant and rave like a lunatic that someone else dared touch her, but I'm already questioning my sanity. I don't need to send her running. I can't believe she's stayed this long. Tears make her gray eyes watery. My brow furrows. "What's wrong?"

"Are you mad I told you I was with someone else?"

"No, Fina. I didn't imagine us together this morning let alone days ago."

I can tell she's still uneasy, so I fist my hand in her hair and once again hold her head in place as I plunder her mouth. She grinds her pussy against me, and I'm ready to spill. I pull her from me and playfully toss her on the bed before crawling on and settling between her thighs.

"Hands above your head, *piccolina*. Move them, and I will edge you until you beg."

I blow cool air over her cunt as I once again trail my fingers along her. She writhes but follows my directions. I tease her, watching her abs flex as she struggles to remain obedient. I push her thighs open, nipping at the inside of her left one. She tilts her hips, pushing her pussy toward my lips. I slap her cunt, but her gaze challenges me. I do it again, and she smiles.

"You want to be edged. Is that what you're telling me?"

I pinch her clit as I watch her. Her chest expands with a deep inhale, then she freezes. Our eyes lock as I flick my tongue into her pussy. I lick her over and over until her eyelids slide shut, and I see her body relax. I pull away. Her eyes fly open. I grin. I lick her again, rubbing her clit between my thumb and index finger. Her hips inch up, but I press down on her belly, pulling away yet again.

"Carmine..."

I cock an eyebrow. She nods but doesn't fight it. I reward her by sucking on her swollen clit. Her moan is my reward. I slide two fingers into her, and she contracts around them.

"Please, Carmine. More. I ache."

"I know, *piccolina*. But I decide."

"Can you decide a little faster?"

I pull back onto my knees and flip her over, just like I did on the sofa. I bring my hand down on her ass before shifting my weight, so my cock presses against her ass, my chest to her back. I reach between us and fill my hand with her plush ass. I squeeze mercilessly.

"Do not prod me."

"I don't want to. I want *you* to prod *me*...with your cock." She twists to look over her shoulder before she finishes. I rock my hips.

"There is no part of you that won't be mine. But I'm not taking your ass tonight, Fina. I want to take you out to dinner, knowing you're wearing a plug I put in there. Knowing you feel it each time you move and remember that it'll be my dick in there by the end of the night. It'll be my cum you feel."

"Promise?"

"Absolutely."

"When? How soon?"

"Tomorrow." I feel her relax and sink deeper into the mattress. I kiss her neck and along her shoulder. I run my hand between her shoulder blades and rub each shoulder.

"Carmine, can I roll over? I want to ask you something, but I want to look at you without straining."

I push up on my hands, but I don't draw back. She turns beneath me, keeping her arms over her head. Her knees bracket my hips. "You are so beautiful." I brush hair away from her temples, which are slightly damp already.

"Is this real, Carmine? Or is this just a scene?"

"This is very real. How do you know about scenes? You've told me you like it kinky. You obviously know about this, but that's usually a term reserved for Dom/sub relationships or BDSM clubs. Do you belong to one?"

"Yes." Her straightforward response makes me want to roar like an enraged lion. "Carmine, you asked. I didn't want to lie. There are four guys who are members who I've been with since I broke up with the boyfriend I moved here with. I don't do scenes with random men. I test regularly. I have an IUD, and I insist upon condoms."

"The guy last week. Was he one of them?"

"Yes. And I can assure you he won't want me again."

"Why? Because you called him by my name?"

"Partly."

"Don't give me half answers, Fina. Unless you want me to lock you in my penthouse and fuck you morning, noon, and night for a month, so you forget this guy and even your own name, you will answer me."

Defiance radiates from her as she presses her lips closed. I press my hand around her throat, but I don't squeeze. I rest my weight on one forearm as my free hand reaches between us and unzips my pants. I push them and my boxer briefs down, then kick them off and out of the way.

"Condom?" I demand an answer.

"Do you test regularly?"

"I haven't been with anyone in six months. I tested right before I went to Sicily and did when I got back."

"No condom. Come in me."

I thrust into her. She cries out, and her neck arches as she pushes her head into her pillow. My hand tightens a fraction, but not enough to be breath play.

"Tell me." I growl beside her ear, but she remains silent. "I will make you sore, Fina. I will keep fucking you until you beg me for a break. I will make sure the only thing you can think about is the feel of me inside you. Is that what you want? Do you want your fucking cunt to be mine?"

"Yes!"

"This isn't a scene. This isn't just dirty talk. Not now that I'm inside you."

"I know. Carmine, the only thing that makes sense right now is that I need you to move until I come. I don't get why I need that so fucking badly or why I'm agreeing to any of this. But I feel like I might lose my mind if we don't actually fuck soon. I—" Tears dampen her cheeks.

"Shh, Fina. I'm sorry. I went way too far."

"No. It's not that. I—"

"What, little one? What do you need from me?"

"Everything. I don't know why I'm being like this. I need it really rough, Carmine. Like break the fucking bed rough. Keep talking the way you are. I like it. But please, don't lie to me about this being more than tonight. If it's just tonight, I'm fine with that. But don't make me need you. Don't make me think there's more to this than there is."

I thrust into her over and over. Sublime. Euphoric. Divine. All of that, and I haven't even come yet. "I've meant everything tonight, Fina. I've meant everything I want to do to you while we're here and everything I want to do in the future."

"You haven't been with anyone else in months, but I don't want to share you."

"You don't have to. But I've already told you I get jealous. I will never begrudge you having guy friends. I don't care if you're friends with those four guys outside your club. But I won't accept you sharing any of this with someone else. Either I'm your only lover from now on, or there's nothing after this."

Her face softens, and the tension slides away. No more tears wet her cheeks. "Only you."

I kiss her, and there's something new about this kiss, and it's different from any I've had before. But I keep thinking that about each type of kiss I share with Fina. I give her what she asked for. We move together, making the bed bang against the wall. She gasps and moans, whimpers when I hit her g spot.

"May I come?"

I cock an eyebrow.

"May I come, Carmine?"

I raise the other eyebrow.

"May I come, Sir?"

I frown.

"I'm not your Dom."

"Then I don't know what you want? May I come, *patrizio?*"

I laugh at that. Patrician. I don't know how she came up with that, but I'm tempted to say yes. My laughter makes my dick twitch. She clenches around me and moans. I rock my hips and lean to whisper to her again.

"Call me what you want, *piccolina*. That's something I will let you decide. But that's it. I lead when we're like this."

"You want me to submit."

"As much as you wish to submit and for me to dominate. You know it just like I do."

She nods. I massage her tits as I move faster. The hand that was at her throat slides up to cover both her hands. She moves them, so my fingers slide between hers.

"*Patrizio*, may I come?"

"*Si, piccolina mio.*" Yes, my little girl. I fuck her harder still. She thrashes beneath me as I feel her cunt spasm around me. I fight not to spill yet. I'm not ready for this to be done.

"Carmine!"

I wonder if her guards have figured out who she's with. If they hadn't before, they will now. They must hear her. I just count on them knowing she's screaming my name in ecstasy. I don't need them breaking down the door. I'll gouge their eyes out before I let them see her naked with me buried in her balls deep.

"Come again. Now." I circle my hips, grinding my pubic bone against her clit. She pushes her heels into the mattress, lifting her hips to meet each of my thrusts.

"I'm so close, *patrizio*. Please don't stop...So close...Yes... Harder...*Harder*."

"Demanding, *piccolina*."

"You promised I'd be sore enough to think about you with every step. I want to think about you with every breath."

"Fuck, little girl. I'm never going to let you go."

This kiss is desperate. That she might want me that much is overwhelming. I almost feel pathetic wanting her to want me like that, but I'll do anything to make that true because that's how I feel about her.

"I don't want to go anywhere, *patrizio*. Please don't let go."

As our gazes lock, I feel her tighten around me with another orgasm.

"If you want me to pull out, Fina, tell me now. Once I spill inside you, you are mine."

"I already am, Carmine."

Chapter Six

Fina

Carmine's lips press softly against mine for a moment before we both demand more. But this isn't the sexually starved kisses we've shared tonight. It's not the possessive kind either. It's so heartbreakingly tender. He's pulling his tie free from my wrists as I feel him pulse inside me. My hands are in his, our fingers entwined as we watch each other come. I'm panting beneath Carmine's weight. He moves to pull away, but I dig my fingers into the back of his hands, and my knees trap his hips in place.

"I'm going to crush you, *tesorina mia.*" My little treasure.

"I'm not that little, *carino mio.*" My cutie.

I giggle as he nuzzles my neck. I don't expect the affection, so it surprises me. I let go of one of his hands and comb it through his hair. He shifts and suckles my breast. He licks my nipple before sucking again. I arch my back, trying to draw him closer. When I press his head to my tits, he pulls back. The moment I stop, he sucks again. I fist his hair, and yet again, he pulls away. I release his hair, and he sucks even harder.

"*Carino*, don't stop. I can come again. Just—" I moan as he circles his hips. How is he still hard? He cups my breast and sucks hard as he rocks slowly. The contrast is driving me crazy. I free both of my hands and grab his ass. "Fucking hell, Carmine. You feel so good. Fuck."

"I'm going to make you come again, *piccolina*. When I do, you're going to beg me."

"Yes, *patrizio*."

His commands make me tingle. I love his assertiveness. I don't feel like he'd be domineering if we weren't fucking. He's a dominant man by nature, and he's dominating me in here. But I have never felt like he'd bend me to his will outside of the bedroom. Just the opposite. I feel comfortable submitting to him in a way I never have before because I don't fear this spilling out of our sex life into real life. I've never felt that confident about this kind of dynamic before. It's why I've always insisted upon not being a sub.

"You're close, *tesorina*. I can feel you."

"So close. Please may I come? I need to so badly."

"Not yet."

"I need to. I don't think I can stop." He pulls all the way out, and I wail. "No! Please don't stop. I need you."

"You need me to fuck you."

"So badly."

"You need me to get you off."

"Yes."

"Who do your orgasms belong to now?"

"You, *patrizio*."

"Whose pussy is this?"

"Yours." I could claim I'm so horny that I don't know what I'm saying, but I do. I know exactly what I'm saying, and I mean all of it.

"I decide, Fina. I will take care of you and give you everything you need in and out of bed. But your pussy and your orgasms are mine. I'll give you pleasure as well as take it away. Can you live with that?"

"Yes."

He thrusts so hard I flinch, but I dig my nails into his back. I try to get closer, begging with my words and my body.

"Why can you live with that?"

"Because I'm yours."

"That's right. Tonight changes everything, Fina."

"I know." We look at each other, and it's the truth. "Fill me with your cum. Prove I'm yours to do with what you want, *patrizio*."

"What I want is to make you come so hard that you never want anyone else."

"Please, may I come?"

"Yes. Now."

I strain until I feel my orgasm tighten in my lower belly, then explode. "Yes! I'm coming."

"Me too." He grunts his response.

We're both panting as he rolls us, so I'm sprawled across him. We lie in silence for several minutes. He strokes my hair while holding my ass. I could almost fall asleep, but I don't want to miss a moment of this.

"Are you all right, *piccolina*?"

"I've never been better. You don't look like you'd be as comfy as you are."

He laughs. "What does that mean?"

"You're hard all over. Not just your dick, which forget about a cock ring. Clearly, you don't need one. But I've never been so comfy as I am right now."

He kisses my forehead as he chuckles. "Then stay as long as you'd like. Who am I to interrupt your comfort?"

I lift my head, resting my hand on his chest, then my chin

on that. He tucks hair behind my ear, and I strain to kiss him. His gentleness surprises me.

"Fina, I know you're worried that you're making more of this than it is. But you're not. Please don't break my heart."

I'm stunned into silence. Never could I have imagined the Carmine I believed I knew could be so vulnerable. He shared things about his childhood and his shit decisions that I'm certain he tells no one else. Now he's worried that I'm going to play him. I swallow the lump in my throat and shift, so I'm straddling him and resting my forearms above his shoulders. I kiss his temples, his cheeks, the tip of his nose, then his lips.

"Carmine, a lot's come out tonight that neither of us expected to share. We've had amazing sex, but it's also been really heavy. What you told me in confidence will always remain with me. I believe I can trust the same of you. But the things I said I wanted weren't just dirty talk. They're what I want with you. I'm going to ask you the same thing. Please don't break my heart."

"Fina, I've fucked up more times than not. But I meant every word I said tonight. I want you. I want an 'us.' You know how I want things. Is that what you want too?"

"Yes. It scares me. I don't understand any of this. I don't get why, after everything you've admitted, you're the first man I've wanted to submit to completely. I don't know why you're the one I trust so completely. What you said wasn't just sex talk, was it?"

"No. I'm not interested in a Dom/sub relationship. I won't tell you what you can and can't do outside of sex. I will make suggestions and ask things, but I won't dictate anything. The only thing I will never bend on is your safety, Fina. That's the only caveat. You're an adult and have done well for yourself long before I came back into your life. But I won't negotiate or compromise when it comes to taking care of you. You're a don's daughter, but it's different being with the don's nephew in the city where you live. Especially when it's New York, and it's me."

"Are we a couple, Carmine? Is that what you mean?"

"I want that. But if you're not ready for that, then I won't push. I'm not going out with anyone else, and I sure as hell am not being intimate with anyone else. I'd like to take you out and spend more time with you besides having sex."

"I want that too." I glance at the clock. I can't believe it's already one a.m. "I have to open the shop in four hours. I'm guessing you have to work, too. But I can cook as well as I bake. Would you come over for dinner tonight?"

"You'd like to cook for me? I'm happy to take us out. I don't want you to have to make dinner after working all day. That doesn't seem fair. I'll make you dinner."

"You cook?"

His chin pulls back, and he looks truly insulted. "Yes, I can cook. I don't order in or eat out every night. I've kept from starving."

I lick along his neck and flick his earlobe before tugging it between my teeth. "I can tell. You're still a growing boy."

I wrap my hand around his cock and stroke. His hand lands against my ass.

"Tell me right now if you're too sore, Fina."

"Not sore enough."

"No. I didn't exaggerate when I said I want you to think about me being inside you every time you move. But I won't fuck you again if I'm going to hurt you."

"Good thing you don't have to fuck me. I'm going to fuck you." I shift and am about to slide down his cock when he rolls us over. I scramble to hold on to him. His fingers thrust into my pussy. His other hand captures my jaw and holds it in place as he finger fucks me.

79

"Little girl, I'm warning you right now. I will give you the rough fuck you want, but you will be honest with me. If you're already sore, then we wait. I will give you all the pain you want with your pleasure, but if you lie to me or don't speak up and I harm you, I will not easily forgive you."

I gaze into his blue eyes, and I see how serious he is. But I see something that lurks in the depths of his gaze. He's truly scared. He's worried not just about hurting me physically, but about losing my trust.

"Time out, Carmine. Let me sit up."

He pulls back and rolls off me. He sits beside me. I shift, so I sit between his legs, mine resting on top of his and around his hips.

"I trust you, Carmine. I'm putting my faith in you that you won't let me down outside of the bedroom. I'm also putting my faith in you to know what you're doing with BDSM. But I need you to trust me, too. I know I want to please you. I can feel it. I want to satisfy you sexually, but I want to make you happy beyond that. Making you feel guilty because I withheld the truth isn't what I want. It actually makes me feel sick. I know my safety in and out of bed is a priority to you."

"It is. I told you at the party that I want to take care of you. I do."

"What does that mean to you? Like, what does that look like to you?"

"When we're like this, it means watching you and reading you. Giving and taking what you need to satisfy you, to build intimacy and trust with you. Outside of sex, I want to make you laugh. Make you feel safe, important, special. I'm protective of the people I care about by nature, especially the women in my life because none of us asked to be born into this lifestyle. It makes all of you vulnerable to men bigger than you and stronger than you. I want you to know that you can come to me about anything and that you'll always be safe with me."

I scoot closer to him and wrap my arms around him. "You're like a life size teddy bear. You're a sweet man, even if you've made shit choices."

"Thank you. I don't know that I'm sweet, but I'll take it."

I cup his jaw in both hands. "You've made fucked-up choices, but you've admitted them. You could have kept all of it from me. Instead, you told me without being asked. You could have kept this all about sex even though you know it means more to me than just the physical. You've admitted you want more, and you've been vulnerable when you could have kept up a wall. I like your idea of being taken care of. It makes me want to curl up with you and ask you to never let go."

"Say the words, and I won't let go."

"What does that mean?"

"Fina, I haven't had a girlfriend since my first semester in college, and she thought we were more than we were. The last time I really thought I could have a relationship with a woman was in high school. You know the man I was, and you know this life. Nothing about who I am or what I do makes my life conducive to a relationship. But for the first time in my adult life, I want to commit to someone. To you. I want to see where this goes."

"Me too." I watch him, and the thought that comes to mind shocks the shit out of me. I glance down between us. What the hell is wrong with me?

"Fina?"

"Hmm?"

"You just retreated. What's wrong?"

"Nothing. I just got lost in thought for a moment."

"And you don't seem to like what you thought."

"Not at all. Just the opposite, and it surprises me." He looks at me inquisitively, but he won't push. "I'm not quite ready to share yet, *carino*. I need to figure out how I feel about this idea. But I like everything you described."

A wave of tiredness washes over me, and I struggle to stifle my yawn. I yelp when he lifts me around the waist and lies back. He slides me onto his cock, and we both sigh.

"Hold on to me, *piccolina*." He moves around until he pulls the covers loose and from under us. We work together to pull them over us. "Close your eyes, little girl. I'm going to make you come just before you fall asleep."

"Are you going to come too?" I rest my head on his chest and close my eyes. His hand on my hip guides me to move along his cock as he keeps his thrusts shallow. His other hand strokes up and down my back.

"Shh. Relax. I'm taking care of you, remember?"

"Mhmm." I let myself relax, and I can't believe how soothing this is. I never once pictured sex putting me to sleep. At least, not in a good way. The closer I feel myself getting to coming, the sleepier I feel.

"Shh, *piccolina*. Let me make you come."

"I'm close."

"I know, my sweet little treasure. Come on me. Make me fill you with my cum." His voice is a deep rattle that warms me like a glass of whiskey. I flex my pussy, and he thrusts harder than he has. "Fuck. Just like that, little girl. Make me come, and I'll get you off."

"I want to take care of you, too." I can barely follow what I'm saying.

"You are, little girl."

"I don't want to fall asleep until all your cum is inside me. It's all mine."

"It is. Let me get you off. That'll make me come."

I yawn again. My body is moving on its own, and I feel myself drifting off.

"You're close, aren't you, *tesorina?*"

"So close. Yes...I'm coming right now."

"Me too. That's such a good little girl. Fuck, Fina."

"I wish you could always take care of me." I'm babbling at this point, and I'm not sure if I'm awake or asleep.

"I will if you'll let me. I know you're out of it, but I mean it."

"I know, Daddy. I mean it too."

He grasps my hips and thrusts hard, waking me. What did I just say? Oh, fuck. I moan, and the memory along with the feel of him coming inside me, brings me fully alert. I push up and ride him.

"Harder."

I'm demanding now that I'm awake. His hand lands across my ass. He sits up and pulls me close.

"Do little girls give their daddies orders?"

Fuck. He did hear me. I did say what I thought.

"That's right, Fina. I heard you. And you remember what you said. I'm not your fucking Daddy Dom, and you're not my little. But you sure as fuck want me to take care of you. That's why you called me that. Right now, that means you want another good hard fuck."

"I've never called any man that."

"And no woman has ever called me that either. But I won't forget it."

"I don't want you to forget. I want you to do just what you described."

Our kiss explodes. We move together, completely focused on moving in sync, our conversation no longer priority. I come yet again, and he does too. How much training does his dick have to last like this? I slip off him. We pant together as our hearts continue to race, but our bodies still. When I catch my breath, I continue.

"I know why I said it. I almost said it earlier."

"Why, Fina? Why do you want to call me that?"

"Because you're the only man who's ever wanted to take care of me without controlling all of me. You might be possessive during sex, and I *love* that. But you don't treat me like a possession. You want to provide what I need and protect me. I feel safe with you. But I don't feel like any of that limits me or makes me feel younger than I am. You're not my father, and you're not a Daddy Dom. But I want to call you Daddy. Does that make any sense?

"Yes. It's the same reason I've called you *piccolina* all along. *Tesorina*, what are you doing to me? I'm hornier than a fifteen-year-old, and I have more endurance with you than I've ever had. I can't get enough. I just want to stay in you and feel you come over and over. How do I even have any cum left?"

"I don't know, Daddy."

We lie together silently for a few minutes before I lift my hips and reach between us to wrap my hand around his cock. He's semi-hard, so I work him until I feel his cock coming back to life. What the hell vitamins or supplements does he take that he can keep going like this? Even the guys I dated in their teens couldn't do this. He's already come, what, twice in like thirty minutes. I sit up to ride him again.

"Fuck, Fina. Say it again. Please." He's begging for the affirmation, for the affection, for the acceptance. I've never wanted to give anyone anything more.

"Daddy."

"Again."

"Daddy."

His fingers bite into my hips. I've lost count of how many orgasms I've had at this point. He thrusts into me and holds me in place as his pubic bone grinds against my clit. Over and over until my fingernails dig into his shoulders as we come together. I collapse forward, truly spent now. He adjusts the covers, and I sigh. Just before I actually fall asleep, I realize he's fulfilling another fantasy—having a man inside me as I fall asleep. I'm glad it's Carmine—Daddy—who does it. But one question comes to me just before my mind goes blank.

What the fuck have we done?

Chapter Seven

Carmine

Fina is sleeping in my arms. I woke a few minutes ago after the four best hours of sleep in my life. I've never felt this rested. I glance down at her as my thumb trails over her shoulder and down to her elbow. She has the most satiny skin I've ever felt. I don't remember ever being so content to just be still. Her arm drapes across my waist, and her left leg presses between mine. I could stay like this for forever, but she said she has to open the shop. I doubt she has work clothes at the bakery, so she'll need to go home.

"*Piccolina.*" I stroke her back as I try to wake her gently.

"No." She mumbles and nestles closer. I smile and kiss the top of her head.

"*Piccolina*, you have to wake up."

"No."

"You're going to be late for work."

"Don't care."

"You're the owner. You have to care." She grumbles and

shakes her head. She feels around and pulls the covers up to her ear. "Fina, you have to get up. I'd rather stay here all day with you, but you have a business to run."

"Shh. I'll call in sick. Be quiet. Your chest moves too much when you talk. You're not being comfortable anymore."

I chuckle. I never took her for being grumpy in the morning. "Come on, sleepy head."

"Are you trying to get rid of me, Carmine? Do you have somewhere to be?"

I roll her over and nudge her legs apart. I settle between her thighs, the tip of my cock pressing against her pussy. The sex last night was mind blowing. The emotions were confusing as hell. The conversation was way too deep, but I've never felt more connected to someone.

"The only place I need to be is inside you."

"That's better."

She shifts to wrap her arms and legs around me. I ease into her, worried she might not be ready for me. But I glide straight in. Her own eagerness mixes with my cum from last night.

"Fina?"

"Are you always this chatty in the morning?"

I laugh a third time. "Hardly. But I don't want you to be late. Don't you have to go home to get ready?"

"My manager has keys. She'll open, and I'll text her I'm running late."

"How do you want it, *tesorina mia*?"

"Slow. I don't want this to end, Carmine."

"It doesn't have to."

"Really?"

I don't like how hesitant she sounds. I kiss her cheek down to her jaw and back to the skin behind her ear. I whisper to her. "I didn't lie or exaggerate last night, Fina. I meant everything. I want us."

She captures my cheeks between her hands. "All of it?"

"Yes. You're still my *piccolina*, and I'm now your Daddy."

She flinches, and I freeze. We stare at each other.

"Do you really mean that, Daddy?"

"Fina, where is this coming from? Why are you so nervous?"

"Because I don't want to think this is more than it is."

"I believe I'm the one who asked *you* not to break *my* heart."

That was hardly my most manly moment. I've felt vulnerable plenty of times in my life, but it was one of the rarest of rare moments I let anyone know.

"Okay."

She lifts her chin, and I offer her a soft kiss. At least, it starts that way. It explodes as we move together. Unlike last night, where we couldn't get it hard enough or rough enough, this morning, we're tender and slow. Our hands roam, and we shift positions, taking turns being on top until she clings to me, holding me down on top of her.

"I know missionary is boring, but I love watching you above me."

"It's not boring if that's what you like. I enjoy watching you riding me."

"I'm close."

"Me too, little one. What do you need to get you off?"

"Just keep doing this. It feels so good."

I thrust and circle my hips over and over until she grabs my ass and strains against me.

"Yes, Daddy... Yes... May I come?"

"Please do because I can't last much longer, Fina. You feel too good."

She moans as her neck arches, and her eyes slide shut.

"Look at me." I don't mean to demand, but it comes out a

command. She turns glazed, passion-filled gray eyes to me. I can't hold back. I thrust hard three more times before I shoot my cum into her. I roll us onto our sides and pull her leg over my hip.

"Can't we go back to sleep for a while and do this again before we go, Carmine?"

"I wish, but you'll wish you'd gotten up on time when you're rushing around. Do you want me to take you home? Or do you want your men to do it?"

"I want you to, but it would probably be better if you didn't."

Sadness creeps into her eyes, and I don't want this after-glow ruined. I toss back the covers and roll to the edge, bringing her with me. I carry her, wrapped around me, to the bathroom. I turn on the water in the shower, and once it's warm enough, I step under the showerhead. She continues to cling to me, her head resting on my shoulder. We let the water roll over us as the bathroom fills with steam.

"Fina?"

"I don't know why I'm being so clingy. I'm not like this."

"Like what? Affectionate?"

"You don't think I'm being—I don't know—ridiculous?"

"No. Come over tonight, Fina. Let me make you dinner. We can have a normal date."

"I'd like that."

She sighs as she lets go of me. I ease her down to her feet. I change positions with her, the water soaking her hair. I move us again, turning her to face away from me. I pump shampoo into my hands and work it into a lather in her hair. She hums and leans back, resting against my chest.

"You're not convincing me to leave. Your fingers are magical."

I rinse my right hand off and slide it between her legs. I rub her clit then move to take my hand away, but both of hers press my fingers back into her.

"Please don't stop."

"Ask properly."

"Daddy, will you please get me off?"

"Yes, little one." I abandon her hair as I massage her tits, going back and forth between them as I rub her clit. She reaches back between us, and her hand encircles my cock.

"May I come?"

"Yes."

She braces one hand in front of her as she continues to work me. I feel her pussy spasm around my fingers as my thumb works her clit and my fingers stroke her g spot. I lean away, allowing the water to wash the shampoo from her hair. When the suds are gone, I press her forward, grabbing her hips in both hands. She spreads her legs, turning her feet inward, as her palms rest against the wall.

I hold her in place as I pound into her. She meets each thrust, pushing back toward me. I'm speeding way too fast toward my orgasm. I want this to last longer, even though I'm the one who keeps telling her we have to go. I grunt as I feel my balls tightening. She pushes my hands away and shifts away from me.

I'm confused until she turns and drops to her knees. She slides her lips down my cock, and I swear I go cross-eyed. She sucks me over and over, her head bobbing until I catch it between my hands, holding her in place. I fuck her mouth. She doesn't fight me, taking me deeper with each thrust. When I'm about to blow my load, I pull out.

"Stroke me."

She obeys, and I come across her chest and throat. She dips her chin and opens her lips, taking the last of my cum in her mouth. I fist her hair and lean forward.

"My cum is inside your cunt and across your tits and in your mouth. My hand painted your ass red last night. You are mine, Fina. Don't question that. If you want this to end, say so. Otherwise, don't doubt it when I say I want us."

I help her to her feet. She reaches for the bar of soap and tears off the wrapper.

"Turn around, Daddy. I can't wash your back if I can't reach."

We take turns running the bar of soap over each other. I lean forward so she can wash my hair. We wind up laughing at how I have to bend almost in half. But I bracket my hands on either side of her on the wall and kiss her while she runs her fingers through my hair. We rinse off and towel each other dry. We don't talk as we dress. We head back into the suite's living room for her shoes and purse. She looks toward the door and back at me. She bites her lower lip, then thrusts her hand out.

"Can you give me a ride home?"

"Are you sure you want your guards to know you've been with me?"

"I've screamed your name at least once. I'm pretty sure the secret is out."

"That's not the same as walking out of a hotel room with me."

"Carmine, how much haven't you told me?"

I consider what she's asking. "There's other stuff, but I told you the worst. I'll tell you the rest if you want to hear it."

"What you did to Anastasia is horrible. There's no two ways about it. You fucked up hard core, Carmine. You're lucky you lived. Does Olivia know what Luca did?"

"Yes."

"You may be guiltier than him, but she's found a way to accept what he did and still be with him. I can accept you did something shitty without believing you are shitty. I'm not ashamed to be seen with you. Are you embarrassed to be seen with me?"

"Never. But if anyone finds out, they're going to expect an explanation."

"Here's the only explanation they need: they can fuck all the way off."

I laugh at her earnest expression and deadpan tone. "All right, *piccolina*. I'll take you home."

She reaches for the doorknob, but I catch her wrist.

"Fina, you must know better than that. You knock and let your guards know you're coming out. You don't open the door until you recognize their voice. They should have a code word for you to know it's safe."

"That's not how we've ever done it."

"How do you know they're still there? How do you know no one's lurking out there for you?"

She stares at me before she nods and steps aside. I ease my arm around her waist and tilt her head up.

"Fina, obviously your men have done an excellent job protecting you. My family just does things differently. I didn't mean for it to sound like your family does it wrong. I just don't like any unnecessary risks when it comes to you."

"I know, Daddy. What you said makes sense. Could you teach me these protocols you use? Is that what *Zia* Sylvia and Maria do?"

"Yes. I can tell you, or they can."

Her brow furrows.

"Maybe you'd feel more comfortable having someone who uses them explain them to you."

"Oh...No. I want you to explain them to me. Then I'd like you to explain them to my guards."

"Fina."

That is not a good idea.

"If they won't listen to suggestions to keep me safer, then they shouldn't be my guards."

"It won't come across as suggestions. They'll think I'm telling them they're doing their job wrong. Who am I to question their methods after one night with you? That's what they're going to think."

"Let them. I trust you, Carmine. If you think this is how it should be now that I'm with you, then that's how it will be."

I kiss her forehead. "Thanks for understanding, Fina."

I open the suite door, and immediately, two guns point at me. One between my eyes and the other at my cock.

"Adriano! Augusto! No. *Metteteli giù.*" Put those down.

Fina tries to step in front of me, but I pull her back. That only makes them train both guns on my head. Once I'm certain I shield her by filling the doorway with my much bigger body, I put both my hands up. She tries to peek past me as she speaks.

"Where are David and Gio?"

I don't know who's who, but it's the one on the left who answers.

"Their shifts ended."

I'm not pleased about that. Fina said nothing about trusting anyone else to know she's here. No one told us one set of guards was handing off her protection to another. I keep my voice low while I keep my eyes on the men. I know they can hear me, but I don't give a shit.

"Fina, is it normal for your guards to change when you're out and not tell you?"

"Yes. Someone's always there, so they don't bother me."

As much as I wouldn't have wanted our sex fest interrupted, this protocol ends today.

"They will from now on. You are to know who your guards are at all times. No surprises. No changes to the schedule without you knowing. It's not safe."

The man on the left seems to be the duo's mouthpiece. I can already tell he's going to argue. "Ms. Carosi is our responsibility, and we've used these protocols for years."

"Fina, after what we talked about last night, what do you want?" I won't be so high-handed as to demand things change right this second. But they are, regardless of Fina's answer. She doesn't skip a beat when she answers.

"Carmine's right. Either someone knocks or calls from now on. If I'm home, and it's a normal shift change, then I'll already know. I thought David and Gio were assigned to me for the entire night. I don't like these types of surprises. If you thought I was in danger, you would have stormed in. It's a bit late to be pointing your weapons at—Carmine. Lower your guns. Now."

She hesitated. What was she going to say? My boyfriend? My lover? My one-night stand? No. She agreed it was more than that. But we never decided what we are. The man on the right finally speaks up.

"We'll take you home now, Ms. Carosi."

She slides her hand into mine and nudges me aside. The guards have holstered their weapons, so I concede and move out of the doorway. She steps beside me.

"Carmine is taking me home."

"Are you both only Ms. Carosi's guards, or is one of you her driver too?"

"I'm her driver."

It's the guy on the left again. Why is he so fucking smug? For Fina's sake, I will try to make nice now. They're going to report to her dad the moment we're in the car.

"I'm Carmine Mancinelli, but I don't know either of you. Who's Adriano? And who's Augusto?"

The quieter one answers for them. "I'm Adriano."

Good to know.

"Augusto, please bring the car around. Adriano and I will

escort Ms. Carosi downstairs once you're in place. Knock when it's time to go."

I close the door in the men's faces. I turn and peer down at Fina, trying to gauge her reaction.

"Why aren't we going in your car?"

"I didn't drive last night. I came with Gabriele and Marco. Gabe drove. I'll have one of our cars meet me at your place. Your guys won't have to take me home."

"You're really pissed, aren't you?"

"Fina, I told you I won't back down when it concerns your safety. What if one of your father's men turns? What if the guy kidnaps you and ransoms you? You wouldn't know not to go with him. I want to know whether David and Gio knew about the shift change and didn't tell you or these guys just showed up."

She pulls out her phone and dials a number. She puts it on speaker.

"Good morning, Ms. Carosi."

"Good morning, David. Did you know Augusto and Adriano were going to relieve you?"

"Not until your father texted to find out where you were."

Fina's gaze meets mine. She's pissed now, too. "Do you usually report where I go to my father? Does he always know if I stay out?"

"No, but he suspected you were with Mr. Mancinelli."

"You've never changed shifts in the middle of the night without warning when I've stayed out before. Why last night?"

"I don't know. Your father didn't offer a reason, and I know better than to ask for one."

I nod and shrug. These may be Made Men, but they're nowhere near high enough on the food chain to ask for explanations.

"*Grazie, David.*"

"*Prego. Addio.*"

"*Addio.*" She hangs up and looks at me. "I thought I shouldn't flaunt spending the night with you in front of my parents, but I didn't think my dad would get involved."

"But you must know why. My past isn't a secret to him. That's what he meant about me speaking on behalf of my cousins about the baby gift. He was taking a dig at me for what I got Luca into."

"I wondered about that at the time, but I figured it out when you were explaining. Carmine, I don't care. I'm twenty-eight. He can't force me to marry someone else while there's an official betrothal contract, so it's not like he can force me away from you that way. He can complain if he wants, but who I date is my choice. The only way it isn't is if he forced me to marry you."

I cup her cheek as we gaze at each other. Would that be so bad? I've never considered marrying anyone, and I'm not ready to propose today—even if we are technically pretty much engaged. But I could see myself with Fina. I could see a future with children when I peer into her eyes. Would they have her eye color?

"Carmine, please don't let him interfere."

"I won't, but neither will I ever ask you to pick between your family and me. I wouldn't let you pick me, either."

"Let me? I didn't know I had to ask for permission for anything outside of sex."

She tries to pull away, but my free hand pulls her closer, then rests on her ass.

"We both know family is everything. Mine would welcome you without reservation, but I won't take you from yours. I don't want that for you, and as happy as my family would be to have you join, they wouldn't forgive me for it."

She slides her arms around me and burrows against my

chest. "Can we think about something else, Daddy? Like dinner tonight?"

"Would you like me to cook for you?"

"Yes."

A knock sounds at the door, so we make our way over. She hangs back and lets me open the door. Adriano's in the hallway, so he leads the way to the elevator. When we enter it, we both automatically rest our hands on our guns. I keep mine holstered at the small of my back since my suit coats always hide it. I know she felt it and saw it last night, but she said nothing about it.

We get off in the underground parking structure. Augusto has the car pulled up to the hotel door. He gets out and opens the town car's back door. Adriano and I continue to shield Fina, so she's barely visible from the front or back. Once she's inside, I slide in beside her. Augusto closes the door with a little too much force, but I say nothing. I hit the button and raise the privacy glass. That would never be down by default if a couple were getting into one of our cars. They already know to take us to Fina's place.

"Carmine, do you have to be at work soon?"

"No. I'm sure Gabriele figured out that I'm skipping the gym."

"Would you come in while I get changed, then come to the bakery with me?"

"Are you worried about something, *piccolina*?"

"No. But there'll be fresh donuts ready, and I thought you might like some."

"Some? Do you need to fatten me up?"

She walks her fingers up my abs to my chest, then she surprises me by tickling me. Unprepared, I can't help but squirm. She giggles, but she bats my hands away when I turn the tide. I reach across her and unfasten her seatbelt before pulling her onto my lap to straddle me. Our kiss is playful, but we're both aroused as she grinds on my dick.

"Take me out, Fina."

"Yes, Daddy."

She hurries to unbuckle my belt and unfasten my pants. I already bunched her dress up around her hips. She moves to line her pussy up with my cock, which is standing at attention, ready to go. She tries to drop her weight straight down, but my hold on her waist doesn't allow it. I tease her, letting her take an inch before pulling her up. Then she takes two inches, and I pull her up an inch. I do this until finally she's seated on me, my shirt fisted in both hands.

"That was torture, not teasing."

"I know. For both of us, little one."

"Then why?"

"Because you know you loved it as much as you hated it. It was the same for me."

"God, you feel good."

"You aren't too sore?"

"No. Every step reminds me of us being together, but it's not enough to stop me from having you one more time."

"Having me? Is that so, little girl?"

"Yes, it is." She grins and tries to tickle me again. I snag her wrists and move them to the head rest.

"Hold on and do not let go."

"Or else?"

"I didn't think you were a morning person when I woke you. But you like to play with fire early in the day."

My hand lands across her ass. She shakes her hips and laughs again. I love this playful side of her. I didn't expect it. She almost lets go when I move us. She wasn't prepared for a good fucking. I thrust over and over, raising her, and dropping her onto my cock. She dares to let go, but she reaches back and unfastens her dress. She pulls her bra down and offers me her tits. She holds them and waits for me. I latch on to her right one, and her hands immediately go back to the headrest. But I bite just enough to make her yelp then whimper. I suckle again. Hard. She does a Kegel that nearly makes me come. I let go of her nipple.

"Thank you for the offer, *piccolina*. I'll never turn your perfect tits down. But I don't recall asking you or telling you to pull your dress down."

"I know, Daddy. But I wanted to offer them to you without you having to ask, to offer them on my own."

"Rather than me take?"

"Rather than you having to take."

"Lean forward." She does without hesitation. I wrap my hand around her throat, but I just let it rest heavily there. "Thank you, *tesorina*."

I kiss her as we move together. I could make a big deal out of her letting go of the headrest or doing something without being told. But I'm not her Dom. I want her to know that our give and take is equal. And to be honest, it might have been a small gesture, but it made my heart swell that she's offering any part of her simply because she knows I'd enjoy it. Of course, I know sucking on her tits arouses her, but she didn't do it because she was in the throes of wanting more passion and stimulation. I pull back and feast on her tits, alternating sides, squeezing them. I know when she's close. Her head is near my ear, and her moans grow longer, even though she keeps them quiet.

"May I come, *carino*?"

"Yes. I'm going to fill you with my cum. You're going to drain every drop from me. Then you're going to keep it inside you until we get to your place. You'll remember what we just did as it drips along your thigh as we go into your place. You'll remember what we did as you wash it away."

"You'll wash it away."

She cocks an eyebrow before her back bows, and she tenses. I thrust hard, despite how her inner muscles spasm around me. Then I'm doing just what I said. Fucking hell. I shoot my seed inside her, and I glance down at her belly. I've lost my ever-loving mind because I just pictured getting her pregnant. Again. As in, not with our first child. She looks down between us, and I know she sees where I'm staring.

"Are you worried?"

I don't look up, but I shake my head.

"No." I slide my hand under her dress until it rests on her belly. "I will never have a child out of wedlock, Fina. I will never repeat my parents' choices, no matter how modern my family might become. I will be married when I have children, so I've always been extremely careful. I've never considered it before you. I won't lie and say I don't enjoy picturing it. But that's a long, long way off, if ever. I know that."

She presses her hand over mine. "Neither of us is pledging love and devotion, but that doesn't mean it's not nice to daydream sometimes."

She leans her head against my chest, and we sit together, with me inside her until my dick doesn't cooperate anymore. When we stop outside her place, I help her arrange her dress. But I'm quick to grab the door handle and pull it shut. I lift Fina off my lap and put her back on her seat as someone tries to open the door again. I don't give a shit if either of her men sees my dick. But I do care if they see it and know I just had sex with Fina or if they see her in a less than presentable state.

"Leave it."

I bark my command. I'm certain they're thinking I'm assaulting her back here. I'm quick to fasten my pants and pull my shirt over my belt, which I leave undone. I glance at Fina, and she's covered up. I push open the door, nailing someone. I step out, but once more I block Fina.

"Do not open the door again until the person inside signals they're ready."

I guess the couples in her family aren't like the ones in mine. I'm certain there's been plenty of sex had in our town cars and limos, and not just by my generation. Hell, I suspect my parents conceived me in one.

I move aside and stick out my hand to help Fina out. I wrap my arm around her waist as we walk to her front door. Her place in Queens is quaint. Nothing about it screams Mafia princess lives here. She lets me in, and I sweep my gaze around the interior. I take in everything. The layout, the furniture I can see, the decorations on the walls, the spacious yard I spy through the floor-to-ceiling windows. I don't like that the curtains are open.

"Fina, you knew you were going out last night. You should have closed your curtains and put a light on before you left. No one should ever be able to tell you're not home, and no one should ever see you in here at night."

"Carmine, I know those rules. I was in too much of a rush and forgot. My mom didn't tell me about dinner until after I left church. I was at the bakery I'm opening in Harlem when she called. I had to rush all the way back here, get ready, and get back into Manhattan."

"All right."

I know she could get defensive, but she steps up to me and grabs my suit coat lapels. Her kiss is fierce and threatens to reignite yet another round of fucking as she walks backwards toward the bedrooms. When we reach hers, she lets go of me.

"Thank you for worrying about me. It's been a long time since anyone has when it's not their job."

"Your parents worry about you. That's why your dad sent Augusto and Adriano. He must have thought they'd give me shit or maybe even intimidate me."

They're both big guys. Adriano is bigger than me and close to Gabriele's size. Augusto and I are equally matched. I don't doubt their training, and I don't doubt their commitment to protect Fina. They wouldn't back down because I'm the don's nephew and a *capo*. I don't believe I'd best them simply because of my name. I'd do it because I'm certain there's nothing I wouldn't do to protect Fina, and being this into her gives me a different motivation from what they have.

"Fina, as much as I want to go another round, aren't you going to be super late?" I point to the clock on her bedside table, and she sighs.

"Yeah. Give me five minutes."

She slips out of her clothes, handing them to me as I put them on the bed. I watch her walk away, and it takes all my restraint not to say fuck it and join her. But she didn't exaggerate when she said five minutes. She's in and out of the shower, and I hear her brush her teeth. After the way I came in her, I don't blame her for the second shower. It took her seven minutes. She comes out with no makeup, and I remember she wore none the day I went to her shop with Maria. She hurries across the room and pulls clothes from her closet. She goes to her dresser and pulls out a bra. She holds up panties, and I scowl, which makes her laugh. She flings them at me.

We're in and out of her house in less than fifteen minutes. While she was getting ready, I texted one of our drivers. I guessed he was at Luca and Olivia's here in Queens. He's waiting for us behind Fina's car.

"My guy can follow us and pick me up once I drop you off. Or we can ride in my car, and your guys follow."

She glances at her men, who're standing on the porch as we walk out. "They can follow."

She's still pissed. Once we're in my town car, we hold hands, but we're both determined not to make more of this car ride. Once we're at the bakery, it takes little for her to convince me to enjoy four donuts. They're as amazing as the cupcakes. She explains that even though her manager opened the shop and baked them, they're her recipe.

"*Piccolina*, do you want me to pick you up and bring you to my place?"

"Are you going to be in Manhattan today or Queens?"

"Manhattan." I don't have any reason to go to Uncle Salvatore's or Luca's, so I'm staying in Manhattan.

"Then I'll come to you. How's six-thirty? Seven if traffic is bad."

"Perfect. Is there anything you don't like?"

"I remember you loved sardines. They're gross." She screws her nose up as I shake my head and sigh dolefully.

"So, you're ruling out half the Sicilian dishes I know." I grin and kiss her cheek as we embrace. "Fear not. I'll come up with something."

I wink and give her a quick kiss on the lips before letting go.

"Have a good day, *piccolina*."

"You too, *carino*."

I turn back to smile at her before I walk out the door. I'm met with two pissed off guards, standing in front of me as an SUV pulls up. I half expect it to be Fina's father. Three men get out, and they're not at all who I expected. They're not even Italian.

Chapter Eight

Fina

Carmine set out to make me sore enough to think about him with every step I take today. Mission accomplished. It's a delightful soreness, not the kind that makes you want to soak in a hot bath. The only reason I want to do that, now that I think about it, is to soak in one with Carmine.

Twenty-four hours ago, and I was celebrating Easter at Mass and wondering if I would see him there. Twelve hours ago, Carmine was doing wicked and delicious things to me in a hotel room. I know Gio and David disapproved, but it's not their job to monitor my dating or sex life. They're the two who I trust to escort me to my club. They're the most discreet and least obtrusive. The four guys I've been with know I come from a wealthy family, but I've never given them my real name. I signed up under a fake one that a forger created for me in college.

The guys know and accept that I don't go anywhere without my guards, who're masked like I am when we're in there. They stand outside any room I go into to scene. The club objected at first, but a sizeable donation to remodel the main playroom convinced them that my men wouldn't cause any trouble. I trust David and Gio have told no one about those extracurricular activities. That's why it shocked me to see Augusto and Adriano outside the hotel room door.

I'm in my office sorting through bills and shipment receipts, but my mind isn't on the work. It's not even directly on Carmine. It's about why David and Gio left, and why my father sent Augusto and Adriano. The last thing I want to do is confront my dad. I'd rather puzzle out the mystery without going to the source because in no way do I want to admit I spent the night with any man. Fucking uncomfortable.

My parents know I'm not a virgin. They can't possibly think I am when I was with Orlando for almost six years. I moved continents to go to college with him. We lived together from junior year on. He moved with me when I went to grad school, getting a job to stay near me. They know nothing about my other sexual exploits, but they never tried to stop me from living with Orlando, even if they disagreed at first. Maybe they really believed we would get married. I knew we wouldn't. I loved Orlando, but he was as vanilla as white paint.

No matter how I tried to spice things up, or how I tried to finagle him into leading during sex, he wasn't into it. It made me realize what I was missing, and that I didn't want to live a lifetime without it. I joined my BDSM club the day I dumped him. I might have joined two hours before I told him it was over. I did it to make sure I didn't back down when he begged me to reconsider. I wasn't cruel, but I was honest.

I'd tried for years to suggest shifts in our dynamics, at least during sex, but really I wanted someone more like Carmine. I wanted someone who made me feel cherished and a priority. Carmine may have shared more sins than the devil could offer one man, but, at the same time, he made sure I knew he would do anything to please me. I don't think he did it just to fuck.

"You've been staring at the same three pieces of paper for an hour."

I look up as Rosella, my manager, enters the office. She handles most of this stuff, but I go over everything monthly. Today's the day I planned to do it, but I can't concentrate.

"Does it have to do with that hottie you arrived with? I remember him from last month. He came in with the brunette and the blonde."

"Yeah. The brunette's his cousin, and the blonde is her best friend."

I try not to sneer as I think about Veronica pressed up against Carmine, trying to make it sound like they'd been in Sicily together. That pissed me off in a way that I hadn't wanted to examine that day. It pleased me beyond belief that she wasn't at the dinner last night. If she had been, would she have flirted with Carmine in front of me? It definitely would have meant I didn't sit next to him. My seat would have been hers. That's enough to make my jaw clench. I believe Carmine that there is nothing between them and hasn't been. You couldn't fake the disdain he radiated. But I still don't have to like her.

My phone pings, and I look down to see a text from Juliana.

JULIANA

You need to see this. I know you spent the night with Carmine.

There's a link in the text, so I tap it. It pulls up a tabloid with today's date. There's a picture of Carmine with some woman he's having lunch with. He's smiling, and he looks so damn hot. I zoom in. That's the same tie he wore last night. The same one he tied around my wrists.

107

I glance at the clock on my computer. It's almost two o'clock. This must have just posted within the last hour or so. He might still be with this woman. I scroll down and my heart stops. The woman's face isn't visible in either photo, but his arm is around her as he kisses her on the cheek. Then there's a third photo of him with his hand at the small of her back as she gets into a town car. One of his town cars. I want to be sick. He left here and within hours he's with someone else. There has to be an explanation. I scroll back up to the top of the article, and the headline only makes it worse.

Playboy life of the rich and famous

Eligible bachelor seen leaving hotel this morning with one woman only to lunch with another.

That's the caption under the first photo. Someone saw us leaving together. They might know about me. Or they saw him and assumed he'd spent the night with someone. Maybe the reporter or paparazzi saw him arrive separately from this woman, and that's how they knew she wasn't his woman from last night. Me.

ME

How'd you get this?

I was scrolling and spotted it.

You know this is a gossip magazine. It's not reputable.

Maybe not but that's still him.

That's true. There has to be a reason. My phone pings again, but this time it's not from Juliana.

CARMINE

I hate to do this but work is going to get in the way of tonight. Tomorrow?

Work, huh? Is he having dinner with her, too? Maybe breakfast? Or is it someone else? I put my phone down. I close my eyes as the tears prick my eyelids. Maybe this is just unfortunate timing, and he's not breaking our date because of the woman in the photo. Maybe there's a reasonable explanation for who she is. When my phone pings for a third time, I don't want to look.

JULIANA

Check this one out.

I click the link. I wish I hadn't. It's definitely Carmine because I recognize the suit and the haircut. There's a chick with shoulder-length blonde hair with her arms around him. The woman's face is obscured just like in the other photos, but I know who it is. There's only one woman with hair that color and length who he'd be with. He fucking lied. He is with Veronica. She wasn't welcome at the family event, so he found someone else to entertain him. But why spend the night with me? Why not go to her? Maybe she had other plans.

The photo is date stamped today. I can't see his tie, but I know that suit. I'm such a fucking idiot. I believed everything he said. He warned me he's a manipulator, and I fell for it all. I feel so duped. So humiliated. I close the browser window and toggle over to my text thread with my sister.

ME

Thanks.

What else can I say?

At least it was only one night.

Yeah. That doesn't make me feel any better. One night to foolishly think I'd found something special. That maybe it was fate or God who'd pushed us together, not our maniacal grandfathers. I run my hands over my face.

I gotta get back to work.

Wanna come over for dinner?

Obviously, I'm not going to Carmine's. It's better than sitting alone at home.

Sure

See you then.

I send the thumbs up emoji. Now I'm more determined than ever to focus on my work. I refuse to allow Carmine to fill one more moment of my thoughts. But he lurks in the back of my mind all day.

It's seven-thirty, and I'm just finishing dinner with Juliana and Ernesto. My phone has vibrated at least five times in the past hour. I help clear the table and excuse myself to the bathroom.

6:25 CARMINE

I'm bummed I don't get to see you piccolina.

6:45

Are you on your way home right now? I wish I didn't have to work.

7:10

Fina?

7:12

Are you all right?

7:17

I'm getting worried. Are you all right?

7:25

Fina answer me before I panic and lose my shit.

7:30

Serafina I'm two minutes away from calling your dad to make sure you're ok.

I don't want my dad involved, but neither do I want to talk to Carmine. Fuck my life. Why couldn't he just discreetly disappear?

7:32 ME

Your plans changed. So did mine. Filling the time with

Do I do it? Do I poke a bear? I won't like the response, but I feel like lashing out. So much for having reined in my temper.

someone else.

That's not a lie, even if the connotation differs completely from the truth. I'm with Juliana and Ernesto. I wait for a response, but nothing comes. Did I expect one? Maybe not. Was I hoping for one? Masochist that I apparently am, yes. Why else would I goad him? I head back into the living room where my sister and brother-in-law are having a cup of coffee. Decaf for the preggers. I decline a cup.

"I'm going to head home. It's been a long day."

They get up to say goodbye. Ernesto gives me a warmer hug than usual, which confirms my sister must have told him. Juliana gives me a tight squeeze.

"Call me if you need me."

"It's not that big of a deal, Jules. It's not the only one-nighter I've had."

"I saw you together last night, Sera. You really like him. From the way he was, I thought he really liked you, too."

"I guess not. I'll see you later."

I leave, and I appreciate the silent drive home. Sometimes I chat with my guards, but I keep the privacy glass up once I tell them to take me to my place. I sigh as I walk in the door, but my heart is still heavy. I glance around as I turn on the living room light. As I close the curtain, I think about what Carmine told me just this morning.

But I didn't come home before going to my sister's, so I couldn't have closed the curtains. I'd planned to come home, shower, and change before going back into Manhattan to see Carmine. I'd considered taking clothes with me, but I wanted to surprise him. I wouldn't have been able to do that since he was in my bedroom just this morning. I walk into my bedroom and flick on the light.

And scream.

Carmine's stretched out on my bed with his arms crossed, ankles crossed, and shoeless. His stare pins me in place, and it takes me a moment to snap out of it.

"What the fuck are you doing in my bedroom? How the fuck did you get in?"

"Your window security is shit, Fina." He swings his legs over the side of the bed before stalking toward me. "Your security team is shit, too. Where the fuck is he?"

"Who?" My tone is snide and antagonizing on purpose.

He's quicker than I expected. He fists my hair and pulls me against his body. His anger pulses from him.

"Whomever you're filling your time and your cunt with."

I push against his chest. He doesn't let go, but he loosens his hold until I can put space between us.

"Don't speak to me like that."

"Doesn't mean I don't deserve an answer."

"You deserve nothing. Let go of me before I scream for real, and my men come in."

"You had a date with me. The minute I have to work late, you pick some other guy to fuck. Who, Fina? Don't make me ask a third time."

"You don't deserve anything from me. I owe you nothing. Go back to fucking the woman you had lunch with."

His expression is one of horror. Fucking guilty.

"Don't be disgusting, Fina."

"Disgusting is you telling me all those things last night, making me believe you, then you banging some chick five hours after you leave me at work."

"I am not banging my mother. What the fuck, Serafina?"

I freeze as I process what he just said. I can't speak louder than a whisper. "Don't call me that. I don't like it."

"It's your fucking name."

"Not with you, it isn't. And that was your mother?"

"Yes. How'd you even know I had lunch with a woman? Spying on me? You trust me that little?"

"No. My sister—she texted me—it looked—"

I burst into tears. When he doesn't immediately comfort me, I start sobbing. He picks me up and carries me to the armchair in the corner of my room. He sits with me on his lap.

"Shh, *piccolina*. What happened today? What did Juliana say?"

I can't stop crying now that the flood gates opened. Carmine rocks me and strokes my back.

"Shh, little girl. Whatever it is, I'll make it better. Just tell me what happened... You're breaking my heart, Fina. What happened? I can't fix it if I don't know... Please tell Daddy what's wrong."

"Kiss me, Daddy?"

Please. I'll beg at this point.

"Of course, little one."

The kiss is everything. It stops my tears as I cling to him. When we pull apart, and I've caught my breath from crying and practically swallowing his tongue, I sit up. I fish my phone out of my pocket and open the texts from Juliana. I know he's reading them, and I don't care. I click on the first link. Carmine zooms in on the tie just like I did before zooming all the way out. He zooms in again, but he's looking at something else.

"Fina, look at that date."

There's a bank clock in the background. The date is last July. I look up at him in confusion.

"But it's the same tie you were wearing today."

"I know. That's definitely not my mom. I was on a date with this woman, but I haven't seen her since three weeks after this was taken. That was nine months ago." He scrolls down to the next photo. It's the one of the woman getting in the car. "This was from today. That's my mom, Fina. I have lunch with her every Monday."

I'm feeling like such an idiot. I go back to the texts and tap the second link. It's the one with Veronica. "Explain why you're with her. You told me you weren't dating."

"Olivia? She and I have never dated. Luca's already come close to killing me a few times. There'd be nothing left of me if I went near his wife. Look. You can see Luca's sleeve in the corner. Zoom in and Auntie Nicoletta's in the background.

They came with my mom for lunch. Luca and I have been on better terms lately, and we've started spending time together. Olivia's been mediating."

"That's not Veronica?"

"Fuck no. Fina, I haven't touched her since that fucked-up night. I truly cannot stand her. I only tolerate her for Maria's sake. She's a fucking hot mess. She's petty as fuck. She taunted you just because she could. She doesn't want me."

"Why would this paper print a nine-month-old photo with this headline?"

"How did your sister find it?"

"She likes to read the magazine during her lunch. She said she was scrolling. Why the old photo, Carmine?"

"Because someone is stirring shit. Either for me in general or with you. They cropped these to look incriminating. It's not the first time gossip rags have done this. They've used photos of me with my mom and aunts, even Maria, but no one's done it in months. Not since before Sicily. I want to know who sold those pics from today." He hands the phone back to me as he wraps both arms around me. "*Tesorina*, I'm sorry you went through this today. I wish you'd just asked me."

"I do too. I feel like such a bitch. But it hurt so much, Carmine. Way worse than I imagined. Thinking you were with someone else right after being with me. I wasn't prepared for that."

"How do you think I felt when you made it sound like you were with another man? First, I was worried for your safety. Then, I was jealous beyond reason."

"Is that why you sneaked in here?"

"Yes. I wanted to know who you chose over me. I wanted whoever it was to know you'd been with me only hours ago."

"We're a fucked-up pair."

"A lot happened last night, and we're moving fast. I know

that. There's still a lot to figure out and a lot about each other to learn."

"I shouldn't have assumed the worst, and I shouldn't have been mean. I'm so sorry."

"I know, little one. I can tell."

"Are you going to spank me?"

"For punishment? Absolutely not. Your hurt and fear were valid, Fina. I will never punish you for that. If you want the spanking as a prelude to us having sex, then absolutely."

"But I jumped to horrible conclusions."

"Based on the man you've known me to be, I understand why. I'm not angry anymore. I just feel badly that you went through it. I'm worried this won't be the last time something like this happens with a tabloid. It makes me worry that next time they might put you in it. I don't want your privacy invaded."

"Like you did my room. Seriously, how'd you get in?"

"Insanely easily. I climbed your neighbor's tree, came over the fence, and jumped to your roof. You have an attic window that needs a new lock. From there, I just came down the stairs. Your guards weren't patrolling. They weren't even listening. I'm not a light man to jump onto the roof. I'm no cat burglar either. I made a thud that should have had them running to investigate."

"It was probably because I wasn't home. They weren't too worried."

"And I'm proof they should be. I got in and was waiting for you. If they won't patrol properly, then they need to do a sweep of the house before you come in. I don't like how lax they are, Fina. Nothing's happened so far, but your dad's the don in Venice. You're dating a *capo* here."

"We're dating?"

"I'd like to think so."

I nod. I'd like to think that too. "Aren't you supposed to be at work?"

"Yes. When you didn't respond to my texts, I left."

"Left? Can you do that?"

"No. I'll hear about it in the morning from more than one person. But Marco and Lorenzo were there too. What needs to get done will get done. Making sure you were safe was way more important. I'm glad I came. I wouldn't want you to have gone all night thinking I was with someone else. I couldn't handle thinking you were with someone else. Fina, if you ever want to end this, I won't trap you. If you want someone else, then tell me. I won't hold you hostage. But please don't throw it in my face like that again."

"I won't. The worst part is I thought about it before I did it. I let my temper get the better of me, and I was vindictive. I'm so ashamed, Carmine. I'm sorry."

"Shh, little one. I know. I'm only partially sorry for breaking in and scaring you. I should probably be completely sorry, which makes me feel guilty."

"No. You made an important point about my safety. I appreciate you putting me first."

"You know better than most that there will be times when I can't. But that isn't by choice. I'll always put you first when I can."

"I know, Daddy." I inhale his cologne as I run my fingers over his shirt's buttons. My brow furrows. "You're in the same suit and tie but different shirt."

"I haven't been back to my place. Gabe lent me a spare one when I went over there. I can wear his suits too, but the sleeves are just long enough to be annoying. He needs the extra fabric to fit around his arms. We're the same height, so his pants fit perfectly."

"Should you go back to work?"

"No. I'm staying with you. I can tell you're still upset. I'm not leaving you alone."

"Will you hold me a little longer? I never imagined I'd be so comfortable as when I sit on your lap."

"Good, because I like you here."

He kisses my forehead. I close my eyes and let myself relax for the first time in hours. Everything feels resolved between us, but who the fuck planted that story? And why today?

Chapter Nine

Carmine

I didn't expect to see Besnik Marku in the SUV that pulled up as I walked out of Fina's shop. I knew immediately that nothing good was going to come from his appearance. It makes me super anxious that he knew where I was, and that I was anywhere near Fina. I can't say I don't want to draw her into this world because she's already in it. But I don't want to pollute it. At least not yet. I want us to have more time to see where this is going before she re-immerses herself in Mafia life.

As I sit with Fina curled in my lap, I think about the impromptu meeting. I knew better than to get in a car with him. I got in mine with my men, and Besnik followed me to my office in Midtown.

"Besnik, what the hell are you doing in New York? I didn't know you ever slithered out of Boston."

"Always a pleasure to see you too, Carmine. I have better things to do than be seen with you. Let's get on with it."

We're sitting in the office on the floor that Mancinelli Devel-

opers uses in the skyscraper we own. The only time anyone comes here is when we need a respectable place to do business. Most of our transactions happen in strip clubs where men can measure their dicks. Now that I have Fina, I'd happily never go in one again. But I own five. Fucking misbegotten youth. Maybe Matteo wants them.

"You came to me. You get on with it."

"Ardit is pissing and moaning about his brother, claiming I let that shit happen. I did not."

Ardit Hoxha is the New York krye for the Albanian Osmani syndicate. He's the equivalent of Uncle Salvatore here in the city. Besnik is his peer in Boston. But they're both really just underbosses to Roel Elezi, the real krye who lives in Albania.

I know some of what he's talking about, so I share that. "I heard some half-Russian, half-Albanian psycho went after Teodor because Teodor bought a car the stupid fuck wanted."

"Yeah. Yuri. He's Roel's son."

"That's a fine little detail I missed when I heard the story the first time."

"Roel's not exactly proud to claim the fuckwad. He's never said it, but I'm pretty certain he wishes the Podolskaya had taken Yuri out a few years ago."

Now there's a name I don't want to hear. The Podolskaya is the bratva that got tangled up with the Anastasia Kutsenko fuck-tastrophe. Anything to do with them means me beating a hasty retreat. I sit back in my chair, as though that could put real distance between me and the Moscow bratva.

"Great history lesson, Bes. What do you want?"

"Ardit plans to make a move on one of your family's restaurants in Queens. The Osmani think they're ready to play at your level. We both know they're not."

"What do you want, Besnik? I'm not asking again."

It shouldn't surprise me when he tells me he wants us to kill

Ardit. I'm unprepared for him to tell me he thinks Ardit and Yuri are sex traffickers. That's not something any of us want to touch with a ten-foot pole. Except he wants me to dig around without the bratva finding out. Hell no.

"I wouldn't have left Boston to see you personally if this weren't a significant problem for all of us. You don't need the Kutsenkos after you, which they will be because your family is guilty by association. Take out Ardit when he goes after the restaurant. Prove to everyone that the Osmani aren't sucking your dicks."

"And in the meantime, you'll make your move to off Ardit's cousin, Zef, and take over New York. You'll put your brother in as Ardit's replacement. And you came to me personally, thinking I'll lick the Ivankov bratva's asses to make up for what happened. I do the manipulating, Bes. Not the other way around."

"The thoughts crossed my mind once or twice."

Fucking hell in a hand basket. He tries to reassure me everything will be fine. I'm certain it won't. Telling Maks and his family could be a path to redemption with them. But the chances of that are smaller than a cockroach's fart in Antarctica melting an iceberg. We don't need them going after Ardit and taking him out, which they will do since they prefer Zef. Fuck my life. Why can't I still be in bed with Fina? Or nearly as good as that would be hanging out at her bakery, eating more donuts.

"I'll look into it, Bes. That's the best I can offer for now."

I wonder why he's taking such a personal interest. But I don't care enough to ask. We shake hands, and I watch him walk out of the office.

"Carmine?"

"Yes, *piccolina?*" Fina shifts on my lap and sits up. How long have I been lost in thought about my meeting?

"You looked a million miles away."

"I was."

"Work?"

"Yes."

Our gazes meet, and she nods. She knows it's the sort I can't talk about. I can tell her about the strip clubs I own, not that I want to. I can tell her about the import/export business I have as long as I don't mention things like tonight's delivery. I can even tell her about the interior design firm I'm now a silent partner in. That was the first business I opened straight out of college. It didn't take long to discover two things. Men who look like me aren't taken seriously in the world of interior design. Men with my last name scare clients away.

Taking a silent backseat while raking in the profits is fine with me. I have a competent CFO and COO. Carmine Ciccone is on the letterhead instead of Carmine Mancinelli. I legally changed my name, or rather legally added my father's last name when I was eighteen. It was an act of rebellion, just like most things I did back then. But I can't tell Fina about this. Not about an Albanian turf war or possible human trafficking. The first of a great many secrets I'll keep from her.

"Did you have dinner, Daddy?"

"No. Did you?"

"Yeah. At Juliana and Ernesto's. Do you want me to make you something? I cooked on Saturday, so I have food for most of the week."

"I bet you only cooked one dish."

"Maybe." She grins at me.

"Does it serve six or eight?"

"Seven. Shows how much you know."

"You ate some already, didn't you?"

"Maybe." Whatever Fina made would be a single serving if she made it for a family. But as a single woman, it'll last her a while. No Italian recipe has ever been invented that's for less than six people. "Are you hungry, *carino?*"

"Starving, but not for food." I lean in to whisper, even though there's no one else here. "There's a pair of tits that I'll have as an appetizer and a very delicious pussy to make my main course."

"Is sex all you think about?" She laughs until I stand, and she scrambles to hold on.

"*Piccolina*, I would never drop you. And it's entirely your fault that I'm hornier than a fifteen-year-old who wants to lose his virginity. Stop being so fucking gorgeous and delectable, and I might be able to think about something else for a few minutes."

"A few minutes?"

"Yes. I'm not easily distracted." I walk past the bed and out of the room, moving down the hallway until we get to the kitchen. The table in the nook is clear, so I put her down there. "Don't move."

She doesn't get off the table, but she watches me as I move around the kitchen, closing blinds and checking windows and the sliding glass door. I shoot her pointed looks that clearly mean we will discuss her home security later. I'll make sure Gabe is here before we leave for work. He'll bring what I need from the hardware store he owns. Between the two of us, we'll have things up to my standards before she's out of the shower. Fuck. Before she's done with breakfast. I intend to enjoy morning shower sex with her.

I return to the table and step between her legs. She peers up at me, and the light catches her eyes. They're the translucent gray that fascinates me. It makes the green flecks stand out. I noticed her eyes turn a darker, steelier gray, in the middle of sex. Perhaps it's exertion or being hot. But they're just as riveting as the lighter shade.

I pick her up again. I love how curvy she is, and I wouldn't trade her voluptuous figure for a more petite woman. But I'm a large man who can fireman carry Gabe, who weighs two-hundred-and-fifty pounds on a skinny day. She's easily sixty or seventy pounds lighter than him, so she's a feather to me. She slides her hands up my chest and around my neck as she hooks her feet around the back of my thighs.

"I think I want dessert after all."

"And what would dessert be tonight, *tesorina*?"

"The biggest *cannolo* I've ever seen."

I can't help but laugh. I close my eyes and shake my head. I'm unprepared for her to push me out of the way and hop off the table. She dashes to the fridge and pulls it open. She lifts out a plate with cling wrap over it. I stare.

"You really meant a real *cannolo*."

"You sound disappointed, Daddy."

That word. It makes my cock ache. I've heard it in porn. I've heard it in strip clubs. I've heard Olivia slip up and use it with Luca. It did nothing for me until Fina said it. Now I want to hear it morning, noon, and night. She puts the plate back in the fridge and pulls out some other containers. She pops off the lids and gets out a plate. I watch as she heaps food onto the dinnerware, then puts it in the microwave.

"Fina, that has to be at least three or four days' worth of meals for you."

"And probably one course for you." She saunters over to me, her hips swinging in the most tempting rhythm. Her hand cups my dick and squeezes just enough to make me groan. "You're still a growing boy. I need to feed you to make sure you have enough energy for your athletic endeavors."

"Athletic endeavors? Is that what we're calling our sex life?"

"You're definitely a marathon runner, not a sprinter."

I laugh as she turns away, but I catch her arm and pull her back. She's facing away from me when I press my hard on against her ass.

"I'm going to need to up my endurance training to keep up with you, little one."

The microwave pings, and she grabs two potholders before lifting out the plate. She grabs a knife and fork before bringing the steaming food over to the table. I grab a placemat from the center of the table and put it in front of me as I sit.

"Thank you, Fina. This looks and smells delicious. I feel badly though. I was supposed to make you dinner."

She shrugs. "Another night. It's the least I can do since me being pissy pulled you away from work. Are you sure everything's going to be all right?"

"Yes, *piccolina*. Don't worry. There are plenty of us in my family. I'm not the only one who can do the job." She watches me for a moment, then nods. I reach out and take her hand. The food needs to cool, anyway. "Fina, how much do you know about how things work for your father and uncles?"

"Enough to know not to ask to know more."

"You know there's a place, right?"

"There's always a place, isn't there? My family in Venice has a place, and my family in Sicily surely has more than one place."

"Yes. Ours is in Queens. Never look for it, Fina. You won't find it, but you'll endanger my family, your family, and you if you poke around."

"Carmine, I know. It won't be on any city records or maps. It'll be somewhere in an Italian neighborhood, but nowhere obvious. I know I won't be able to reach you when you go there. You and everyone else will have your phones off. I know that if you see me twice in one day, and you're not wearing the same clothes, it was because you went there."

"I'm glad you know that last part. I never want you to think I've changed clothes to hide being with someone else."

She stares at me for so long that I get nervous and take a bite of food that's still way too hot.

"You admitted a lot to me last night. I suspect there's still a shit ton more to come. But the one thing I think you take more seriously than just about anything else is fidelity. You're not a cheater. Plus, I think your family would kill you if you cheated on your girlfriend or wife."

"You would think." I set my fork down. "Fina, my family is as good Catholics as any Mafia family can be. We don't break sacraments once they're made. That means divorce is out of the question. It also means that couples turn blind eyes at times. My parents separated the day after I left for Stanford. They haven't lived together since. They've both had other people in their lives. I know neither of them has been faithful. It's always been by mutual agreement, so some would say it's not cheating. But just like I will never have a child out of wedlock, I will never be unfaithful. I will not make the same fucked-up choices my parents have or that were forced upon them. Sacraments are not to be broken. Not even bent or twisted."

I watch her, and I think she realizes how unwavering I am about this. I will remain single my entire life if I think for a moment I cannot be a worthy husband and father. I won't put Fina or any woman through the misery I watched my parents endure, and I will never make a child grow up in a house with the tension I grew up in. My parents didn't yell when they argued, but there was never a doubt when they didn't get along. Half the time, they just didn't talk to each other.

Some would say people shouldn't stay married for the sake of the kids. But I can appreciate the sacrifices my parents made to give me a stable home life. They never shuffled me between houses. I never wondered who I was spending holidays with. I never had to alternate weekends or weeks with just one of them. And for all their faults between them, they were devoted parents to me. My parents came to every game I played. They came to every violin recital. They listened to every science fair presentation.

They did it with pride, and those days and events were the only time they were happy together. They were when I was happiest. Unless work kept my father away, we always had dinner together until I left for college. Neither of them has ever said a negative word about the other to me. So, no, I don't think it's always better to divorce for the kids. I would have been even more jealous of my cousins and their happy homes if they had.

"I'm glad to know that. There are couples like your parents in my family, and I never want that. I'd rather not marry at all. But I saw your parents last night. They seemed happy, even when they were together. They sat next to each other."

"Mama and Papa will probably always resent being forced to marry and being forced to spend so many years under the same roof together. I know the sacrifices they made for me. I knew it as a kid. It didn't shock me or upset me when they separated. I've accepted that they've been with other people. But now that they don't live together, they're actually pretty close to being friends. My dad fixes things around my mom's place and brings her food. She's a phenomenal cook but hates to do it. My dad's a bit more than a passable cook but loves it. She'll take his dry cleaning when she takes her own. She'll drop off groceries. They're more compatible now than they ever were living together."

"I'm glad they have that."

I take a few bites, savoring each one. Then I dig in with gusto. I'll marry Fina right now if I can spend a lifetime enjoying her cooking and baking. "This is wonderful, Fina. Thank you for sharing."

"I'm glad you like it."

"Love it. My God, is there anything you can't do?"

My phone buzzes in my pocket, but I ignore it. A minute later, it goes off again. My shoulders sag. I don't want to deal with this right now. I know it's my family because it only buzzes twice before it goes quiet each time. I pull it out, and I see Gabriele's name.

"What's up?"

"We need you back. We think we found something."

I watch Fina, and I know she understands without me saying anything. She whispers to me. "You have to go."

I nod. This fucking sucks. When I've had to leave women in the past, I haven't cared that much. Or rather, my dick cared if I didn't have time to get off. But I never invested emotionally, so it didn't matter that much.

"All right, Gabe. I'll be there as soon as I can."

"Sorry. You know I wouldn't call if it weren't important."

"I know. Bye."

"Bye." I put my phone back in my pocket. I look down at the plate.

"Do you want to take it with you? Maybe eat in the car?"

"I drove myself. But yes, can I take it?"

"Of course."

"Thanks. I intend to make them all feel guilty that I got pulled away from my dinner with you and have to spend the night with them instead."

"How long do you think you'll be gone?"

"I should be around tomorrow. I'll let you know if I'm going to be unreachable for a few days." I stand and watch Fina put everything into a divided container before she walks me to the door. "Fina, I'm sorry."

"You don't have to apologize. I get it."

"I know, but it still blows. Especially after the evening you had, thinking I was playing you. I also wanted to change your locks and latches in the morning."

"Rome wasn't built in a day, Daddy. We'll get to everything, whether it's you making my house into Fort Knox or a dinner date."

I take the food from her, and we share a passionate yet sad kiss. We're both disappointed. She watches me walk out to my car, and I wave before I get in. Once I've pulled away from her house, I hit my Bluetooth button in my Alfa Romeo Giulia. It's hardly my flashiest car, which is why I drove it to Fina's. It stands out in her neighborhood if someone's looking. But it doesn't draw attention like my sports cars.

"Gabe, what the hell's so urgent?"

"It's Maria. She's been taken."

"What?" My heart's racing.

"She went down to Miami for the conference. She took Veronica with her since their vacation got cut short a few weeks ago when Maria had to come back to work."

"I know all that. What the fuck do you mean she's been taken? Who? She only got there this afternoon."

"We don't know. Matteo was with them. They went to a club tonight, and he was outside the bathroom door. When they were in there for fifteen minutes, he pounded on the door and called to them. Some other women had come and gone, but there'd been no sign of Maria or Veronica. He almost got thrown out for barging into the ladies' room. Neither of them was there. There was what looked like a broom closet in the corner, but he discovered a door leading outside. There were a couple minutes when he believed they were alone in there between other women going in. He found Maria's earring in the closet and one of Veronica's shoes outside. Maria's tracker isn't pinging. We don't know where she is."

This is my worst nightmare come true. Until yesterday,

Maria was my most favorite person in the world. Gabe's my best friend, but there's no one I love more than her. She has her faults, but she's been the sweetest person I know since we were babies. She's six weeks older than me and loves to remind me that with age comes wisdom. She's always listened to me and offered me sound advice. I just haven't always been smart enough to take it.

I'm doing my best not to panic, but I'm swerving and speeding to get to Uncle Salvatore's house. Thankfully, it's only ten minutes from Fina's. I'm not going all the way to the garage. That's where we go to handle things. Fina was right. It's not on any records or plans. The neighbors conveniently forget about us because we pay well for their memory problems.

I barely slow down long enough for the gate at the end of Uncle Salvatore's driveway to open. I pull around the semicircular drive and push the ignition button. I run to the house and don't bother ringing the bell. Partly because Pia and Natalia are already in bed. Partly because we're family and don't have to ring the bell. And mostly because I'm not waiting another second to find out what happened to my cousin.

I storm into Uncle Salvatore's office, and everyone is already there. My cousins Luca, Lorenzo, and Marco are pacing in different directions. Maria is their baby sister. Gabriele's standing by the window, staring out into the darkness. Uncle Massimo looks wrecked. He loves all my cousins equally, but Maria is the only one he's always been openly affectionate with. Uncle Domenico stands like a statue in the corner. Uncle Salvatore looks like he's ready to throw something. My dad comes to stand next to me when I stop at the end of Uncle Salvatore's desk.

"Carmine?"

"Yeah, Matteo. I'm here." I look at the phone on Uncle

Salvatore's desk. Matteo's voice comes through, and I close my eyes as he speaks.

"Carmine, you were the last one to talk to her before we took off this morning. Did she say anything at all?"

My eyes fly open. "She would not ditch you, Matteo. She wouldn't do that regardless of who's guarding her. Someone took her."

They argued about something at dinner last night. I don't know what, but Matteo can be overbearing. At least, Maria thinks so. She believes he still sees her as the kid sister that needs sheltering. He sees her as his best friend's sister who doesn't realize her own magnetism. We all worry about her because she's beautiful, intelligent, funny, and has a kind heart. She doesn't see her own charisma and how it draws people— both good and bad—to her. She's not naïve. She just doesn't think she's any more special than anyone else. But she is.

I look at my dad and my uncles before looking at my cousins, then I lean toward the phone. "Did you send the jet back? We can be at the airfield when it lands. I'll call Luigi and get him to meet us there. He's on standby. Raphael can swap over with Luigi and be his copilot."

We all freeze at the knock at the door. Uncle Salvatore calls out. "*Entrate.*" Come in.

Olivia sticks her head in. "I'm sorry to interrupt, but I brought the stuff Luca asked for."

She pushes the door open and lugs two bags in. Luca and Lorenzo hurry to help.

"Did you bring my entire closet, Livy?"

She shrugs. "You didn't tell me how long you'll be gone. You just said grab some stuff for you and the guys." She glances at Gabriele and winces. "I don't know if Luca's stuff fits you."

"It does. Thank you."

Gabriele shoots her a quick smile, but Luca huffs. "Try not to rip all the seams on my shirts."

Gabriele smirks. "Try hitting the gym more than Auntie Carlotta's cookies. Maybe you'll hit a growth spurt and finally fit in my clothes."

"*Fanculo*." Fuck off.

Olivia tsks playfully, and it helps lighten the somberness in the room. "Luca, be nice to Gabriele. If you're not, your flan will go missing again."

"You did give him my slice." Luca's eyes widen as he stares at his wife before he glowers at Gabriele. Olivia shakes her head.

"Play nice with your friends, Luca." She stands on her tiptoes, but at five-feet-two, she's a foot shorter than Luca. He picks her up and whispers something in her ear before kissing her cheek.

"Thanks for bringing this over. The guys and I appreciate it."

She nods. I can see her swallow before she takes a step back. We all know fear is hitting her as it suddenly gets real for her. This is the first time Luca's traveling without her. He's gone to the garage several times since they got together, but he's never been away from her for days and in another state. He looks at Uncle Salvatore and Uncle Massimo. They nod, and he leads her out of the office. It makes me think of Fina. She's surely gone through this with her dad. But will it be different for her now that I'm in the picture? I guess I'll find out. I have to let her know I'm going out of town. It also means letting Uncle Salvatore know we're together. He watches me as he speaks.

"Get your gear together. The SUVs'll be here in twenty minutes. Matteo, how long until the jet's here?"

I almost forgot he was still on the phone.

"At least another hour. I sent Raphael back the moment I realized Maria and Veronica were gone. Even before I called you, Uncle Sal."

Matteo's not actually related to us by blood, but he pretty much is. Not only is he Marco's best friend and two-and-a-half hours younger than Marco, his dad is my mom's, Uncle Massimo's, and Uncle Salvatore's second cousin. But Uncle Domenico was adopted as an infant. All of us have always called him Uncle Domenico. He's Uncle Massimo's best friend. His wife, Auntie Carlotta, is Auntie Nicoletta's—Uncle Massimo's wife's—best friend.

Uncle Massimo and Auntie Nicoletta are Luca, Marco, Lorenzo, and Maria's parents. Everyone in my generation has always called the older generation auntie and uncle, even if it's honorary. Only Aunt Sylvia goes by aunt instead of auntie. She married into the family when my generation were already adults. I listen to Uncle Salvatore hang up with Matteo, and everyone else files out of the room except for my uncles and my dad. I turn to Uncle Salvatore.

"Serafina and I are together. I need to tell her I'm going out of town. Her dad will shit, but I want men at her place. People have seen her with me, and someone is fucking with me. Someone planted a story in *UsToday*. They used photos of me with Mama and Olivia, along with a photo from nine months ago with a woman I haven't seen since three weeks after it was taken. They made it look like I'm jumping from one woman to another. The headline said I left one woman this morning for another. People know about Fina, and her security detail is bullshit. I don't trust them. Her house needs every lock and bolt changed. I—"

Papa puts his hand on my shoulder. "Carmine, calm down. Mama saw the story and called me. We've already taken it down. I dealt with it."

"I need to know who planted the story, but I can't if I'm away. What if they print something even worse while I'm not here to explain to Fina?"

"Car, I'll monitor it. You know Mama will too. She'll go to Serafina if anything else gets printed. She'll explain."

I nod, then shift my gaze to Uncle Salvatore.

"Piero is going to hate it, but if she's your girlfriend, then she's entitled to our men guarding her."

I run my hand through my hair. I don't want to share anything about Fina with anyone, but I have to. "The two guys, Gio and David, who were assigned to her last night at dinner, brought her back to the hotel. We stayed there, but when I opened the suite door this morning, two other men were posted. Fina didn't know the men were swapping over. No one told her before, during, or after. She knows why that bothers me. Then the stupid tabloid story. She saw the photos, so me having to work late fucked things up even more. I went over there before she got home. Let's just say it was way, way, *way* too easy for me to get onto her property and into her house. I know she's been fine so far, but she also wasn't dating the Mancinelli family shitbag."

"Carmine." Four deep voices bark my name at the same time.

"I know what people think of me. You know why it didn't bother me in the past. If this were just about me, I would say I deserve whatever's coming. But I can't let Fina end up in the middle. I also can't not go find Maria. I need to know Fina's going to be safe while I'm gone."

Uncle Salvatore steps around his desk to stand in front of me. "Go and help your cousins. I'll make sure Serafina is safe, and I'll deal with Piero. He should be relieved someone worries as much about his daughter as you do."

"Uncle Sal, he's going to try to break the betrothal. I'm

certain of it. Let him. I'll pay whatever penalty there is if he insists. If Fina and I are together, it's because she chooses me."

Uncle Domenico, Uncle Salvatore, and Uncle Massimo give me loose embraces before my dad pulls me close and thumps me on the back. He puts his forehead against mine, the same way he did when I was little and played peewee sports and was headed onto a field for a game.

"Be careful. Try not to get any grass stains or blood stains on your clothes. Mama hates trying to get those out. Do your best. I'm always proud of you."

It's the same things he's been saying to me since I was five and played in my first soccer game. I hear women's voices, and I know all the moms are here. I pull away from my dad.

"Thanks, Papa. I'm not coming home without Maria."

The five of us head into the living room.

"Mama."

My mom spins around from giving Gabriele a hug. My parents have been like second parents to him since we were kids, and especially now that his parents moved back to Palermo. She opens her left arm and waves me over. She embraces both of us, nearly disappearing between us.

"*Vi amo, ragazzi. Fate attenzione. Mi mancherete ogni minuto di più, quindi tornate presto a casa.*" I love you, boys. Be careful. I'm going to miss you more and more by the minute, so come home soon.

Another ritual. It's the same things she's been saying since we started going on missions. She lets go of Gabriele and practically smothers me. I don't mind in the least. I cling to my mom and whisper to her.

"Serafina's the one. If I'm gone longer than a couple days, please go see her, Mama."

"I will, *polpettino mio. Ti amo.*" My little meatball. I love you.

She's been calling me that since I was born. I was nine pounds, four ounces, and nearly two feet long. When the doctors held me up, I was still curled in like a meaty little ball. All she could see were my arms and legs. She said she had a moment of irrational fear I had no torso. She said it was labor hormones. But she's called me her little meatball ever since.

"*Grazie, Mama. Ti amo.*"

I say goodbye to Aunt Sylvia, Auntie Nicoletta, and Auntie Carlotta before saying goodbye to my dad, Uncle Massimo, Uncle Domenico, and Uncle Salvatore. Uncle Massimo is staying here for Auntie Nicoletta's sake. She needs him since her daughter is missing and all three of her sons are going into God only knows what. We all are.

We pile into one SUV, and we'll have other men meet us at the airfield. They'll bring our weapons. I look out the window and consider whether it's too late to call Fina. A text seems like a shitty copout. I dial her number, and it rings several times before her voicemail picks up. I glance at my watch. It's after eleven, so she's probably asleep. I make myself stop panicking.

"*Piccolina*, I have to go out of town. I'm not sure how long I'll be. It's a family thing and serious. I'll try to call or text, but I don't know when. I'm going to miss you. Bye."

As I end the call, I watch my phone. When the screen dims, I have the worst feeling that everything is about to blow up in my face.

Chapter Ten

Fina

I got Carmine's message when I woke this morning. I'm in the town car on the way to work now. He sounded horrible. His voice was raspy and despondent. It scares me enough that I call my dad to see if he knows what's going on. This is a mistake I won't make twice. We've been arguing in Italian for the past five minutes. Or rather, for the past five minutes, he's been rambling off a list of all Carmine's faults. He's repeated several.

"Papa, I know you're annoyed that I'm seeing him, but—"

"You are not seeing him. You had an indiscretion that won't happen again. I won't hear any more about this."

"Papa, you will. Either we have this one phone call, or I'll keep bringing it up."

"You do not give me ultimatums."

"Then don't be unreasonable. It was not an indiscretion, so don't call it that. I'm twenty-eight. You do not tell me who I can date."

"I'll ship you back to Venice."

"And I'll come right back here. I'm a U.S. citizen now. You can't have me deported. Papa, put Carmine aside for a moment. Something's happened in the Mancinelli family. Something bad. Do you know what it is?"

The moment the words leave my mouth, I regret it. Not only was calling a bad idea because my dad's bitching at me, I just realized I shouldn't have aired any of Carmine's family laundry in my dad's backyard. Fuck. There's a protracted silence before my dad speaks again.

"What do you mean something bad?"

"I don't know. That's why I called. I just know Carmine had to go out of town."

"Where to?"

"He didn't say. I think this is more than work."

"I'll look into it and let you know."

"Thanks, Papa."

I've fucked up. This was such a bad idea. I would have done better to call *Zio* Salvatore and butt straight in there. I've just washed my hands when my dad's name pops up on my phone screen. I point to my office, and the two employees I have working today nod. I close the door behind me.

"Papa?"

That was fast. Is that good or bad?

"He went to Miami with his friends."

"Miami?"

"Yes. He and a group of guys went down there. It's seven a.m., and they're already at a bar. They've been to three nightclubs since they arrived."

This feels like yesterday all over again. Is this some fucked-up coincidence? Did he really play me last night?

"You said he was with a group of guys. His cousins?"

"I don't know."

"Yes, you do, Papa. If you know where he went, then you

know who was with him."

"The places were crowded, and he was talking to women not men. I know Gabriele was with him. Of course." He tacks the last comment on with an extra sneer. What the hell is going on?

"Thanks, Papa."

"Now do you see why it was an indiscretion?"

"Don't call it that, Papa."

"Serafina—"

"If you keep calling it that, then I'll tell you all the other indiscretions I've had."

"Sera!"

"Thanks for calling back, Papa. I have to go. Customers are coming in. Love you."

I barely hear what he says. Maybe I love you too and good-bye, or maybe a slew of indignant exclamations. Don't care. Didn't listen. I shove my phone in my pocket and head back into the kitchen for another two hours of rolling dough and stirring batter. I wash my hands again before I head out front and greet customers. The day moves slowly compared to the ones leading up to Easter, but I have plenty to do. I spend the morning at my Manhattan location before going up to Harlem to check on the site's progress.

I did this on my own. I bought both shops and am remodeling the second on my own. *My* money got me where I am. I worked as a real estate agent in yuppie parts of Connecticut after grad school. I made a shit ton of money making sure young families could keep up with the Joneses. I bought the house I live in, even though Juliana shared it with me until she got married.

I did this. I didn't ask Papa for help. I didn't hire any Mancinelli connected contractors. I have taken no bribes nor given any. Everything has been on the up-and-up. And I'm fucking proud of what I've accomplished. But truth be told, I've been lonely since Jules moved out. She knows about my membership at a BDSM club. I even took her a couple times. It was only sorta her thing. Once she fell for Ernesto, he satisfied her in that department. My club is fun for the night, but it's not true companionship. I thought I'd found that with Carmine.

But he's in Miami, living it up with his boys and calling it work. I need to call him and give him the benefit of the doubt. I pull my phone out on the way home. Thinking about my place reminds me of what he said about needing better security. I guess I'm on my own for that.

"Hey, Carmine. It's me. Just checking in to see how things are going. I hope it's nothing too serious, and you'll be home soon. Talk to you later. Bye."

What else do I say to his voicemail? If he's partying while I pine for him, I sure as shit won't admit I miss him. One fucking night. I shouldn't miss anyone as much as I do him. I know better than to ask where he is because a) he wouldn't admit it if he's in Miami partying, and b) he wouldn't admit it if it's for Mafia business. I'm not playing my hand and letting him know I know where he is. I want to know what vestige of the truth he'll tell me. I want to trust him because he confessed so much. But the very things he confessed make it hard to trust him.

Did I mention how much this blows?

It's been a week. I haven't heard from him. Not a fucking peep. My dad won't talk to me if I mention Carmine's name or the Mancinellis'. My mom is no better. I thought I might ask for myself at Mass on Sunday, but the entire Mancinelli family was missing, not just Carmine—he's never there. That's pretty unusual. At least one couple usually attends, if not all four. But

Zio Salvatore and *Zia* Sylvia, Nicoletta and Massimo, Carlotta and Domenico, and Paola and Cesare weren't there. People I barely know filled the three pews the family can occupy. I'm over this. It's Tuesday again, and I want answers. I look out my living room window as I listen to a phone ring on the other end.

"*Ciao, Sera.*"

"*Ciao, Zio.* Where's Carmine?" I'm not playing games. There's a long pause before my uncle-in-law answers. I wonder if I can believe him. Was he debating over telling me the truth or fabricating a lie? Will I be able to tell the difference?

"He hasn't talked to you in a few days?"

"A week. Where did he go?"

"He had a business trip."

"To Miami? Not a bad business trip."

"How do you know that?" I don't answer. "Did you get your papa involved?"

He's getting pissed. Oh, well.

"Yes."

"Sera, you could have called the moment you got suspicious."

"Who said I was suspicious? Maybe I'm worried."

"You were worried the first few days. That's why you asked your dad. You're asking me now because you're suspicious. He isn't doing anything wrong."

"And by what standard are you judging wrong? As a mafioso? As an uncle whose nephew caused trouble his entire life? As someone else's boyfriend?"

"All of those. Sera, come over. We can talk about this in person. You know I won't say more on the phone."

"Some of us have jobs we have to go to." Ouch. I scrunch my eyes closed. Fuck me. "I'm sorry, *Zio.* That was completely inappropriate and unkind."

"That's your mother's temper."

"*Zia* Sylvia's too."

"Don't I know it? Come over when you can."

"I have plans for the next few evenings, and I have the new site opening on Saturday. I don't know when I can make it."

That's sorta true. I'm going to make plans since Carmine ghosted me. I'm not sitting around alone anymore. I'm aiming for the movies with Jules, a girls' night out with some friends, and maybe go to... I bite my top lip. I'll give the last idea more thought before I truly consider it. I should find out everything from *Zio* before I go down that road. I'll think about it later. I want answers, but I don't want a confrontation in person. They'll know just how much this hurts, and I don't want anyone to see that.

"*Zio*, if I come by, can you really tell me anything more than what you have?"

There's that pause again.

"No. Not yet. But I thought you might feel better looking me in the eye."

"Thanks. I really do hope he's okay. I'm still worried." I can admit that much without feeling too vulnerable.

"I promise you, Sera. He's all right. He and the others will be back soon."

"Others?"

"Your papa didn't tell you he went with his cousins and Gabriele?"

"He mentioned Gabriele."

What the fuck is Luca doing at nightclubs as a newlywed? Do I ask that? I close my eyes and exhale. I want Carmine to answer these questions. I regret getting my dad involved, and I don't feel much better about calling my uncle.

"*Zio*, if you talk to him, let him know I'm thinking about him."

"I will, Sera. He'll be home soon and will explain what he

can. Just be patient."

Ha. Be patient while my maybe-boyfriend is out at night-clubs in Miami, where even the ugly people are more beautiful than the best-looking people anywhere else. The place where Brazilian bikinis are more popular than anywhere but the place they were created. Where they consider pasties with a little thread around the neck and back are halter tops. Easier said than done.

After we hang up, I check the mail, and there's a manila envelope with no return address. The postage stamp is local, but I don't know who it's from. I don't open things like this. I want to groan as I glance over at Augusto. Fuck my life. He's been making subtle digs about Carmine for days. I don't want to talk to him, but he's the one on the porch. I'm not taking this in the house until someone checks it. Why couldn't he have the backyard and Gio could be out here?

"I don't know who this is from. Can you check it, please?"

I duck into my home office and grab a black light and a kit the guys use to test for residues. The only fingerprints are from where I held it. He does some other things to test for chemicals before he walks down the driveway to the street. I watch him ease it open and pull out what looks like eight by ten photos. He looks through them, and I'd like to knock the smug expression from his face when he comes back to the porch. He practically shoves them under my nose.

They're photos of Carmine in Miami. He's in some swanky hotel lobby. He's in five photos at some nightclub, talking to different women in each of them. Then the last photo is him meeting with some guy at a villa. There are women walking into the house behind them. Work trip, my fat ass.

Fuck him.

He ghosted me, and no one has the balls to just tell me. Except for whoever sent these. But why would they? Who are they? Someone is definitely stirring shit between Carmine and me, and the list of people is longer than I'd like to admit. The top of the list is my parents. The last thing I want is to call them and ask if they sent proof that Carmine's probably cheating on me. But he swore he would never do that. He doesn't want to be like his parents. Is he drunk in these photos? Does he have a selective memory when he drinks? No. That's not possible. Neither he nor any of the men in his family would get drunk in public. It's too dangerous to slow their reactions and dim their senses. He's sober.

I say nothing to Augusto as I enter the house. I want to be angry because I feel like that's justified. Instead, I'm miserable. I pull out my phone again and stare at it before I tap his contact. I don't bother to hide that I'm crying.

"Carmine, call me. Unless you're at that place or somewhere like it, you have your phone. Someone sent me photos of you in Miami. You are not on a work trip. It's been a week, and you've ghosted me. I'm giving you until tomorrow night. If I don't hear from you, then I'm taking your silence as a sign. We're done, and you've moved on. I'm going to do the same thing."

I hang up. I tilt my head back and look at the ceiling, exhaling a slow breath. None of this feels right, but I don't know enough to figure it out. The photos are odd and definitely meant to cause trouble. I don't want Papa more involved because it won't do me or the Mancinellis any good. I'm pissed at Carmine, but I don't want to hurt his family. Our families are on good terms, but that doesn't mean there isn't rivalry and the constant search for any exploitable weakness. I'm not calling *Zio* Salvatore back, and I definitely don't want to go over there now that I've seen these photos. But why? Why any of this? The trip? The evasiveness and ghosting? The photos?

Fuck if I know, and that's breaking my heart.

Chapter Eleven

Carmine

All I want is to get home and see Fina. It's been a week since I left New York, and we're finally on our way home. I've left three voicemail messages, asking her to call Gabriele since my phone isn't on. But I've heard nothing from her. Unfortunately, I've only had time to call at night. But she must be getting them. I told her she could text if it was easier since I wasn't sure if Gabe or I could answer when she called. Not a fucking peep.

The past week has seen us spinning our wheels. Fernando Alvarez, the man who helped kidnap Maria and her friends, took off to Cuba, but we heard Yuri Preobrazhensky is lurking somewhere in Miami. I glimpsed him on a boat docked at Fernando's place. I knew it was him because I heard someone call out to him in what I'm pretty certain was Albanian. Seeing his face reminded me we'd met years ago in Boston. It was when Besnik broke my nose, and I broke all his fingers.

We went back the morning after we rescued Maria and her friends and tried to negotiate for the other women, but Fernando'd already moved them. We tried the warehouse we learned about, but no one was there. A guard Gabriele "questioned"—yes, air quotes—knew nothing useful other than several women, including the Russian woman, Larisa, went to Texas. She was a captive at the villa too, and she stared me in the eye as I got Maria out. But there was nothing I could do then. My guilty conscience won't let me forget how I turned my back on her desperation.

We're on the jet and almost ready to land. I've been putting out feelers, and even called in some favors through Luca's in-laws. But no one knows where all the women went. I'm uncertain if all of them left Florida or even Miami. But I haven't given up my goal to rescue all of them. My conscience won't let me. I ignore Veronica, who's sleeping. Maria leans her head against my shoulder while the guys continue to strategize. Her appetite has been shit, and her friends were the same. We've done what we can, but three out of four of them are doctors, and they've all said rest is the best medicine. I suppose I can believe them.

"Are you ready to see Sera?"

"So ready. But she hasn't returned any of my calls. Not even shot back a text to tell me to fuck off. She's just gone completely radio silent. I don't get it."

"That's weird. I didn't take her for the type to ghost you. I wonder if she didn't get the messages. Maybe she didn't recognize Gabe's number, so she hasn't listened to them."

"I get sending it to voicemail then checking it later if it's an unknown number. But it's been nothing. I'm worried about her. I grabbed a charging cord at the store this morning. I'm hoping seeing my number will get her to pick up."

I forgot my cord, and no one else's phone charger is compatible with mine. My phone died on the flight to Miami.

"Good luck, Car."

"Do you need anything?"

"No. I'm good."

"Okay. I'm going to the cabin to make this call. I don't need everyone and their grandmother listening."

Maria nods, and I slip to the plane's aft, where there's a private cabin. As I sit on the bed, I picture bringing Fina on here as we escape for some exotic vacation. I'd lock the door and make love to her the entire flight. I miss her. And not just the taste and touch of her. I miss her expressive face and her voice. I miss the way she makes me feel.

I turn my phone on now that it's charged. Voicemails ping left and right. I wonder if she's left me a message. I skip through until I get to the ones from her. My heart sinks. Fucking hell. She thinks I'm the one who ghosted her. How though? She doesn't mention my voicemails. She says she's heard nothing from me. The last one is a gut punch. It's from an hour ago.

"It's me. Again. I'm over this, Carmine. I know you went to Miami. I know you were out at nightclubs with Gabriele and your cousins. I know you've been chatting up women and even went to some house party. You're a liar and as manipulative as you admitted. I'm done. If you're going out on the town and having a good time with one woman after another, then I'm not sitting at home pining for you. I have options too. Goodbye."

Options too? What the fuck does that mean? Is that one of her empty threats, like the night I had to work late? Or does she really mean it this time? I grip my phone so tightly I fear cracking it, but it's all that's keeping me from hurling it across the room. I force myself to take a deep breath and calm down. We're thirty minutes away from landing. I text the guy I know is on her security detail. He's one of ours, not one of those lazy fucks her father employs.

ME

Where's Serafina?

There's a long wait. Like fifteen minutes. I let myself out of the cabin and join the others. I look down when my phone vibrates.

TONY

You're not going to like this.

Then you better tell me fast. Is she safe?

Yeah. She's with Gio and David. It's where she went.

Fucking tell me.

I'm forced to wait almost five minutes for the next text.

Cries and Whispers.

I stare at my phone. You have got to be fucking kidding me. Oh, the hell no. She went to a motherfucking BDSM club.

Fina, I swear to God.

She thinks we're done. She thinks I dumped her without giving her the courtesy of telling her, and she thinks she ended things officially with me. She believes she's single and ready to mingle. I can't blame her for that. If she didn't get my messages, I can see why she's doing this. But no. She's either going to tell me to my face that we're done, or she's going to accept that this is life with a mafioso. It blows big chunks, but I am certain beyond a doubt that men in her family have disappeared for a week or longer without a fucking peep.

"Carmine?" I look up to find Gabriele and everyone else

staring at me. My best friend cocks an eyebrow. "Is everything all right?"

"No. I'm not going to Uncle Sal's. I have something else I need to take care of."

"Carmine, that's—"

"I don't give a fuck, Marco. I'm taking care of something else. I was with all of you the entire time. There's nothing I did that someone else can't explain."

I turn to look out the window, staring into the dark. A reckoning is coming, *piccolina*.

Chapter Twelve

Fina

I've waited around long enough. I know the Mancinellis have men guarding my place and following me. At first, I appreciated it. Just knowing they were there made me feel connected to Carmine while he was away. Then they became an albatross around my neck, a constant reminder that I'm just another duty and assignment for these men. Hell, *Zio* Salvatore probably organized and ordered them. But tonight, they can tell Carmine where I'm going. They probably have a way to be in touch with him.

I don't want to have dinner with Jules and Ernesto after all. I'm going out. After I called John—one of my four BDSM partners—Carmine, that arrangement soured. Now I'm kicking myself. But I'm meeting Henry inside. David and Gio have their masks in place, and so do I. Mine is a masquerade style black one. It covers my forehead to my cheekbones. It's dark enough inside that I don't worry that anyone can clearly make out my eye color.

"Hello, Henry."

"Hello, Eve."

Yes, as in the origin of women. I preferred it to Jane Doe. For a sex club, Eve seemed appropriate. But I'm not getting any of us kicked out of this garden. I follow Henry—also an alias—as he follows a Dungeon Master. Gio and David walk on each side of me. The DM shows us a room, and Henry and I are soon alone. It's my favorite one here, with a large chandelier and what looks like a dining room table that seats at least eight.

"Undress."

"Yes, sir."

I'm wearing a wrap dress with no bra and no panties. What's the point? Tonight is not about seduction. It's about getting off the way we both enjoy. I slip off my ballet flats and drape my dress over a chair.

"On the table."

"Yes, sir."

I climb on, and Henry binds my wrists and ankles to the table.

"Close your eyes. Do not open them until I give you permission."

"Yes, sir."

It's a test in submission to him and dominance over my own body. Rather than using a blindfold to ensure I can't see, I must control myself. It's often a struggle, but it's been years since I've failed. I close them and relax. His hand rests on my calf, but my brow furrows. For a moment, I thought the door opened. I didn't agree to voyeurism tonight. I hear Henry shift and step away and his hand leaves my calf. I wonder if he's getting a toy. It's at least another minute or two. Then his hand moves to my pussy. The pads of his fingers run the length of it as he kisses the inside of my calf.

He inches along my leg, licking, sucking, then kissing.

Normally, I never agree to being marked. But the sensation is beyond erotic. He moves over my hip, nipping at the bone before surely leaving love bites all the way up my belly. His tongue swirls around my nipple, and I arch off the table. He suckles, and it reminds me of Carmine. He had this way of doing something with his tongue while sucking at the same time. I don't remember Henry ever doing that before. It tempts me to open my eyes, but I suppress the urge.

He moves back down to my feet and yanks my left leg open. His fingers caress my inner thigh. The gentleness in opposition to the moment of roughness. Then two fingers slide through the dampness between my pussy lips. Again, I arch my back. When a Wartenburg pinwheel glides up my calf, thigh, then along the outside of my pussy, I realize he must have stepped away after all to grab the implement. I can't help but shiver as the sensation continues as he rolls it on my belly and over my nipple.

With my eyes closed, I can picture whomever I want. When I first started coming here, I pictured Orlando as I wanted him to be. That didn't last long. Usually, I just picture the man I'm with. But right now, it's Carmine. And that pisses me off enough to threaten to ruin my mood. I don't want to think about him. I don't want to wish it were him arousing me. I don't want to because it makes me miss him. But whatever plan Henry has for me tonight feels so much like what Carmine would do. We only had one night together, but I'm sure of it.

He only gives me those two fingers, and they're shallow thrusts. My hips undulate, begging for more, then his mouth is on my clit. I gasp, unprepared, then reveling in the sensation. This takes me back to the hotel room. My hips lift off the table as I form an even clearer picture of Carmine, and I'm no longer on a table in Cries and Whispers. I'm back in that bed at the Waldorf.

"Mmmm... Yes... Oh... Mmmm."

All I can do is moan and whisper. Not too far off from the club's name. Obviously aptly chosen. My restrained hands flex and fist, then grab the edges of the table. I want to reach for the man between my thighs and press his head closer. His tongue delves deeper into my pussy.

"Daddy."

It comes out a breathy whisper. I didn't realize I said anything until I get an annoyed grunt. But I'm too close to coming and too deep into my fantasy to care. A riding crop thwacks across my pussy, eliciting a moan then whimper. He does it three more times.

"Carmine."

The moment I say his name, I want to kick myself. I'm going to lose half my sex partners if I keep doing this. Two digits thrust into me as strong fingers tweak my nipple. Warm breath and a cologne I recognize move close to my ear.

"Daddy is here for what's his, *piccolina*."

My eyes fly open. But his fingers work my g spot, and his thumb rubs my clit as his lips ravage mine. I can't help it. I moan as I writhe. He pulls his fingers from me and slaps my pussy with the crop four more times.

"You didn't ask to come."

"You knew you were going to make me even if I wanted to stop. Untie me, Carmine. I want to sit up."

"I rather like you like this. At least I know you won't slip off into the night to fuck someone."

"Carmine." I infuse as much warning into my voice as I can. He leans over me, his lips inches from mine.

"You came here to get tied up and fucked. What does it matter who does it? That guy or me? Close your eyes and dream of him. Oh, wait. It was my name you whispered. You only want me."

"And you're going to exploit that to get yourself off and to punish me. I'm not the one who ruined this. Let me go, Carmine." I yank at the restraints. I'm surprised when he releases my right wrist. I loosen the rope enough to slip my other one out. But I don't get off the table.

"I left you three messages, Fina. But you claimed I never tried to get in touch with you. I did. I might have used Gabe's phone, but I called. You didn't listen to them. Or you lied as an excuse. Too horny to wait a few more days?"

"You did no such thing. You're the liar. About it all."

His hand rests around my throat. "I haven't lied to you, and I won't. I went to Miami to rescue Maria from some fucking sex traffickers who drugged her and her friends. My phone died, and I didn't have a charger. I don't have the same operating system as everyone else, so none of them were compatible. I'm trying to keep my cousin from being raped and sold. You're trying to get off."

The anger pulses from him, but I'm not scared. Despite being naked while he's fully dressed. Despite having been restrained and shocked that it's him. Despite his hand resting on my throat, large enough and strong enough to strangle me. All I want to do is curl my body around his and hang on.

"Is Maria all right? Did you get her in time?"

"Yes. And even though I was out of my mind worrying about her, I still thought about you. I still worried about you, too. You assumed the worst of me, *piccolina*. You took what I shared with you and turned it on me."

"You were gone for a week, and I didn't hear from you. *Zio* Salvatore was vague as hell, even when he invited me over to talk. My dad told me you were in Miami at nightclubs, talking to women."

He rears back, his face a thundercloud. "You involved your father?"

"I was scared for you, Carmine. You sounded horrible in the one message I got from you. I knew it was a mistake the moment I did, but I thought he might know."

"And I bet he loved telling you half-truths. I bet he loved knowing something was going down in my family. Fina, I guarantee he fucking knows what happened to Maria if he knew where I went. That begs the question did he know before or after?"

"You think my dad had something to do with this?"

"No. But I think he understands as well as any of us that knowledge is power."

I sit and stare at him. I nod as my gaze falls to the floor. "Carmine, someone sent me photos of you in Miami. There were pictures of you at some nice hotel, at nightclubs talking to women, and at a villa with women around. That hurt so much."

He releases my ankles and lifts me off the table and carries me to a chair. He slips off his suit coat and wraps it around me.

"Do you still have them?" I nod. He holds me tighter. "Little one, I need to see them. Do you have any idea who sent them?"

"No. There was no return address, but the post office stamp was local. Can you put yourself in my shoes? I don't hear from you—and I'm not saying you didn't try. I just didn't get any messages—then I get photos that make it look like you're partying instead of working."

"Fina, you know the type of businesses my family has. You know what types of products come in and out of Miami. Even if I were partying, it would be business. It would be what needs doing to secure the deal. Fina, you jumped to some awful conclusions. This can't be the first time a man in your life went away for a week, and you didn't hear from them."

"It's not. But none of them were the man I—"

"What? The man you what?"

I squeeze my eyes shut. I can't believe what I just thought. Fuck feminism and the horse she rode in on. I may as well be saying that. My thought is positively prehistoric and sets women back about a thousand years.

"What, Fina? Do not make me ask a third time."

"The man I want to belong to. There. I said it."

He stands so abruptly that his coat falls on the floor. I watch it as he brings me back to the table and puts me down.

"Roll over, little girl."

"Yes, Daddy."

We fall back into our roles without dropping a beat now that our power exchange has really started. His hand comes down on my ass, and it burns.

"You have every right to be hurt. You have every right to think I ghosted you. You have every right to be pissed." His hand lands again, and I flinch. "What you don't have a right to is accusing me of something without proof. Those photos didn't prove I abandoned you. Those photos didn't prove I was cheating on you. How do I know? Because I didn't fucking leave you to go fuck someone else. But you sure as shit came here to fuck someone else."

"But—"

"No."

I snap my mouth shut.

"I got your message about ending things. Sure. You thought you were single and free to mingle. Maybe you were lonely, too. But you came here to be vindictive, even if I never found out. You did it to get back at me."

His hand lands across my horizontal crack, pushing me forward, making my clit rub against the table. He knows it because he pulls me up onto my knees before pulling my hips back. He stands at the end of the table, and his stubble grazes my pussy. Then his tongue is doing things to me that make me moan while my toes curl.

"Daddy."

He ignores me. Or rather, he doesn't answer with words. He redoubles his efforts as his tongue slips in and out of me. He sucks hard on my clit as he thrusts three fingers into me. His thick fingers still aren't enough to replace the feel of his cock. I push my hips back to him, offering him more, hoping he'll take more. He withdraws his fingers to my mewling disapproval. But both his hands grip my hips as his fingers bite into my flesh. Then he's teasing me with the tip of his cock. He must have used his free hand to undress.

"Daddy, please. I can't... I need you."

"I know."

"Don't you need me too?" God, how desperate I sound.

"More than you know." He thrusts hard, sliding in until he's balls deep. He pounds into me over and over, making his point even before he says anything. "You belong to me, Fina. All of you. Not just your pussy. Every single inch. Your mind, your body, your fucking heart and soul. Do you know why?"

I shake my head as I pant.

"Because we belong together. We belong to each other. I've given myself to you as much as I want you to do the same."

"I didn't know. I thought—"

"I know, little one. We both fucked this up. I should have tried harder to get in touch with you. I should have sent texts instead of expecting you to listen to voicemails from a strange number."

"Wait, Daddy." He stops thrusting at the urgency in my voice. I shift to kneel and look over my shoulder. "I truly received nothing."

He wraps his arm around my waist and kisses along my neck. It must be something in my voice or my expression.

"Baby, I believe you. I'll ask Lorenzo to look into it. He'll know what happened. He can hack anything and find how anything was hacked. Someone is meddling."

"Are you still angry with me?"

"No. I admit I'm still hurt, but I think you feel that too. I'm going to get you off more than once, then I'm going to fill your cunt with my cum. Then we are going to go out to the main room and finding whatever you want to do and fuck until sunup. You will never come here with or for another man, Fina. If you want to return, then it's with me. I will cancel my membership to my club. I will never go there without you."

When he tells me to bend forward, I follow his instructions, and he thrusts hard, but he's agonizingly slow. He grabs my ass and kneads the flesh. Before Carmine, I was always self-conscious the first time a guy saw me naked or in this position. But the unadulterated lust in his eyes each time we're together gives me confidence I used to lack. He wants and enjoys every inch of me. It empowers me, even when I don't have the power in our dynamic.

"Do you know how much I want to fuck your tight little ass?"

"It's yours. Take it."

"Not tonight."

"But now that's all I'm going to think about."

"I know." His chuckle is dark and seductive. My pussy clenches. He reaches around me and rubs my clit.

"May I come?"

He pulls out, and I whimper. But he flips me around, lying me back before grabbing my ankles and pulling me to the edge of the table.

"I'm going to watch you every time you come. And you're going to watch me, knowing I decide when you orgasm. Why is that, little girl?"

"Because I belong to you."

"How do you want me to get you off?" I'm surprised by the question. "How, Fina? I belong to you. What do you want me to do?"

Love me.

"Will you be rougher?"

"Don't close your eyes."

The opposite command from earlier. It's so much harder to obey. My back arches as I fight the urge to close them.

"I can't help it. This is so intense."

"Look at me." He barks the command, and I try to obey. I gaze into his eyes, and while there's fierceness, there's something else too. Kindness? Concern? I don't know. I can't name it, but it's something deep. I can feel it. I scream as I come. My eyes scrunch shut again. It's almost too much. I struggle for each breath, overwhelmed. How can the same act I've engaged in with other guys be so fundamentally different with Carmine?

He lifts me off the table and guides me to ride him. I don't know how he does it. I marvel at his strength each time he carries me anywhere. I am not a little girl, despite what he calls me. I watch his abs flex and run my hands over his bunching shoulder muscles as he continues to surge into me. I guess the reasons are literally right under my fingertips. It wouldn't surprise me if he could carry Gabriele, and he has to be two-forty or two-fifty soaking wet.

"Kiss."

He grunts his demand, and I'm only too happy to oblige. Everything shifts again when our mouths meet. We're slower. We're savoring each moment rather than desperate to pleasure each other. My left hand roams over his neck, shoulder, and chest while my right hand cups his jaw. We surge into ecstasy together, leaving us dazed. He puts me back on the table. He laces his fingers with mine as I lie back, and he follows me. One more thrust, and my fingernails press into the back of his hands. My legs tighten around his thighs. My pussy squeezes him as he pulses inside me. We kiss over and over.

"Daddy, can we just go home? I don't want to go out there and do anything else. I really just want to be alone with you."

"Fina, you sound sad. What just happened?"

"Nothing. I just don't want to share your attention with anyone else."

"I can promise you, no one but you has my attention. I don't want to look at or talk to anyone but you. We can do whatever makes you happy. Let's get dressed. I don't like you being at your house, Fina. Even if I'm there. I'm going to ask Gabe to go over tomorrow and fix everything. But I also don't like that someone sent you mail there with no return address."

"Augusto tested it."

"That motherfucker?" Carmine scowls so deeply that he looks like a pissed off bull.

"It sucked so hard, Daddy. He smirked as he gave me the photos. He saw them. They were so incriminating."

"We are going to your place. You're going to get at least a week's worth of stuff. You're going to give me those photos. Then we're going home."

Our gazes lock, and neither of us misses the significance of what Carmine said.

"That's exactly what I want."

We hurry to dress, then head out to Carmine's SUV. He drove his own Audi here, which I hadn't thought about. But I'm immensely appreciative that he did. I don't want any of his men to know where we've been. But that makes me think.

"Did you ask your men where I was?"

"Yeah. I asked Uncle Sal to assign men to you. I knew I couldn't insist they be your primary guards, but I didn't want you anywhere without Mancinelli men nearby. I know who was assigned tonight, so I texted and asked."

"So, your men know I come to a BDSM club?"

"Only him and his partner. They know better than to breathe a word. If they do, it'll be their last."

I know he's not exaggerating. I look over at him as he drives. "Once the afterglow wears off, are we really going to be okay, Carmine?"

Chapter Thirteen

Carmine

That's a good question. I refuse to consider any answer other than the one I want. But I have to accept Fina must have a say too. "What do you want for us?"

"I don't know, Daddy. But it must be something if that's what my gut tells me to call you."

"What made you decide to leave your old boyfriend after so many years together? Why'd it take so many years of dating to know what you wanted?"

"I loved him, but something was always missing. We were happy together, and I liked not living alone. But what I really needed just wasn't there. I thought I could live without it, but the longer we were together and the more often I tried to explain it, the more incomplete I felt. Maybe I could live without it, but I couldn't live without it with him. Not once I really understood what I needed."

"What was that?"

"Someone more dominant. Someone who makes the world

disappear the moment I step into his arms. Someone who doesn't decide everything for me, but someone who can ease the burden of making simple decisions. It would free up my mind for the bigger ones. I would come home from grad school classes, and I'd be the one deciding on dinner. I'd be the one deciding on what to do on the weekend. At first, it felt like he was being so considerate, letting me choose. But I realized he just wasn't the one who was going to lead in our relationship. When I tried to encourage him to at least be more dominant in bed, it didn't happen. I know he never stopped desiring me, but that wasn't—enough. That sounds so fucking vain."

She looks out the window, but I slide my hand under hers, palm up, and entwine our fingers. She shifts her gaze to me. I give her hand a squeeze, encouraging her to go on.

"Once the foundation cracked, I couldn't ignore it. I preferred being single and living alone to living with someone who, every time I looked at him, came up short. It wasn't fair to him. It scared me to leave, especially since I'd just graduated and hadn't established my career yet. I admit part of it was just selfish logistics. It's not like I didn't work during grad school and didn't contribute, but being financially responsible on my own was intimidating. I went into real estate, and I soon started making more money than I needed. I wasn't scared anymore. I wasn't going to stay for the wrong reasons."

"Fina, what do you need now?"

I want to know. I need to find out if I can be that man. She needs to consider whether I am. Her response is so soft I strain to hear her.

"You."

"Why?" I glance over at her, and I see tears brimming in her eyes. Am I pushing too hard?

"Because all those things I felt were missing and haven't found with anyone else, you have in spades. When you hug me, nothing else exists. Everything I worry about, all the decisions I have to make, they all fall away for a few moments. I'm not a business owner who has to pay a mortgage and make payroll. I'm not a single woman living alone in a huge city. I'm not a Mafia daughter with constant shadows and a father who is too controlling one moment and too absent another. I can just be me, and I can live in the moment."

"What about the decision-making part? I'm not interested in true domestic discipline, and I'm not interested in being a Daddy Dom, despite what we call each other."

"I don't want those either. I'm not a child, and I don't need to have moments where I can feel like that. I don't feel like I need you to guide me because I can't decide for myself. But I like that you can tell when I need you to step in. And it makes me happy to know I can give you the control you need. So much about this life is beyond our control, and I know how badly you need it to stay alive. But there's no guarantee that you'll have it anywhere outside the bedroom."

"Our bedroom." I test the water with that. Her grip on my hand tightens to almost painful. "Is that what you want, *piccolina*?"

Again, her whisper is so quiet, I almost don't hear her. "Yes."

"We're moving fast."

"I know. But I'm more certain about you than I was about moving to America. About where to go to college or grad school. About my careers. About buying the shops. About being with Orlando. Being with you is the only easy decision I've made. But that's also why thinking you played me hurt so much. I felt like such an idiot. No one said the words, but everyone in my family was saying I told you so."

"Fina, I will not lie to you if I don't have to. I hate how

much of me I'll keep from you. You could have a man who can give his whole self to you. I can't do that."

"I know. But having part of you is better than none of you. This week taught me that."

"There will be many times in the future when I can't tell you where I'm going or for how long. Sometimes it'll be because I don't know, but a lot of times I'll choose that."

"I know, Daddy." There's sadness in her tone, but there's acceptance from a lifetime of this shit. That makes me sad for her.

"I will do better to stay in touch when I can. I will tell you as much as I feel is safe for everyone involved. I need to find out why my mom didn't see you. I told you if I was gone for more than a few days that you should see her."

"I forgot."

"But I told her too."

"I don't know."

That's something for me to consider. I won't get angry at my mom without reason. Her health hasn't been great lately. I don't want to upset her, and if she's been unwell, I can't fault her. But if nothing's wrong, I want to know why my family abandoned Fina.

"Carmine, I talked to *Zio* Salvatore. I was angry, and I made it clear nothing he could say would be good enough. Maybe your mom already knew that. Maybe she didn't want to make it worse."

"Maybe. I'll sort that out tomorrow. Right now, my only concern is us."

We arrive at my building in Hudson Yards, the most expensive neighborhood in Manhattan, after stopping at her place to grab a week's worth of clothes and her toiletries. I earn far more than the median income, so there's no question I can afford to live here. The moment I moved home from Stanford, I bought the place. I'd been playing the stock market throughout college and making big money. Lorenzo isn't the only one who knows investments. I was a millionaire in my own right by twenty-two. I'm a billionaire now, but no one—not even members of my family—know that. I'm richer than Uncle Salvatore, which was a goal I achieved when I turned twenty-five. I gleefully enjoyed great smug satisfaction from knowing that, even though I never boasted.

The one thing I did to celebrate was pay back Uncle Salvatore for the money he spent to get me out of trouble at the end of high school. But that's something I never think about, and no one ever talks about. That was my greatest fuck-up ever.

Fina squeezes my hand as we cross the lobby, and I look down to meet her gaze as she speaks.

"I want an 'us'. I know you make snap decisions all the time. And I know they aren't done impulsively, but out of necessity. You may have decided about me and us with ease, but I've given it a lot of thought over the past week. I considered what it would be like if we did commit, and that made it even more painful to think you hadn't or wouldn't. Despite thinking over and over that you'd walked away, I kept wanting us to be together. If you really are the man you let me see, then I want no one else."

If.

She still has doubts. Massive ones. I'm uncertain if she said that intentionally or even caught what she said, but she hasn't corrected herself. I don't think I need to pump the brakes, but I need to ease off the accelerator. Let's see if we can get through the next few days of spending our nights together.

As we get in the elevator, and I use biometrics to push the button for the top floor, I wonder if I should have Fina added to the list of people who can come and go freely to my condo. I glance at her, and now my doubts start. If she isn't as committed to me as I am to her, then what's the point? We step off the elevator, and it takes us directly into my living room.

Her gaze sweeps the sprawling open floor plan. She takes in the comfortable furniture that is hardly high end or luxury. I don't want it to be. I want my home to be my sanctuary. I want to be at ease here. She looks at the spacious kitchen with a practically industrial size fridge. It might be excessive, but Gabriele's here as often as I'm at his place. We both can eat.

I know what she's staring at now. She takes a step forward, but then stops herself.

"Go ahead."

She crosses the living room to a little nook that gets the morning light. She walks directly to the glass display case on top of the bookshelf and leans forward. Then she turns her head to look at the only uncomfortable piece of furniture in my house. The upright chair isn't inviting, but I've spent hours sitting on it. She stares at the music stand and the closed instrument case before looking back at the display.

"Is that a Stradivarius?"

"Yes. An original. It's not The Messiah, as much as I wish it were. I never hear about it in time to bid at auction."

"The Messiah?"

"It's the rarest violin in the world. Not only is it a Stradivarius, it's never been played and is in mint condition. It's pretty much priceless."

"What about this one?" She points to another case that's on the adjacent bookshelf.

"That's a Giuseppe Guarneri. He was the second-most revered violin maker. Many would say his instruments are as incredible as Stradivari's. I'm one of them."

Both instruments are worth millions. And not just one or two, but upwards of ten million apiece. She turns toward the chair where the closed instrument case sits. She points to it.

"What about that one?"

I unlatch it and lift out a violin I've had since I was a freshman in high school. Since it's been over a week since I played it, I tune it and tighten the bow. Then I put it against my left shoulder. My chin sits in the smooth black rest, and it's as natural a position as walking upright. I begin Brahms's Violin Concerto in D Major solo. I could play it in my sleep. I've certainly dreamed it enough times. I serenade Fina for a couple minutes before lowering my bow and violin.

"That was amazing, Daddy. When did you start playing?"

"When I was four."

"They make violins that small?"

I chuckle. "Yes. When I was just a little boy in Queens, I thought I would be the next Itzhak Perlman. I had his 1978 performance DVRed from when it replayed on TV. I would stand in the living room and play along with him."

That was before I knew I had a life sentence from birth. That was when I thought I could grow up to be what I wanted. That I could grow up and leave my judgmental and uncaring family behind. I lumped them altogether, but who I really wanted to escape were my grandfathers, their siblings, and friends.

I put the violin back in its case. When I stand up, Fina wraps her arms around my waist. She leans back, so we can see each other.

"How old were you when you realized your path was preordained?"

"Eleven." That was when everything changed. It was when I committed my first monumental sin.

"Why then?"

I stare down at Fina. Until a few weeks ago, I hadn't spoken of that day to anyone. I let it loom over Luca's head to control him. But after what he went through with Olivia and how much seeing them together made me realize I didn't want to be the family shitbag anymore, I talked to him about it. We made amends, and we're on better terms than we have been in seventeen years. It's put me on better terms with everyone, even though they still don't know what happened. I run my hand over my face before I lead Fina to the sofa. We sit, and I wrap my arm around her shoulders, but she turns to face me. I shift to use the sofa's arm to rest my back against.

"When I was eleven, I liked this girl named Iskra. She was a bratva Elite Group member's daughter." The Elite Group is the upper echelon. The senior-most leadership. The Kutsenko brothers fill those positions. Their cousins from both sides of the family fill the positions just below them. "I thought she might like me too, so I met her at a park one evening. I wasn't supposed to be there. But I followed Luca and Emilio, Matteo's older brother. They're the same age and were best friends until that night."

For years, I believed I caused that irreparable rift. But I know now that I contributed to it, but Emilio made his choices on his own.

"Iskra had a crush on Bogdan Kutsenko, the youngest brother. But she told me she'd be my girlfriend if I could kiss better than Bogdan. When I leaned in to try, her sister appeared and freaked out. Klara accused me of attacking Iskra and trying to molest her. Iskra bolted, and Klara put a gun to my head. She was high like she often was after school and on the weekends. Luca was with Klara and one of her friends who he had a crush on. He and Emilio ran over when Klara started screaming at me. I was frozen. I could only stare at her and try not to piss myself. She had the gun pressed right between my eyebrows. Luca tried to talk her down, but when her finger moved on the trigger, he launched himself at her. They fell to the ground, and he did what he could to keep Klara from getting hurt. But the only way to stop her was to turn the gun on her. She'd already fired a shot that barely missed me."

That night is one of my most vivid memories from my entire life. As I sit with Fina, I may as well be eleven and back in that park.

"When the gun fired the second time, it was between Luca and Klara. I didn't know who pulled the trigger and who was hurt. Emilio pulled Luca off Klara and turned a knife on him. He slashed Luca from his cheekbone, down his neck, to below his collar. I'd never seen so much blood. But despite all of that, we knew we couldn't leave Klara in the park. We couldn't let the Ivankov bratva know three Mancinelli kids were involved in an Elite Group member's daughter's death. We got Klara to her car and put her in. Luca wiped the gun and wrapped her fingers around it. It looked like she killed herself, and we've never corrected anyone."

"But what about Luca? How did he not pass out?"

"Sheer fear. He was fifteen. He'd never killed anyone before. None of us had. But we knew our lives were forfeit if anyone ever found out. Emilio helped me get him to his house, but he went upstairs and passed out in his room. He was still drunk off his ass. We're lucky we didn't die just trying to get to Auntie Carlotta. He dumped Luca in the living room, and I wasn't big enough to hold him up on my own. While Emilio disappeared, I was left screaming for Auntie Carlotta to help. There was so much blood on the carpet and sofa. I sobbed the entire time she stitched him up. Uncle Domenico had to take me in the kitchen because he thought I was going to pass out. Once Auntie Carlotta was done, they asked what happened. I refused to speak. The family only learned Emilio did it because Uncle Dom found the bloody switchblade on Lio's bedside table."

I close my eyes as I choke back the tears. I still have never been as scared as I was that night. Not other times when guns have been put to my head. Not when I've been shot and stabbed or beaten to within an inch of my life. The only time anything came close was what just happened with Maria.

"You refused to tell on Emilio? You protected him?"

"No!" I bark my answer. I take a breath. "If I'd told anyone Lio hurt Luca, I would have had to confess why. That would have put Luca in more danger. We've kept each other's secret ever since. Luca has never forgiven Lio. It's not so much about the scar as it is that Lio didn't choose family first. He picked Klara, who he claimed he loved. He didn't. He loved getting high and fucking her."

"I've never met Emilio."

"He's the true black sheep of the family. Uncle Sal relegated him to Jersey to deal with the lowest level shit. We can trust him on big missions, but he's rarely called. None of us trust his judgement to act on his own. For all my faults, my family never doubts that I put them first."

Fina sits back and watches me. She waits to see if there's more. There is.

"Luca violated the cardinal rule of never hurting women and children. He didn't do it intentionally, but I exploited the fuck out of that once I realized the power it gave me over him. All I had to do was threaten to tell Uncle Sal, or worse, one of the Kutsenkos. With everything that happened to Anastasia Kutsenko and the Moscow bratva kidnapping her and our role in taking her hostage before that, I violated that commandment. But I figured I'd only done it once. It made it twice for Luca, and I reminded him of that any and every chance I had. I've never wanted to be the underboss or don, but I wanted to control them. Now, I just want a quiet life where I do my legit jobs most of the time and only handle *Cosa Nostra* business when I'm called upon. That's not how life works, but that's what I wish."

"That's a monumental secret to carry from being eleven."

It was. But I don't know how to interpret that observation when she says nothing else. I sit silently, waiting for her to make the next move.

"Is there anything else, Carmine? Any more cardinal sins I should know about?"

I nod. I close my eyes and inhale. I have no remorse for what I did, but I have remorse for the fall out. This was why I had to pay Uncle Salvatore back so much money and why he exiled me for college.

"During the winter of my senior year, the Irish created a lot of trouble. Gabriele and his parents had been here legally for six years, and they'd begun the process of becoming citizens. Liam O'Rourke led the mob back then. He stirred up shit and planted evidence that caused Gabriele and his family to be deported. Then he released Uncle Domenico's sealed adoption papers. No one—not even Uncle Dom—knew he'd been adopted. His birth father assaulted a nun when he stumbled into a church one night drunk. Uncle Dom's parents had tried for years and couldn't have children. Their priest knew of their struggles, so he suggested they adopt the baby. They came up with an excuse to go back to Italy for six months, saying they were going to travel. They returned with a newborn."

I remember how devastated Uncle Domenico was to learn his parents kept that from him, but they were both dead. His entire identity came into question—at least in his mind. He was no longer related by blood to my mom, Uncle Salvatore, and Uncle Massimo. It meant Lio and Matteo were no longer our blood cousins. But it didn't take long to assure him that nothing changed. He was family. Full stop. Period. End of sentence.

"It made several people question what other family secrets we held. People tried to exploit it as a weakness. All it did was make us rally. My contribution to supporting the family was revenge. It was Uncle Dom who introduced me to the violin, and I've always been close to him. Seeing how Liam hurt him pushed me beyond reason. Fina, I was eighteen, but I'd already killed before. But what I did went way further. Liam hated winter, so he snowbirded to the Caribbean every year. It was no secret, and his travel plans were so predictable that it still shocks me that no one else did what I did. I bribed FAA officials at the airfield in Connecticut that he used. They turned a blind eye while some mechanics I knew helped me tamper with the plane. They were on Liam's payroll, but I paid a lot more. It wasn't my money, though. I borrowed it from Uncle Sal. I just didn't mention it."

I really thought my life would end when he discovered what I did. The only reason it didn't was because he banished me—and he couldn't kill his little sister's only son. But it was the first real beating I got. I never underestimated how my uncle kept his position and power as the don ever again.

"Liam's wife and kids were already in St. Lucia, but he'd come back to New York to deal with some union issue in Upstate. The plane crashed thirty minutes after takeoff. He knew he was going to die. It was a Cessna, but not the kind that is popular among skydivers. It was a private jet. But the pilot parachuted out of it. Liam was the only person aboard, and according to the pilot, didn't realize what the man was doing until it was too late to stop the pilot."

Fina remains silent as I watch her throughout my story. Her expression is neutral, so I can't tell what she's thinking. I can't tell if she horrified and hiding it or completely unmoved. My guess is the former.

"It took months, but the FAA figured out what happened. It cost Uncle Salvatore two million dollars to clean up that mess. He paid more bribes in a week than he probably had his entire life. They wanted to try me as an adult for domestic terrorism. The DA wanted to take down a Mancinelli, so the death count went from one to twelve. Supposedly, I'd plotted the murder of some O'Rourke associates who were foreign nationals. None of that was true. I watched who boarded that plane. It was the pilot and Liam. But Donovan, his son, wanted to burn it all down. He wanted his revenge for my revenge. I'd been accepted to all the Ivy Leagues and a few other top-tier schools. Stanford was the farthest away, so Uncle Sal sent me there. He didn't allow me to return at all during those four years. Part of it was to keep me safe from Donovan, but most of it was Uncle Sal couldn't stand to look at me."

"Because you'd killed someone or because you'd killed Liam?" Fina's brow furrowed.

"Because I cost him two mill. No one regretted Liam's death. But it cost Uncle Sal a fortune to keep my name out of the press and out of the gossip. Most people still don't know that I put the hit out."

"So, you were alone for four entire years?"

"My parents came out for all holidays and breaks. We went on European vacations, and I saw family if they were there too. But I didn't step foot on the Eastern Seaboard until after I graduated. Plenty of people thought I'd gone to prison or was dead. Needless to say, my resurrection shocked everyone who wasn't immediate family."

"So that's what really sealed the deal that you were the black sheep of the family. Emilio became a nonentity to almost everyone, but you were the one that people claimed was trouble all along."

"Yup."

She nods before shifting closer and resting her head against my shoulder. My shoulders lower, and I realize just how tense

I'd been throughout that story. I'd been waiting for her to reject me.

"Would you put the hit out on Liam again if you had the chance?"

"Yes. But I'm more experienced now and wouldn't have made the same mistakes. I should have picked the crash site better, and I should have had a team there to remove the incriminating evidence and replace it with parts that would tell the story I needed. I had the team clean up but didn't plant the right evidence. I wouldn't get caught this go around. I don't regret protecting Uncle Dom and my family, even if it shook the hornets' nest. The Irish had to reorganize and recover, so they were weaker while Donovan took over. It meant Uncle Sal could strike and do more damage. I opened a door he was only too happy to pass through. I'm certain that's why he allowed me to return, and I didn't wind up on Elba like Napoleon."

"But Napoleon escaped his exile and returned to Paris."

"For one hundred days. That's not very long. Not quite who I'd model my escape after." We laugh together, and the air lightens. But I have to ask. "Fina, what are you thinking?"

"That you've faced some shit experiences from way too young, and you've done the best you could to navigate them when you didn't have nearly enough life experience to really know what to do. That you've put family first even when your family hasn't supported you like they should have. That resentment blinded you too much to appreciate the members of your family who would have stood beside you. That you're not really that old in the grand scheme of things, and you're trying to make amends. You could be in your sixties and still proclaiming you're right. You're not even thirty."

"Can you forgive me for what I've done?"

"It's not a matter of forgiveness from me. You didn't wrong me. But I can accept the things you've done. I understand them, even if I don't agree with them. I can't pass judgment on things I wasn't there to witness. Even if you're telling me first-hand, there's still been a lot of time that's passed since then. For all the ways you've erred, they've made you the man I'm sitting next to. I'm not running away, and I'm not demanding you take me home. I'm still here."

She pulls her knees up and turns, so she can sit on my lap.

"Daddy, your mistakes haven't made you more flawed or weaker. Just the opposite. You've learned who you do and don't want to be. You have way more years ahead of you than behind you."

That's not a given in the *Cosa Nostra*. I hope so. I hope I have way more years with Fina than without. But no one can promise me that.

"Daddy, you must be exhausted. Can we just go to bed?"

"Yes, *piccolina*."

Who knows what's next? For now, I'm curled around Fina in my bed. Where we belong. As Scarlett O'Hara said in *Gone with the Wind*, "I'll think about that tomorrow." Not a quote I'd ever admit to remembering.

Chapter Fourteen

Fina

When will we have a light and breezy conversation? Everything is always so heavy with Carmine. Yet, that doesn't seem like a bad thing. He seems committed to telling me his darkest secrets, and I know he's doing it to make sure I know I have an out, to make sure I'm with him without reservations or the wrong impression. It moves me that he already trusts me enough to confide in me.

"Good morning, *piccolina*."

"Morning, Daddy. Did I wake you?"

"No. I've been up for a while."

I wiggle my hips back against his hard dick. He draws my top leg back over his before maneuvering my hips so he can slide into me. He kneads my breasts as he rocks in and out of me. I sigh.

"Every morning should start like this, little one."

"With sex?"

"Sex with you."

"Mmm."

I hum as he kisses along my bare shoulder and up my neck. I twist my neck to welcome his kiss, sucking on his tongue with the same rhythm he's fucking me. He pulls out, and I roll over. He shifts until I'm beneath him, my legs open to receive him. He lifts my arms over my head, holding my wrists in one hand as the other guides his cock back to my pussy.

"May I come?"

"So soon?"

"Yes."

It's a plea. I can't believe it. I knew I was aroused, but I didn't think I'd get off this fast. But I can't get close enough. I strain and lift my hips to meet each of his thrusts, to keep our bodies close. His free hand slides beneath my ass after he pulls my leg over his hip.

"You have the most amazing ass ever created."

Hardly. I know my imperfections, of which there's plenty of evidence on my ass and thighs. I still work out daily, but I've had dimples on the wrong cheeks since I was thirteen.

"You don't agree with me, little one."

"I think you exaggerate."

Before I know what's happening, I'm flipped over, pulled onto my knees, and his cock is pressing against my back door.

"Do you have toys, Fina?"

"I'm throwing them out. I don't want to reuse anything from my past."

"Then we are doing some shopping on the way to work. By tomorrow night, you will have a plug in your ass, spreading you for me. I'm fucking all of you tomorrow, Fina. I'm leaving my cum in and on you. I value what is mine, and I like to have the best of whatever I want. If I say your ass is the best, then it is."

His hand lands across my ass. It smarts but doesn't hurt. This isn't a punishment. This is playtime. I shake my hips, and he swats the other side. He thrusts into my pussy and pulls all the way out. I can feel how my juices coat his cock when he slides it along the division between my ass cheeks.

"Don't wait until tomorrow night, Daddy."

"Ask me, *piccolina*."

"Daddy, will you fuck me in the ass?"

He thrusts into my pussy again, over and over. Then the tip of his cock presses into my asshole. I relax as best I can, knowing what to expect. He's so careful.

"What's your safe word, Fina?"

"Fondant."

"Is this just uncomfortable or painful?"

"Uncomfortable for right now. Daddy, please don't hold back."

It'll be more comfortable once he's all the way in. He eases in inch by inch until I feel his lower belly pressed against my ass.

"Slide your hands forward and lie down, *piccolina*."

I follow his instructions, and his chest presses mine into the mattress. His fingers entwine with mine as he rocks. He doesn't withdraw, then thrust. He just tilts his hips back and forth. He lets go of my right hand and slides his beneath my hips. His fingers play with my clit before rubbing it.

"May I come, *carino*?" Cutie. I haven't called him that often, but I like it nearly as much as Daddy. There are other endearments I'd like to use, but maybe it's too soon despite how we keep saying we want to commit. At some point, we have to stop talking about what we want to do, and just do it. Either shit or get off the pot.

"Yes, *tesorina*."

"Yesss... I'm coming... Oh, yes."

"I am too, baby. Fuck, you're so fucking tight... Yeah... Just like that. Squeeze. Fuck, Fina."

He stops rocking and thrusts over and over until I feel his cum. He's careful as he withdraws. I lie on my belly, panting as he moves onto his side next to me. His hand sweeps up and down my back. I turn my head to look at him as my cheek rests on my forearm. He kisses across my shoulders.

"I told you last night that all of you is mine, Fina. It wasn't the heat of the moment. I know you're not ready to agree to that. I'm okay with that. But I will not share you either. I might not have your heart and soul, but I won't share your body with anyone."

"I don't want anyone else, Carmine. You know I was fantasizing about you last night. But what do you mean you know I'm not ready?"

"You said 'if' last night. If I'm the man you think I am. You have doubts, and I accept that. I've shared things with you that anyone who didn't grow up how we did would never understand. At least not accepted them as easily as you did. I've confessed my faults, so you know the worst about me. But I've had little time to prove I'll be a good man to you."

"I know you'll be good to me. I've questioned that. I've questioned whether you were as committed to me as I am to you. But I never doubted how you would treat me when we're together."

"Then I haven't had much time to prove to you I'm a man you can be proud to call yours."

I twist onto my side. "Carmine, you don't have to prove yourself to me. I'm the one person I hope you know you never have to prove anything to. I picked my words poorly. I don't have doubts. If I did, I wouldn't have had sex with you at the club, and I wouldn't have come to your place with enough clothes to last me more than a week."

"Fine. You might not think I need to prove myself, but I feel I do."

"But I don't want you to feel that way."

"I can't help it."

It's easy to look at Carmine's handsome face and his chiseled body. It's easy to sense his aura of confidence and power. It's easy to fall for his charisma. But he's so very vulnerable. His exterior may be made of stone, but he isn't on the inside. I think there're a lot of hollows that need to be filled with love and acceptance. As he continues to hold me, I'm certain I want to be the one who does that. I drift off to sleep in his arms for another hour, and I wake there. I offer him a sleepy smile as I long for more time tucked away with him.

"I wish I had sick days."

"Me too."

The sun hasn't risen yet, but the sky outside Carmine's bedroom window is lightening. We climb out of bed and make our way into the shower. It takes great restraint not to fuck again as we wash each other. We dress quickly since it's approaching five, and I need to get to the bakery on time.

"Can you drop me off and come inside? There'll be fresh donuts again."

"I have never counted carbs or calories, but I'll have to start if you keep feeding me those donuts. It's humanly impossible to only eat one. Like it would be a mortal sin not to have more than one."

"I thought gluttony was the sin."

"Nope. Who am I to deny the manna God sent down in the form of your donuts?"

I laugh. "You are ridiculous." He steps away from me as we enter the living room. My brow furrows. "What?"

"I'm not standing too close when God smites you for denying His heavenly creations. That ass and your donuts are divine."

I roll my eyes, then yelp when I find myself pressed against the wall. His kiss is everything. It's intoxicating. It's arousing. It consumes me. And I'll gladly go up in flames. I rest my head against his chest when we pull apart. Then I place my hands on his chest as I pant, and I feel his racing heart beneath my palms.

He steps back and takes my hand. We walk over to where I put my purse and the manila envelope. We agreed to wait until this morning to look at it. We had other things to sort out, and it was too late to do anything about them. He opens it and pulls out the photos. I watch his jaw harden then tick as he goes through them. He presses his lips into a thin line, and it makes me realize just how much I like them when they're more like Cupid's bow. He slides the photos back in and shifts his gaze to me. I don't expect the worry I recognize.

"Fina, I'm so sorry you got these alone. Obviously, that's what the sender intended, but I'm sorry you had to wait for me to get home and deal with this. No wonder you thought I'd walked out on you. We went straight to those nightclubs because the first one was where they took Maria and her friends from. The others were next door. We went to bars in the morning and asked around. That villa is where we found Maria. That picture was most likely taken by a drone. I'm negotiating Maria's ransom in that picture."

"Carmine, I've been so self-absorbed. I haven't asked how Maria is or what happened. I'm sorry."

"It wasn't being self-absorbed. Fina, our relationship is a priority to me. That's why I tracked you down rather than going to Uncle Salvatore's with everyone else. We had things to sort out that couldn't wait and fester any longer."

"I feel like you're absolving me, and I don't deserve it."

"I could have told you this last night, and there wouldn't have been any more to do then than there is now. But if I hadn't found you, we would have remained suspicious and hurt. That wouldn't have helped. We might not be standing here right now if we hadn't put us first."

"Will your family be mad that you came to me rather than going to them?"

"Maybe. But they're going to have to understand that they still come first, but you're a part of that now."

"I'm not your wife."

"I'd like you to be my girlfriend."

I nod. "I'd like that too." I glance down. "What about those?"

He sighs. "Let me take you to work, then I'll go to Uncle Sal's and start figuring this out. I also want Lorenzo to look at your phone sometime today."

"Can we go to the bakery, let me make sure everything is set for today, then we could go to *Zio's* together?"

"That's a good idea. It still sounds funny to me whenever I hear you say *Zio* Salvatore and *Zia* Sylvia when I call them uncle and aunt."

"Why don't you use the Italian?"

"I don't know. That's on Luca and Emilio as the oldest. They both learned Italian before English. We all did. I just called my aunts and uncles what I heard everyone else call them."

"I suppose it's not so bad that I use the Italian and you use the English. If we were both calling them the same thing, it would sound pretty incestuous for us to not be married, but both of us call them our aunt and uncle. At least using different titles maybe makes it clear we're from opposite families that joined by marriage, not by blood. Or I'm totally overthinking something pointless."

"I get it. It's easy to forget that you're Aunt Sylvia's niece."

"With everything that happened, she's always been considerate about spending time with me separate from your family. Now she doesn't have to juggle anything."

"I don't go other than when my mother insists, so do you see my family every week at Mass?"

"I don't go as often as my mother would like. I definitely go when they're in town, but it's hit or miss after that. But I usually see at least one of the older couples, if not all four. We keep our distance. Do you not believe anymore?"

"I do. I always have and always will. Fina, you know the worst of my sins, but there have been way too many to count. It feels like the ultimate act of hypocrisy to ask for absolution only to intentionally commit the same sins all over again. God might be merciful, and He may have granted Man free will, but I don't think He intended us to break His commandments, say a couple prayers, then go on our merry way to do it all over again. It just feels wrong. It feels like I'm flaunting my sins and thumbing my nose at our faith. I'd rather keep my relationship with God private."

"That makes sense. After what I did to retaliate for *Zia* Sophia's murder, I get it. That's my worst sin, and that was years ago. I still feel like a hypocrite even though I want to believe He's forgiven me. There's comfort in the rituals, and I still feel better after praying, so I usually go to Mass at a church closer to my place."

I only go to the same church as Carmine's family when it's an important holy day and my parents are in town. In fairness, Carmine isn't the only one who usually isn't there. His male cousins, along with Gabriele and Matteo aren't there either. Only Maria shows up with her parents. It'd been months since I'd gone there before Easter. I don't enjoy going into Manhattan on Sundays when I can go five blocks to the church near me in Queens. They only go into Manhattan because some

Mancinelli a few generations back wanted to flaunt his family's wealth. It became a tradition.

"Fina, the more I think about this, the more uncomfortable I'm getting about you being on your own. I'm still going to have guys assigned to you, and I'm glad you're going to stay here. But for today, until I figure out what's going on with your phone and these photos, I'd feel better if I didn't leave you anywhere. I know nothing's happened, but I'm worried someone will do something worse now that I'm back in town."

"Wouldn't they do that while you're gone and can't get to me?"

"They would. But the icing on the cake would be that I'm close enough that I could have gotten to you and didn't. It feels like someone wants to punish me, and they want me close enough to see what happens, not hear about it later. Either I stay at the bakery, or you come with me for the day."

"I don't want to get in the way, Carmine. If you have family business to handle at *Zio* Salvatore's, then I shouldn't be there. *Zia* Sylvia will be at work, and the girls will be at school. I don't have an excuse to stay."

"I'm your excuse. I wouldn't back down. I won't. Not with your safety. I have a bad feeling now that I've seen those photos."

I can tell he's more upset than he wants me to see. This is a bigger deal than he's letting on. "All right, Daddy. Let's get you your donuts, then we'll go to *Zio's*."

His lips purse and twist side to side. "I suppose I should take donuts for the rest of them. But I'd really rather gloat that I had them and they didn't."

"Are you eight instead of twenty-eight?"

"When it comes to bragging about my girlfriend and her donuts, yes."

He winks at me as we walk to the door. There's a town car waiting for us. It only takes us fifteen minutes to get to the bakery. It's still early, so I let us in and go straight to the kitchen. It was Carmine's guy who drove us. I stopped to talk to Gio and David, who stationed themselves in the lobby overnight. Carmine made it clear last night that they weren't welcome to come up. At first, I didn't understand. But once I saw the elevator opened directly into his place, I got it. I didn't want either of them in there with us. They followed us here, but now two guys Carmine hasn't met are on duty. I can hear them talking while I turn on the ovens and get things going for the bread and donuts.

"I'm Francisco, and he's Nicholas. We're assigned to Ms. Carosi today."

"Ms. Carosi and I are going to the don's once her employees are here. Mr. Scotto is going to change all the locks on the doors and windows at Ms. Carosi's place. She won't be staying there for a few days, so there's time for him to do any updates that aren't quick fixes."

"Mr. Mancinelli, we—" That's Francisco. I can tell he's picking each of his words carefully. "—don't report all of Ms. Carosi's movements to her father, but—" I hear him sigh. It's that loud. Maybe it's more of a groan. "—Look, only one of us has a problem with you. He's going to be a problem for Ms. Carosi. The rest of us think it's a good sign that you've assigned extra men. It shows you're serious about her. Only Augusto is taking it as an insult, and that's because he wants something to bitch about to our don."

"Does he want her?" Carmine's question stops me in my tracks. I'm standing with batter dripping from the spoon I'm holding. It's Nicholas who answers.

"Like he's the dog in heat."

Gross.

"Do you know about the photos?" Carmine sounds testy,

but not enough to antagonize either of my guards. Francisco sounds pained when he answers.

"Yeah. Augusto couldn't wait to tell everyone, especially Don Carosi."

"Was it either of them?"

There's a long silence. I'm back to working the batter, but I want to know the answer.

"Francisco and I don't know. But it's possible. Mr. Mancinelli, we're telling you the truth, but we wouldn't confirm it if it were true. You must know that."

"I do. But I play a different role than you. I've spent my adult life finding people's tells. Deciphering how people telegraph their lies. I'm great at it. I wouldn't fault you for being loyal to Don Carosi, but I would know. That said, if you lie to me and it risks Ms. Carosi's life, you won't enjoy how I extract the truth. I understand your loyalty to your don, but I don't give a flying fuck about it if it endangers Ms. Carosi. I will put her ahead of her father any day of the week and twice on Sundays. And when you relay this conversation to him, which I'm certain he'll force you to do, be sure you don't leave out that part. Maybe even start with it."

Oh, fuck.

"When's Augusto scheduled next?"

"Tonight."

I cringe. Fucking hell. I can imagine how that's going to go if he has to spend the night in the lobby.

"Is Adriano with him?"

Nicholas answers for the pair. "No. Gio will be back."

There's another pause, then I hear Carmine, but I have to strain to make out what he says. "Can I trust Augusto? Or is me being with Ms. Carosi going to push him into acting on his —feelings?"

Carmine's voice is mocking when he says the last word. He

just doesn't want to say lust or something equivalent. Francisco glances over Carmine's shoulder and meets my gaze. Carmine spins around. Busted. He stares at me, but what am I supposed to do? I can't walk away from the batter right now. I won't hang my head in shame for listening. And I don't really want to invite them into the kitchen. I shrug. The look he shoots me tells me my ass will hear about this later. That sends a shiver down my spine and makes my pussy clench.

Nicholas shifts his gaze from me back to Carmine, but Carmine's still watching me. "You can trust him to keep her safe. But he will tell Don Carosi everything. He always does. He thinks being up the don's ass will make the don consider him suitable. That's never going to happen. Even if Don Carosi did, Ms. Carosi's never shown any interest in him. That's his real motivator. It's his ego. He thinks he can wear her down. Until today, I'm pretty sure she was oblivious. But he will lash out at you. He'll make it hard for you to see her, either by conveniently changing the plans or making sure you get the wrong information. Something. He's been a little bitch since we were kids."

"You've known him long?"

I wince.

"He's my brother."

Carmine's head whips back around. "Your brother? And you just spoke against him to me?"

"Mr. Mancinelli, I love my brother. We're really close. But right now, we're talking about work." It's Nicholas's turn to wince. He steps to his right so he can see me clearly. "Ms. Carosi, that sounded bad. I know the privilege it is to be your guard. It means your father trusts me more than most men. But during this conversation, we're talking about how your safety is my duty and my job. Anything that gets in the way of that is serious enough that I have to consider you before my family

190

and my friends. His feelings for you are real, but so is his jealousy. He knows Mr. Mancinelli isn't going anywhere. We all do. That means Augusto perceives him as a threat to him. No *Cosa Nostra* or *Mala del Brenta* man is trained to ignore a threat. Just the opposite. We're all trained to neutralize them."

I drop the spoon in the bowl, and it splatters onto the counter. I stalk out of the kitchen. "Are you telling us Augusto will try to kill Carmine?"

I shift my gaze from my bodyguards to Carmine. He wraps his arm around me and pulls me close. "Shh, *tesorina*. He'll come to his senses."

"What does that mean? You'll beat the idea out of him?"

Carmine stares down at me, but he doesn't answer. Is silence agreement? Or is he pissed I said that?

Fucking perfect. I hear Rosella and Hillary come in through the back door. I step away from Carmine, but he catches my hand. "Do they both speak Italian?"

"Only Rosella. She's not *Cosa Nostra*, but her family is from Sicily. She knows about our families."

Carmine switches to Italian, and we continue the entire conversation in it. "I'm not doing anything to him unless I'm defending you or myself. He might be jealous, but he isn't stupid. If he endangers you, your father will kill him. I won't have to. If he comes after another don's nephew, he has to know my family won't retaliate against him. They'll go after his don. Your father doesn't want that."

I watch Carmine as he speaks, but I shift my gaze to Francisco and Nicholas. They're nodding. "What are you going to tell my father?"

Nicholas shoots me a reassuring smile. "You have a new boyfriend. It's not our place to have an opinion, so there's nothing more for us to say, is there?"

"*Grazie.*" I appreciate that, but it doesn't make me feel

better. Augusto thinks he's—what? In love with me? He or my dad could be responsible for the photos. No. How could Augusto do that? He might have enjoyed my discomfort, but I don't think he has the means to cause it that way. But he will be a pain in the ass and tattle to my dad. "Are my parents still planning to go home next week?"

The day can't come soon enough. They haven't been in New York the entire time they've been away from Venice. While Carmine was in Miami, my parents went up to Montreal for a few days. My dad had business up there, so my mom went too. While I went to Sicily the first time, they went to LA for some fundraiser. But they've been gone for almost two months. That's longer than my dad usually likes to be away. It's not good for the king to be absent from his kingdom.

"*Si.*" Both guys answer together.

"Then I'll be back to overseeing the schedule you guys make. Once they're gone, Augusto can take a well-earned vacation." I glance over my shoulder at Hillary and Rosella. They both know what to do. Hillary's taken over the donuts, and Rosella is working on the bread. They're both super experienced, so they're quick and need no supervision. I close my eyes and sigh. "If only. I know that won't work. It's just wishful thinking. I can't avoid him."

Carmine kisses my forehead. "Between your men and mine, you won't be alone with him. If he wants to start trouble, then he's going to do it regardless of his shifts or a vacation. *Tesorina*, we'll sort it out. At least, now I know."

"I don't worry about me." I wrap my arms around Carmine's waist rather than resting my hands on his back and stomach. I feel badly that Nicholas is caught in the middle. But it's not new for him. I've known the brothers since we were all kids.

"Nicholas, do you think he'll come to his senses? Or is that the real wishful thinking?"

"He's been into you for years, but he's never felt threatened before. I don't think he'd do anything to actually hurt Mr. Mancinelli, but he could make life difficult between you or for Mr. Mancinelli."

Wonderful. We've had the entire conversation in Italian, but I switch back to English.

"I'm going to check on the girls. Then I'll be ready to go. We're going to *Zio* Salvatore's."

That announcement makes my guards uneasy, but they nod. What else can they do?

Chapter Fifteen

Carmine

Hearing that Augusto's in love with Fina wasn't how I wanted my morning to go. Fortunately, Fina appeared shocked, then appalled, to find out. There wasn't a moment when she appeared to consider Augusto as a possibility. Just the opposite. My heart and my ego were glad to see her reaction, but the practical side of my mind is screaming at me that there is bound to be far more trouble ahead.

What did Augusto tell Piero about Fina and me? Did Fina telling her dad that I suddenly went out of town encourage him to spy on me? If that's the case, that's an issue on multiple levels. He's Venetian. We're Sicilian. He needs to keep his fucking nose out of our business. The only reason Piero's even in the picture is because Fina's mother is Sicilian, and her sister married my uncle. Otherwise, he'd have no reason to be nosing around in our business. And that's why I'm sitting in Uncle Salvatore's office right now.

"Carmine, is everything all right with Serafina? She didn't look upset when you arrived."

I look over at my dad, who's sitting on a sofa on the other side of Uncle Salvatore's desk. He and Uncle Massimo are facing Gabriele and me. Uncle Domenico isn't here. The rest of my cousins and Matteo spread out on a third sofa and several chairs. Uncle Salvatore is on his throne—the most inviting looking desk chair I've ever seen. Except for the one I have. It's the same as his, but in royal blue instead of tan. What can I say? I was twenty-three when I bought the thing and thought I was hot shit.

"Yes. We had a long talk last night. We cleared the air about a lot of stuff." I look at Luca, who's watching me. Our gazes meet, and his eyebrows shoot straight up. He knows I told Fina what happened between us. I'm certain he told Olivia too, but definitely not as early in their relationship as I did with Fina. Then again, early in their relationship, they were trying to make sure a Mexican Cartel didn't murder Olivia. My dad draws my attention back.

"Mama's asthma has been flaring up ever since she had the flu. She wasn't up to seeing anyone, but now she feels badly that she didn't make more of an effort to check on Serafina."

My parents have never said your so-and-so. No *your* mama or *your* papa. Despite how they fought, they were always clear that we were a family first. So, it's always been Mama, Papa, and Carmine. They really did their best with a shit situation.

"Should I see her today?"

"She'd like that. The wind's been too chilly for her lately. She's been staying home, but she doesn't have anything contagious, so I think she'd enjoy the company."

"Can I take Fina?"

"She'd love that."

Uncle Salvatore hangs up the call he was on, and everyone turns their attention to him. "Matteo, recount everything from when you landed until you found Maria."

Turns out, everyone was too tired to debrief last night, so we're doing it this morning. Matteo looks like death warmed up. He barely dozed from when Maria disappeared until we found her. My bet is he didn't sleep last night either. He spent the night at Auntie Nicoletta and Uncle Massimo's. He has his own room there since he and Marco were inseparable as kids. My cousin has a room at Uncle Domenico and Auntie Carlotta's house. I don't think he was ready to leave Maria's side in case something else happened. The guilt is wreaking havoc on him as he recounts getting off the plane, checking in, running into Maria's friends, and going to the club. Matteo frowns as his gaze drops to the floor. His eyes drift shut as he collects himself.

Matteo rests his head in his hands with his elbows pressed into his thighs. His fingers are in his hair, and it's going in every direction. That is not Matteo. He doesn't do messy. He's no neat freak, and he's not metro. But he's always what he deems presentable—ready for a board meeting. The more he shares, the more upsetting the situation becomes for Uncle Massimo. It's as though the women just vanished. Matteo'd searched everywhere in the clubs and along the way back to the hotel. He finishes by acknowledging me.

"If Carmine hadn't been there to negotiate, I don't think we would have gotten Maria without killing everyone else there."

I nod to my cousin's best friend. Matteo and I haven't gotten along since he turned ten and became too old to hang out with Maria and me. He only wanted to hang out with Luca and Marco. Lorenzo was welcome with them or with Maria and me. He went back and forth since he's the easiest going of all of us.

Maria hung out with me because she felt sorry for me. I knew that then, and I know it now. Once Gabriele moved here, she was off the hook. She suddenly had other friends she was always with. But she was sweet to Gabe, so I never begrudged her hanging out with people who had more in common with her.

Luca takes over, telling the story as Matteo remains hunched over. He lets our uncle, my dad, and his dad know how we searched, rescued Maria, and then were forced to go back to get Veronica and the two other doctors because we couldn't save them at the same time as Maria.

When I'm not watching Matteo, I'm watching Uncle Massimo. Anyone who didn't know him would question how he could appear so unmoved by the story of his only daughter's abduction and near sex trafficking. Anyone who knows him can easily read that he's about two wrong words away from exploding. If Auntie Nicoletta is easygoing, then Uncle Massimo is a powder keg. Which is funny because, of his siblings—Uncle Salvatore and my mom—and him, he's the easygoing one. I glance over at Uncle Salvatore, and I can practically see the hamsters running in his mind. He's plotting. It surprises me when Uncle Salvatore looks at me.

"Good job, Car. I'm glad we had you there. Thank you for getting Maria free of that madman. But what about the photos Serafina received? What were those about?"

I mentioned them when we arrived. "She got worried and called her dad to see if he knew anything about why I went out of town. He didn't at first, and she regretted it as soon as she brought it up to him. But she was concerned about me. A few days later, photos of me in the nightclubs, at the bars, and at Fernando's house arrived. I saw them. They're incriminating as fuck. I'm talking to a group of women in the club, and you can see me smiling. I was schmoozing. I'm talking to a woman in a bikini top and Daisy Duke's in the bar photo. Then there's a parade of women standing behind Fernando in the photo at his villa. The thing is, whoever took those photos knew not to get anyone else in them. Even though the others were close enough to be in them, somehow they never were. They took them to make me look bad."

I know this shocks the guys. I didn't talk about it because I knew nothing about them. Lorenzo sits up to see over Matteo's back.

"Did anyone else see these?"

"Yeah. Her bodyguard, Augusto, who opened the envelope. It had no return address on it, so she had him test it. It came up clean, but he still examined the contents first. I'm certain it thrilled him to wave them under her nose once he recognized me."

"Does he dislike you?"

I snort at Lorenzo's question. "I didn't know why Fina spending the night at the Waldorf pissed him off so much until this morning. I thought he was just following Piero's orders and was a kiss ass. His brother is one of Fina's guards today. I discovered Augusto's in love with Fina. He's been sucking Piero off, hoping the don will consider him suitable. He has to know about the betrothal contract, so either Piero has said in the past that he'll break it, or Augusto wants to convince him to."

My dad speaks up when I finish. "Did his brother tell you how far this *stronzo* will go?" Asshole.

"He doesn't know, but he's certain Augusto won't accept this gracefully. He's going to cause me shit or try to break Fina and me up. Nicholas doesn't think Augusto would do anything to endanger Fina, but he's uncertain. I foresee Augusto trying to get to me, and Fina getting caught in the middle."

Uncle Salvatore's been silent while I explained. Now he leans his right arm on the chair's armrest, covering his chin and mouth with his hand. He's still plotting. "What did Serafina have to say to this when she heard it?"

"It shocked her. She's worried he's going to be trouble. Her parents are returning to Venice in a few days. She'd like to send Augusto on vacation, but she knows that won't make it better. It'll just antagonize him."

"She's likely right, and none of us want her caught in the middle. Keep our men on their detail for her, and you can handle Augusto as needed. If it comes to it, then do what you must. I'll deal with Piero. In the meantime, we need to strike Fernando and his *amigos*. If word gets out, it'll destroy Maria's reputation and make her a target again. You know what people in our world will think. It's shit like this that makes me feel like we're still in the Middle Ages, but we can't risk her or any of the other women. And we have to make it obvious that an attack on any of us will rain hellfire on anyone near our enemy."

I listen to Uncle Salvatore as my gaze sweeps the room. I can tell everyone agrees with him. Of course, we do. The idea of a woman's ruined reputation may seem archaic, but if our enemies think she's already been assaulted and used, then she'll just become an object to them. An object they can take and do what they want with. If they think we can't protect the women in our family, then they will go after more of them. I speak up as I point out something that's been on my mind and that none of my cousins or friends could answer.

"We don't know why they took Maria and the others. We're assuming Maria was the real target because she's related to us and rich. But what if it was about one of the others? We know Veronica, but we don't know the other two women. Regardless, have these fuckers been watching their targets and grabbing them specifically? Or was it a moment of opportunity?"

We go back and forth as we try to answer those questions.

Uncle Massimo, as the *consigliere*, is often the voice of reason and Uncle Salvatore's conscience. He wonders what will happen to the other women. The best we can do is find out what they want and do what we can to help them.

I glance at Gabriele. If I hadn't led him down a path of ruin, he would have gone straight to law school after undergrad, and he would have been Uncle Massimo's likely successor. Law school interested none of my cousins, so no one pushed them. But becoming an attorney is something Gabriele's wanted since he was a kid. I fucked that up so many times that it makes me ashamed now. What makes him such an ideal candidate to one day be *consigliere* has also been his downfall. Loyalty. He's been way too loyal to me, and it's held him back.

It's not that he's a follower. He's not. He can lead as well as any of us, but he's understood me better than anyone since the day we met. We were both outcasts for different reasons, but it drew us together. We're the same height now, but until we were seventeen, he was always several inches taller than me. He's the broadest of all of us and definitely the strongest. His loyalty meant that he was always there to defend me, usually by knocking someone out. I can fight and have plenty of times, but Gabriele's always been that extra set of eyes and fists. I've done the same for him, but he outgrew his bitterness years ago. I only did a couple months ago. My mind has wandered, so I focus on the conversation, hoping I missed nothing too important.

Uncle Massimo states the obvious. "Once we deal with them, we let the Kutsenkos help the Eastern Europeans, and the Diazes help the Latin American ones. We walk away."

There's a problem to that, though. I point it out. "You know they're all going to be pissed if we wait until after the fact to tell them. I mean, the Diazes clearly already know what's going on since they helped us find Fernando. So, they won't want to wait and let us have a go first. The Kutsenkos are going to be pissed as fuck."

I can't get the blonde woman who was next to Maria when we found her out of my mind. It's guilt, not attraction. The way she looked at me, so hopeful. But I walked away. When we went back for the others, she was gone. I missed my opportunity, and it's haunting me. I saw other women who needed rescuing just as badly. But I didn't lock eyes with them. I didn't see them silently plead with me. I didn't know Maria helped her until she mentioned it on the plane. Before Uncle Salvatore suggests anything, I speak up because Javier, Jorge, and Joaquin may be the solution.

"*Tres J's* have a way to reach Fernando through their mutual acquaintance. I think I can lure him back from Cuba by saying I saw a woman I want. It's not like I can do a bank transfer or wire. Cuba's not an easy place for us to strike, so it's better to get him back to America. Even if we let the Diazes deal with him personally, we still need him back here to really make our move. The best thing we can do is free those women. We end his business that way. That's how we get our revenge. Take his money. No women, no money. Come after one of our own, and we will take it all from you."

If ever there were a family motto or creed, that is ours. V is for vendetta. Wrong us, and we will hunt you. V is for vindictive. We will make it hurt. Both words come from Latin. It's the Italians who gave us words to remind everyone that we neither forgive nor forget. Everyone's looking at me, but I'm watching Uncle Salvatore. He stops drumming his fingers and nods.

"We might not end this tomorrow but make it fast."

That's our sign the meeting is over. Luca will lead from here. As the underboss, he'll say yay or nay to anyone who presents ideas. My uncles remain in the study while the rest of us file out. I wonder what Fina is doing to keep herself occupied. I look at my watch and realize we were in there for over an hour.

"Carmine?" I turn toward Lorenzo when he calls my name. "You negotiated all of this so far. Do you think you can convince *Tres J's* to give us a direct contact in Cuba?"

"I don't know. Maybe. If not, we know some people there. They can probably find out."

"Will you deal with Fernando? You know the rest of us have things coming up that we can't leave behind."

"Yeah. I figured. If Luca's all right with that, then that's fine with me."

Luca nods as he looks at his phone, texting someone. Probably Olivia. They don't go more than two hours without checking in with each other. They know it's excessive. They even admit it, but after all the threats made to Olivia, they're both cautious. The Culiacán Cartel isn't after her anymore, but Dillan O'Rourke was involved. We struck back hard, and they're licking their wounds. We know it's only a matter of time. I pull out my phone and start a group text to the *Tres J's*.

ME

> Maria's home safely. This isn't over. I need to get in touch with Fernando in Cuba. Can you make that happen?

I force myself to phrase the last sentence as a question, not a command. When nothing comes in immediately, I drop my phone in my pocket and search for Fina. I find her in the living room, curled up on the couch, asleep. There's a movie on the TV, but I don't recognize it. I scoop her into my arms and sit with her on my lap.

"Fina?" She nestles closer. "*Piccolina*, I'm done with my meeting. Wake up."

It takes her a moment, but she sits up and looks around. "I

texted Maria while you were in the study. She didn't answer right away, but she said she feels better after a solid night of sleep. I know she's a doctor for real and this isn't exactly what the adage means, but doctor heal thyself. Do you think she'd see someone to talk this through? There has to be someone safe that's connected to the *Cosa Nostra*."

I grimace. "Emilio's longtime girlfriend is a therapist. Her dad was *Cosa Nostra* until—he made some bad choices. She knows this life. I'll suggest it to Maria."

"Would it be better coming from me? I know she and I aren't close, but I also know she brought you to my bakery. She made sure I sat next to you for Easter. Maybe coming from another Mafia daughter, it might go over better. I don't know. I know you're close, but I thought I'd offer."

"How about together?" I smile.

"I like that idea."

"We can text or call her later. Are you ready to go home?"

Her cheeks pinken when I say home. Not my place.

"You shouldn't be so comfortable. I don't want to move."

"We can stay here for a while."

"Just hang out in someone else's home?"

"It's not like we broke in, and they're strangers. Neither of us is Goldilocks. Uncle Sal isn't going to kick us out."

"No, but I feel like that's an imposition. Don't you have work to do?"

"It can wait another day. All of my businesses have managers who handle the day-to-day. I don't ignore them, but I don't have to be in the thick of it either. Do you need to get back to the bakery?"

"I should."

She sits up and looks around. I heard my cousins filter out, and so did Gabriele and Matteo. That makes me stop. I have an idea that I'd like to discuss with my uncles before I chicken out.

"Actually, do you mind waiting a moment? I need to ask my uncles something."

"Of course."

"Be right back." I head back to Uncle Salvatore's office and knock. When I hear him call out, I go in. Uncle Salvatore watches me while Uncle Massimo and my dad look at something on Uncle Massimo's phone. Probably kitten memes. I'd die before my next breath if I told anyone that they text each other ridiculously cute memes and videos. "Uncle Sal, I wanted to talk to you and Uncle Massi about Gabe."

I launch straight into it. From the way all three men sit back, I can tell none of them are thrilled. Oh well.

"We all know I'm the reason he isn't a *capo*. But he's proven his loyalty time and again. Not just to me, but this family. He got shot twice a few weeks ago protecting Olivia. He's as much a part of our family as anyone related by blood. I fucked up his chances to work with Aunt Sylvia, but we all know he'd be wasted there. And there's a canyon between Aunt Sylvia handling our legal businesses as a woman and Gabriele trying to when everyone knows or will easily guess he's deep in *Costa Nostra*. No one doubts he'll pass the bar. He should work for you, Uncle Massi."

Six eyes stare at me. I'm trying not to hold my breath. Part of me wants to ramble to fill the silence, but I wait. Uncle Massimo begins slowly.

"We've all seen the new leaf you've turned over. Whatever was at the heart of your issues with Luca seems to be gone. You're getting along with everyone better, and you've shown your intelligence positively. But Gabriele has always followed. He never stopped you or refused to go against you. He isn't a leader. That's why he's well-suited to be our enforcer."

Fuck. More confessions. I pray Gabriele doesn't get pissed.

"Do you remember how Gabriele and I suddenly quit playing soccer when we were fourteen?"

My dad answers for them. "Yes. You refused to tell anyone why."

"I forgot a cleat one day after practice, so I went back into the locker room. Gabriele was as tall as he is now, but still lighter and weaker than Coach. I walked in to find the man about to assault Gabriele. He had Gabe pinned face down on his desk and his dick out. Gabe was fighting with everything he had to get free. He was making progress, but neither of us knows if he would have succeeded alone. I stabbed Coach in the kidney, and that allowed Gabe to slip out of his hold. I gave Gabe my knife, and he sliced the guy's junk. Coach claimed he got jumped leaving the sports complex at night. He didn't leave until almost ten because we beat the shit out of him, then knocked him out."

I let that sink in for a moment before I continue.

"Gabe and I were always best friends. But that incident cemented that there's nothing we won't do to protect each other. It also changed Gabe. He's not a follower because he's weak. His size already makes him stick out. He'd rather not. It made him retreat into himself for a lot of years. He still doesn't like to be the center of attention. But he can lead. We've seen him do it plenty of times, but he isn't bossy about it, so no one really takes notice. He leads by example, and when he gives orders, he never barks them. But people obey. He's more subtle than people give him credit for. Now that I'm not fucking things up out of spite, he's not having to keep me from setting the world on fire. He's ready to take his rightful place. There is no one more loyal than Gabe, and that's the most important quality a *consigliere* can have. He will support Luca no matter what."

My dad and two uncles sit in stunned silence. Neither

Gabriele nor I have told anyone, not even our moms, who knew something happened. They sensed it, but we swore we would never tell. For how much loyalty means to Gabriele, I hope he doesn't think I betrayed him by finally revealing what happened. It was fourteen years ago, and the guy's dead. We made sure of it two years later when we found out Gabriele wasn't his only victim. Uncle Massimo looks at Uncle Salvatore before he looks back at me.

"What does Gabriele know that none of us do about why you made the choices you did?"

"He doesn't know what happened between Luca and me. No one but Luca, Emilio, and I knew until recently. Olivia and Fina know now, and it will stay that way until the day Luca can make peace with Emilio. If he never does, then no one besides the five of us will know."

My dad interjects, obviously asking what they're all thinking. "You told Sera?"

"Yes. She knows about all of my major fuck-ups. I didn't want her to hear about them from someone else. I didn't want her to feel like I keep more secrets than I have to. And I don't want to trap her. She needs to know who I was and who I am."

The three older men look at me as though I sprouted a second head.

"Gabe knows some things both my *nonnos* told me that I've never repeated to anyone but him."

It's my dad's turn to look at my uncles before his brow furrows. I've confessed more in the past two weeks than I ever have in church in my entire life. In some ways, it's lightened the weight on my shoulders. But it's also left me raw.

"Let me get Fina. She may as well hear all of this, too. I know Piero doesn't want us together. It wouldn't surprise me if he already knows some of this. If he doesn't, he still has plenty to hold against me. I expect he's going to disapprove of me no matter what."

The men remain quiet as I go to the office door and call to Fina. She comes, and I slip my hand into hers before we walk to a sofa.

"Fina, you already know a lot of my past. But there's some stuff about why I did what I did that I'm finally going to tell Papa and my uncles. You should hear this too. It involves our grandfathers."

Her eyes widen before she looks at the three men watching us.

"It's no secret both my *nonnos* called me *spazzatura illegittima*." Illegitimate trash. "*Nonno* Vicenzu swore Papa forced himself on Mama. Since we're Catholic, he claimed they had to force her not to get rid of me. When no one was around, he called me *figlio del diavolo*. Son of the devil. Devil's spawn. However you want to translate it, I don't remember a time when he didn't call me that. He couldn't kill you, Papa, and he hated that. He hated he had to accept me because he believed Mama was so far above you. *Ragazzo di strada*. That was his other favorite. Guttersnipe. Street urchin. That took me longer to understand."

Decades of disgust and loathing make my belly roil.

"*Nonno* Andrea-Mario wasn't any better. He swore Mama trapped Papa to get away from *Nonno* Vicenzu. He called her a whore long before I knew what that meant, too. He called Papa *cazzo d'Orro*, and that's why Mama trapped him. She couldn't get enough."

The Golden Prick. The term basically means a guy who marries a rich woman, who wants him because he's a good fuck. It wasn't a compliment to my dad.

"When he was with friends, he'd call me *mi fa cagare*."

That translates roughly to it makes me shit, or it's disgusting, repulsive. In my head, I'd call him *faccia de cazzo*. Testicle face. I figured his were shriveled up and useless since I knew my *nonna* had her own room.

My father's face has gone a shade of gray I didn't know was possible when someone is still alive. "Car, why didn't you tell anyone?"

"What was I supposed to do when I was five or six, and they swore me to silence? They'd both tell me I'd make you and Mama angry because you didn't care about me and didn't want to deal with me. I knew that wasn't true. I never thought it was. But they scared me. By the time I understood they were both hateful old men, I was used to it enough that it seemed pointless to say anything. Who was going to stop *Nonno* Vicenzu? Who was going to stop *Nonno* Andrea-Mario? Only *Nonno* Vicenzu could have, and he wouldn't have. He might have pretended to come to my defense for Mama's sake—or let's be real, for appearances—but he didn't give a shit about me."

I almost forgot Fina's sitting next to me, but she's squeezing my hand so tightly that I flex my fingers. She doesn't ease her hold. I move our hands to my thigh, and I cover them with my other hand, surreptitiously prying her fingers off. She gasps and looks down as she loosens her hold.

"Carmine, if I'd had even a clue, Mama and I never would have sent you there every afternoon."

My mom's mom used to babysit me after school while my parents worked.

"She made up for a lot."

Not nearly enough, but she made it tolerable. She couldn't stop my grandfather any more than I could, but she kept me away from him. She protected me as best she could. I watch my father, and he's still so pale it's scaring me. He looks on the verge of tears. He couldn't have stopped either of my grandfathers any more than anyone else. I never told my parents because of that. I didn't want them to look the way my dad does now. What good would it have done them to know they couldn't protect their only son? After what happened to Gabriele, I would remind myself that my life could be way worse. That they were only words. Words that fucked me up for most of my life.

Uncle Salvatore doesn't look much better than Papa. "Car, I wish I'd gotten even a hint. I would have stopped Papa."

"Uncle Sal, you couldn't have. You tried to keep *Nonno* from making Mama marry Papa, and that didn't work. I know you didn't agree with *Nonno* arranging my betrothal to Fina, but he wouldn't listen. That man did what he wanted. He couldn't get Mama to marry the man he wanted, so he was intent upon making me. *Nonno* Vicenzu knew Fina's grandfather needed our support in Sicily, but he also knew her family would hate me because of that. Fina's grandfather knew it too, but he was as happy to use me as anyone ever has been. It didn't matter to *Nonno* at all what anyone said. Not what you said as underboss. Not what Uncle Massi said when he became *consigliere*. Why cause arguments that no one but he would win? Why put people in the middle of something that didn't end until he died? Same thing with *Nonno* Andrea-Mario. They were two peas in a pod despite how they treated each other."

Fina's resting her free hand on my forearm, her thumb stroking my skin through my sleeve. It's not pity. It's not even sympathy. It's courage. That's what she's giving me. Silent strength to not run now that I've shared all of this.. Each of the three siblings looked enough like *Nonno* Vicenzu that no one could question their paternity, but they really favored *Nonna*. But I look just like Papa, and he looked just like *Nonno* Andrea-Mario. It meant whenever I saw myself, I saw a man I hated.

Uncle Massimo meets my gaze as he speaks. "They used a little boy to fight a petty war. Papa loved to flaunt his power in Andrea-Mario's face since it was his father who took out Andrea-Mario's father and became the don. Andrea-Mario never forgave our family for that, but he was stuck working for us. They couldn't strike each other, so they took it out on the person who most reminded them of their enemy but who could do nothing about it."

I shrug, and my eyebrows twitch up and down. That's exactly what it was. I figured that out around thirteen. By then, I was so bitter. *So, so bitter.* I hated seeing how well *Nonno* Vicenzu treated my cousins, how much respect he gave my uncles while looking at Mama with disgust. I wanted nothing to do with my male cousins and Matteo, but we're a tight-knit family. What could I do?

"Now you know what happened. Growing up keeping secrets like that, being manipulated every time I saw them, taught me a lot. As much as they hated me, they crafted me in their own image. I knew that, and it was its own type of revenge. I was just like them despite how worthless they said I was. If I was worthless, then what did that make them? But it was seeing Lucenzo beat Luca at the vineyard that finally made me realize I disgust myself. I didn't want to be like Lucenzo, who reminded me of both *nonnos*. I didn't want to be like them anymore because they're both dead, and I can't have revenge on men sharing an *apéritif* in Hell."

The five of us sit in silence as everyone else digests what I share. I don't feel better for having shared. Just the opposite. Their guilt radiates from them, and Fina's miserable because she's horrified and sad for me. I absorb it all before I stand and help Fina up.

"Now you know. I remember hearing as a kid 'secrets, secrets are no fun. Secrets, secrets hurt someone.' Yeah. In the singular. Some things are better taken to the grave. None of you could have changed anything, so there's no point wishing you had."

I shrug again. Fina and I say our goodbyes, and I can't get outside fast enough. The crisp breeze soothes me, but the moment we're in the car, I can't stop but think what's next?

Chapter Sixteen

Fina

I'm lucky I didn't break the skin the way my nails bit into the back of Carmine's hand. I had no idea what I was doing until he had to pry my fingers loose. Every time he told us one more thing those fucking bastards called him, the more I wanted to dig them out of their graves, resurrect them, and kill them myself. Even my grandfather. I knew he was using me. How couldn't he be if he forced a betrothal on his granddaughter in this day and age? But I didn't realize how badly he wanted to punish Vicenzu and that he purposely used Carmine to do it.

There's no way, in an Italian family—a *Cosa Nostra* family —that Carmine didn't spend hours each week with either or both of those wretched men. There is no other way to describe it than emotional abuse. My heart breaks for that little boy. My heart still aches for the man Carmine grew into after hearing those things day after day, week after week, month after month, year after year.

It doesn't excuse his major fuck-ups, but I get now why he

acted how he did. He wasn't a dog licking for scraps, going back to the same master who kept kicking him. He took what they gave him and turned it back on them. But I can't ignore what that must have done to his child psyche. It makes me wonder if he would have abandoned his family if he weren't part of the don's closest relatives.

"Fina?"

"Hmm? Sorry. Just thinking."

"It's enough to give you a headache, isn't it?"

His tone's casual, almost flippant, or irreverent. But he's had twenty-odd years of practice. My mind's wandering, and I'm glad. It's keeping me from picturing Carmine as a kid. I watch the buildings go by as we approach the bakery. I need to stop by the new Harlem shop either today or tomorrow and check the display cabinets that were installed yesterday. We'll see how things go at the main shop, then I'll decide whether we should make our way toward the top of Manhattan and the new store.

I groan as Carmine passes the shop and turns into the nearby parking garage. I'm not thrilled to see Augusto standing outside the shop. What's he doing here? He's not assigned to me today. This has already been a long day, and it's barely noon.

"How about a long lunch, Daddy?"

"I saw him, Fina. We may as well deal with it. You said you need to be at work."

"I do. But I don't want a confrontation."

"There won't be one. I will not argue on a street or in a store with him. He won't touch me with you and my guards with me."

"I know. But now I can't stop thinking that he's feeding information—even lies—to my dad to fuck things up for us."

"He can if he wants to. As long as you're okay with me, then I don't care what anyone else thinks."

"Until he makes life miserable."

"Fina, we'll cross that bridge when we come to it."

He's right. But that doesn't mean this doesn't add to my stress. He walks around to my side of the car and opens the door. As always, he's looking in every direction, constantly scouting for any threat. Once I'm out of the car, he wraps his arm around my back and locks the car. We head out to the sidewalk and turn left toward the bakery. I slide my arm around him, and I can feel the tension in his body. Is he just hyper alert because the street is crowded? Or is he gearing up to deal with Augusto? Probably both.

The pain in my ass blocks the door. I glance over my shoulder at Nicholas, who was in the car that followed us. My guards hung out with some of the Mancinellis' men while I was inside *Zio* Salvatore's house. Francisco left to go to his daughter's play, so Adriano replaced him. Right now, Nicholas appears no more pleased to see his brother than I am. When Augusto doesn't step aside or open the door for us, Nicholas moves forward. I hear him hiss at Augusto.

"Don't make a scene. Move."

Augusto's glaring at Carmine and doesn't budge.

"If you don't want a one-way ticket back to Venice, don't do this, Augusto."

I infuse all the authority I can into my voice. These men work for my father, which means they work for me vicariously. The only time they're to give me orders is when it pertains to my safety. I give the orders the rest of the time. I just rarely have. He does nothing. He doesn't shift his gaze to me. He continues to stare at Carmine, who appears unperturbed by it all. His voice is normal when he addresses my insubordinate bodyguard.

"Augusto, Ms. Carosi needs to get inside to work. We can talk while Nicholas and Adriano go with her."

"Augusto, listen to Mr. Mancinelli. If you cost me a customer because they can't get in or they're too scared to approach, I will send you back to Venice. Move."

My voice isn't as neutral as Carmine's. It's what finally makes Augusto budge. He recognizes that tone. It's the tornado siren before the storm strikes. Adriano and Nicholas escort me inside, only for me to find Heather and Rosella staring at the scene outside. Heather's never outright asked, but she's bright. She's figured it out. Now my asshole babysitter and my way-more-patient-than-me boyfriend confirm it.

I cock an eyebrow and head toward the back. Rosella stays out front while Heather follows me back. I go straight to the sink and wash my hands. I'm trying to hide my curiosity better than my two employees, but I'm dying to know what they're saying. Instead, I check what's in the ovens before I do a quick visual check of the dry and wet goods. We're lower on flour than we should be, but nothing catastrophic.

Heather comes to work beside me. "Sera, any chance your boyfriend has a single brother? A single best friend?"

"He's an only child." And I assume Gabriele is single. These guys don't date for the same reasons it's always been hard for me to date.

Where's your family from?

Italy.

What brought them here?

Business.

What do they do?

This and that.

Do you always have bodyguards?

Yes.

Why?

Blank stare.

That's about as far as it gets. That's as far as it would get if I introduced Heather to Gabriele or even any of Carmine's cousins and Matteo. They're better off finding their own partners. But Heather's persistent.

"What about a single best friend? Rosella said he came in with a big guy that first time they came with Carmine's cousin. You know I like them all muscly."

"He's not on the market."

Take that to mean whatever you want. I've poured ingredients into the industrial mixer, so I flick it on. Perfect timing. It drones out any conversation we can have. Heather goes back to work. Maybe she took the hint. As the minutes tick by, and I get further into making a gender reveal cake, the more anxious I become. Carmine still hasn't come inside. Every time I look out to the storefront, I look at the door. He's still talking to Augusto. I notice this last time that Carmine's guards are a lot closer, even though they appear busy on their phone or window shopping.

Do I intervene? No. Like it or not, I know my place in this. They might argue about me, but my place isn't in the middle. This is no longer really about me. From the length of the conversation, it's escalated to a machismo standoff and a power struggle between the *Cosa Nostra* and the *Mala del Brenta*. The last thing any of us need is some *soldato* starting a blood feud with a *capo*. That'll fucking go over like a house on fire. It tempts me to step in, after all. But I can't. Augusto will say Carmine needed me to rescue him. And Carmine'll be infuriated that I put myself in the middle of something that could get physical at any moment. Fucking hell.

I pour the batter into the baking pan and slide it into the oven. I'm ready to help Heather with the bread people will come in for on their way home. That's a huge portion of my business. People love picking up fresh Italian and French bread for dinner. Donuts in the morning and bread in the afternoon. They're the least expensive things I sell, but they make the bulk of my revenue. I can't not help Heather; otherwise, I'm sabotaging myself.

I grab a bowl of dough that's been rising and punch it down a few times. I'm working where I can still see the door. They've moved aside to let some customers in, and they don't look like they're arguing. Fuck, I want to know what's happening.

"Sera? Can you come out here?" I hear Rosella call to me.

"Just a moment. Let me wash my hands." I set aside the dough that I can't ignore for too long and clean up before walking out of the kitchen. Rosella has her saleswoman smile plastered across her face. Saccharine sweet. Customers love it. I think it looks patronizing as fuck. Whatever sells.

"Sera, they'd like to set up a wedding cake tasting."

"Wonderful. Do you know what you have in mind?"

I spend the next fifteen minutes talking to the two men, suggesting different cakes, fillings, and frostings. I make notes and set an appointment for them to come back in a week. I've been playing hooky too much since Carmine and I got together. I have to buckle down and keep to my work schedule. More people trickle in while I'm talking to the couple. It keeps me occupied enough that I don't notice Augusto leaving. Carmine comes inside as the fiancés leave. Our gazes meet, and he shoots me a reassuring smile. It does nothing to make me feel better since it could all be for appearances. He approaches Rosella, which surprises me.

"Could I have that dozen red velvet cupcakes and four pieces of the brownies without the nuts, please?"

He's ordering desserts? I walk over to him.

"Don't tell me you plan to eat those all by yourself."

"I might."

"You'll be sick."

Maybe it's because I've been a baker and pastry chef so long that I no longer crave sweets at all. Maybe I just have common sense. There's no way anyone should eat all that.

"I don't mean to eat them all in one sitting, Fina. I would be sick, and that would be a waste. Though I know this phenomenal baker who might be willing to make some goodies just for me."

He waggles his eyebrows. I go onto my toes, and he bends sideways so I can whisper in his ear. "I'll make something all right. I'll make you come."

He chuckles. It isn't a humorous one. It's dark and sensual. It tests my resolve not to give up my business and tie him to the bed to have my way with him. It's his turn to whisper to me. "Bring home some frosting, and you'll be every course of my dinner tonight."

I clench my ass and pussy. Fuck me if that doesn't make me wet. He thanks Rosella when she puts the boxes on the counter. When he moves toward the register and pulls out his wallet, I snap back to reality.

"Carmine, you don't have to."

He looks at me as though I'm nuts before he turns back to Rosella, waiting for her to ring him up. She looks at me.

"It was a dozen cupcakes and four brownies. Do you take app payments or is a card easier?"

Rosella's still looking at me while Carmine pulls out his phone, too.

"Carmine, you really don't have to. It's my treat."

His gaze hardens to that look he gives me when we're being kinky. It makes me want to say, "yes, Daddy."

"Thank you, Carmine."

I concede. Rosella rings him up, and he carries his boxed pastries to a table in the corner. His expression changes as he looks at the brownies. Now I know what six-year-old Carmine looked like. I can't help but laugh. He looks up at me guiltily. But only for a moment. He takes a bite, and his expression is completely unrepentant. I shake my head and make my way back to the kitchen.

I come out four hours later, flushed and tired. But everything is done. Kasey and Maggie arrived for their afternoon and evening shifts. They're only part time. Rosella and Heather take off. I help the two new arrivals during the after-work rush, then it's time to clean up and lock up. The afternoon flew by.

"*Piccolina*, do you want to text or stop by Maria's?"

"Let's text first. If she's around, then maybe we can go over."

Carmine pulls out his phone. I notice none of the brownies are left, and three cupcakes are missing. I stare at him, eyes wide and slack-jawed. He shrugs.

"You have all the ones you could want here, and Gabriele doesn't like brownies. There are enough cupcakes left for Maria if we go over there."

"Don't you think taking nine cupcakes will make it obvious you ate some?"

"Like she doesn't already know I'd do that." Carmine pretends to roll his eyes and shoots me a look like I'm the one making no sense.

"I suppose you aren't in a rush for dinner."

He has such an expressive face when he wants to. The gleam in his eyes as he looks me up and down is purely predatory.

"Where's that frosting, Fina?" He was serious? "I'm definitely starving for dinner."

I step closer, and he wraps his arm around my waist. He offers me a quick kiss, aware that we aren't alone.

"Get the frosting."

I hesitate. He lets go of me, spins me around, and gives me a little push. I look back over my shoulder.

"But it's for tomorrow." Those might be the saddest words I've ever said.

"Pity. That means Maria's out of luck for the cupcakes. I'll use the frosting from those and eat the cupcakes for breakfast."

I just stare. I gather my senses and say goodnight to the women. They leave, and I lock up. We head to the parking garage. I need to learn the names of the men who accompany Carmine. Adriano, Nicholas, and Carmine's men get into town cars. They wait for us as Carmine texts Maria. We got a little distracted earlier.

CARMINE

How're you doing? Can Fina and I stop by? I have cupcakes.

We wait a few minutes since her answer will determine where we go.

MARIA

At work. Leave the cupcakes in the kitchen. Don't eat any more of them.

Carmine chuckles.

Uh uh. In person delivery only. You feel okay enough to be at work?

Better than being home alone. I prefer being busy. Looking at people's innards is better than thinking about what happened.

Just checking on you. When can Fina and I stop by?

I work the next three days. Then I'm moonlighting for two then back here.

Can you make time?

Why?

I look at Carmine. He doesn't seem surprised or perturbed by her evasiveness.

You should talk about this. You know you can talk to Gianna.

So she can blab to Emilio who'll blab to Matteo who'll blab to Marco who won't leave me the eff alone. I'll pass.

Can't you invoke doctor patient confidentiality?

Picture me snorting. That's what I'm doing. Don't be dumb.

Then would you talk to Fina?

I don't want to talk to anyone right now Car. Let it go. I'm not saying never. Just not yet.

Would you talk to me?

Carmine!

Fine. You know I worry.

I love you too.

> Love you. Text me tomorrow. Then it doesn't count as me bugging you.

She sends him the eye roll emoji then a thumbs up. Then she sends him a kissing emoji. He sends the face with hearts and a kissing emoji back.

"Home?"

He looks at me as he plugs in his phone and turns on the engine.

"Yeah."

"I'll let you scrape the frosting off, *piccolina*. Then I'm licking you everywhere."

It's been two weeks since Carmine's unexpected trip to Miami and the disaster that came with it. My parents are—blessedly—back in Venice. I've hung out with Juliana several times and even done some baby stuff shopping. At first, she was wary of Carmine, but she's come around. I explained what I could, and she understood not to ask for more. Out of the past two weeks, he's been to that place twice. Once for two days and another for three days. He was exhausted when he returned each time. I've been back at my place while he's been away, and the improvements Gabriele made are noticeable.

He changed every lock and even put doorknobs with locks on all of the ones inside. I know it was Carmine who ordered and authorized the window replacements, but Gabriele made the recommendations and oversaw their placement. That shocked me. Carmine and I argued about it. I felt like it was too extravagant. I could buy my own windows. He just had to tell me which ones. He said it was no big deal. It ended with me over his lap for arguing about my safety. That spanking wasn't a punishment, and we put to use almost all the toys we ordered. It happened on a Sunday, and we went to bed at one in the afternoon and didn't leave until five the next morning.

He's spent the night at my place a lot, but I've also gone back to his penthouse almost as often. It almost feels like living with a guy again. I like it. I'm getting used to it much faster than I did when Orlando and I moved in together. He's hinted at making it a permanent arrangement, and I'm onboard with that. But we don't want to rush any more than we already have. He's at that place again, so it surprises me when my phone rings midmorning, and it's his number.

"*Carino?*"

"Hi, *piccolina*. How're you?"

"I'm fine. I didn't think I would hear from you yet."

"I know. I have to leave again. I don't know how long I'll be gone."

"Can I know where?"

"Boston."

I wonder what happened up there, but I know better than to ask. "When are you leaving?"

"Right now. I'm on the way to the airfield with Gabriele. I'm sorry, Fina. But this can't wait. My cousins and Matteo are going to be part of your detail again."

Any time Carmine isn't with me, someone from his immediate family is. He's been unobtrusive about setting that up, and I've gotten used to the other guys. The weather has gotten really nice now that it's May. They often go outside, looking like they're waiting for someone. Or they bring their laptops and work at a spot on one of the kitchen counters.

"Do you need me to do anything, *carino?*"

"No, little one, but thank you. If I'm gone more than five days, Uncle Salvatore and Aunt Sylvia want you to stay with them. It means something went wrong."

Five days? Just what does he expect to do up there?

"Is there anything I shouldn't do while you're gone? I mean, it's safe for me to do my regular everyday stuff, right?" Since I have no idea what this involves, I ask.

"None of this should touch you. You should be far removed, so don't worry."

I keep my voice low. "Daddy, that's like telling the sky to stop being blue. Of course, I'm going to worry."

"I'll be home as soon as I can, Fina. I miss you already."

"I miss you, too." There's more I want to say, but this isn't the right time to declare myself. It's too soon and over the phone when he's about to leave town. That isn't how I want to do it. And if he says I love you back, I want to see him and touch him when he does.

"Fina, if anything happens at all, go to Uncle Salvatore. I trust all your men but Augusto. But we have more resources than you do."

"I won't be anywhere without one of your family with me, anyway."

"I know. But they aren't there at night, so I have to rely on your men for that shift. Or if something happens, and my cousins or Gabe or Matteo can't protect you. You go straight to Uncle Sal. If you can't get there, then my dad, Uncle Dom, or Uncle Massi. Promise me, Fina. I have to hear it."

"I promise, Carmine." I already know these things. But it freaks me out a bit to hear how urgent his tone has become. "I won't do anything to put myself at risk, Daddy. I know you can't promise the same, but be careful."

"I will, *piccolina*. I already spoke to Matteo."

I glance out the back window and see Matteo in the alley near the closed backdoor. Then he disappears. He must be coming back to the kitchen. When he opens the door, I mouth

"Carmine." He nods and goes back to his spot across the industrial kitchen.

"I know you have to go. I can hear the plane."

"I do. We're about to take off. I'll be back as soon as I can. Bye, baby."

"Bye, Daddy."

I watch Matteo to see if he notices. I don't think he heard me, but these men have ears like dogs. If he did, he does nothing to acknowledge it. I hang up and slip my phone into my pocket. I want to grill Matteo, but I know he won't answer. And it's not cool to put him in that position. I'm just going to have to wait. But for what? Nothing good came out of Carmine's last trip.

Chapter Seventeen

Carmine

It's going down. Or, at least, it will be soon. We picked Boston because Besnik is up here, and I'm certain he knows more than I realized. He owes us some product that he's supposed to run down to New York. We can get that while we sort this shit out. While I was at the garage, we learned he made the grave mistake of lying to us. He told us someone stole the shipment. Nope. He sold it to Dillan. The Albanians and Irish get along pretty well in Boston, and I suspect Besnik's hoping to expand his drug running all the way to New York. But without us.

Gabriele looks at me as we walk into the hotel suite. "First thing in the morning?"

"Yeah. I just want to sleep. I'm going to call Fina and let her know I got here safely. I know it's the last time I'll talk to her until this is over."

We checked into the suite that has a bedroom for each of us. Since the men we're using are locals, they'll go home. Four will rotate here at the hotel, one standing out front and one in the back, with one at our door, and the other at the elevators. I hang up the suits and shirts I brought, but there isn't enough of the rest of my stuff to bother unpacking. I'll just grab what I need as I go.

"Hi, Daddy." That voice. I sit on the end of the bed with my eyes closed. Life's a little better now.

"Hi, *piccolina*. I wanted to let you know I got here safely."

"Thanks. I've been thinking about you."

"I've been thinking about you, too."

"What are you wearing, Daddy?" She purrs the question. I glance at the bedroom door, which I've shut. Gabriele said he was going to study for the bar for a few hours before we figure out dinner. He won't be interrupting.

"I just took off my suit coat and kicked off my shoes. Now I'm loosening my tie."

"Mmm. If I were there, I'd help you unbutton your shirt."

"And my pants."

"Of course."

I'm stripping as fast as I can without dropping the phone. "And what would I do with my tie?"

"Blindfold me with it. Or wrap it around my wrists. Could you use it to tie me to the bed?"

I look at the headboard. No, I couldn't. But that bit of reality has no place in this fantasy. "Yes. But first we need to get you naked, little girl."

"Oh, I already am. I was about to get in the shower, but Daddy came home early."

I grin. I'm down to my boxer briefs, which she's threatened to burn since I refuse to let her wear panties. I pull them down and free my cock, which is pulsing.

"You're not nearly dirty enough yet, *cuore*." Sweetheart.

"You just haven't looked close enough. I'm very dirty."

The fucking dirty, dirty things I want to do to her. "Get on the bed, *piccolina*."

"Yes, Daddy."

"Put your right hand over your head and grab the bottom of your headboard. Don't move that hand. Imagine my tie is around both your wrists." I'll let her have one hand free. She has to do what my mouth ought to be doing.

"Yes, Daddy."

"I'm naked now too as I climb into bed. You're so beautiful, Fina. I can't help but watch you. Your nipples are getting hard as I look at you."

"They are."

I don't know if she's rolling them or just this role playing is doing it. I don't care. I have my hand around my dick, and I'm stroking myself.

"I'm whispering in your ear. You're mine, *piccolina*. Mine to do whatever I want with. Your mouth, your hands, your pussy, your glorious fucking ass are all mine to fuck. Open wide. I'm straddling your shoulders as you suck on me, getting my cock nice and wet. Yes. That feels amazing... Let go now, little girl. I'm titty fucking you... Stick your tongue out... Yes. Lick the tip."

She hums, and I know she's picturing exactly what I'm describing as I sit propped up against the headboard.

"Daddy, can I taste you again?"

"Do you want to suck me off?"

"I want whatever you want, Daddy. But I definitely wouldn't mind that."

I chuckle. "Open wide again... Fuck, Fina. Your mouth feels so good. So warm. So soft. But the way you suck me off is enough to make me come the moment you start. Slow down... So good."

My eyes are closed as I imagine each thing I say. I'm going

to get myself off way too soon. If only my imagination weren't so vivid.

"Let go of Daddy, *piccolina*. I'm not ready to come yet." I'm not, but I will if I don't move onto something else. "I'm kissing you, and you're sucking on my tongue just how I like it. The way that makes me want to be inside of you, spilling and filling you with my cum."

She hums again.

"Touch yourself, Fina. Slip your fingers into your wet little pussy. You're soaked, aren't you?"

"Yes, Daddy." It's a breathy answer followed by a moan.

"Those are my fingers inside you. Do not rub your clit. Do you understand me, little girl?"

"Yes, Daddy."

It's fine with me if she is. Whatever makes phone sex good for her is all I want.

"You can't help it. You keep lifting your hips, trying to get me to play with your little clitty. To get me to stroke your g spot, but not yet. Patience is a virtue."

"Then I'm the least virtuous person I know. I'm close already."

"Do not come, Fina. I'll spank you if you do. I'll remember it for when I get home."

"Yes, Daddy." Need fills her voice, and I know the threat of a spanking turns her on more than any of this.

"You haven't had a spanking recently. I think you're overdue. Roll over."

"Yes, Daddy."

"Your ass... Fuck, Fina. I want to pull you up onto your knees and slam my cock into your pussy just thinking about you like this. I want to watch it move each time my balls slap your ass, and I can't get any deeper."

"Daddy, please let me come. When you say shit like that, I can't stop needing you and needing to come."

"No. You're mine, Fina. All of you. I told you that already. That means your orgasms are mine to give and to take. I'm not ready to give you your first one."

"First. That means there'll be more than one. What's the harm in letting me have a little one now if I'm just going to have more later?"

I chuckle again. She moans. I know how she responds to it when it's not about humor. It's about letting her know I'm about to do way more to her. "That is not how it works, little girl. That just reminds me you're overdue for your spanking. Now I can't stop picturing you on your knees, leaning forward. Do that now."

"Daddy, can we pause for a moment? I want to get my hairbrush."

"Fina, we're just playing right now. I don't want you to hurt yourself. If you miss because you can't see—"

"Daddy, I need you to trust me on this. I know what I'm doing."

Fucking hell.

"Daddy, do not think about that. Stay here with me. I've only ever spanked myself alone. May I get it?"

"Yes, *tesorina*. Grab the nipple clamps too and put those on."

I hear her moving around. I switch us to a video call. This is stupid not to see each other when we can. I watch her pinch and roll her nipples into nubs before she applies the clamps and tightens them.

"Daddy?"

"Is this better?" I hold the phone so she can see my face and my hand stroking my dick.

"So much better."

"Get back on the bed, Fina. Ten. No more, no less. Count them and say thank you. Then ask for the next one."

"Yes, Daddy." The sound of the back of the hairbrush hitting her ass comes through the phone. I can't take my eyes off her. "One. Thank you, Daddy. Can I have another?"

She continues to spank and count until she gets to the tenth one.

"Put the brush down and finger yourself."

"Yes, Daddy."

That word. I know some people will never understand why that's hot to me. I don't give a fuck about them. The more she says it, the more I want to hear it. She knows that, so she indulges me. And I think the more she says it, the more she wants to do it again. I suppose it could be some other word, but it's what it signifies. She's trusting me, and it's been a long time since I've earned that or deserved it. She's vulnerable to me by choice. That means the world to me. She not only wants me to take care of her, but she's letting me. That's what being a daddy means to me. We don't need to go as far as age play.

She's watching me as I watch her. It's nowhere near as good as being together in person. But fuck, she's hot no matter how or where I see her. Everything about her. Her broad hips I love to hold on to. Her thick thighs I want wrapped around me. Her soft belly with the smoothest skin I've ever felt. Her arms, toned from her work, that cling to me when she needs me. Her perfect handful of tits that I could suck all day. And her lips. So plush and soft.

"Roll onto your back." She obeys, but she's slow. She's teasing me. "*Piccolina*."

I infuse warning into my tone. She grins.

"Yes, Daddy?"

She winks at me. I growl.

232

"We are getting you one of those phone tripod things. You're still supposedly restrained."

"Hold on." She arranges pillows and props up her phone. She puts her right hand over her head and holds onto the headboard.

"That's much better, little one. Let me see you rub your clit."

I stroke faster as she rubs. She arches her back as though I were there and able to suck on her perfect dark nipples. Perfect. The word keeps coming to mind over and over. She's perfect for me. I won't put her on a pedestal where she's destined to fail to live up to perfection. But there's no one better for me to love. I pray one day she feels that way about me. I wanted to tell her on the phone earlier, but then and now aren't the right time.

"Let go of the headboard and tug on the clamps." I watch her nipples darken as she plays with the nubs while rubbing her clit.

"May I come, Daddy?"

"Yes, *piccolina*."

"Are you close too?"

"Always, but I'm not ready to be done with you. Those are my fingers getting you off."

"I know. I need your cock." I watch her as her body tenses, and she squeezes her eyes shut. Her chest rises and drops. She turns her head to look at me. "Thank you, Daddy."

"Keep going."

"Um... I have something... Could I get it? Would you want to watch me?"

"Of course."

She scrambles off the bed and moves away from the phone's camera. But she's back quickly. She sits on the bed cross-legged with a box. She looks at me before peeling back a seal and tugging a little. She gets the packaging open, and I realize it's brand new. It wasn't something we ordered together.

"What is that, Fina?"

"So, I kinda bought it while you were at that place last time. But you came back, so I haven't used it."

"You bought a vibrator that you planned to use to get off when I'm not available?"

"You make it sound bad."

"I didn't know you were in control. I thought we agreed I decide when you do and don't come."

"You do. But I really missed you, and it was an impulse." She gets it out and holds it up. It's fucking enormous. She bites her bottom lip. "It's still not big enough to be you. But I thought it would let me feel like you're with me when you're gone, and I don't know when you'll be back."

"Fina, you flatter me. I am not like that."

Her brow furrows. She wraps her hand around it and slides it a couple times. "Carmine, I promise you, you are more endowed than this."

I look down at myself. Maybe it's the angle she's holding the thing at. Or the only angle I'm able to see myself at right now. I grin. "You do wonders for my ego, little one."

"You need no help with that in this department. We both know you fuck like a porn star. Are you mad I got it without at least letting you know?"

"No, Fina. While I'd rather you be as hungry to come as I am after we're apart, I won't insist that you not use it."

"Can we compromise? I only use this when you're away, and we can be on the phone together. Okay?"

"You don't have to—"

"That's what I want. I told you. It was an impulse. But I don't want to get off without you, Carmine. I didn't actually play with myself either time you were gone. Tempted, but I didn't."

"Lie back and turn it on. Or does it need charging?"

"I hope it doesn't need charging. Fucking cock tease."

We laugh, but not for long. The moment we hear it turn on, we're back in the scene.

"Lie back, *piccolina*. Ease it into you... Slowly... Yes. Just like that. How does it feel?"

"You're so big. Fuck... Daddy, I need it harder. Please. Fuck me harder."

"Turn it up, baby."

She does, and the vibrator gets a little louder. I watch her slide it in and out of her pussy. It doesn't take much to imagine the feeling of her on me, the feeling of me inside her.

"Daddy, I'm close again."

"Keep going." I can barely get the words out as I fight not to come yet. She's moving it around, finding just the right spots.

"Daddy, please." She's begging. I love it.

"Five. Four. Three. Two. One. Come, *piccolina*."

I watch her strain and hold the headboard tighter. Her legs go stiff, and I see the muscles in her belly flutter. They tense, and her shoulders come off the mattress as she throws her head back. She moans, and I can't stop.

"Fina, look at me." It's a command, and she obeys. I erupt with a groan. So much cum. It covers my hand and across my lower abs. I don't know how I didn't get it on the sheets. "Next time, my cum's going to be inside you, little girl. Where it belongs. You will sit with it inside you. Sleep with it inside. Who does your pussy belong to?"

"My daddy."

"Fina, thank you."

"*Thank you.* I still miss you, Carmine. I know not to ask anything, so I won't. But I want you to know I miss you, even when I'm not horny." She hesitates. "Do couples live together before they're married in your family? I caused a massive fight with my parents when I told them Orlando and I were living together. We'd been in the same apartment for six weeks before I told them. But they eventually came around."

We've danced around the topic but never discussed it outright.

"No. The only exception was Luca and Olivia, and that started because he was protecting her." She nods. "Fina?"

"Would you consider breaking that family tradition?"

"Only for you."

"You would?" I like the excitement in her voice.

"Yes."

"Carmine, I'm not suggesting right this moment. But I'd like us to consider it in the future. Near future."

"So, do I. We'll talk about it when I get home."

"I'd like that." She glances at the clock. "I'm going over to Jules and Ernesto's. I'm already going to be late, and I really have to shower now."

"Is your phone case waterproof?"

She grins. "Absolutely."

"Let's take a shower together, *piccolina*.

"Yes, Daddy."

Chapter Eighteen

Fina

It's barely been two days since I had the most unreal phone sex of my life. I keep replaying it in my mind as I work and when I'm at my place in the evening. As much as I want to act all of that out as soon as Carmine gets back, I miss more than just the sex. I miss his company. I miss his companionable silence as much as I do the corny jokes he sometimes cracks. I miss the smell of his cologne or how he helps make dinner. I really miss listening to him serenade me with his violin. He's truly gifted.

My doorbell rings, and I head to the door to answer it. I think it's Lorenzo's turn today, but he isn't here yet. He should arrive in like ten minutes, but maybe that's him. I'm not going to the shop this morning. Jules has an ultrasound, but Ernesto has a big meeting he can't miss. She asked me to go with her. I can't wait. She calls it baby-vision. I'm so excited.

I open the door, and there's a courier standing on my porch. I look past the guy to where David and Augusto sit in a car parked in my driveway. Gio's out back. He's doing one last sweep before his night shift is over. I have a den downstairs where the guys can watch TV or whatever when they have to be here overnight. Carmine insisted. It's been a while since I've routinely had a guard in my house or on my property at night. Usually, they're in a car halfway down the block.

"Ms. Carosi?"

"Yes."

"Sign please."

I look at the envelope. Once again, there's no return address. I don't like this. I glance at the car in the driveway again. Fucking hell. Is this round two, and Augusto's here for that again? I haven't seen him since Carmine left. I still don't know what they talked about outside. I didn't have a chance to ask, and Carmine didn't bring it up. I decided that might be for the best.

"Can you hang on a moment, please?"

"Sure."

I close and lock the screen door before I hurry to the back door. "Gio, there's a courier here. It's another envelope with no return address. Can you check it, please?"

He comes inside and goes straight to my office. I unlock the screen door, sign for it, and Gio takes it once he has gloves on. That's something Augusto didn't do last time. Did he know before he tested it that the envelope was safe? My suspicions grow by the day. The courier takes off, and David and Augusto get out of the car. Lorenzo pulls up as Gio starts testing the envelope.

"Ms. Carosi?"

"Morning, Lorenzo."

"What's going on?" He must know what happened between Carmine and Augusto because he's practically breathing flames at my least favorite guard. I'm surprised Augusto doesn't go up in smoke.

"It's clean, Ms. Carosi."

Gio hands me the envelope, but Lorenzo reaches past him and takes it before I can. He walks forward, forcing Gio to step aside lest Lorenzo slam into him. I take several steps back, and it allows him to enter my house. He pushes the door shut in my guards' faces. Lorenzo hands me the envelope. I stare, blinking at him, for a moment before I stare at the envelope.

"Ms. Carosi, the last time something like this arrived, it was to frame my cousin."

I already thought about that. I take a fortifying breath before I break the seal. More photos. If the first round was bad, these are horrible. It's like a paparazzo took these. It's one shot after another. There's got to be at least two dozen photos.

Carmine getting out of an SUV with his arm around a blonde. Carmine's arm still around her as they go into a hotel, then an elevator, then a hotel room. There are photos likely taken by a drone that show them in a suite's bedroom, then they're walking to the bathroom together. There are pictures of the woman in the bed, and it's obvious she's naked. They're having breakfast together. They're headed back out to an SUV. Then it looks like they're at a car rental place. I can't tell who it is, but they have a driver, and Carmine is sitting next to her in the backseat. The woman is striking. She looks like she's a little pale, but she's still really attractive.

"Ms. Carosi—"

"Unless you're going to tell me the entire truth, don't."

"I don't know what the entire truth is. But I know Carmine."

"Yeah, and until a couple months ago, you hated him. And with reason."

"I never hated my cousin. He's family. But you're right, I strongly disliked him. But there has to be an explanation for this. I don't know if he's told you or not, but Carmine loves you,

Serafina. It's obvious. He has never loved anyone outside our family."

"Sure as hell doesn't look like it."

"Those other photos didn't look like he was rescuing Maria, but he was."

I inhale and release it slowly. Lorenzo is right. I won't jump to conclusions. But this still sucks. "Lorenzo, can you find out what's going on? Can you call him?"

"I'll try." I watch him pull out his phone. He's listening to it ring, but it must go to voicemail. "Car, it's Enzo. Call me. It's urgent."

We stare at each other as we wait for the phone to ring. Nothing happens. I slide the photos back into the envelope. Thank God none of my guys saw them. My father would already be screaming at me on the phone. We've had some horrible arguments in the last two weeks. I haven't told Carmine, but my dad's been trying to bribe me into breaking up with him. I suspect he's one more pissed off call away from fucking up shit for the Mancinellis.

I put the envelope in my office, and I head out to the car with Lorenzo. The day drags on and on, even though I spent the morning with Juliana at her ultrasound. Before I lock up, I approach Lorenzo. I saw him on the phone several times today.

"Did you hear from Carmine?"

"He's headed back to the city."

"Can I call him?"

"I don't think that's a good idea."

I narrow my eyes. "Why not?"

"Because he isn't finished with work yet."

Work? That woman hardly looked like work. That makes me pause for a moment. No. Definitely not. Carmine did not pick up a hooker. That wasn't some sex worker. Forgive me,

Father, for I have sinned. That was horrible to even let that cross my mind.

"Do you know when he will be?"

"I don't know any more than that, Sera."

The guys in Carmine's family call me by my name in private most of the time. But they never do in front of my men. I think it's reminding my guys that they are with me to protect me, not be my friends. Or protection first, friendship second.

"Can I call *Zio* Salvatore? Would he know?"

"Sera, there's still some unresolved stuff. I don't know what it is. If I don't know, Uncle Salvatore won't tell you. I'm sorry, but you're going to have to wait until Car gets back. I know you must hate this now that you've seen those photos. But I'll tell you the same thing I did this morning. My cousin loves you. He isn't going to fuck that up."

I nod. If he says so. "Can we go home?"

"Sure."

Lorenzo said Carmine's headed back here. Hopefully, he'll come see me, and I can ask for the truth.

Carmine was supposed to be back last night, but I didn't hear from him. But I see his name pop up as a text comes in. I'm getting ready for work, but I drop my eyeliner pen and open the message.

> **CARMINE**
>
> I miss you piccolina. I'm back in the city but I still have something I need to do. I just wanted you to know I'm back. But it might be a few more days until I can see you.

Is he with that woman? I desperately want to ask. I want to

confront him. But I want to look him in the eye. I want to watch him as he either tells me the truth or lies.

> I miss you too Carmine. I'm glad you're back.
> Let me know when you're free.

His response is almost immediate.

> What's wrong Fina?

Fuck. That's what I get for texting while pissed and hurt.

> Nothing. Why?

> I call you piccolina and you call me Carmine.
> What's wrong? I won't ask a third time.

As desperately as I want to hear him say that in that voice—the one that makes me sopping wet and willing to do anything he says—I'm not feeling that vibe today. He doesn't feel like Daddy. He feels like someone I'm not sure I can trust. He feels like the Carmine I used to know. The man I believed he was. I hadn't been wrong until we met again.

> I'm getting ready for work. I'll be late if I don't
> hurry up and I'm still putting my makeup on.

> That doesn't tell me what's wrong.

> Nothing. I'm looking forward to seeing you.

So, I can know if you played me. Fucking-a. This refrain is getting tired even to me. I wish I could shut my brain off.

> Something is wrong. I can't force you to tell
> me but I wish you would. I can't fix it if you
> won't tell me.

I want him to make it all better. I want him to take control of this situation, give me a reasonable explanation, show me he loves me as much as I love him, and fucking end my suspicions.

> The opening is tomorrow. My mind is
> occupied. Will you make it?

> I'm going to do my very best little girl. I can't
> promise though. Like I said work isn't done
> yet. I may not be able to get away. Please
> know that isn't by choice. I want to be
> with you.

It's like I can hear him in my head, and he sounds so sincere. But don't most cheaters? I don't know. Orlando was the only other guy I was serious enough about to consider being in a long-term monogamous relationship with. I dated other guys, but I rarely considered them a serious boyfriend.

> I understand.

> I know you do but that doesn't mean this
> doesn't suck.

That one sentence actually makes me feel way, way better. I don't think he'd regret not being with me if he preferred being with someone else. At least I don't think he'd say that. I think he'd find some way to be evasive instead. Like he was a moment ago.

> I miss you piccolina. When I'm done how about we go away somewhere for a long weekend? I know you have the new shop so maybe not right away but soon.

> That would be nice.

I almost said I'd like that. But with my uncertainty that won't shut the fuck up, I don't want to be the liar in this conversation. An entire minute goes by before he responds.

> Yes it would. I'll see you soon.

> See you soon.

Whatever that means.

I'm up to my eyeballs in inventory at the new shop. I made sure that none of the perishable items got delivered until today. But the dry goods arrived too. That was a slip up on my part since I thought I scheduled it for yesterday. I'm checking everything against the shipments' packing lists.

I look over at the island counter when my phone buzzes. A text just came in. Carmine? I doubt it. He made it sound like he won't be done today. But maybe something changed since this morning. It's an unknown number. There's a video, and I immediately recognize Carmine. I tap play. I watch him enter a walk up building with the woman from the other photos. There's a time lapse, and thirty minutes later, they come back outside. His hand was at her elbow when they arrived, but now it's at her lower back. They stop at the bottom of the steps to talk. I have no idea about what. Then he opens the door to his

Alfa Romeo and waits for her to get in. He walks around to his side and gets in.

What the fuck? As though whoever sent this knew I needed time to watch it, another text comes in. I tap the new video. My jaw practically hits the ground. They're at a restaurant like a block away.

UNKNOWN

They're there right now.

I look toward the front door. Do I go? Do I watch or confront them?

"Hey, I'm going to step out for a moment, Sam. I'll be back in a few. A friend of mine is around the corner."

I don't wait for my new manager's response. What's he going to say? No? I hurry along the street until I'm across from the restaurant. They're sitting outside together. Not a care in the world. Obviously, they're not skulking around. I watch Carmine pay, and they stand up. They embrace, but it doesn't seem intimate. More like friends. Maybe they got all their lust out of the way while they were banging in that apartment building. Instead of getting into his car, which I passed, I watch her get into a town car. Is it a Mancinelli one? It sure looks like it. My heart races. Before I know what's happening, I'm practically sprinting to the restaurant.

"Who the fuck was that?"

Carmine spins around. A smile spreads across his face as he reaches for me, but I step back. "Fina?"

"Who the fuck was that woman, Carmine?"

"A friend."

He gets cagey real fast.

"What's her name?"

He stares at me for a moment. "It's work, Fina."

"I didn't know fucking other women was part of work."

"What? I'm not involved with her."

"Then why did you go into an apartment with her and not come out for thirty minutes?"

"Are you spying on me?"

"Don't answer a question with a question, Carmine. Tell me the truth."

"I can't. I told you. It's work. You know what that means. I wish I could, but I can't. At least, not yet."

"Not until you officially dump me for her."

"I am not dumping you for anyone. What the hell is going on, Fina? You were evasive in your texts this morning. Now you're accusing me of shit."

"Give me something, Carmine. Can't you see how this looks from my perspective? I know you went into a building with her, an apartment in the building. You spend half an hour in there after you cupped her elbow to lead her in. When you come out, your hand is at the small of her back. Then you're here having a cozy lunch."

"Yes, to all of those things. She's been unwell, and I didn't want her to fall on the steps."

"And?"

"I cannot tell you more, Fina. Why can't you see this from my perspective?"

"Because I'm not the one who looks like the cheater."

"Serafina—"

"Do not call me that. I am not a child. I'm pissed, but I'm not someone for you to scold."

"Then be reasonable and tell me what's going on."

I look around. We're not yelling, but it's obvious we aren't having a friendly conversation either. I need to get back to the bakery before I turn into a raving lunatic.

"I've told you what's going on. I know where you've been, and I just saw you with her. Until you can give me the reasonable explanation, I don't want to hear or see any more of you. Leave me alone, Carmine."

"The fuck I am. We are going to talk about this."

"You mean, I'm going to talk, and you're going to keep staring at me when I ask things you don't want to answer."

"I never said I don't want to. Of course, I do. But I can't."

I huff. "Whatever, Carmine."

"Fina, if this is how it's going to be when I have to travel or work comes up and I can't explain, then this isn't going to work."

"You're right. I won't be some stereotypical Italian woman whose man is philandering, and she lets him back into her bed every time he remembers to come home. I won't let you turn me into a jealous bitch, either. I don't like who I am right now, and that's because I'm with you."

He stands there shocked. Then he's hurt. It makes me wonder if I went too far. It gives me a moment of doubt. I wait, but he says nothing to dissuade me of my fear until I'm ready to turn around.

"I told you, I would never be unfaithful. I told you the first night we were together. I will not be my parents. I've broken practically every commandment other than adultery and honoring my mother and father. You don't believe I've changed. I know what I was, Fina. I know I've made my bed, and now I'm lying in it."

I cross my arms, waiting for anything more. But he slides his hands into his trouser pockets. He watches me, and I have nothing else.

"Goodbye, Carmine."

"Fina."

I shake my head. When I turn around, I spot Lorenzo. I didn't even think about him when I left the shop. Carmine looks devastated, and Lorenzo looks enraged. He stalks forward but ignores me.

"Fix whatever you fucked up, Carmine."

I head back to the shop with Lorenzo walking beside me. When we get to the shop, I'm so used to the Mancinelli men opening the door for me, I wait. Lorenzo doesn't move.

"I don't know what you just did since you ran out without telling your guards or me. I'm certain Carmine is guilty of something, but you hurt him with whatever you said. You better be fucking right about why those photos were taken. You're family because you're Aunt Sylvia's niece. We won't stop guarding you, especially not with shit like that showing up. But if you're wrong, and Carmine gives up trying to be better, I will lay the blame at your feet. He's my cousin. I'll defend him from anyone who might hurt him, including you, Serafina."

He practically yanks the door from its hinges. I blow out a slow breath as I head back to the kitchen. Carmine once warned me it takes a shit ton to get Lorenzo pissed, but once he is, watch the fuck out. I felt like I was going to shrivel into the concrete the way he glowered at me. I better be right, or I just ruined my happily ever after.

"Thank you for stopping in."

I hand over the hundredth cupcake of the day, having given that one away free to the little girl with her dad. The grand opening has been a success. It's three o'clock, and we're pretty much sold out. It helped that I posted the hell out of the opening all over social media and asked pretty much everyone I know to do the same thing. I had a sign twirler out there during the morning commute and during lunch. Now I'm putting out the loaves of bread for what I hope will be the third rush of the day.

"Fina?"

I freeze and turn around slowly. "Carmine."

"Congratulations. It looks like today's been a success. I hoped to get a dozen cupcakes and some brownies, but it doesn't look like you have much left."

"I'll see if we have anything in the back." I hurry into the kitchen. I know we only have a few things, but I take my time. I need a moment to breathe. I cried all night and the entire way to the shop this morning. I slipped into the bathroom a few times because I thought I would burst into tears. Now he's the one who looks good enough to eat.

"Fina?" Lost in thought, I didn't hear him follow me into the kitchen. His hands rest on my waist, and he presses his chest to my back. I inhale his cologne. "You've been crying, *piccolina*."

"What makes you think that?"

"Because I've seen you tired and when you haven't taken your allergy medicine. Your eyes are never red and puffy like they are now. Tell me what's wrong. I need to fix it."

I hear it in his voice as much as the words he chooses. Is it guilt or sorrow? Both?

"Until you can tell me more of the truth, you can't fix it. I know you can't tell me everything, but there has to be more."

"Soon, Fina. I need you to trust me again and for a little longer."

I turn around. "There were photos again, Carmine. And videos."

"What? Why the hell didn't you mention that yesterday?"

"Why should I have to? You should have come clean without me having to tell you I have proof."

"Proof. You have circumstantial evidence at best. How do I know? Because I haven't fucking cheated on you, Fina."

"Why was she in your bed?"

He sucks in a breath.

"She was in a bed in a hotel room. That was not my bed that night. I shared Gabriele's room."

I bite my bottom lip, then shake my head. "I need to get back to work. I'll box up your cupcakes. I don't have a dozen red velvets, but I can give you chocolate or strawberry."

"Never mind. I told you, if you can't have faith in me when you know this is how *Cosa Nostra* couples have to be, then it won't work. I can't change, Fina. It has to be you."

"Just tell me enough, so that the photos of you going in and out of a hotel together, and in and out of an elevator and hotel room don't make me question you. There are photos of you getting in and out of cars, going in and out of apartments, and who knows what else. Someone is doing this to hurt me and to break us up. They're succeeding because you won't give me enough to make me trust you again."

"I shouldn't have to make you trust me. That's not how trust works."

I nod my head. I squeeze past him and box up the cupcakes. He didn't say what he wanted, I just give them to him. He looks down at the box as he takes it. I watch him swallow before he goes out to the register. Sam starts to ring him up.

"Sam, Carmine doesn't have to pay."

Carmine looks at me as he reaches back for his wallet. He doesn't take his eyes off me as he pulls out a one-hundred-dollar bill and hands it to Sam. He leaves without saying another word.

I'm going on day five of Carmine withdrawal. He hasn't approached me, but he's assigned himself to my detail. He's been on the rotation twice. Both times, he says nothing. He's waiting outside when I leave my house. He rides in the front passenger seat. He remains outside the shop most of the time or stays in a corner of the kitchen on his laptop, working. He watches me walk to my door when I get home. I know he told Lorenzo to check my phone, but Lorenzo had no luck figuring out who hacked it. He knows someone deleted the messages while Carmine was in Miami, and he knows how. But he can't pinpoint who.

Carmine's driving me crazy, and he knows it. I got screen-shots of a text conversation last night. It did nothing to make me feel better, especially since he's back again this morning. He's across the kitchen from me, and we're pretending like we don't exist to each other. Yet neither of us can stop glancing at one another. Because I'm a masochist, I look at the photo again as I wait for three pies to cool.

UNIDENTIFIED WOMAN

Thanks for taking me to the apartment the other day. I can't wait to move in. I'm glad you suggested it. Thanks for lunch too.

CARMINE

I think it'll work out well for now. Good thing it was available.

I look forward to seeing you again once I'm settled.

But it won't be for long will it?

No. I can't wait to finally have a life with the person I love. You made that possible. We're so close.

> A couple months and then you'll have everything you want.

> I wouldn't have it without you.

> I'm glad I can be a part of it.

That's where the messages end. "Unidentified woman" is what I'm making myself call her instead of "that bitch." I threw up when I read it. I want to throw up again as I reread it. I like pain—but only during sex when it's inflicted by the right partner. I dash my glance at him for the umpteenth time. Fuck this. I cross the kitchen and drop my phone in front of him. He looks up at me before picking up my phone. He reads everything I have. Then he's holding my phone so tightly I fear he'll crush it.

"And I assume you believe this is more proof that I'm involved with someone else."

"Not someone else. *Her.*"

"Fina, you are going to regret this when I can finally explain."

"No. After today, I'm done with you and your family guarding me. I texted *Zio* Salvatore, and he agreed to stop sending your family over. I don't want them or you near me anymore."

"You couldn't tell me you wanted my family to stop. You went behind my back to our uncle. You are not who I thought you were, Fina. I thought I was the mess. I thought I had to live up to being good enough for you."

It's what's left silently dangling in the air that hurts so much.

"Get out, Carmine. Leave."

"No."

"Leave before Augusto and Adriano make you."

He laughs. He stands up and towers over me. "Besides the fact I'm stronger than both of them, little girl, they won't lay a hand on the don's nephew and *capo*. It's why that shitbag did nothing outside the other shop, and it's why he won't do a damn thing today. You'd cut off your nose to spite your face. Did you stop to think that the fact some stranger can get those photos of me and screenshots of my texts and send them to you also means they know a fuck ton about you too? They're watching you and know this hurts you. They're manipulating the fuck out of both of us, and you're letting them. They want us apart. Why? If it's to get to me, fine. But what if they're going to hurt you, Fina? You don't want to see me anymore, fine. But you are keeping the extra guards. It's that or you ask your father to assign more men. Have fun explaining that."

He gathers his stuff and hands back my phone.

"I think deep down you know I would never cheat on you. You know there's a reasonable explanation. But you're pissed that you can't control me or this situation. You're pissed that you can't make me do what you want, which is tell you shit that could get you, my family, and me killed. Is that what you want? You want me dead?"

"Don't be ridiculous."

"Don't be naïve."

"I'm not naïve, Carmine. I'm sick of being manipulated. By you because you refuse to tell me enough for me to believe you. By whoever the sick fucks are who keep doing this. The list of candidates is way too long. You're right. I do want control. I want my life back to normal. I want what other normal couples have. I want a lot of things."

"Don't we all? Even poor little rich Mafia *principessas* can't get everything all the time. You can learn to be like the rest of us. I haven't gotten shit that I want since I was five and my dad got me a firetruck, which Marco broke that afternoon. So tough shit that this life isn't giving you everything you so clearly believe you deserve. Right now, from the way you're acting, you're getting exactly what you deserve."

He looks at me with such disgust that I want to punch him. I'm as pissed as I was when we were twelve, and I broke his nose. I'm as pissed as I was when we were eighteen, and he humiliated me in front of New York's high society.

"Never speak to me like that again."

"Or what? You'll break my nose again? Go fuck someone at your club? Hmmm. I guess I'm single again."

He cocks an eyebrow. My chest heaves as I force myself not to say anything or hurl anything at his head. We've both gone too far. Way, way too far. He walks out the back door, and it's like all the oxygen's been sucked out of the room. The afternoon drags until I finally get home. There's a box on the porch, and I recognize a sweater I left at Carmine's. It didn't take him long to return my shit.

"It's fine. I recognize my stuff."

I wave Adriano away. I carry it into the house and into my bedroom. I take the sweater out and freeze. There are a few other pieces of clothing, but there's a note next to the bottle of lube I brought over one night.

Figured you'd want this back if you only have Little Carmine.

The fucking vibrator I got and used while we had phone sex. He remembers I said it wasn't as big as him. He knows I don't bring guys back here and that the only men I fucked were the four from my club. And I ruined it with two of them. Rather, I ruined it with one, and Carmine sent away the other. Most likely, even the last two guys won't have anything to do with me because John and Henry probably warned them away.

I sink down onto my bed. He's hurt and lashing out. But so am I. Fuck him. If I didn't feel so fucking exhausted suddenly,

I'd go to my club. Shit. I can't do that because I canceled my membership. I get changed and head back downstairs to make dinner. As I open my pantry, I notice I have everything I need for a cake. A very particular fucking cake. Baking is work, but it's also cathartic. I'm going to feel a shit ton better after I finish this. I pull everything out, and I know I have a ridiculous smile on my face. But this is the most excited I've been in days. This is going to be so good. Epic even. I can't wait to share. I hope they enjoy.

Chapter Nineteen

Carmine

I didn't sleep for shit last night. I just stared at Fina's spot. I'm so pissed. Part of it is at her, but most of it is at life. I thought I finally had something good. Something that made me want to continue to be better. I thought I had something that could give me a reprieve from life. Instead, this fucking Mafia life ruined the only good thing I had going. Gabriele and I resolved things in Boston. Besnik knows not to fuck with us, and we rescued Larisa. She's with her sister and the Kutsenkos. We realized Dillan fucked us all by doing a deal with Besnik to pit him against the New York Albanians. The bratva will deal with him. We'll see what happens with Yuri.

It disappoints the fuck out of me that Fina wouldn't be more patient. I'm frustrated that she wants things she knows I can't give her. She's known that her entire life. But I also know it's a lot different when you're a kid watching grown up problems compared to being the grown up with the problems. It's fucking history repeating itself. My mom and dad had similar arguments to what I had with Fina. But before they split up, my mom always knew my dad would never be unfaithful to her. The moment he moved out, it was game on for both of them.

Mama knew how close my dad and I are, so it terrified her she'd one day tell me he was dead. She wanted reassurance that it wouldn't come to that. But even when she begged for him to tell her more, to reassure her more, it was never because she thought he was cheating. That cuts me to the quick. But what else is she supposed to think? I'm actually not at all angry or even that hurt that she thinks I'm with Larisa. I would too from what she described seeing in photos and from the text screenshot. I'm pissed that she's trying to take control of a situation she knows she can't control. Fuck. Even I can't.

I can't fault her for wanting control. Who wouldn't? But she's paralyzed by this need, and it's for something she can never have. It's only going to spin her in circles. And I did a shit job explaining that. I didn't even really try that hard. I couldn't. I was too close to making a fool of myself by bursting into tears and begging her to forgive me for sins I'm committing against my will.

I blow out a long breath as I only half listen to the conversation going on around me in Uncle Salvatore's office. We had a bunch of shit come up because some of our men thought they could skim off the top. When I wasn't at the bakery, I was at the garage. This is the first time we've discussed our next steps. They're going on about the issue with Dillan, but I have to tell them about what's happening with Fina. Even though it cost me Fina. My heart aches. Once I can tell her, is there even a way to come back from all this? If we do, will it just happen again? I blow out a long breath.

My dad's sitting next to me. He's attended more meetings lately than he has in years. He and my uncles have always gotten along. They've known each other since they were kids, but they weren't friends. Shit was rough when I got exiled and my parents split up. But the years have calmed things, and my uncles trust him. But he usually sticks with his day job as an insurance adjustor. It comes in handy.

Papa can tell something's bothering me, so he asks during a lull. "What now?"

"Someone sent photos to Fina again. I haven't seen them, but they were bad. They were of Larisa and me. It makes it look like I'm cheating. She got a screenshot of a conversation Larisa and I had. It was ambiguous enough to look incriminating. And someone sent her video texts showing me with Larisa at Katerina's apartment in the Bronx and of me having lunch with Larisa. Fina confronted me there. It's only gotten worse."

Lorenzo grimaces. "I saw the photos. They are really incriminating, especially the one that makes it obvious Larisa slept naked in the hotel. You can see Carmine's bag in the corner."

"I—" I don't get to answer because someone knocks on the door.

"Come in."

One of Uncle Salvatore's men is carrying a box I immediately recognize as coming from Fina's bakery. The guy is trying hard not to laugh. I cross the room and take it from him. He grins and shakes his head, but quickly leaves. I flip open the lid.

She didn't.

I close my eyes, then open them again.

She fucking did.

"Is that something from Sera's bakery?" It's Matteo.

"Yeah. I'm going to put this in the fridge."

"What'd she send you?" Now it's Gabriele asking questions. I don't flip the lid down fast enough. He hoots with laughter.

"Oh, my God. I can't believe I'm saying this, but I want a slice."

"*Fanculo.*" Fuck off.

Gabriele doesn't relent. "You may as well let everyone see her artistry. I'm just going to tell them about it, anyway. Though I don't know that my description could do this justice. *Ho-lee* fuck."

I glare at him, but I know I have no choice now. No one is going to leave me alone until I show them. They'll just go in the kitchen and look in the fridge. They'll look in the trash if I throw it out. Aunt Sylvia would say it's a waste of perfectly good food. I walk over to Uncle Salvatore's desk, put the box down, and flip back the lid. The laughter is immediate. Every crude joke my cousins and friends know fills the air. Papa, Uncle Salvatore, Uncle Massimo, and Uncle Domenico are laughing so hard I can't understand their Intanglese—Italian-English.

I can only stare.

The cake fills the entire box and must be close to two feet long. It's an *enormous* penis with balls. She's textured the frosting to make it look so fucking real. It has a tip with a small hole and white frosting coming out. It has a line to make it look like a realistic mushroom-shaped head. There are veins too. Along the entire perimeter are tiny plastic penises stuck into it. Like the shit you'd see at a party favor store for a bachelorette party or something.

But that's not the pièce de résistance.

Oh, no. She's left me a message in raspberry glaze, or whatever it's called.

Eat a dick, Carmine.

If anyone else in this room received it, I would laugh the hardest. It is hysterical, but I'm not loving that it's at my expense. I nudge Gabriele and Matteo out of the way since they crowded me to see better. I heard Luca say something about getting plates and forks. I mean, it is food. And I'm certain it'll be delicious. I pull my phone out as I swipe my finger through the cum frosting and snap a pick of me licking my finger. Then I pull up my texts.

ME

> You made my dick so big. How'd you get it to fit? I knew your frosting was delicious. But it's even better now that it's been so long since I had it. There's enough for me to share. Do you want just the tip? Or would you lick my balls?

I attach the photo and hit send. I don't expect a response, but I want one. Even if she tells me to fuck off. I know this isn't conciliatory humor on either of our parts, but she knows it's as funny as it is insulting. Nothing comes back. I can admit I'm disappointed. It tempts me to text her again or even call her. I accept a piece Luca hands me, and it's even better than I imagined. You'd think we were having an orgy in here with the sounds that are coming from all of us. When my phone vibrates, I wake the screen. I see her name and grin.

Then it all comes crashing down.

FINA

911 Help.

I hit her contact, then put the phone to my ear and bark at my family.

"Shut the fuck up. Something's wrong."

"Daddy?" I can barely hear Fina.

"What's happened? Where are you?"

She's still whispering. "Harlem. I don't know what's going on, but there were gunshots from inside the shop. Then stuff breaking. I locked myself into the walk-in pantry. Carmine, I stabbed someone."

I'm already pointing to my cousins, along with Matteo and Gabriele, before I gesture for them to come with me. "I'm coming, *piccolina*. I'm in Queens. I'll be there as soon as I can. Call your guys."

"I can't. Nicholas and Augusto went to Atlantic City for the weekend. Gio's wife is having a baby. Francisco's in Venice. David and Adriano are already here."

"All right. I'm sending my men. You'll know it's them because they'll say *elefante*."

Elephant. They're her favorite animal. I hear Gabriele on the phone, explaining to someone that's the safe word for Fina. We didn't expect to go anywhere, so the SUVs aren't at Uncle Salvatore's place. We all came in our own cars. Luca, Marco, and Lorenzo usually drive on missions. I handle gathering intel. Gabriele assigns the men their duties, and Matteo oversees the weapons. I get into Luca's car while Matteo jumps into Marco's, and Gabriele goes with Lorenzo.

"Fina, tell me what you hear?"

"Nothing I can make out. I'm all the way in the back. Should I go closer to the door?"

"No. Is there anything you can hide behind?"

"Not really. It's like an oversized butler's pantry, so lots of shelves, but nothing to hide behind."

"I'm putting you on speaker, *piccolina*. I'm in the car with Luca. I need to look some stuff up. I'll keep talking to you, but Luca can hear us."

"Okay, Daddy."

I glance at Luca. Fina must be terrified. The whole point of why I warned her Luca could hear us was so she wouldn't slip up. My cousin shrugs and whispers to me.

"Don't tell a soul, but Livy calls me that too. I won't judge."

It doesn't surprise me since I've heard him call his wife *piccolina* too. I suppose that's where I got the idea.

"Carmine?"

"I'm here. I'm trying to get into the city cameras. Hang on, little one."

It would be a fuck ton easier to do this on my laptop or better yet surveil the place with one of my drones, but that's not an option. I shake my head. My phone isn't a computer. I can't do it. I didn't think I could, but I wasn't going to not try. Fina's shop is almost in Spanish Harlem, which, before it became known as El Barrio, had strong Italian roots. That's why she picked it as her second location. I checked to see if it was in an area any of our rivals claim, but it's not. Could it just be a robbery gone wrong? Did whoever this is not expect Fina to have armed bodyguards? I don't know.

"Daddy?"

"I'm here."

"Someone's getting closer, and they're speaking Spanish."

That could be plenty of people. There are enclaves of Puerto Ricans, Dominicans, Cubans, Mexicans, and Salvadorians. Could it be Fernando? Could he or some Cuban associate of his be striking back? Could shit with Olivia's family still be unresolved? Could it even be Enrique? I'm pretty certain Enrique isn't sending any Colombians after Fina. Not after Enrique's nephews, *Tres J's*, helped us with Maria and Larisa. But Olivia's mother grew up with and had family connected to a Mexican Cartel. There's too much unknown, and I have no eyes in the area yet.

"Can you tell what they're saying?"

"No. Even if I could, I don't speak enough Spanish these days to remember much."

I hear someone banging on a door then a man's voice. "*Signorina Carosi, elefante.*" Miss Carosi, elephant.

She calls back to him. *"Di che colore sono gli occhi della figlia minore di Salvatore?"* What color are Salvatore's younger daughter's eyes?

"Uno è verde e uno è marrone, signorina." One is green and one is brown, miss. Pia got Aunt Sylvia's green eyes, while Natalia inherited Uncle Salvatore's heterochromia. They both have a green left eye and a brown right eye.

"You can open the door, Fina." We're only five minutes away, but I can't get there fast enough.

"Ms. Carosi, are you all right?" I recognize the man's voice. It's Giuseppe, who often guards Olivia. I see Luca nod out of the corner of my eye.

"I'm all right now. Carmine?"

"I'm almost there. Just a few more minutes."

"Should I stay in the kitchen or go see what happened?"

"Giuseppe?" I want his opinion since I'm not there.

"Ms. Carosi, you should stay here until Mr. Mancinelli arrives."

Fuck. That means there are bodies. If it was just a mess, he would have said so and let her decide.

"Fina, I'm a few blocks away. We're going to come in through the back door. Have one of my men unlock it for us."

"Okay." She still sounds so frightened. I hate this.

"Da—darling, I'm going in my office." She catches herself.

"We're pulling up. Go in and close the door. I'm coming straight to you."

I'm out of the car before Luca has it in park. Lorenzo and Marco pull into the alley behind Luca. I'm sprinting to the backdoor while I trust the others to sort out the front of the shop. The door opens as my hand touches the knob. I nod to Giuseppe as I bolt past him. I knock once before thrusting the office door open. Then Fina's in my arms.

"Daddy, I'm so sorry. Please forgive me. I fucked everything up. I'm so sorry."

I lift her, and her legs come around my waist. I sit on the end of her desk and press her head to my shoulder.

"We'll sort all of that out later, little girl. I'm here now, and you're safe."

"This wouldn't have happened if I hadn't sent you away. You warned me. This is all my fault."

"Shh. No matter whether or not I warned you, no one has the right to break into your business and terrify you. It's not your fault. I shouldn't have given in, but I let my pride get the better of me."

"Because I was horrible to you. I can't believe you came."

"I will always come. No matter how things stand. But we're done with the bullshit. We're getting your stuff, and you're moving in with me."

"What?"

"Living together won't allow me to tell you more, but if I'd come straight home to you, you would have known there was nowhere else I wanted—needed—to be."

"You could have come to my place. That doesn't mean we move in together."

"You'd have known exactly where I've slept every night since I've been back. It would have been beside you. In you would be preferable."

"Daddy." She whispers the name as she nuzzles my neck. "You were right about it all."

"About what, *piccolina?*"

"That I should understand how this works. That neither of us has a choice. There's no point in me fighting what I've known my entire life. You were also right that I was desperate for control. It scared me and hurt me to think you were cheating. But then it felt like you weren't doing anything to defend us, protect us against whoever this is. It felt like our relationship —me—didn't mean as much to you. I wanted you to be in control, and instead of saying that, I expected you to just make it happen. When it didn't, I wanted to call the shots. But I'm so in over my head, Daddy. Which is all the more reason I wish you were in control."

"And that's why you're moving in. Fina, I am doing what I can to figure out who the fuck is tormenting you and trying to fuck me over. It's slow going because other shit keeps coming up, but I'm working on it. This is way more urgent than anything else. I want us as much as you do. Never doubt that. Neither of us has control of this shitstorm, but I can give you that sense of calm when we're alone. When you let me be in control of us when we're having sex, then you can let go for a while. When you lean on me outside our bedroom, you know I'll support you. You can be free and just focus on what we're doing, what we're sharing. I'll always take care of you. You know that. You've told me that's what you need."

"And I was so hurt that you were spending time with this woman instead of finding out what I needed."

I lean forward and whisper in her ear. "Until they sweep this place for bugs, I can't explain anything. I will tell you everything I can once we're home."

"You always say home. Never my place."

"Because it's been your home since you walked off the elevator the first time."

She nods and burrows closer to me. "I'm so ashamed of myself. I was such a colossal bitch to you. I'm sorry."

"I didn't handle this well at all. I probably could have told you at least a little, but I don't know what's safe. I haven't had a girlfriend in more than a decade. I wanted to protect you."

"I know. I always knew, but I didn't get what I wanted, so I lashed out."

"You also didn't get what you needed from me. I'm sorry for that. We both fucked up. I shouldn't have said what I did."

"I sent that cake, though."

"Which was hilarious and what I deserved."

"No, you didn't."

"If not for this incident, then for when we were twelve and eighteen."

There's a knock at the office door, then Marco's voice. "Carmine?"

"Five more minutes."

"Fine."

I cup Fina's cheek, and we finally kiss. We both sigh, and I feel her smile like I do. But we don't stop kissing. A moment later, we're fumbling with our clothes. She slips off my lap and drops her jeans as she kicks off shoes.

"No panties?" She shrugs. "Good girl."

I unfasten my belt, and I see the interest in her eyes.

"Do you want me to spank you with this later?"

"Yes."

"Why?"

"Because we both know I won't feel better until you punish me. I was a bitch, but I also disregarded your wishes for my safety. I knew how you felt. I knew I would make you worry. But I was so mad I didn't want anyone to remind me of you. Now look what's happened."

"Fina, I will punish you for that. But I will not punish you for feeling hurt and angry over what happened between us. You have every right to those feelings. I will never hold that against you, even if they're misplaced or hurt me. You were hurting too."

I help her onto the desk, then pull her hips to the edge.

"Tonight, I'm going to remind you that all of you is mine. You will jerk me off. Then you will swallow my fucking cock and cum. I am going to fuck you in the pussy hard enough that every step you take tomorrow will remind you I belong inside you. You will remember you belong to me. And just so I can be sure you really understand that I'm going to fuck your ass."

"Daddy, please."

"Please what, little girl?"

"Fuck me now, Daddy."

I thrust into her. We both know everything I said is true, and we both believe in it. But how I said it arouses us both. We're returning to our version of homeostasis. Our hands roam over each other as I keep slamming into her. I'm certain anyone nearby has guessed what we're doing. I don't like the idea of other men picturing my girlfriend having sex, but I can get over it.

"Daddy, may I come?"

"Yes."

Her pussy contracts around me, and I can't stop. We come together, and I gaze down at her. Soon. I'll tell her soon. It's tempting now, but it's not the right time or place. I help her sit up before lifting her again. I sit on the desk, still buried inside her.

"Daddy, I love how you can pick me up. Most guys couldn't."

"I can carry Gabriele's ass up and down stairs. You, *piccolina*, are a beautiful feather compared to his heavy ass."

"What would the guys think if you carried me around on your dick for the rest of the day?" She grins, but we both wish that were possible.

"Nuh-uh, little one. The only guy getting off seeing your ass is me."

"We have to go out there, don't we?"

"Yes. Are you scared?"

"Yeah, but I also just want more time with you."

"You're going to have it. Fina, shit's definitely not done now. But I'm taking tomorrow and the day after off. We need the time together."

"But—"

"They'll all understand. Don't argue."

She cups my cheeks. "Carmine, you will always be enough for me. I'm sorry I made you doubt that or think I believe you're not. There's no one better for me."

She gazes so earnestly into my eyes that I know the time is right. The place is right. We speak at the same time.

"I love you."

This time, our kiss is languid. We infuse all the emotions we haven't said aloud into it. When we pull apart, I set her down. She pulls her pants back on and puts her shoes on too while I fix my clothes.

"Come on, *piccolina*. We'll deal with this together."

"You lead, Daddy. I'll follow."

"No, we do this side-by-side."

"Carmine, thank you."

"Always." I open the office door, and we walk through the kitchen, holding hands. Before we get to the storefront, she puts her free hand on my forearm.

"Can I have the drawers on the left side of our dresser?"

I turn and fist her hair, tugging her head back. "We don't have to live in Manhattan. We can go to your house in Queens or get something new. But from tonight on, there is no yours and mine, his and hers. There is only ours. I will not let you go again, Fina."

"That assumes I'd ever let go long enough for you to have to come get me. Carmine, we're back in our roles, and it feels right. But I think I proved I'm prone to possessiveness too. Do not doubt I will do whatever I have to, to protect us."

I remember what she admitted to doing to avenge Aunt

Sylvia's sister, her *Zia* Sophia. She said she stabbed someone today. I don't doubt her at all.

"Fuck, you're hot. I love you, little girl."

"I love you. And you're pretty fucking hot, too, Daddy."

"And I'm all yours."

"In that case, I think I'm going to lick all of you tonight."

We smile, then brace ourselves. We step into the storefront, and Fina screams. Holy hell. I wish my cousins prepped me before I brought Fina in here. I wouldn't have. Marco rushes forward, and we move to block Fina's view. Marco whispers so others can't hear.

"Sorry. You took more than five minutes, so I figured it was best not to interrupt again. I didn't hear you come out. I would have warned you."

Fina tries to peer around us, but Marco and I are each twice as broad as she is across the shoulders. She can't see between us, over us, or around us.

"Let's go back in the kitchen, Fina." I try to steer her away, but she bats at my hands.

"No. I want to see what they did. I want to see what they did to my men."

There's blood splatter across the walls, and it pools on the floor. The display cases shattered when someone either shot them or swung an object into them. The cash register is gone. The storefront windows and displays are still intact, which tells me whoever did this wants the message to remain private. They know we won't call the police, and they don't want passersby to wonder what happened. Marco shakes his head and points behind her. I follow his finger while Fina twists to see where I'm looking.

"Oh, thank God."

She rushes toward where Luca's bandaging Adriano's arm, and David sits with an icepack over his left eye. We both take in the open suture kit next to Luca's right side. He became a paramedic during college. Somehow he juggled everything: regular classes, Uncle Salvatore's tasks, and paramedic training. He's our doc when we're on missions. He can't do everything Auntie Carlotta can since she's a general surgeon. We go to her for wounds serious enough to need a doctor, but not so serious we'll die without a hospital.

Fina leans forward to see David's face. It's clear something nailed him, but since neither of Fina's men are lying in those pools of blood, they came out the winners. My family's *soldati* cleared the dead bodies. I step away to speak to Marco and Lorenzo, but I watch Fina the entire time. I can't hear what she says to David and Adriano, but they both nod.

"Who did this?"

Lorenzo motions me a few more steps away from Fina before he explains. "We don't know. They took their dead with them."

I assumed wrong. That makes it way harder to know who did this. I listen as Lorenzo continues.

"Adriano and David said they wore masks but spoke Spanish. They don't know enough about accents to recognize where they were from. They don't speak the language, so they couldn't tell us if there was any slang or other giveaways. But they shared these were pros. They came in and started smashing shit. Adriano was in the alley, and David was in the kitchen. These fuckers strolled in through the front door. When one of them rushed straight to Sera, she sliced his face, then stabbed him through the throat. David got her into the pantry as Adriano came inside. He and Adriano used the narrow entrance from the kitchen into the storefront to keep the men from passing. The way they built the walls, the guards got several shots off without making themselves targets."

Marco points to bullet holes in the metal islands. I saw the ones in the drywall around the archway into the kitchen. Since it's too narrow for more than one person to pass at a time, if the attackers wanted to enter the kitchen, they would have to go single file, making each of them a target for two gunmen.

"Did either of Fina's men catch these fuckers saying anything in English?"

"No."

I watch Fina as she now stands quietly as Luca applies butterfly bandages over David's eyebrow and on his cheekbone. I tilt my head toward him. "If they fired from the kitchen, how'd he get hurt? My guess is a bullet grazed Adriano's arm."

Marco nods as he answers. "Yeah. The bullet injured him enough to need stitches, but nothing more. David got nailed by some flying drywall. He's lucky it only scratched him and caused some bruising. I saw the piece. It could have taken an eye out. Our men got here just as the attackers fled. Giuseppe said they had a van outside the front door with Serafina's logo on it. The sliding door opened as they fled. Giuseppe sent men out to scout the street to see if anyone stopped to look. No one noticed. Or they didn't care enough to stop and look long enough for our guys to spot them."

I shift my gaze away from Fina and scan what I can see of the damage before I look at Lorenzo and Marco. "Did they leave a calling card?"

Lorenzo points to the floor between the display cases. "No. Nothing to claim this. Adriano said they bagged their guns to catch the casings. They're pros, Carmine. This wasn't some broad daylight smash and grab."

"I didn't think it was. The most obvious are the Colombians, Cubans, and Mexicans. I don't want to think Enrique would sanction something like this. But Fernando is pissed, and there are plenty of Cubans in this neighborhood he could hire. Jesus swore he'd leave us alone for Olivia's sake, but that doesn't mean someone else in the Culiacán didn't take it upon themselves to retaliate for how Luca protected Olivia."

Marco frowns and furrows his brow while thinking. He suggests what I've already considered. "The strongest explanation is Fernando. He thought he could strike back and make a bigger statement by doing it in our territory. Since you negotiated with him both times, he took it personally and went after the person who means the most to you."

"That's my theory too. I hate that means someone's been watching Fina long enough to know she's my girlfriend. But we can't rule out Besnik or Yuri, either. Regardless of whether they did this, it's a reminder we need to finish that shit."

Besnik is more troublesome than Yuri. He's a necessary evil to us. We don't want Ardit to expand his influence into Boston. We don't want Besnik to go free since he's likely to harbor Yuri again, and he sided with the O'Rourkes. But his replacement is weak. While we could control Besnik's cousin, he doesn't have the balls to run things without a babysitter. We don't have time for that shit.

The intel I've gathered shows Yuri in the Baltics. It's tempting to let the bratva handle him after all, especially since we learned a little more about Yuri's attacks on Katerina while they were in university together. Larisa told me when we had lunch. I offered to take her to Katerina's apartment that day because I wanted to check on her, and she convinced Maks to allow it. What Fina clearly didn't see were the five men Maks sent with us. The videos omitted that, and she obviously wasn't looking when she approached me at the restaurant.

Lorenzo brings us back to the most likely culprit. "If this was Fernando, then we have to tell Enrique. *Tres J's* needs to get back to Miami and end this while we deal with our friends in Boston."

Marco shakes his head. "Guess who's back in town."

My eyebrows shoot straight up. "Alejandro?"

"Yup."

Enrique has three siblings. His younger brother, Luis, is Pablo's father. Pablo is equivalent to Luca, but he's their chief enforcer, like Gabriele. When it comes to what happens at the garage, we all take equal turns. That's not how the Diazes roll. We've all changed since we were kids, but Pablo the most. The darkness in him. There's not a scrap left of the kid I played soccer with.

Enrique has two younger sisters. One of them is the *Tres J's* mother, and the other is Alejandro's. He's been in Colombia for the past year, overseeing shit for Enrique. Enrique's brother, Luis—Pablo's dad—makes trips down to Bogota every so often and always gets himself arrested. Really, he greases palms to get himself in and out of jail to deal with anyone who forgets how long Enrique's reach is. The *Tres J's* spent some time "helping" —yes, air quotes—Luis after the shit they pulled with Aleksei's wife, Heather. They allied themselves with some Irish chick, and they paid the price for their choices. That's why it shocked the shit out of all of us they helped with Maria and Larisa.

Marco's expression grows tight. Alejandro is most like Lorenzo. They're both the pretty ones. The ones who are too good looking to be real. They're also the most mellow and hardest to anger. But, just like Lorenzo, when Alejandro reaches the point of being pissed, he rivals the *Tres J's* in what he's willing to do to fuck someone up—and there's only one of him. He's spent too much time in Colombia, seen too much shit down there. *Tres J's* saw it as kids, and it warped them. Alejandro's had to survive it as an adult.

None of the syndicates have small families. I suppose it's because three out of the four of us are Catholics. I guess the Eastern Orthodox aren't that different with family planning. It means each family tree has a lot of branches. For those who don't know, the names can all run together. But we each have our roles, and no one confuses that. I ask what I know my cousins are thinking.

"Could Alejandro have done this?"

Marco shrugs. "Maybe. I don't think Enrique would sanction any of his nephews going after a woman, but none of them came in through the kitchen. That tells me Serafina wasn't the actual target. If they wanted her, they would have surrounded the place and overrun David and Adriano. Serafina's men were better than the attackers assumed, but they didn't plan to kill her or take her hostage. That makes me think it could be the Diazes."

I hold out my hand as Fina approaches. I shoot my cousins a speaking glance, and our conversation ends.

"Carmine, I don't know what to do. I avoided using any of your family's companies to do the renovations. But I can't ask anyone else to do this unless I want to deal with the insurance company and a foreman asking too many questions. Neither of those is appealing. Do you know anyone?"

I pull her into my embrace and tuck her head against my chest, kissing the top of her head. "We'll have all this taken care of by the time you open in the morning. Where were your employees during all of this?"

"It's Sam's day off, so I was the manager. The two others were out making deliveries for a wedding and bridal shower. One of them dropped off your cake. I called them a few minutes ago and told them we're closing early today. They didn't need to come back to the shop once they finished their deliveries. I assured them I'd still pay them for a full day."

I glance at my cousins, remembering the mention of a van with Fina's logo. "Do they just drive their own cars?"

"No. I pay for rideshares. I don't want them to have to use their cars, and I don't have a van or truck."

Marco, Lorenzo, and I share a look. That amps this up to yet another level I never imagined. Fina sighs, and her body relaxes against mine. I stroke her back as her arms tighten around me. Luca and Matteo join us, and Luca gives us the first update.

"David called Nicholas. He and Augusto are coming back. David didn't give them all the details. Said he couldn't talk about it over the phone. David told me he'll fill Nicholas in, but no one will tell Augusto the full story. There was a fire in the kitchen, and David got Serafina out. But he and Adriano are both recovering from smoke inhalation. That's why the brothers need to come back."

That's a plausible story. I don't know who came up with it, but it'll get Nicholas and Augusto back without Augusto having anything to tattle to Piero. The idea Piero or Augusto caused this and hired Spanish speakers has crossed my mind several times, but I haven't wanted to voice my concerns. Certainly not around Fina. I saw Matteo on the phone the entire time I spoke to Lorenzo and Marco. He gives the second update.

"Our guys are five minutes out. They'll have everything back to normal before Serafina arrives in the morning. You can tell your employees the same thing David's going to tell Augusto. You closed early because it was too smoky and smelly to continue. You didn't want to worry anyone, so you didn't mention the fire. But it turned out to not be a big deal."

Fina nods as Luca and Matteo talk, but she says nothing. I look down at her as Matteo finishes. Her eyes are closed, and tears leak from beneath her lashes.

"It's time to go home, *piccolina*."

She just nods again. Matteo points to the back door. "Alfonso's already waiting."

"Thanks." I guide Fina outside and slide into the car after

her. She reaches for her seatbelt, but I lift her onto my lap. That false sense of security. I know I shouldn't have it, but I'll hold on to her and not let go.

"Daddy?"

"Yes, baby."

"Who did this?"

"I don't know yet. When we get home, I'm going to explain as much as I can about Boston. There's a good chance that has something to do with it. Boston and Miami are connected too. Now that you're not terrified, you must be sleepy. We'll be home in fifteen minutes. We can soak in the tub while I explain. Then why don't we take a nap?"

"That sounds good. I'm just going to rest my eyes for right now."

I kiss her forehead as I stroke her hair. I feel her fall asleep almost instantly. Whoever did this is about to see a side of me I haven't let loose since I ordered the hit on Liam O'Rourke. But I'm older and wiser. I won't be as sloppy as I was with the plane crash. But these fuckers will know they're about to die, and there won't be a damn thing they can do to stop it.

Chapter Twenty

Fina

"Come on, Fina. Let's get in the bath."

He settles in, then I straddle him. He eases his cock into me, and I sigh. I'm home. He pins me against his chest as I pull my arms in and curl my legs around his hips. His left hand rests on my ass while his right hand cradles my skull.

"Shh. I'm here, and I'll do whatever you need."

"Just keep holding me, Daddy. I'm so fucking tired. All I want to think about is the feel of being in your arms and you being inside me."

"Do you want me to get you off?"

"Not yet, if that's okay."

"I told you, *piccolina*, I'll do whatever you need. Being like this—no end and no beginning, just one—is what I need too. I've never been so scared in my life as I was on the drive to you. I never want to hear you frightened like that again. I never want to know you're that unprotected ever again."

"I will never argue with you about my safety. You obviously

know way more about this than I do. I've taken for granted that no one really knows I'm a Mafia daughter in New York, and I underestimated how valuable my protective duty is. You warned me I was being foolish. I'm so sorry. So, so sorry."

"It's forgiven, Fina."

"No. Not until you spank me."

"Little one, you need that to forgive yourself. I've already forgiven you."

"I want to show you the photos when we get out. You need to see them, and I hope it helps you understand why I freaked out."

"Lorenzo described them to me. I get it. But I do need to see them because all of this is likely connected."

"Then can we take that nap?"

"Of course."

I still don't feel close enough to Carmine, even though I know that short of climbing into his skin, we can't get any closer.

"Fina, were you scared I wouldn't come for you? I'll hold you as close as I can for as long as you want, but I get the feeling your need isn't because you're still scared someone is after you. You're scared I won't stay."

"No. I knew you would. That's why you were the first and only person I thought to ask. I didn't doubt that for a moment. I doubted that you'd talk to me beyond getting the details of what happened. I didn't think you would comfort me or forgive me."

"My love is unconditional, little one. It will never depend upon you always agreeing with me or doing what I say. You're still your own person, free to make your own decisions. I'm not your Dom and never will be."

"I didn't know I had such a possessive streak in me. But it was visceral. Logically, I know your missions could involve women. But—"

"Fina, I get it."

"Thanks."

"I love you, *piccolina*."

"I love you, *cuore mio*." My heart.

We move together, our conversation over for now. We cling to each other as we crest and drift into bliss. It's over too soon. I whimper as he withdraws, but he soon wraps me in a fluffy towel, rubbing me dry. I do the same before hanging my towel next to his. We go back into what is now our bedroom. He hands me one of his button downs because he knows how much I love wearing them. He loves seeing me in them. I scowl when he puts on a pair of boxers.

"I'd rather you went naked."

"I bet you would, little girl." He puts them back in the drawer. Fucking shameless.

"You said we'd look at the photos together. How'd you know I have them? I've kept them in my office at home."

"I saw the manila envelope folded in your purse."

"I was going to send them along with the cake, but I didn't want anyone to get them accidentally or have any of the guards see them."

He grabs a pair of basketball shorts and slips them on. We head out to the living room, and I feel a hundred percent better than I did when we arrived.

"Are you hungry, Fina? It's after noon, and I doubt you had lunch."

"Not really." I try to stifle my yawn, but I fail miserably. I barely cover my mouth in time.

"All right. Let's sit on the couch. I don't want this in our bedroom. It's the one place the outside world should never touch."

"Agree." I grab the envelope and sit beside him. He takes it when I offer it. I watch his expression as he goes through each one. It remains completely neutral. But everything in the air shifts. Rage pulsates off him. He practically vibrates with it. His curse comes out as a hoarse whisper.

"Fucking hell, Fina. I'm so sorry you went through this alone. Enzo said they were bad. He said there were about two dozen. There're thirty. I can't believe how close up these are."

He slams them onto the coffee table and picks me up. I squeak as I land on his lap. He cups my face and kisses me. It's desperate and needy. I cling to him, not letting him pull away until we're both breathless. It's my turn to comfort him, and I press his head to my chest.

"We're talking about it, and we'll make it better together."

He leans back and runs his hand over his face. "Enzo should have taken photos of the photos and sent them to me."

"Lorenzo probably didn't want to distract you."

"No. He knows this is a threat."

"They meant to break us up."

"Fina, if whoever this is got this many photos this close up of me, then they can do it to you too. It's a warning. They want me to know they're watching, and they want me to believe there's nothing I can do about it. This is way more serious than someone just trying to fuck me over. To them, I didn't heed their warning, so they took it up a notch by coming to your shop."

He looks at the photos, then at me. I can practically see the wheels turning in his head, but I can't guess what he's thinking.

"Tell me what happened."

"I was in the kitchen slicing loaves into halves. I heard them come in because they were noisy. I looked out and saw them smash a display case and go for the register. Before my guys could do anything, one rushed toward me. I sliced his face when he reached for my throat. He raised his gun, so I stabbed him. That's how blood wound up on the entryway to the kitchen. He was dead when David got to me. He moved me to the pantry."

"Get up, Fina. We're going to my mom's."

"You're freaking me out, Carmine."

"Those fucking photos are freaking me out. The fact you had to kill to defend yourself is freaking me out. Let's get dressed. Now, Fina."

I hurry to keep up with his longer legs. Since he returned the few things I had here, I put my clothes back on from earlier. Carmine pulls on jeans and a fitted t-shirt. This is not the right time to be getting wet. But his ass...holy fucking shit. And the way every ab shows through his shirt. And his pecs. And his biceps.

"No. Change, Carmine. I'm throwing those shirts out unless you promise to only wear them at home."

"What?"

My lips twitch, but I force myself not to smile. "You're wearing the equivalent of lingerie. It covers just enough to tease. No."

"You can't be serious. I wear these all the time."

"That was when you were single. If you didn't want to show off, you would have bought shirts the right size instead of three sizes too small. No more flaunting what's mine. Not unless you want me walking around Manhattan in a teddy."

He chuckles and strips off the shirt. I reach past him and pull out a polo shirt. I know it won't be a ton better, but it's not the t-shirt.

"Tell me again how you don't have control."

I glare at him, but my lips twitch again. "You know I'm right, playboy. Remember, I know your reputation. I saw the photos in the gossip magazines. You don't need to prance around practically naked for women—for everyone—to know you're hot.

"Fine. But no more of those leggings you like."

"That's not the same at all. They're comfy, but they aren't flattering. Why do you think I always wear an oversized shirt with them or have something tied around my waist?"

"Fina, I've seen the way men look at you. You're gorgeous. It's taken all the restraint I can muster not to have shredded them before now and not to gouge those men's eyes out. I didn't want you to think I was a psycho, but I hate them." He rolls his eyes. "Or rather I hate you wearing them out. I don't like men ogling you."

"They do not."

"Yes, they do. I know exactly what they're thinking."

I'm almost dressed as I respond. "And what's that?"

"They wish those thighs were wrapped around their waist. Or better yet, their face was between them. They wish they were the ones making your ass bounce while they fuck you from behind."

"You're making shit up. You think way too highly of me. I think the old fashion word was plump. I'm pleasantly plump."

I forget how fast he can move. He has my back against the wall, and his hand in my hair.

"Fina, I get you might not see what I do. But I know exactly what I fucking see when I look at you and when I watch other people look at you. Curvy. Voluptuous. Rubenesque. Fucking sex on stilts. You will not criticize yourself. I wouldn't allow someone else to do it, so I won't hear it from you. I get you see flaws I don't. I'm not saying they aren't real to you. But I will never encourage you to speak negatively about yourself. To me, you're as perfect as anyone can be."

The intensity of his gaze tells me he's not exaggerating. It's definitely a confidence booster. I see plenty of flaws, but I don't talk about them. Who wants to hear them, anyway? But I think them. I feel like Carmine can read my thoughts a lot of the time, and I suspect he knows exactly when I'm feeling self-conscious. He'll kiss me somewhere or put his hand right where I'm uncomfortable about and show me he likes it. It shouldn't surprise me he won't tolerate me putting myself down. With time, maybe I won't think those things without needing his reassurance first. I'm not there yet. But he's definitely good for my ego.

"All right, Daddy. Maybe you should add these to my spanking."

He groans. "Fuck me."

"Okay." I run my tongue over my lips. The hand in my hair goes to my throat, resting heavily there.

"Don't tempt me. We really have to go."

Why am I so nervous about meeting Carmine's mom? Or, rather, talking to her again after so long. It's been years. While I've seen *Zia* Sylvia plenty of times, I've only seen Paola, Nicoletta, and Carlotta a few times at church. I think Paola and Cesare avoided me as much as I avoided them, neither side wanting to make uncomfortable small talk. Now we're pulling up to Paola's house, and my palms are sweating. She didn't care for me when Carmine and I were twelve, and I punched him. She was angrier at him, but I could tell she didn't approve of my problem-solving skills back then. She pitied me when he and I were eighteen, and he humiliated me.

Maybe it's because we've only prolonged the inevitable. She was supposed to see me while Carmine was in Miami because of how long he was away. She was too sick, and I was too angry. That makes me reflect on my behavior, and I'm so ashamed. It makes tears sting behind my eyelids.

"Fina?"

"Yeah?" I swallow several times and try to compose myself.

"What's wrong? What just happened to make you sad?" Carmine nudges my chin toward him, and I blink rapidly against the threatening tears. "Fina, you're scared."

I nod against his fingers. He presses a soft kiss to my lips.

"Are you afraid my mom's going to disapprove of you?"

I nod again.

"She's liked you since you and I were kids. She spent most of my college years trying to get me to see why you'd be the perfect wife one day. She was right about everything she told me. She's told me over and over that I would regret my choices and flaunting my bachelorhood because one day my past would hurt the woman I love. I know she always hoped that would be you."

"How could she have known all that?"

"Because you didn't put up with my shit and decked me. Because you possessed such dignity when I was clearly a lowlife."

"Carmine, never say that again." That one word pulls me out of my stupor. I have the same reaction as he did when I talked down about my appearance earlier. "I will not hear it anymore. You've called yourself a piece of shit, a shitbag, a stupid fucker, and now a lowlife. I understood why when you explained your past. But that's done. I know it, and I accept it. You made shitty choices, but you've proven you're not a shitty person. Stop it."

He stares for a moment before he launches himself at me. I fall backwards against the backseat of the town car, and he hovers over me. Thank God the privacy glass is always up by default. His kiss is everything. But it's over too soon. We get out of the car, and he holds my hand. When we get to the door, we share a kiss that leaves him hard again.

"Christ."

"Don't take the Lord's name in vain, Carmine."

My head whips around as the door opens to Paola's voice.

"I don't know why you're swearing, but you won't do it around my ears."

"Yes, Mama. I'm sorry." He looks rightfully chagrined as he leans forward to kiss each of his mother's cheeks before wrapping his arms around her. He lifts her off her feet before giving her another kiss on her left cheek.

"Ridiculous, boy. I'm happy to see you too. Put me down before you suffocate me."

"Sorry, Mama." He's careful as he puts Paola back on her feet. He keeps an arm wrapped around her shoulders as he turns to me and wraps his arm around my waist. "Mama, you remember Serafina."

I grit my teeth. I know why he used my full name. It just feels so odd to hear it. I relax with the next breath.

"Fina, you know my mama, Paola."

"It's nice to see you again, *Signora Ciccone*." I have a moment of panic because I can't remember if she took Cesare's last name or kept Mancinelli. After what Carmine told me about his birth, I suddenly have doubts.

"I'm only Mrs. Ciccone at the bank. I'm Paola."

She smiles, and we lean forward for air kisses. Then she surprises me and hugs me. It's genuine. It's better than my mom's hugs have been since I left home. I return it, and I feel far more at ease than I did a few minutes ago. I feel accepted.

"Carmine, please bring the tray into the living room. And wash your hands first."

"Yes, Mama."

Mother and son grin at each other, and it's the most relaxed I've ever seen Carmine. I suspect Paola's been saying the same thing since Carmine could walk. He strikes me as the kid who always found a mess to make. I follow her into the living room, and she offers me a seat on the sofa. Carmine soon joins us with a tray overflowing with antipasto and pastries.

"I didn't know if you'd prefer sweet or savory, Sera. Carmine prefers anything edible."

Keep your mind out of the gutter. Keep your mind out of the gutter. Fuck it. I know he does. He's made a meal of me plenty of times.

"Paola, these are amazing." I turn to Carmine. "Why do you get cupcakes from *Morso Migliore* when you can have your mom's desserts?"

His intense gaze threatens to send me up in smoke. My cheeks radiate heat since I know Paola's watching us. He cocks his left eyebrow, and I have to look away.

"Are these Mancinelli family recipes?"

Paolo beams. "Of course. Mama brought them with her from Sicily. I'll make copies for you."

I stare at her for a moment before shaking my head as I look at Carmine then back to Paola.

"Car, fetch something from the kitchen."

"Mama—"

"Carmine."

"Yes, Mama."

I cover my mouth with my napkin and try not to laugh. He's a foot taller than Paola and probably a hundred pounds heavier. But he rushes out of the room at his mother's bidding. I don't get the sense that he's a mama's boy so much as he has a healthy fear of the woman.

"Two things, Serafina. Both come with the same explanation. You're welcome to the recipes, and when the time comes, don't be shocked if you get a wooden spoon at your first baby shower. Both are Mancinelli traditions. Carmine's been avoiding you as much as you've avoided him for ten years. But he's never brought a woman over. He's never insisted on a security detail for a woman. You're already part of this world, and you are part of our family. But you've remained on the periphery until now. If you both didn't intend to have a future together, you wouldn't be sitting on my sofa. I'll wait for you both to tell me how things will proceed, but we both know your future is with Carmine, and not because of that ridiculous betrothal. You love each other."

This is the Paola I remember. Blunt. It's refreshing compared to how veiled and conniving so many Mafia women are. I can't blame them. I'm like that when I must be. I trust few people outside my family, and today's shitshow proves why. There's always someone ready to finish their enemy.

"Mama!"

I look over my shoulder at Carmine's horrified expression. He flushes to his ears when he looks at me. I didn't know the man could blush. Seeing him with just his mother is endearing. This is the Carmine he's hidden from the world for so long.

"Hush, *polpetta*."

Little meatball. Hardly in any context. Since Paola can't see me, I look at his groin and waggle my eyebrows. He's positively fuchsia now. I laugh, and he scowls at me. His eyes tell me he'll remind me of this later. I fucking hope so.

"Did I lie, Carmine?"

He scowls at his mother. I test the waters and wrap my arms around his biceps as he sits next to me. He kisses me on the forehead before pulling his arm loose and wrapping it around my shoulders for a quick squeeze. Then he fills a heaping plate for me, then puts his arm back around my shoulders.

"Fina, you missed lunch. You'll be starving by dinner. Have some more."

I laugh at him. "You'll make a good *nonnina* one day if you insist upon feeding me because I might starve."

He playfully scowls. "I'll remind you that you called me a granny the first time you're called that for real."

"And that's why you can expect a wooden spoon." I swing my attention back to Paola, my brow furrowed. "None of the mothers actually strike their children with the spoon. But by the time the children realize that, we mothers find more creative punishments. They end up wishing we had used the spoon. It's a rite of passage and confirms you're truly a Mancinelli."

"Paola, we—"

"I'm not counting nine months from today. Carmine would never."

She shoots us a speaking glance, and my heart breaks for my boyfriend. She doesn't have to say it aloud for it to hang in the air. Carmine would never be careless, like Paola and Cesare were. Carmine glances down at me, and his arm slips down around my hips. I can't read his expression, and I almost choke on my cookie when he speaks.

"Have Piero and Allegra insisted on breaking the betrothal yet? Uncle Sal hasn't said anything, but I expect them to approach you and Papa first."

Paolo looks at me before her gaze meets her son's. "Yes. Piero called Papa while you were in Boston. Papa agreed to break the agreement as long as Piero does nothing to end your relationship."

"What?" I set my plate down a little too hard and wince.

"Fina, I saw how your father looked at me on Easter. He sent Adriano and Augusto to the room. I know you've argued with him about me."

"How do you know that?"

"You had your windows open more than once. My cousins heard the conversations."

Well now, that's not embarrassing. Fortunately, they could

only hear my side of the conversation. "Carmine, he figured your side of the family would insist that it end, then they'd have to pay for breaking their word."

Carmine looks at Paola, but I don't understand the silent exchange. I turn to him when he responds. "Fina, I want the contract to end. I don't want anyone to think your family or mine forced you to be with me. If we're together, it's because you chose me."

"We chose each other."

"Uncle Sal's been willing to pay a penalty for years. We figured your father would break it when you found someone you'd rather marry. Uncle Sal wasn't going to contest it."

"He knew about Orlando. Is that why?"

Carmine shrugs. "No one told me you were living with a guy. I didn't know you were seriously involved. I—" He can't meet my gaze.

"Didn't care what I did as long as I left you alone to do what you wanted. It's okay, Carmine. I was the same way."

"I'll tell Uncle Sal to call Piero in the morning. The betrothal ends tomorrow. No more arranged marriage." He kisses my forehead, and it's a reminder we aren't alone. Paola's been unobtrusive, eating a cookie and sipping her lemonade.

"Car, do you want me to invite Papa over for dinner?"

"Yes, please. I'd like that."

Paola shoots off a text, and it's only a moment later that her phone pings. "He'll be here at five."

That's still a couple hours away. I don't know how we're going to fill the time. As we finish our late lunch of sorts, I suddenly feel like I'm going to overstay my welcome. Paola offers me a kind smile. Carmine rubs the outside of my shoulder as he speaks.

"Fina, do you still want to take a nap?"

"That would be great."

Paola points toward the stairs as she speaks. "I don't know if you brought anything with you or if you'll go back to your place, but there are fresh toothbrushes in Carmine's bathroom. If you don't like his shampoo and body wash, let me know. I have some better smelling stuff I can give you. Carmine still has clothes here, but there should be plenty of space in the closet and dresser for however long you're here."

I guess that means I'm allowed to sleep in Carmine's room. Or is she giving me his, and he'll be in a guest room? That doesn't make much sense. The house is nowhere near the size of *Zio* Salvatore and *Zia* Sylvia's. The entire family could stay there. But this is definitely spacious for a family with an only child, and it's enormous for one woman. Paola stands and gathers our plates. Carmine and I immediately move to help her, but she swats our hands away.

"You both look exhausted. Go take your nap before Cesare gets here. He can still eat as much as Carmine. It'll take me two hours to make enough food."

"Mama."

Carmine huffs, but he gives her a kiss on the cheek. I think they're adorable together. I'm certain Paola knows her son's flaws, and she's probably had plenty to say about them. But it's also clear she loves her son more than anything. He takes my hand and leads me upstairs. As we head to the stairs, I notice what must be the master suite is downstairs. If we do get up to anything, I'm not so worried Paola will hear us. He leads me into a room that's a deep cobalt blue. It feels masculine, so I doubt this is the same paint as when he was a child.

"I know you're tired, Fina, but we still need to talk more."

"I know."

We kick off our shoes and climb onto the bed. He sits with his back against the headboard, and I lean against him. He wraps his arms around me, and I listen to his heart, then feel the deep rumble as he talks.

"I went to Miami because someone drugged and abducted Maria, Veronica, and two of Maria's friends. These people were sex traffickers. We got her and her friends free. They weren't the only women there. The woman you saw me with was one of them. We tried to free those other women, but it came down to just her. She had a personal connection to the people running this ring. I needed to take care of something in Boston anyway, so I arranged for an exchange up there. We were going to buy all of their freedom, but in the end I could only rescue her. It turns out she's Misha Andreyev's girlfriend's sister. The day you saw us together, we went to her sister's apartment to check it out. She wanted to take me out to lunch to thank me, and we stopped there first, so she could see it. She had five bratva guards with her. The things in the texts between us weren't about us. She has someone in Canada she's going to. She's staying at her sister's temporarily. I felt—still feel—guilty that we couldn't rescue her while she was still in Miami. The people running this trafficking ring sold her. I was going to buy her. It makes me sick to say that, but I would have just to set her free."

I listen to everything he says. Never in my wildest dreams did I think this would be the explanation. I can hear the shame in his voice when he talks about his role in buying and selling someone. I think of it as more of a ransom, but I understand why it's not.

"Fina, the people involved in this come from more than one country and more than one syndicate. I didn't want to say anything because things aren't resolved. But I want you to know as much about the truth as I can tell you. With what happened today, I'm worried one of these people targeted you to send me a message. But I swear to you, nothing about helping this woman had anything to do with attraction. It was just the right thing to do."

I sit up and turn to look at him. I take his right hand in mine.

"Carmine, you're a good person. I know your family would never countenance slave trading. That's not what you did. Even if you'd paid for her, it was more a ransom than not. Truly. I'm proud that you took a personal interest. In our world, you've been morally gray. To the rest of the world, we're all morally black. They will never understand, and they don't need to. I do. I love you even more for it."

I tighten my hold on his hand.

"If ever this situation were to happen again, I don't want you to fear I'll freak out and assume you're cheating, Carmine. Everything in our Mafia lives is always so amplified. How we love. How we fight. All of it. And it's still really early in our relationship. I wasn't secure in it, but I am now. Your mom's right. You wouldn't have brought me to her home if you didn't want me permanently. We wouldn't be living together if you didn't. Because I'm from this world, I know breaking up wouldn't cause the same complications as it would with a woman who didn't grow up in it. But you haven't had a girl-friend in more than ten years. Now you pick me. I get how significant that is. I let fear make me forget that. I won't do that again."

"Thank you, Fina. And I'm not used to letting anyone in. I know you understand these things, but I'm not sure which details are safe for you. Part of the reason I'm telling you this is that I don't want secrets when there don't have to be. I want you to understand what's been going on. The other part is I need to tell you who's involved. I didn't want to at first, but now I think you need to know. I need you to be aware of where the threat could come from."

"Okay."

"The least likely, but still possible are the Colombians. I don't think Enrique would sanction this, and I don't think the Diazes are interested in either you or me. But they could be. The most likely is a Cuban named Fernando Alvarez. He's the man who kidnapped Maria. He also took Larisa from Moscow. But he didn't work alone. There's a half-Russian, half-Albanian named Yuri Preobrazhensky. He's the one who had a personal stake in Larisa's kidnapping. He holds a vendetta against Larisa's older sister, who's with Misha. He hurt Katerina years ago when she rejected him. He wanted his revenge by toying with Katerina through her sister. Yuri has ties to a bratva in Moscow, and his father is the strongest syndicate leader in Albania. This same bratva is enemies with the Kutsenkos and the Andreyevs. They were involved in Anastasia's kidnapping. The head of the Boston Albanians, Besnik Marku, is in the thick of it, too."

"Complicated to say the least. So, I need to be on the lookout for a Cuban named Fernando; an Albanian named Besnik; and a half-Albanian, half-Russian named Yuri." I bite the left side of my lower lip. "Did Larisa see or hear me go apeshit?"

"I don't think so. She was in the car by the time you approached me."

"I hope she didn't. I can't believe I made a scene in public. That's so embarrassing, and I humiliated you." My head throbs. Reflecting on this is making me feel worse and worse. I'm the least likable person I know. I can't even sympathize with myself. I'm such a fucking idiot.

"Get up, *piccolina*. Strip."

I know what's coming. My heart speeds up. My pussy aches. And my mind finally moves toward calm. I climb off the bed after Carmine does. I watch him unfasten his belt as I shed my clothes as fast as I can. He sits on the bed and pulls me onto his lap. His hand strokes my hip as our gazes meet.

"Fina, this is a punishment. Not only am I going to spank you with my belt, I'm going to edge you. I will not make you come until later. Pain and pleasure may go together, but punishment and pleasure do not. But to be clear, this punishment is because you haven't forgiven yourself. You want the penance. I've already forgiven you. I don't think you need the penance. You feel badly enough already. But I think this will make you feel better."

"It will, Daddy. Most of me believes you forgive me, but I haven't even started to forgive myself. I need you to do what you feel is right."

He helps me stand, and I turn around. I lie flat over his lap.

"You know to keep your hands out of the way. If you're tempted to reach back, hold on to my leg. If it's too much, use your safe word. Fina, if you keep taking it because of your guilt or you think it will please me, and I harm you, that's something I will struggle to forgive."

"I promise, Daddy. The last thing I want to do is upset you. I know the difference between hurt and harm. I won't put you in that position. I love you."

"I love you, too. That's why I can't stomach the idea of injuring you, whether it's physically or emotionally. If it's too much for you mentally, safe word. What is it?"

"Fondant."

"Good girl. How many do you think you deserve?"

"Twenty."

"No."

"Thirty."

"*No!* Wrong direction, Fina. Ten."

"Fifteen."

"Twelve. I will not negotiate any further with you."

"Yes, Daddy."

I already know the temptation to reach back will be too much, so I grab his ankle. His hand rains down on my ass, warming the flesh. He alternates sides and presses my ass up as he hits my horizontal crack. I get ten on each side and two across the bottom of my ass. I've closed my eyes, so I can only sense by his movements that he's wrapped the belt around his hand.

"Are you ready, *piccolina?*"

"Yes, Daddy."

The first blow lands across my ass, and I jerk upward. His steely arm wraps around my middle and pulls me back against him. He's hard, and I want to suck him off or fuck him. He knew each time he spanked my horizontal crack, he pushed my clit against his thigh. He's landing blows there now, making me rub myself against him. I kick my feet, forcing myself not to scream. I fight to keep my moans quiet. By the fifth one, I break into a sweat.

"Open your legs, *piccolina.*" I follow his instructions. "You're so wet and needy, aren't you?"

"Yes."

"Yes, what?"

"Yes, Daddy."

"Do you need me to finger you?"

"Yes, please."

"Do you need me to eat you out?"

"Yes, please." My answer is a strangled plea as he plunges his fingers into me. His free hand rubs my shoulders, helping me to relax.

"Do you need me to fuck you?"

"So badly, Daddy."

He tsks. "Such a shame you were so naughty, little girl."

"I know. Please, can I have the rest of my spankings?"

"When I decide it's time."

Fuck me. Like seriously. Please fucking fuck me.

I keep quiet. But my breathing increases until I'm panting and fighting not to come. When I'm on the cusp of being unable to talk myself out of it, he pulls out. A moment later, the belt lands across my ass with a particular force that makes me tremble.

"Fina?"

"I'm all right, Daddy. I promise. Keep going."

The next one is just as hard. The tears begin. It hurts so much. So much it's almost excruciating. But what would have been truly excruciating is ruining things with Carmine and him not taking me back. My guilt reaches a head with smacks eight, nine, and ten. I continue to tremble as I sob. Then I go limp. The heat radiating from my ass and the burn that comes from the inside out is all I can focus on. Paying attention to that instead allows my mind to calm. My worries about my mistakes slip away as he pauses to finger me again.

I can't ignore how he makes my body feel. It fills my mind and keeps my attention riveted on everything he does. I have no control over this, and finally, I feel at peace. He decides what happens next. He'll make sure I have what I need. He'll take care of me. The tears continue, but I don't sob anymore. They just trail unbidden down my cheeks.

"Two more, little one."

"I know, Daddy."

He makes them quick but searing. I exhale all the air from my lungs as I hear him drop the belt to the floor. He rubs my back to where my ass begins, but he's careful not to touch the punished flesh. I take a shuddering breath before he helps me up. I move to kneel between his legs, but his hands go to my waist and stop me.

"No. You will never pleasure me after a punishment. I am

not that kind of Daddy nor am I a regular Dom. You don't have to show you truly repented or thank me for my forgiveness. It comes unconditionally because I love you. When the spanking is done, the punishment is done."

"But I want to say thank you."

"Then let me hold you while you kiss me."

He opens his legs wider, so he supports me, but my ass doesn't press or rub against anything. I do everything I can to make sure he can feel my love through the kiss as easily as he knows when I say it.

"I love you, Carmine. I love you for who you are and who you help me be."

"I love you just as you are, but I will always be here to help you and take care of you."

I close my eyes since I'm exhausted all over again. Drained is really the right word, but I feel like I could sleep for a month of Sundays. "Do I still have time to take a nap?"

"Yes. Plenty of time."

"Are you going to sleep too?"

"I'm going to hold you."

"You can do both."

"I'd rather be awake to enjoy it, little one."

"I would never tell anyone, but you really are such an over-sized teddy bear. I loved seeing you with your mom. She's so sweet, and you're adorable with her."

"Sweet? She's terrifying."

I hear the humor in his voice.

"You have no idea how much trouble I *didn't* get into because I feared how she'd react. For all the ways my parents were dysfunctional, they really were unified with parenting me. There was no easy parent or hard parent. No strict one or indulgent one. They were both strict. Looking back on it now, I think everyone believed they were too indulgent. I think they understood it was better to let people think they spoiled me and let me have my silent rebellion than to drop the hammer on me. That would have totally isolated me, and my rebellion would have been far more destructive."

"They knew you needed to know someone loved and accepted you."

"Yes. I made my worst choices as an adult, Fina. Long after they could punish me. Before that, people just thought I was lazy. I acknowledge I manipulated people into thinking that because it meant most people left me alone. It meant my time around my grandfathers was short. It wasn't until the last couple years that I started maneuvering people into doing what I wanted."

I shift to straddle his lap. "You've trusted me from the very beginning. You've shared things I know you haven't with anyone else. I promise I will give you the same level of trust going forward."

"I know."

I help him take off his shirt then cling to him when he stands to drop his pants. I'm still wrapped around him as we climb into bed.

"Daddy, this cannot be comfortable. I'm squashing you."

"Fina."

"Carmine, I am not small. I'm a lot to be resting on your chest and stomach."

"I'm glad you're not what you might consider small. But you are still a lot smaller than me. I'd be terrified of hurting you if I rested on top of you instead. Besides, if you were smaller, there'd be a lot less of you to touch. That would not make me happy. The more, the merrier."

"That is not what that phrase means."

"Sure, it is. The more of you, the merrier I am."

"You're ridiculous, Daddy."

"I'm just crazy for you, *piccolina*."

I laugh and shake my head as best I can while it rests against his chest. I kiss the spot over his heart. My eyes drift closed, and I'm soon asleep. This is so much more preferable to reality. Who the hell knows what's coming next?

Chapter Twenty-One

Carmine

Dinner with my dad went really well. He charmed Fina, just like I knew he would. Mostly, he told stories about me as a kid that made me flush and Fina giggle. He and my mom get along better than ever. If I didn't know better, I'd say they could reconcile. The problems come when they live together. I've spent the last two days with Fina. We ran back to her place the morning after we had dinner with Mama and Papa. We gathered enough stuff for two weeks. Hopefully, it won't come to that. I don't think it will. I'm at the garage right now.

I look at the guy stripped naked in front of me. We stretched his arms overhead, and they're tied to a garage bay door. I've already opened and closed it several times, surely making it feel like his arms are about to be ripped from their sockets. I've dislocated plenty, but I'm yet to see one actually rip away. We don't quite draw and quarter people, though I've made that threat plenty of times. I know many a man probably would have preferred I just cut off their arms.

"If you cooperated, this wouldn't hurt so much." The metal pipe smashes into his left kneecap. I've already nailed it a few times. The next one will land against the right one.

"I don't know anything, *tipo*." Guy. "*¡Vete pa la puñeta!*" Go to hell. The heavy Cuban accent fills the air.

"You really are hanging onto that lie. Do you know how I know you're lying?" He stares at me mutinously. "When you lie, right below your left eye twitches and narrows it for a flash. But without fail, every time. So, who sent you?"

The guy's name is Miguel. He was in a heavily Puerto Rican neighborhood in Queens but guess what he parked in his garage. The van with Fina's logo. The van that isn't hers.

"No one."

"You don't have the money to buy a van, and you definitely don't have the money to pay for the custom paint. I checked. I've seen all your financials. But you know that because I've already told you. But let's say—hypothetically—you're not working for anyone, then why do you have the van?"

"My buddy asked to park it there. The detailer said it shouldn't be out in the sun for too long. Paint isn't set or some shit."

The pipe whacks his right knee, and he howls. I moved faster than he expected.

"Your eye twitched." I hit him again. Then I do it a third time. "I will keep swinging until the bone completely shatters. I'll move on to something else after that. It can all be over if you just tell me the truth. Imagine I'm your priest, and you're at confession. Forgive him, Father, for he has sinned."

"I don't know who hired us. My buddy asked me to keep the van because he doesn't have a garage. He offered me a wad of cash to do the job with him. I didn't ask questions."

"Now, see. You really should have. You should have found

out who you targeted. You know what I am, don't you?" He nods. "Say it."

"*Cosa Nostra.*"

"Do you know whose bakery you hit? My girlfriend's. She's *Cosa Nostra* on one side of her family and *Mala del Brenta* on the other. Ever heard of them?"

"No."

"Not surprised. They're the Mafia in Venice. So, you see, you really pissed off three different groups. Her *Cosa Nostra* side of the family is still in Sicily. Her Venetian side of the family is still there. Then you really fucking pissed me off, and I know you know I'm a Mancinelli. Any regrets?"

"Plenty!" The man screams his answer as I thrust the bat into his belly like a battering ram. Then he pants because I knocked every molecule of air from him. He swings several times before he comes to a stop.

"I got a great night's sleep, so I can keep going for hours. See the guy over there? The big one. He'll be my replacement when I get tired or bored. You'll beg for me to come back."

Gabriele's munching on an apple as he watches me work. He's leaning against the door frame to the office, his ankles crossed, and his left hand in his pocket while his right holds the apple. I'm certain he's enjoying it, but it's staged. We do shit like this. We make it look super casual, like it's an everyday thing. It's not quite that frequent. It fucks with their minds though, which is its own valuable type of torture.

The guy's been hanging here for ten hours, so I know he's hungry. He's got to be thirsty too since he's pissed himself several times. That's a part I hate. So disgusting. But you learn to live with the stench. Watching Gabriele eat something as meager as an apple is tormenting him. When his eye isn't twitching with each lie, he's watching my best friend, practically drooling.

"Your buddy hired you to do the job and to stash the van. How much did you get?"

"Fifteen hundred up front and fifteen hundred after."

"Did all of you get that much?"

"Nah. I got extra for the van. Just in case shit like this happened. I want my family to have a little extra cash once I'm dead."

"At least you understand that part. I don't have to explain you aren't leaving. But once again, you can decide how painful this is going to be. I'll keep going until I get what I want. Then, because you're making me wait longer and longer, I'm going to make your death more excruciating. I'll show you some mercy if you end this."

He glares at me. His funeral.

"Gabe, light the furnace."

My friend tosses his apple core in the furnace before he turns it on. It's an industrial size one that you'd see in an old steel factory.

"You can get a bullet between the eyes and be dead before you go in. Or I'll burn you alive. Death isn't instant that way. We'll hear your screams. Music to my fucking ears. Now, stop being a little bitch and speak."

When I swing the bat and hit his face, I'm careful to only shatter his cheekbone and break his nose. If I break his jaw, he can't talk. He howls in pain.

"I truly can break every bone in your body. But that won't keep you from feeling your skin melt off those bones."

I draw the bat back again.

"A'wight." He wheezes as tears stream down his face. Now that's better. "No one told us there'd be guards. We had the guns to scare the *pu*—woman."

"Good catch. Go on."

He was about to call Fina a *puta*, a bitch.

"It was just supposed to be a smash and grab this time."

"If it was just to scare her, then why'd you bag your guns? You made sure you left no casings behind."

"My buddy said the guy who hired him told him to."

"You really are a stupid motherfucker, aren't you? If the guns were just to scare my girlfriend, then there wouldn't have been a reason to worry about collecting the casings. The guy who hired you knew you'd have to shoot. Why would you have to shoot? Because someone else would be shooting at you. Who's your buddy?"

I already know. We have a walk-in fridge in the back of the garage. While this fucker passed out earlier, we brought his friend in and stored him in there. It's cold enough to be dangerous, but we won't keep him in there long enough to freeze. At least, not until after we get what we want. He scowls, and I know he's thinking about what a mistake he made. He's just crossed the threshold into no longer caring about any of this. He's accepted his death, but he's pissed. He doesn't want to die. So, he'll take everyone down with him. Final-fucking-ly.

"A guy called Emmanuel—Manny. We went to school together. We still run with the same crew."

"I'm sure. You may not have planned to shoot anyone, but this definitely wasn't your first job. You knew to only smash the inside."

"Yeah. No need to draw attention until we were done."

"This Manny, he tell you how much he got?"

"Fifteen up front and a grand after."

"Anyone else?" He goes silent again. "Brother? Cousin? Who're you protecting? It's too late. We'll just round up all the men in your family and kill them."

We would if we had to, but it won't come to that.

"You live with your *abuelita*, don't you?" His granny.

He remains silent.

"Your dad's dead from a drive-by. Your mom's at Bedford Hills."

A women's correctional facility in Upstate. Not exactly luxury living since it's the biggest women's pen in the state. But it could be worse.

"So, your sweet *abuelita* will be all alone if we take your three uncles and ten cousins. Who's going to take care of her then? Don't believe we'll round them all up? Look up. We have plenty of hooks."

We have meat hooks in the garage door opener chains. We can accommodate plenty of people at once.

"Fine. It was a friend of his. Some Cuban dude. His family owns a restaurant Manny likes. He's fucking the dude's sister. This guy's the one who set things up. He knows the most."

"What do you know about him other than he's Cuban and his family owns a restaurant? Which one?"

"Havana Cantina."

I know the place. It's in Spanish Harlem, not even ten blocks from Fina's shop. "What's his name?"

"Pedro something or other."

My chest expands as I force myself not to respond immediately. "Has Pedro been to Miami recently?"

"Yeah. Like a month ago. He runs drugs into the city for some guy down there."

"Anything else he helps run?" Miguel's looking everywhere but at me. I let my head fall forward and cock my left eyebrow. "You know he traffics women, don't you?"

"Yeah."

"And you're down with that?"

"No. But I'm down with making money to support my *abuela*." Grandma.

I can't fault him for that in theory. But there are other ways to make money that don't include working with slave traders. I look toward the office, and I know Luca can see me. He's in there alone right now, but he steps out with his keys in his hand. I know he's already showered and changed after his turn with Miguel. He's going to pick up Pedro. I wave to Gabriele, and he orders two guys to pull Manny out of the fridge where we've kept him waiting.

I gag Miguel, so he can't talk while I interrogate Manny. I want the latter to see the damage I've done to his friend. Miguel fucked around, and now Manny's finding out. Manny's already naked, so he goes up on the hook. His teeth chatter, and his skin's tinged blue. Good. Gabriele hits the garage door button with Manny on the track next to Miguel's. The sound of the metal door rattling drowns out Manny's screams. Not that it matters. The people in this neighborhood know better than to care. When he's just swinging and twirling, I ask my first question.

"Who hired Pedro?"

"Don't know."

"If you say so." I grab a set of pliers from the table near me. I walk over and catch his right nipple. "Do you really want a titty-twister with these?"

I get the same mutinous glare from Manny as I did Miguel. I turn my wrist until I've almost made the pliers go in a circle. I've ripped the skin.

"I can take it all the way off. I've done it before. Don't prolong your agony. Just tell me the shit I want to know."

I nod to Gabriele and tilt my head toward Miguel. He orders the same guys who got Manny to get Miguel down. He struggles against them, but in his condition, he's like a wounded lamb to my two wolves. They shove him forward, making him limp, and stumble to his own crematorium. Gianni opens the furnace door before grabbing Miguel's feet. Luigi scoops him up under his arms. They swing him five times, building the momentum before they toss him in. Miguel's screams fill the air, and I'm certain that's a leg flailing around in the flames. Manny watches it all.

"I'll tell you whatever you want. Just put a bullet in me first."

"Very well."

"Pedro works for some guy named Fernando in Miami. Pedro mostly deals drugs. But sometimes he gets the women jobs at less-than-reputable strip clubs and massage parlors up here. Something pissed Fernando off enough that he told Pedro to fuck you over. Pedro decided to go after your woman. Me and Miguel warned him this was a fucking disaster, but they'd already paid us half. We couldn't get out."

"Why the van? That's a lot of money to spend for one job."

"Nah. It looks like paint but just a good magnet. Probably didn't cost all that much. It covers the Havana Cantina logo. Pedro figured no one would ask questions if a business had its own delivery van parked out front. We wore aprons."

This is going way faster. Thank God. I'm starving, and it's past noon. "Miguel said you were supposed to fuck up the place. You didn't know there'd be armed security."

"We didn't. We bagged the guns, so we wouldn't leave any casings if we decided to shoot the display cases. We took bats with us. It was when those two *guidos* pulled guns on us we pulled ours."

I ignore the term. Whatever. Not the first time I've heard it. Not the last. I'm not offended. It's not like I'm from the Jersey Shore or Staten Island.

"That's not what I heard. You came in with your guns out."

"Pedro and the other two guys he brought did. Me and Miguel didn't, and neither did the third guy your girl stabbed. But we got them out fast. Shit load of good it did those two guys since they're dead."

"How much did Pedro make off this?"

"Like five g's."

"For busting up some display cases. I don't buy that B.S. What else did he do?"

"He took some photos. The guy likes expensive toys. He has some high-end drone he uses to spy on women. He said he fucked with you and your girl."

"And Fernando paid him to do this?"

"No. Fernando was only the bakery shit. Someone else paid Pedro for the photos."

Interesting. That begs the question: Who? *Tres J's* come to mind immediately since they knew about Fernando and some other unnamed Cuban. My guess is Pedro if he's bringing drugs up here. He's doing it for the Colombians. But why? They helped us free Maria and Larisa. Why come after me while doing that?

"He get paid while he was up here or in Miami?"

"Don't know. He just got his money and the cash he gave me and Miguel."

I wonder how long it's going to take Luca to drag Pedro in. I'm eager to finish this shit. Lorenzo, Marco, and Matteo are at the Manhattan bakery with Fina. Giuseppe and Alfonso are there, too. I feel better with them all with her. Marco's inside in the kitchen. Lorenzo and Matteo are in one car in the alley, and Giuseppe and Alfonso are in another parked out front.

Nicholas knows the truth, but Augusto still thinks there was a fire. He believes Adriano burned his arm, and they told him David got in a fight at a nightclub while he was off. It's Gio and Adriano on duty today, so they're in the kitchen, too. During the two days Augusto's had a shift, our cars parked farther away but still within sprinting distance. I'm taking no more chances.

"Anything else you want to share? After all, sharing is caring."

"That's all I know. I did what I was told to get paid."

"Fair enough."

I pull my gun from the holster under my arm. I'm not wearing my suit coat since those are too constrictive when I need to fuck someone up. I point the gun at Manny's head. He closes his eyes and takes a deep breath. I point it down and shoot him in the junk. His scream would be blood-curdling if I weren't so desensitized to violence.

"Only a man with no balls targets women. Men with real dicks measure them against each other. You told me to put a bullet in you. You just didn't say where. Get him down. I'm done."

I step back as I holster the weapon, knowing I spoke about my past as much as about what he did. I turn my back on him, appearing like I don't care what happens to him. I don't. But I turn back in time to see him pass through the furnace door. Luigi snaps it shut. Gabriele walks over to me with hand sanitizer. Like that's going to do much about the blood that's splattered on me, but at least my hands are clean enough for the sandwich he hands me.

"This shit's giving me a fucking headache. Besnik's still breathing because he's a fucking necessary evil to keep the power balance. Yuri's somewhere in Albania hiding like a little bitch. Roel won't hand over his son, so the bratva may have to take him. They have the reach to get him if he goes to Russia. I'm staying the fuck away from any Moscow bratva."

After the shit that happened with the Podolskaya and Anastasia, I want nothing to do with anything in Russia. Gabriele nods as he eats a sandwich now, too. He swallows his bite before talking.

"Misha fucked up a lot of shit for the O'Rourkes. I gotta

say, I'm actually pretty impressed. There wasn't a brick left standing after what they did to the O'Rourkes' fucking ancestral home."

When the O'Rourkes arrived in America, like many immigrants four generations back, they didn't have much. Three brothers or something scraped together enough money to get a house where they all lived with their wives. It's become—it became—like home base to them. Misha made a statement by going after the place.

All the syndicates are violent. It's just our way of life. The Mancinellis are vindictive in how we punish. The Diazes have the *Tres J's*, who we'd all thought were psychopaths. But they claimed during the little tête-à-tête at Maks's after we freed Larisa that they've been playing a role. A little too well if you ask me. I think they're legit fucking batshit crazy.

The Ivankov bratva were all trained by former KGB and Soviet soldiers, so they are methodical. Like only the Germans and Chinese can rival them for how precise every movement is. And the Irish—well, there's a reason they're called the mob. Though, with Dillan now leading it and his brothers and cousins finally in leadership positions, they're a—concern. We still have bad blood with them over how they tried to use us as the scapegoats for the shit they pulled with Pasha Kutsenko.

They made us look pretty fucking guilty, and it might have made sense if Luca, Gabe, and I weren't in exile in Sicily. It was Pasha's wife, Sumiko, who figured shit out. Forensic accountants come in handy. They think we let that pass, but we have shit in the works. The mercenary they hired disappeared. At least, that's what everyone else thinks. I hand Gabriele a bottle of water from a mini fridge, then look toward the door.

"How soon do you think Luca'll be back?"

"Like twenty probably."

I consider showering and changing then driving a few miles

away and calling Fina. I know she has the best men with her, but I'm still nervous. Plus, I just like hearing her voice. Her accent is still strong, and I love it. Gabriele's has lightened after being here more than fifteen years. I have one with certain words since Italian was my first language. I didn't speak English until right before kindergarten. Maria and I used to sit together with our mozzarella and salami sandwiches and little containers of olives. The worst was when we both wound up with sardine sandwiches. There were no halves to swap.

I finish the sandwich I have now and reject the idea of leaving. Let's just get this shit done. I won't use the satellite phone for a personal call, and turning on my phone in here is absolutely not an option. We'd each die before doing that. Nothing that can lead anyone here. When Luca returns, I finish my second water bottle and toss it in the burn can—I wish we could recycle, but no DNA evidence and all. I recognize Pedro. Looks like Luca had to rough him up a little to get him to cooperate.

Gianni strips him and gets him strung up. I look at Pedro and laugh. Not only is he completely manscaped, he has a crown on the inside of each of his hips. Basically, right above his crotch. King of Munchkinland maybe. Nothing there to brag about. I don't wait around. I get the pliers and go straight for his nipple, nearly ripping it off.

"You really pissed me off, Pedro. You get involved with my cousin's kidnapping. Then you go after my girlfriend. Never mind the whole helping to buy and sell humans. You are not my favorite person right now. What do you have to say for yourself?"

"*Vete a chingar.*" Go fuck yourself.

I pick up a narrow, hollow metal rod that's about two feet long. I hold it in front of him. "The only person getting fucked is you. Without lube. Tell me what I want to know, and I'll rough you up a bit, then be done with you. Make me play twenty questions, and this is going up your ass."

He hesitates before he radiates defiance. His silence makes me smirk.

"Fine." I spin him around. Gabriele and Gianni hold him still, each grabbing an ass cheek. There's no modesty in this line of work. Pedro kicks and thrashes.

"I wouldn't do that. You don't want me to miss my aim."

The tip of the rod touches his asshole. He tries to clench while spewing a slew of curses in English, Spanish, and Spanglish. "Get the fuck away from me, you ass fucker."

"I'm not fucking your ass. This rod is." With him held in one place, I press a little more.

"Stop. I'll talk. Get that fucking thing away from me."

"Once you tell me something satisfactory."

"There's not much to tell. I got a text that Fernando's body washed up near his dock in Miami. No obvious signs of what killed him. He's already on his way back to Cuba. No one needs an autopsy that's going to show he's been snorting coke like some '80's rock star at CBGB."

"Who'd he piss off that much?"

"Friends of yours. *Tres J's*. They put a hit on him. No one got it done, so they went down there themselves. From what I heard, they were there less than an hour before Fernando disappeared. They left before it was dark."

"You're the contact who led them to Fernando, aren't you? You let them know about the sex trafficking to see if they were interested. What made you think they would be?"

"If we branch out to Colombia, then we can give those women better lives than they have there."

"No one here believes that load of shit. Not a single Diaz does either."

The rod's tip goes inside him. He flails again, but between

having his arms tied above his head and Gabriele and Gianni holding him in place, he lodges it deeper. He did that on his own. I just held it steady.

"Unless you want this in your fucking intestines, calm the fuck down. Otherwise, I'll shove it so far up that no one can find it. Why my girlfriend?"

"Because she's your *zorra*. Nothing personal to her. If she wasn't with you, then no one would care."

"You call her a slut, and you want me to think it's nothing personal about her? Bad choice."

I spin him and punch him in the junk. It makes his asshole contract, which must shoot unbearable pain up his ass. He gags; it hurts so much. Good. I draw back my fist as I talk.

"Tell me who, or my friend shoves the rod farther up your ass while I keep punching you in the junk." I drive my fist into him again as Gabriele's hand moves. I can't see to where, but I know what he's doing.

"If I tell you, they'll go after my family."

"Don't tell me, and I'll go after your family."

"Yeah, but the shit he'll do..."

We went from "they" to "he." Pedro's genuinely terrified. There's no faking what I see in his eyes. That makes me think bratva. The shit the Kutsenko and Andreyev brothers survived as kids is worse than any fucking psychological thriller. Their old leader believed to torture someone properly, you needed to have felt it yourself. I know this because Niko told me that years ago. We were in high school, and there was a huge melee with guys from all four syndicates. All the leaders' families. We all caught so much fucking shit for it. Uncle Salvatore couldn't stick with one language. He changed every other word.

Niko and I were circling each other with knives. He boasted that there was nothing I could do that was as bad as what he'd already survived and what he'd already learned to do.

He said that the reason his family would one day run New York was because they were individually unbreakable, and as a family, they were indivisible. They'd survived too much shit together. They have a bond through blood, but I think the one forged through shared trauma is probably stronger.

"You scared of the big old mean Russian bear?" I use a mocking voice. Confusion flashes across his face. "Which one is it? Maks? Aleks? Niko? Bogdan? Misha? Pasha? Sergei? Anton?"

"You mean the bratva? Fuck no. I don't have shit to do with them. My family escaped the Communists. I'm not going near those bastards."

My brow furrows in condescension. Bogdan, Misha, and I are all the same age, and they're the youngest in their family. We were born after the Soviet Union fell. Their family fled Russia. Stupid fuck. Whatever. The point is, I believe he isn't working for the bratva.

"That brings us back to *Tres J's.*"

He's panting between each word, and sweat drips down his brow as he continues to speak. The agony hasn't let up. He just knows it'll get way worse if he stays quiet.

"No. They focused on Fernando. I slipped away and kept my head down. They might come for me, but they didn't have me do any jobs for them that didn't involve drugs."

"No one's coming for you because we already came for you. You know you aren't leaving."

I watch him, and it's like the truth sinks in for the first time. He really thought he might get out of this. Not when he refused to talk from the very beginning. He had to know the moment Luca approached him that the end was nigh. I need him to at least admit which syndicate this fucker is from. I have to narrow it down that much, so I know who to watch. Better yet...

"Get his phone."

Luigi digs in the discarded pants and retrieves it. Gabriele gets Pedro's right hand down and forces him to unlock the phone. I hit the text message icon and scroll. I tap on some, but most are nothing more than people trying to get tables at his family's restaurant or him setting up women to fuck at those questionable strip clubs and massage places. This is a burner, but he sure texts a lot on it. I scroll back to around Easter since that's when Fina and I got together. I see a contact listed as DA.

DA

> He oído que CM se está tirando a una chica nueva. Incluso la llama su novia. ¿De qué se trata?

I hear CM is banging a new girl. He even calls her his girlfriend. What's the deal?

PEDRO

> No sé nada específico sobre el cabrón. ¿Quiere que lo averigüe, jefe?

I don't know anything specific about the bastard. You want me to find out, boss?

> Sí. Averigua quién es, dónde vive y a qué se dedica.

Yeah. Find out who she is, where she lives, and what she does.

> Entendido. Dame unos días.

Got it. Give me a few days.

> No me jodas ni me hagas perder el tiempo ni
> el dinero.

Don't fuck around and waste my time or money.

That text thread ends. But another one starts a few days later.

PEDRO

> Tengo esas fotos. Hace que el cabrón
> parezca que ha estado con dos mujeres que
> no son Serafina. Tuve que pagar mucho para
> conseguir la de UsToday.

I got those photos. It makes the fucker look like he's been with two women who aren't Serafina. I had to pay a lot to get the one into UsToday.

DA

> ¿Cómo reaccionó?

How'd she react?

PEDRO

> Me sorprende lo rápido que se enteró su
> hermana y le mandó un mensaje. No se
> asustó pero está disgustada.

I'm surprised how fast her sister found out and texted her. She didn't freak, but she's upset.

There's a break in the conversation when DA doesn't respond. Then Pedro sends another message. I smirk, but it pisses me off Pedro knows what he included in the next text. It means he was watching way too closely.

PEDRO

> Probablemente se la esté follando ahora mismo. Se metió en su casa y la estaba esperando cuando llegó a casa. Ella no lo echó.

He's probably fucking her right now. He got into her place and was waiting for her when she got home. She didn't kick him out.

DA

> Pues esfuérzate más.

Try harder then.

The next message comes in the day they attacked the bakery.

PEDRO

> Hoy hemos perdido a tres chicos. La mierda se fue de lado. Ella lo dejó ayer. Se suponía que esto haría parecer que él estaba enojado con ella. Tenemos que escondernos un poco antes de atacar.

We lost three guys today. Shit went sideways. She dumped him yesterday. This was supposed to make it look like he was pissed at her. We gotta lie low for a bit before we strike again.

DA

> He vuelto a la ciudad. Si tengo que lidiar con esto yo mismo vas a desear que CM llegara a ti primero. Estás haciendo este lío. Odio los líos, especialmente cuando tengo que limpiarlos. Arreglate tu mismo.

I'm back in town. If I have to deal with this myself, you're going to wish CM got to you first. You're making this messy. I hate messes especially when I have to clean them the fuck up. Fix your fucking self.

Back in town? I look at Gabriele then Luca. I jerk my head toward the office. Before I turn around, I look at Gianni.

"Deal with him. His phone's more useful." My cousin, best friend, and I go into the office. "I know who the fuck it is. I just don't know why."

Gabriele's eyebrows shoot up. "What'd you find?"

"Here."

I hand the burner to Gabriele, and Luca steps closer to read beside him. I watch him scroll from the beginning of the thread to the end. I cross my arms. While they read, I watch Gianni and Luigi take Pedro to the furnace. It's going to be even more extreme with a metal rod up his ass. After all, metal conducts heat. I wonder if Gabriele and Luca can guess like I did.

"Who's been out of town lately?" Luca glances up at me before looking back at the phone. "Dillan was up in Boston to see Besnik right before Easter."

"Nope. Who else?"

Gabriele shakes his head. "No way. This cannot be sanctioned. Enrique wouldn't go along with it. DA. Fucking Alejandro Diaz. He's back from Colombia."

Luca nods. I'm certain that was his next guess. He watches me, his eyes narrowing. "Why's Alejandro pissed enough at you to target Sera?"

"Because he's petty as fuck. This has to go back like five or six years. There was that Brazilian chick I hooked up with. Apparently, they were dating. I seriously had no idea. It's not like I checked her social calendar to see who else she was seeing. We were free to do what we wanted when we weren't fucking. I guess he really liked her and thought I purposely tried to steal her away. I told him he was welcome to have her. He thought I was being a prick and mocking him about sloppy seconds. I just genuinely didn't give a shit. He's fucking getting back at me for that."

"It can't be something that fucking old and stupid." Luca looks unconvinced. I'm not a hundred percent, but I'm pretty damn positive it at least has something to do with that.

"I'm trying to think back to Easter when his family saw me with Fina. What could they have told him?"

Gabe grins at me as he answers. "You two were in a world of your own while dancing. The fucking building could have burned down around you. It was obvious you were totally into each other. It was kinda sweet, actually."

"Yeah, well, I just remember Javier nearly saw me checking in. He probably did and told Alejandro who they assumed I was with. I didn't think about it until now, but the crew working on the sewer line that morning also had a few Colombians I recognized. They probably saw who I left with."

Luca shakes his head, his lips turned down in a frown. "I can see being petty enough to send the photos and the text screenshot, but I don't think he'd actually attack her or smash up her business. There's something else there."

Fucking hell. Please don't let me be right.

"Let's get cleaned up. It just clicked. I know who really doesn't want us together."

"Piero."

Gabriele and Luca speak at the same time. I just raise my eyebrows before stripping. We each take a shower stall and scrub ourselves. Once we have on fresh clothes, and we bagged our old clothes to be burned, we head out. Would he really do that to his own daughter?

Chapter Twenty-Two

Fina

Carmine's voice floats to me from the living room as I enter Paola's home while Lorenzo, Marco, and Matteo talk outside. It's been a long day, and I just want to put my feet up. When I hear Carmine say my dad's name, I consider hiding and eaves-dropping.

"Could Piero be working with Yuri or Enrique? If he is, and it's with Enrique, is he using Augusto to arrange everything?" He hears me gasp and turns. He rushes to me and pulls me into his arms. "*Piccolina?*"

He looks at his family and leads me up to our room before we continue.

"Daddy, I heard what you said. The stuff about my dad, Yuri, Enrique, and Augusto. Do you really think my dad could have done this? Ordered men to destroy my store?"

"I don't know, little one. I can't rule that out as a possibility. But I think it's someone else."

"Who?"

"Alejandro Diaz."

"Is he related to Enrique?"

"Yes, he's another nephew. Enrique has a brother and two sisters. Pablo is his nephew through his brother, and the others are through his sisters."

"So, Alejandro isn't *Tres J's* brother? He's their cousin."

"Yes."

"Why him?"

"There's only one reason that comes to mind, but it has to be more. Years ago, I hooked up with a woman he was dating. I didn't know until after the fact. I told him I would back off, and he could have her. He thought I tried to steal her, then I was offering her to him once I'd fucked her and gotten bored. We've never been fond of one another, but that cemented our rivalry."

"He's going after me because of some other woman?"

"Maybe. I don't know. Right now, from what I know, it looks like he's the culprit. But, Fina, your father really doesn't want us together."

"I know. I always thought he didn't want us together because you weren't who I wanted. Then I thought he was worried about me because of your reputation and that you might leave me broken-hearted. But when I just heard you talking, I realized he'd try to break us up if it were bad for business. If an alliance with your family no longer suits him, then he would break the contract. What I don't get—if he's involved that is—is why he's trying to push me away from you. If I demand the contract ends, then he'd pay the penalty. Why isn't he trying to get you to break the contract?"

"If it is him, then that's exactly what he's trying to do. He probably believes I don't have enough honor to walk away, but Uncle Salvatore does. If you're in danger with me, then Uncle Salvatore would insist I end things for your sake. He would pay the penalty."

"And he needs me to have enough reason to go along with it. If I'm in danger with you, then it would relieve me to be done with you. How do you know all of this?

He hesitates, and I know that's a question I shouldn't have asked. I know better. I'm treading into dangerous waters even having this conversation with him. It might pertain to me, but it's the men's business. Patriarchal and archaic, yes. How we do things, definitely.

"Fina, I know what you're thinking. I'm going to tell you what I can, but I'm figuring out what that is."

"You don't have to, Daddy. I trust you to handle this."

"Fina, we tracked down the men who vandalized your shop. I found evidence that points directly to Alejandro. It's pretty irrefutable, but until it's confirmed, I won't say it's absolute. But it begs the question why. Maybe it is purely about Alejandro having revenge. Something feels off about that, though. It feels like it has to be more."

"If it's Alejandro or my dad, what are you going to do?"

"I told you the other day that Uncle Salvatore is going to sever the agreement. *I'll* pay the penalty for reneging. If you're with me, then it's by your free will. I never want anyone to question that. I don't want people to pity you or call you weak for not standing up to your father. Times are changing. In some families, a daughter can stand up to her father. Anyone outside our world would assume you can."

"I'm going to break it. I'll pay. Then I'll marry you the next day." Did those words just come out of my mouth? We're lying on the bed, and his smile is sensual as he pins me in place.

"Do you think you give the commands now? You are mine, Fina. I am yours. But do not confuse who is in control. We are marrying and fucking soon. But you are not getting in the middle of this. You will piss your father off more, and he's likely to take you and hide you. Then I will have to find you. And, little girl, I will burn everything in my path. So, unless you want me to destroy your father, you will not get involved. No one will keep you from me, Fina. Don't make me have to prove it. If you choose your family, then I respect that. But if you tell me you want me, then I *will not* let go."

His eyes are ablaze, and the certainty in his voice makes my pussy ache. That's probably the hottest thing I've ever heard. Possessive as fuck and perfect.

"I am yours, Daddy. I'm not giving commands, but that is my preference. Don't mistake my willingness to follow you for me being unable to fight for us. You are not the only one willing to do anything to keep us together. You are mine. I will not let you go, Carmine. I may not do the things you have to, but you know what I'm capable of. Don't underestimate me or ever believe I don't want us as much as you do. That's why we had the fucking fight that almost broke us."

"I should have said it sooner then. The moment you let me inside you, you became mine."

"Daddy, I've been yours since you came into my bakery. I couldn't stop thinking about how different you were. Then at Easter, I thought my heart would break because I wanted you so much. I didn't think we would spend the night together. I thought the meal would be one perfect evening, and that would be all I had. I knew I was committing to you the moment I said I would spend the night. I don't know how or why I knew. It defies reason. But I did."

"It was the same for me because we're soulmates. It terrified me you would reject me or that you would walk out in the morning and not look back. But I couldn't *not* take the risk. I'll do anything to protect you and to make you happy, *piccolina*. I knew that, that night. I'm so sorry you ever had reason to question my commitment to you. I will never let that happen again."

"You don't have to prove yourself to me."

"But I will."

"Carmine!"

He closes his eyes and shakes his head. "That's Enzo."

"Carmine!"

He looks at me and frowns. I climb off, and he slips off the bed. He goes to the door and opens it a crack. "Give me a minute."

"Hurry! It's urgent!"

There's something in his voice that freaks us both out. I follow him out of the room and down the stairs at a run. I immediately recognize David, and he's bleeding badly. It's pouring out of a gash across his right temple. His arm isn't in good shape either. It looks broken from the way he's cradling it.

"I'm calling my mom."

I watch Matteo pull out his phone. His mother's a surgeon, but I don't know if she has the day off. I rush forward as Lorenzo and Marco help him into the kitchen. I hurry to pull out a chair as Carmine yanks open a drawer and pulls out dish towels. I don't know whether I should get ice or what. It's obvious the men know what to do as they work in silence. They soon have ice on David's ribs, a towel pressed against his forehead, and an improvised sling to take the pressure off his shoulder. I stand there, trying to stay out of the way. Once Carmine has David's arm in the sling, he comes over to me. I gawk at him in stunned silence. When he hugs me, I turn my gaze to David. The words tumble from my mouth.

"What the fuck happened?"

"Augusto."

I glance up at Carmine, then return my attention to David. "Why?"

"I overheard him talking to someone, giving the guy your schedule for the next week. He was telling him which shop you'll be at and when. I confronted him. I didn't expect him to draw his gun. As soon as I saw his arm go to his back, I reached for mine. But he got it out and pistol whipped me. We hit the ground, and I felt my arm snap. I kept fighting, finally getting the gun away from him. Nicholas came in just as I got it. He pulled us apart, but Augusto snatched Nicholas's piece. He pointed it straight at my head. I didn't want to do it, but he took the safety off and put his finger on the trigger. I raised the gun I had. The moment his finger twitched, I shot him. His bullet grazed my temple that was already bleeding. My bullet went between his eyes."

I listen in disbelief. I stare at my guard, and once more words leave my mouth without thinking. "Where's Nicholas?"

"He drove me here and dropped me off. He went back to deal with Augusto."

Carmine speaks up as I cling to him. "Where were you?"

"At their place. I came to pick Nicholas up. We were going to the shooting range together."

Gio and Adriano were my guards today, along with Carmine's family and two men. I don't know what to make of this. Nicholas watched his brother die, then drove the man's shooter to get help. Now he's gone back to deal with the body. We live in the most fucked-up world. I whisper to my boyfriend, but I'm certain the others hear.

"What now?"

Carmine doesn't answer me, instead asking David another question. "Who was he talking to?"

"Some guy named Alejandro. I don't know anything else, but that's the name I saw on his phone when he dropped it. Do you know who that is?"

"Only too well."

Carmine looks at Lorenzo, Matteo, Marco, and now Gabriele and Luca. I don't know where they were when David first came in. I know they're who Carmine was talking to when

I got here. I watch the Mancinelli men, and they're communicating without saying a word. Carmine's hold on me tightens before he lets go.

"Fina, Marco and Gabriele are going to stay here with you. I have to go for a little while, but I'll be back as soon as I can."

I open my mouth ready to launch a barrage of questions at him, but I know better. All I can do is nod. He leads me out of the kitchen and into the living room.

"Fina, we are ending this today. You will not live in fear anymore, and I won't risk someone else coming for you. If Augusto was a traitor and pulled a gun on a man who trusted him with his life, then he got what he deserved. David did not. This won't end until we find and deal with whoever ordered Augusto to talk to Alejandro. I don't think he did this on his own."

"Me neither. He wouldn't turn on David unless someone with the authority ordered him to."

"And that leads us back to your dad."

"I know. I hope it's not true. I really pray it isn't, but if he's responsible, then he's the real traitor. He turned against me, his own daughter. He didn't get what he wanted by arguing with me, so now he's trying to intimidate me by having someone else do his dirty work."

"We don't know that for sure, but it seems like it, Fina. I'm sorry."

I see the worry in his eyes, and I know what he's thinking. "Carmine, my past was with my family. My future is with you. Maybe one day I can forgive him, but not yet. If this was him, he was willing to terrify me, make me miserable, and damage my business to get what he wants. It's not even about him wanting to get between us. It's what he will do to accomplish it. That's what I have the real issue with."

"Fina, I'll do the least I have to, to resolve this. But something is going to happen. I won't kill your father or order him killed, unless it's my life or one of my men."

I swallow as tears fill my eyes. I don't want to picture my father dead, and I definitely don't want to picture Carmine doing it. I don't want him to live with that.

"Fina, if it comes to that, I'll understand."

My brow furrows, then my eyebrows shoot straight up before I narrow my eyes. "Understand what?"

"That you won't forgive me. That we'll be over."

"Don't put words into my mouth, Carmine. That is not what will happen. You are the only person I'll turn to, so you better be ready."

He stares at me without blinking for a moment, maybe waiting for me to recant. Then he nods. He pins me against him for a fiercely possessive kiss. Each time I think I can't feel more loved, protected, and desired, he shows me I am to yet another degree.

"I love you, Daddy."

"I love you, *piccolina*."

"I know you can't make me any promises that you'll come home, but promise me you'll do your best."

"No other outcome is acceptable. I'm coming home, little one."

I nod as I swallow the lump rising in my throat. I choke it down as I go up on my tiptoes, wrapping my arms around his neck. "Bye, Daddy. I'll be here when you get home."

"I like the sound of that." He gives me a quick, hard peck. Then he's leaving, and I'm left watching him walk out the door. I pray it's not the last time I see him.

Chapter Twenty-Three

Carmine

I kept my shit together for Fina's sake, but the moment I'm in the SUV with Gabriele, Matteo, and Luca, I let loose a stream of curses.

"*Fottuto pezzo di merda succhiacazzi. Spero che il fottuto Diavolo lo caghi dal suo fottuto buco del culo. Fanculo a lui,*" Motherfucking piece of fucking cocksucking shit. I hope the fucking Devil shits him out of his fucking asshole. Fuck him.

"Feel better now?"

I glare at Luca. "No, I don't fucking feel fucking better. Did you feel better while Gabriele was protecting Olivia in the fucking treehouse? Don't fucking patronize me, Luca."

"I'm not. I was genuinely asking."

We've spent too many years at odds for us to take anything on face value. I nod and shoot him a tight smile.

"Thanks. No. I'm terrified I'm going to find out it's Piero and have to put a bullet through his heart. I don't doubt for a moment that he'll shoot me given the chance."

"He won't have the chance. And he may be a pissed off father, but he's not stupid enough to take out Don Salvatore Mancinelli's nephew. No one is that dumb. That's why you've lived to the age of twenty-eight."

"Maybe in the past. But this is his daughter. I'm not good enough for her, and I know that. I can tell myself I am, and I can even try to convince Fina, but I know what I am and what I have been."

Lorenzo grunts with annoyance before he argues the opposite. "Fuck this shit, Carmine. You might have used your genius for evil within our family, but you've been a bigger help than any of us realized for the past six years. You're sly and clever. You led without us realizing you were. You're the type they make movies about."

"Wonderful. I'm fucking Don Corleone. That doesn't do shit to make sure I don't have to kill my girlfriend's father."

"I meant, you're worth more than anyone—particularly you —have given you credit for. You might have rebelled against your *nonnos*, but you believed most of the shit they told you. If you hadn't, you wouldn't have been so bitter. You felt like the shit they called you. You're not. Fina's a fucking good judge of character. If she loves you—which it's obvious to a blind and deaf man she does—then you're good enough. Fuck Piero. Fuck him and his family if they don't see it. She's made her choice, and her family has to live with it. If they won't, then it's their fault that they lose her. Don't take on their baggage. Our family has more than enough of its own."

I nod when Lorenzo finishes. I look at Luca and Matteo and see their agreement. It's going to take a long time to undo the damage I did to my family, and probably just as long, if not longer, to undo the damage the old generation of my family did to me. But it's nice to not be at odds with everyone, to know I'm wanted for more than just being able to hack shit and liking expensive toys like drones. That they want me for more than being the whipping boy or the shitty lackey. It feels odd to be accepted. I hold my phone to my ear when it buzzes and raise my eyebrows. My cousins and friend fall quiet.

"Nicholas, where are you?"

"Dealing with the body. I assume you know what happened."

"I want to hear your side. I'm putting you on speaker. I'm with Luca, Lorenzo, and Matteo." I tap the button.

"Where is Ms. Carosi? Is she safe?"

"Yes." I won't tell him anything more. If he wants to know, he can talk to Adriano or Gio.

"Fine. I came home to meet David to go to the range. I walk in, and they're rolling around on the ground. I can see Augusto has his gun out, and David's fighting to keep it from being turned on him. He still had his gun holstered at his back. When they rolled, and Augusto was on top, I pulled him off. David had Augusto's gun, but he didn't point it at either of us. I didn't expect Augusto to go for my piece, so I wasn't prepared to stop him. He whipped it out from the shoulder holster. He was ready to kill David. I understand why David shot him."

"You seem very calm for someone who watched his brother die."

"You don't know me that well."

"Fair enough. Maybe you're an actor worthy of an Oscar. Or you aren't surprised it came to this."

There's a silence before Nicholas sighs through the phone.

"The moment you came into the picture, I knew this was the only ending. I just never imagined it would be one of us. I figured you would be the one to pull the trigger."

"Have you talked to your don?"

"Fuck no. Not until I have a handle on this shitstorm. The timeline's gonna be a bit different from reality to make up for not calling right away. But this shit needs squaring away before Don Carosi gets involved. I need to know what the fuck Augusto got all of us into. Because no one is going to believe he acted without at least me knowing. We're brothers and roommates."

"You've been forthcoming with me. I don't believe you're involved in this. But if you prove me wrong, Nicholas, I will make your death miserable. If you have any part in putting Ms. Carosi in the middle, I will rip your throat out, then reach in and pull your heart out before I shit down your guts."

"I don't doubt that. Carmine, I'm not involved in this. Augusto was convinced he loved Ms. Carosi. Obsessed, not in love. But Don Carosi knew that, and I think he played my brother to get him to work with someone else to fuck with you. I just don't know who."

"Does the name Alejandro mean anything to you?"

"No. Should it?"

"David said he saw it on Augusto's phone when it fell to the ground. Your brother was talking to Alejandro Diaz, the Colombian *jefe's* nephew."

"Does that mean Enrique Diaz is involved, too?"

"We don't know. We don't think he is directly, but he may have turned a blind eye. We're headed to Uncle Sal's right now. Then we're meeting with you. I want to see the body."

"I have him, and I'm headed to Mario's."

"You know about Mario?" He's our mortician. He doesn't ask questions when a body arrives with holes. He patches them up enough that the guy looks presentable for his open casket wake.

"Yeah. Don Carosi told us about him when we first started guarding Ms. Carosi. I gotta make Augusto look good enough for my parents. This is going to wreck my mom, so the least I can do is make it less obvious how he died."

"Do your parents live here?" I assumed they were in Venice or around there.

"Yeah. They moved here about three years ago. With Augusto and me here, working for Don Carosi and guarding Ms. Carosi, it made sense."

"Where's David's family?"

"They're all here. His family's been in New York for three generations. They're *Mala del Brenta*, too. Half his family is still near Venice, but his grandfather came over after World War Two. Don Carosi picked him because he already knew New York."

"Explains his name." David isn't the most Italian of names, even if one of the greats carved a statue by that name. Nicholas snorts.

"Yeah. So much for his family blending in and leaving the Mafia behind."

"What's your father going to do when he finds out?"

I hear a turn signal through the phone, then it sounds like Nicholas's car drives over train tracks. He's almost at Mario's.

"There won't be some feud. He won't seek revenge. Augusto's always been the hothead. It'll destroy my parents, but it won't surprise them. Augusto did this to himself. He could have lied to David or come up with some other solution. The moment he drew his gun, he signed his own death warrant. He was too fucking smug. He assumed he was untouchable. And he died for it."

His voice trembles on the last sentence, and I can't blame him. Augusto may have been a shitbag, but he was Nicholas's brother. I just hope he's right about his father and David. I like David, and I trust him the most with Fina. I don't want to see more shit happen to him for this.

"Stay with him. Don't leave Mario's. We'll go there when we're done with Uncle Salvatore."

"I have to call my parents soon. I can lie about the times to Don Carosi, but I can't lie to my parents. The moment Mario tells me Augusto is ready for my mom and dad to see him, I have to make the call."

"I know. The Mancinellis will corroborate whatever you tell Piero."

"Thank you. I gotta get my parents past the shock. Then I gotta help them with the shame."

Luca's been watching me throughout the conversation. Lorenzo and Matteo are a little less obvious. Luca speaks up. "Don't take on that shame, Nicholas. You aren't your brother. You are not a reflection of his choices. Don't blame yourself or fear we'll think you're the same."

Luca's gaze locks with mine while he talks. He's speaking to me as much as he is Fina's guard. I'm not a reflection of how fucked up our shared grandfather was or my dad's dad. Six months ago, I never imagined he'd be so understanding. I didn't think he could be so forgiving. Matteo and Lorenzo look at me and nod at the same time. Since reconciling with Luca, the others have accepted me. It makes life a fuck ton easier being *with* them rather than *against* them.

I hang up with Nicholas, and we ride the rest of the way to Uncle Salvatore's in silence. None of us are eager for this conversation, but it's unavoidable. I lead the way into the house and find Uncle Salvatore in the kitchen with Aunt Sylvia. He's in a t-shirt and gym shorts, helping his wife make dinner. Outside of this house, no one ever sees him in anything less than an Italian tailored suit and tie. He looks so normal right now. And I'm about to rip him away from being a typical husband and father and force him back into his role as don. It tempts me to turn around and run.

"Uncle Sal."

He looks up, sees the four of us, and wipes his hands on a

dish towel. He nods, and we head to his office in silence. It's a converted den because he needs a room large enough to accommodate at least seven, if not ten, large men.

"What happened?"

I launch into it. Explaining what happened to Augusto and David. How we discovered Alejandro's involved in this. How this is just getting worse rather than better. Uncle Salvatore's eyes narrow as he listens. He stands with his arms crossed while I recount what I know. I remember how he looked when I was a kid. He's not as bulky as he once was since he doesn't go on missions that often. But in a t-shirt, it's still easy to see he's fit. His forearms ripple with muscles, and I don't have to imagine his strength. I was on the receiving end before he sent Gabriele, Luca, and me to Sicily. It's a reminder that he leads our family, and it's always by example.

"Carmine, it's time to call Enrique."

I pull my phone out and unlock it. How fucked up is that we have the members of the other syndicates on speed dial? That's how it is. We hate each other with the fire of a thousand suns, but we can make nice when we must. Right now, until I know exactly what the fuck is going on, I have to play nicely. I tap Enrique's contact. It rings four times, and I expect voicemail to pick up.

"Carmine."

"Enrique."

There's a pause, then I hear his voice again. "You called me. What do you want?"

"What's Alejandro been up to since he got home?"

There's another pause. "Working. Why?"

"So, he did this for you since all of his work is for the Cartel."

"Did what, Carmine? What the fuck are you getting at? I'm

in the middle of making dinner. I don't need fucking indigestion before I eat."

"Did Alejandro take up photography while he was in Bogota? Or is he hiring someone? Did you hire someone?"

"To do what? Stop fucking asking me questions since I obviously don't know what the fuck you're talking about. I'll hang up."

"Pedro Pérez."

"Don't know him."

"His family owns Havana Cantina. Alejandro's favorite restaurant, apparently."

"Salvatore, tell your nephew to spit it out, or I'm hanging up."

Uncle Salvatore circles his hand, gesturing for me to get on with it. Not yet.

"You say you don't know him, but he was on your payroll."

"Salvatore, do you know every single person your family has ever paid for a job?"

"Yes." My uncle does not. But that isn't the point.

"Bullshit. I don't know who the hell Pedro is. Carmine, what the hell does Alejandro have to do with this?"

"He paid Pedro to hire a couple guys to fuck up my girlfriend's business."

"Girlfriend? The pretty woman from Easter? She's too good for you. But isn't she forced to marry you? Not exactly a girlfriend. More like a hostage."

I grit my teeth. "How she wound up with me isn't the point. The point is Alejandro hired Pedro, who hired a couple guys, to bust up Serafina's shop. He's also hired someone to take photos and sent text screenshots that made it look like I was unfaithful to her. I'm a lot of things, Enrique, but I'm not a cheater. At least, not on women."

"That's not what I remember."

"Fuck you and Alejandro. I didn't know she was banging Alejandro, too. I walked away when I found out. Your nephew was too butt hurt to realize I did the gentlemanly thing."

"Gentlemanly thing." Enrique scoffs.

"Whether any of you think that is irrelevant. You've sworn up and down that women are off limits. You doubled down on that after the fucking shitstorm Juan caused. If Alejandro doesn't leave Serafina alone, what the Kutsenkos did to Juan will look like mercy. Do you really want to lose two nephews in two years? I'll fucking make it happen."

Enrique's tone shifts just like I expected. "You don't issue me threats, you *pequeño chupapollas*." Little cocksucker.

"I'm not threatening you, *jefe*. I'm merely giving you a heads up. That way you can pick out his casket now. Keep him away from Serafina and out of our relationship. You don't want to make an alliance with Piero Carosi, Enrique. That won't be good for business."

"Piero Carosi? What's Serafina's father got to do with this?"

"Alejandro's doing Piero's dirty work. Alejandro hates me, so he's more than okay with fucking shit up on Piero's behalf."

"Alejandro doesn't even know Piero. They've never met."

It's my turn to scoff. "Like that matters."

I hear voices in the background, and as they get closer, I recognize Alejandro and Pablo. Suddenly there's silence. Enrique must be signaling them to be quiet. Uh-uh.

"Put me on speakerphone, Enrique. Alejandro either shows us he has the balls to own this shit, or he can lie, and I'll kill him sooner rather than later."

The sound quality changes, and I know everyone on the other end of the call can hear. Good.

"Alejandro, we don't like each other. Fine. What-the-fuck-ever. But you were the least like Juan, yet you're fighting your wars through women, just like the little bitch your cousin was."

There's silence, then muffled Spanish. Alejandro speaks next, and I assume Enrique commanded him to. "I don't know what you're talking about."

"Now that's a pile of shit we can all smell. You're the smartest person in your family, so don't play dumb. It doesn't suit you. Why the hell are you working with Piero Carosi to get back at me?"

Alejandro laughs, and it grates on my nerves. I wait for him to answer, but he remains quiet. I infuse warning into my tone. "Enrique."

"*Responde a sus putas preguntas. A mí también me gustaría saber.*" Answer his fucking questions. I'd like to know too.

"I'm not working with Piero Carosi, but I am fucking up your life a little at a time."

"You think you're going to drive Serafina away? She's already picked me."

"Because she has to."

Uncle Salvatore interjects. "I canceled the contract a week ago."

My eyebrows shoot up. I don't like that kind of surprise. Is this why Piero's upping the ante? My uncle shakes his head. He scribbled a note while Alejandro's been on the line.

> *Nothing was definite until I paid yesterday. I broke the contract, so it was on me, not you.*

I gesture for the pen and respond.

> *You should have told me.*

"Alejandro, if you want to come for me, fine. Leave Serafina alone."

"Like you did with Giselle?"

"Exactly like that, motherfucker. I found out you wanted her. I walked away. You found out I'm serious with Serafina. You walk away. That's how this is going to fucking work, Alejandro. Fuck with me any more on this, and I will destroy you."

"You don't issue me threats." Alejandro talks over Enrique, so I don't hear what the *jefe* says.

"I just fucking did, motherfucker. Fuck with me and find out."

"You're not the one paying me the good money. Beat what I'm offered, and I'll consider it."

"You're not blackmailing me, *hijo de puta*. Enrique, control your mongrel, or I will put him down." Son of a bitch.

Enrique snaps at us. "Enough out of both you. If Alejandro says he's not working for Piero, then he isn't. He'll back the fuck off, won't you, *sobrino*?" Nephew.

"Eh."

Something bangs on their end, and I imagine Enrique throwing something at Alejandro's head. He plays old man rec softball and still pitches. Better Alejandro than me.

"He'll back off, Carmine, and you'll calm the fuck down. The past is the past."

"Nope."

"Carmine, for fuck's—"

"If the past were the past, Enrique, this shit wouldn't be happening. If it's not Piero, then who the fuck is it?"

Alejandro's tone mocks me when he answers. "There's someone else in the *Mala del Brenta* who hates you even more than Piero. This person's way more creative. Shit's going down you don't even know about."

As though this conversation isn't going badly enough, Fina's calling. I decline it but open my texts.

ME

> I'm on a call. I can't talk right now. You okay?

I wait for her response.

FINA

> Someone drained all my bank accounts. I'm the only name on any of them. Business and personal. Just got an alert from my bank. Went to check on my app and someone racked up my credit card too. Maxed it out. They're trying to ruin me.

I show my phone to my uncle. He takes it and turns it off speakerphone.

"Enrique, take me off speaker. It's just me now."

Uncle Salvatore's quiet for a moment, so I assume Enrique's talking. Maybe he's turning off speakerphone too.

"This is going too far. Serafina's Carmine's girlfriend and a *Mala del Brenta* daughter. Your nephew knows to stay away from the women. Serafina just texted Carmine that someone's stolen all her money and maxed out her credit card. Alejandro's going to destroy her business. Do you want us to retaliate? Do you want us to go after your sisters? He puts the money back, and we call it a day. Or he doesn't, and this escalates."

Fuck. I wish I knew what Enrique was saying right now. I only hear my uncle's response.

"You know I can make sure every single property in escrow falls through. Your sister's business will be done. No one will hire her as their real estate agent again."

Silence again. I run my hand through my hair. I want my phone back to see if Fina texted me again. I didn't get to respond. I mouth, "give me your phone," to Lorenzo. He hands it over, and I open the texts and punch in Fina's number. She's one of the few I have memorized.

It's Carmine. I'm on Enzo's phone. Are you still at my mom's?

I wait, and it feels like forever.

FINA

We're headed to my bank. I have to get there before it closes. I have fifteen minutes to get to the branch near her place. We're already in the car.

I don't like this. My Spidey-Senses are tingling.

Who's with you?

Gabe and Marco with three guys. We're in an SUV.

Stay in the car until they clear the building. I don't want you in there with anyone but the bank manager. Understood?

They can't make that happen.

The fuck they can't. I swear to you you will not like it if you don't agree.

Even though I'll delete all these texts, I'm aware this isn't my phone. I won't call her little girl or say that I'll spank her. But she knows.

I'll tell them.

I'm on my way.

> You don't have to. I have five guys with me. No one will even see me go in and out. I'm too short.

I'm on my way.

There's a pause. Either she knows better than to argue, or she's telling the men with her. Probably both.

> Fine.

She shoots me the name of the bank and the cross streets. I hold the phone up to Uncle Salvatore, so he can read the thread. I was only half listening to him. Now I pay attention as I point to the phone screen. Lorenzo, Matteo, and Luca read the messages. They nod, and I delete the thread and hand it back to Lorenzo. I need my phone back before I can leave, so Uncle Salvatore needs to end the call. I point to the others and me before pointing to the door. My uncle nods.

"Enrique, we're going around in circles. Fine. Alejandro isn't working with Piero. I'll buy that. But he's working with someone. Cage your pup and housebreak him. If anything else happens to Serafina, I won't stop Carmine. We all know he can't kill Alejandro, but he'll make your nephew wish he had."

Uncle Salvatore hangs up and hands me the phone as I speak. "Can you handle things with Nicholas? He's going to have to tell Piero."

"Sure. Carmine, think things through. I know you're angry, but you're smart. You're not rash, but I get this is about the woman you love. I mean it. Think things through. She needs you alive. I don't buy for a minute that Piero isn't involved. If he'll do this to his daughter to win, then he's ballsy enough to kill you."

"I know. Uncle Sal, Fina knows what it might come to.

344

We've talked about it. She says she'll understand and that she'll choose me, even if I have to kill her father. You know that's not true. She won't let me near her if that happens. Make sure she's safe and has whatever she needs until she finds someone else." I want to say someone better, but I don't need platitudes. I need to hear him promise what I already know but am desperate to hear.

"She'll always be safe with us. She's already family. She knows to come here, right?"

"Yeah."

If anything goes sideways and I can't protect her, or she gets separated from her guards, she knows to come here. She has since before we got together. It's Aunt Sylvia's policy. Women from any family are welcome here and have sanctuary until their family can get them. She refuses to let the same thing happen to another woman that happened to her sister, Sophia, so the door is always open to the women and children. Uncle Salvatore supports her, but she'd do it, regardless. He's smart enough to know not to fight her, even if he disagreed.

"Carmine."

I've turned toward the door, my phone now back in my pocket. I stop when my uncle says my name. He jerks his chin toward the door, and the others leave. They shut it.

"I know you're in a hurry, but there's someone you haven't considered."

"Yeah, I have. Allegra."

"Yes. I know what Serafina did to the men who attacked and killed Sophia. No one else does. I have an informant in their family. Sylvia's aware. She told me who to pick. The man followed Serafina that night. Serafina didn't get her ruthlessness from Piero. Allegra and Sylvia are the same in what they can and will do to protect their family. But my wife would never hurt one of her children to get her way. Allegra isn't doing this to protect Serafina. She has other plans. I don't know the details yet, but she's using Serafina."

"Doesn't she love her daughter?"

"Very much. This isn't about protecting Serafina from you. It's about making sure Serafina is the next matriarch, the next Godmother—*la madrina*—of their family. Allegra knows Sylvia's life is in America, and this is where our girls will stay. Julianna's the oldest of all the daughters, but she doesn't have the same temperament as Serafina. She's not suited to the role, but Serafina is. Allegra wants her back in Italy and back in Sicily specifically. I just don't know who she wants Serafina with or what lengths she'll go to do this for their family."

"And Piero is fine with this?"

"I doubt the fucker knows half of it. He's up to his eyeballs in shit in Venice. It's not a good time for him. Shit's brewing there, so he's not thinking about Allegra's side of the family. He also trusts his wife as much as I do mine. Allegra and Sylvia could run their families and their syndicates, with no one ever knowing there wasn't a man at the helm. They were raised to since it could be their only means to survive if anything happened to a husband or son. Don't underestimate her, Carmine. She's far smarter and strategic than Piero, and she can concentrate on more than one thing at a time. He probably thinks she's focused on helping the *Mala del Brenta*, but I guarantee she's just as attuned to the *Cosa Nostra*."

"Fuck my life."

"Exactly, nephew."

Chapter Twenty-Four

Fina

The last thing I want is this brewing confrontation. I know exactly how this is going to go, and my anger burns throughout my chest and into my belly. I can't tell the guys what's coming because, if I do, they'd never agree to take me to the bank. I want Carmine with me for support, but he's going to lose his ever-loving shit when he gets here. He won't cause a scene. I'm not worried about that, but it's going to be ugly. Marco's on my left, and Gabriele's on my right. We've just pulled into the bank parking lot, and none of the guys open their doors. Marco turns to me.

"We can wait until Carmine gets here."

"I know. But believe me, it's better if we don't."

"He texted me. He wants the bank cleared before you go in."

"He texted the same thing to me. But doing that means waiting until after it's supposed to close. We only have ten minutes left. I can't guarantee they'd stay open for this. I'm certain they wouldn't."

Marco cocks an eyebrow as though I'm slow. Yeah. I know. They're Mafia, and plenty of people in banking know that. But I'd rather not throw that around unless we have to. I also don't want video security showing us there after closing.

"I want this on the up-and-up, Marco. Check out the place, make sure it's safe, then I go in. But we don't have time to waste. As is, I doubt we'll resolve anything before the bank closes, but at least I can get the ball rolling."

"Believe me, when my cousin gets here, nothing is closing until this is resolved."

I get inside, and my eyes sweep my surroundings. I spot who I need, and I fist my hands. I step around Marco and make a beeline for a man I haven't seen in two years but would recognize anywhere. I know my guards aren't pleased that I led the charge, but I won't look weak.

"Serafina."

"Orlando."

I sense Gabriele's and Marco's shock. They know the name. Good. I step right up to his desk, the edge pressing against my thighs. I keep my voice low.

"Why the fuck did you do it?"

"Do what? And nice to see you too, Sera."

"Don't, Orlando. I know you're lying. It's not nice to see me, and you know exactly what. Don't waste our time. You know my temper, and it's about to boil over. I haven't been this livid in years. You know better than to test me."

"Sera—"

"No. I know that tone. Don't fucking patronize me. Answer me."

He knows my tone, too. He knows he's reached the limits of my patience. I've never been violent toward any man I've dated, and I will never be violent with Carmine. But Orlando's familiar with my temper. He knows I can keep it in check, but let loose? He'll cry the entire way home. There won't be a person in this bank who doesn't know his deepest darkest secret. There won't be a person in this bank who doesn't know what he's done. I'll make it impossible for him not to be arrested, then I'll make sure he never posts bail, and I'll absolutely make sure he spends time in prison. I'm not a man, but I have resources too. A few kids' birthday cakes for the right judges weren't by accident.

"What was I supposed to do?"

"Fucking say no and be a man for a day in your life." Now I'm prodding his temper. He doesn't think clearly when he gets pissed, and he always says way more than he intends to, and it's never the shit to hurt my feelings. It's unintentional confessions.

"Serafina, you know it was impossible for me to say no. My family is not what yours is."

"Bullshit. It's not like your father and grandfather aren't senior *Mala del Brenta*. Your father's a *capo*, and your grandfather is *consigliere*. You could have told Papa and let him deal with it. You could have told your dad and grandfather, and they would have gone to Papa. But your balls still haven't dropped. I waited six years, and they were still stuck up inside you. I thought they would have by now, but you're still a pussy."

"You never said shit like that, Sera. Did you learn that from your new boyfriend?"

"I didn't say it out loud, but I definitely thought it all the fucking time."

His face flushes like a radish, but neither of us can say more because the door swings open and bangs against the window. I raise my hand over my head.

"Carmine, I'm here."

He barks one word, and I'm certain the security guard jumps.

"Move."

He's beside me before I expect it. I look up at him while he surveys our surroundings. He looks at Lorenzo and juts his chin toward a security camera. I don't know what's going to happen, but I pray it doesn't involve Carmine's cousin shooting any of the cameras. Instead, Lorenzo makes his way to a teller and clearly has a convincing one-sided conversation because the man runs to the locked door leading to the back offices. We all wait until the red flashing light turns off on all of them. Carmine wraps his arm around my waist and eases me back three steps until I'm almost behind him.

"You know who I am."

It's a statement, not a question. Orlando glares at Carmine, insolence written across his face. This is not the right time for his *cojones* to descend at last. He crosses his arms, and Carmine laughs. The other guys follow suit. Orlando isn't little by any stretch, but he's not stacked like a pro bodybuilder like Carmine and his relatives and friends. Carmine puts his hands on his hips, and I know Orlando can see both guns holstered against Carmine's upper ribs. I can't see his face anymore, but I can guess he's cocking an eyebrow. He must have learned it from his mother. It's very convincing. Orlando takes the shovel offered and starts digging his own grave.

"I know you're the piece of shit her grandfather tried to force her to marry."

"She's had ten years to marry someone else, but she never did."

Orlando's gaze flashes to me, and I know Carmine went straight for the scab that still hasn't healed. I don't believe for a moment that Orlando still loves me. He's engaged. But he's bitter that he wasted six years with me. At least, that's what he claimed the night before he proposed when he called me to brag. But I don't need them in a pissing match right now. I need my money back. I shift to Carmine's side, and he slides his arm around my waist again. He squeezes, and it's not reassurance. It's a warning. I'll deal with my punishment later.

"Orlando, put my fucking money back."

"I don't know what you mean."

"The fuck you don't. Don't play stupid. It doesn't suit you."

Carmine chimes in, and I want to squeeze his waist in warning. "Are you sure he's playing? He can't be that bright to go after a Mancinelli's woman."

This is the absolute wrong moment to get aroused by his possessiveness. I know in this moment, he'll kill for me. I don't want it to come to that. He's never the type of possessive that would keep me from doing what I want with whomever I want. But he is the type who will do anything to protect me and to make me happy.

"Now you want her. You didn't while you fucked most of New York."

I lean forward and lower my voice. "Who says I didn't do the same thing?"

Orlando's face turns a deeper shade of red. I twist the knife.

"I had a lot to make up for. Now, give me back my money. Take it out of whatever account you transferred it into and put it back into mine. Do you want me to wake your grandfather in the middle of the night?"

My father and his grandfather have a love-hate relationship. My dad trusts him and relies on him as his counselor, conscience, and lawyer. In return, Riccardo chooses his battles wisely, but he will put his foot down when needed. I consider this one of those necessary times. I pull my phone out and hold it up. I shake it side to side.

"Sera, by all means. Call *Nonno*. There's not a damn thing he can do."

Carmine squeezes my waist again before he draws his gun. With one arm still around me, he points the pistol at Orlando's groin. "Call Allegra."

"What?" I practically squawk.

"Fina, it's obvious calling his grandfather doesn't scare this dipshit. That's because there's nothing his *nonno* can do to convince your father because your father isn't responsible. Call Allegra."

I stand in stunned silence. But the pieces fall into place. I wondered why only my father argued with me about Carmine. My mother didn't think she needed to. I feel like such an idiot not to see it. The plan was for Orlando and me to eventually move back and go to Sicily. At least, that was my parents' plan. I hadn't been so sure while Orlando and I were together.

Once we broke up, and I had the first bakery, I knew I wasn't going back. My mother thinks to force me. If I have nothing, then I'll turn to them. Then they can give me the ultimatum. Be broke in America or go to Sicily and have support. But I'm not as destitute as they think. I listened to my mom more than she thinks. I checked my investments, and no one's touched them.

I also have some offshore accounts and two accounts in Switzerland no one knows about. I let my family think I used some of my inheritance from both sets of grandparents to pay for part of grad school and the bakery. I didn't. I squirreled that shit away for a rainy day. It's fucking monsoon season right now.

"Call my mother, Orlando. Now."

I watch as the employees shuffle into the back, Mancinelli men fan out, and someone turns the power off to everything but the computers. How'd they do that? When Orlando makes no move to do what I say, Carmine nudges me.

"Call your mom, Fina."

"What the fuck kind of nickname is that? Her name is Sera."

"Carmine means more to me than anyone ever has. I like that he has a name for me only he uses."

"Fucking bullshit."

Orlando mutters under his breath. Let him. I watch Gabriele and Luca drag him into an office, and Lorenzo takes his seat at Orlando's computer. I hit my mom's speed dial number. It only takes two rings before she answers. Was she expecting me? We go back and forth in Italian.

"Serafina, it's the middle of the night. What's wrong?"

"You made a lot of money tonight, Mama."

"What do you mean? Serafina, I was asleep. Don't speak in riddles."

"You stole my money and made Orlando do it."

Her pause is one heartbeat too long, and I know she's lying.

"Is *he* blaming me? How do you know it wasn't him? His uncle broke the contract. They want the money back."

"That's ridiculous. The Mancinellis don't need a penny from me. *Zio* Salvatore would never do this. He wanted to break the contract years ago, and you know that."

"Then he wants you dependent on him, so you can never leave. He may as well steal your shoes to keep you."

I thought I was livid before. My anger is swirling with hurt and disbelief, pushing me toward an edge that I might not pull myself back from. Carmine senses it and holsters his gun. He pulls me into his arms and presses my head against his chest. He can't hear my mom's side of the conversation, but I'm certain he can guess. My forehead rests in the divot between his pecs. When he tries to take the phone from me, I don't fight him. I wrap both arms around his waist and cling to him. He continues the conversation in Italian.

"Allegra, you can blame me for what we all know you did. She doesn't believe you. Don't do this to your daughter. You'll push her away."

When my mother responds, I can hear her. I realize Carmine must have heard everything, too. "Since when do you care about family? You've done everything you can to ruin yours."

"Do not mistake my dislike of some of my family members for me not putting my family first. There's nothing I won't do for my family, and that includes Fina. For now, out of respect for Fina and Aunt Sylvia, I won't do anything. But push Fina any further, and I will retaliate. I will take it all. Everything you have from the *Cosa Nostra* and *Mala del Brenta*."

"Don't threaten me, little boy."

"Don't manipulate your daughter."

"You're a distraction. You won't last."

I pull the phone from Carmine's hand when I hear that. I was exhausted a moment ago, but the adrenaline pumps through me in another surge.

"*Ci sposiamo.*" We're getting married. I blurt that, then consider what I said. My gaze meets Carmine's, and I never imagined he could look so happy or excited about anything. He nods several times.

"Don't lie, Serafina. You will not coerce me or give me ultimatums."

"I'm not. I'm telling you what's happening. Either you accept this and Carmine, or you don't. But you will not make me run back to you and beg you to support me. You will not choose another man for me. You will not force me to move to Sicily. My life is wherever Carmine is, and that's New York."

My mom introduced me to Orlando. It took a couple years before I realized why she'd done it. It wasn't because he was a nice young man she thought I'd be well-matched with. She recognized I had the stronger personality from the beginning. Even though he's Venetian Mafia, she knew he would follow me to Sicily if I insisted. She thought she'd picked a man who would take a spot in the *Cosa Nostra* in Palermo, and I would rise in our family.

Since she had no brothers, her cousin became don when her father died. None of her male cousins married strong women. They married the ones who don't ask questions. They may run their homes, but they aren't the type to be *la madrina* —the Godmother—of a dynasty. I know Mama has groomed me for that. I recognize it now. It's those qualities that made me so good as a real estate agent and a business owner. My future is still in the *Cosa Nostra*, but it's here in New York with Carmine.

My mom goes silent, and I can only imagine what she's doing. My dad has to be awake and listening by now. I pray she isn't telling him to put a hit on Carmine. While Orlando glares at me from within an office where Gabriele and Luca hold him hostage, Lorenzo gives us a thumbs up. He spins the computer monitor, and I lean forward. I squint before my gaze jumps to his. All my money is magically back in my accounts. I just stand there and blink before I whisper to him.

"How'd you do that?"

"I have a degree in computer science." That doesn't explain this level of hacking skills. This is crazy. I know better than to ask anything more. I knew better than to expect a real answer. But I couldn't help myself.

"Serafina, what the hell did you just do?" That was fast. She must already know.

"Nothing. I've been on the phone with you. Go back to sleep, Mama. I'll talk to you later."

I don't wait for a response before I hang up. I know my smile is smug, and she can't see it. But I feel vindicated. At least, until I look up at Carmine. Fuck. This isn't nearly over.

Chapter Twenty-Five

Carmine

I'm proud of Fina. I know there were moments when she wanted my support, and I was happy to offer it. But I knew she didn't need it. Not really. She might have thought she did, but she's stronger than she realizes. I watched her and listened closely. Even at her angriest, her tone remained level, except for when she blurted out that we're getting married. We are, but I thought I'd at least have a chance to propose. But the rest of the time, she remained collected.

I understand now what Uncle Salvatore meant about Allegra's plan for her daughter. I saw what Allegra must have known her daughter's entire life. No one will ever easily cow Fina. She'll always fight back. She's willing to accept help and allow others to use their skills. But in the face of a threat, she won't back down. She's just like Aunt Sylvia.

I draw her away from Orlando's desk, where Lorenzo is finishing his hacking. I keep Orlando in my line of sight, but I trust Gabriele and Luca to subdue him if needed. I want a private moment with Fina.

"What do you want me to do with him? Let him go? Scare the shit out of him? Or..." I let my words trail off. She knows what I mean. She looks at her ex-boyfriend as she mulls it over.

"I don't want to act in haste and repent at leisure. But he needs to know this isn't okay. Don't take him to that place. I don't want him dead, and my father won't be able to ignore you killing his *consigliere's* grandson. Do what you have to short of that."

"Do you want him to go back to Italy?"

"Maybe... I don't know... Yes. I don't want him where I can run into him or where he can do this again."

"Consider it done. He'll be back in Italy by the day after tomorrow."

Her eyes lock with mine. She knows why he isn't leaving tomorrow. I have some convincing to do. She nods and whispers when she speaks again.

"Daddy, what about my mother? She won't give up just because this didn't work."

"I know. Fina, do you want to go to Sicily?"

"For a visit. But I don't want to live there. I've never wanted that. I've always considered myself more *Mala del Brenta*. That's who I grew up around. I know my mother's family as well as I do my father's, but Sicily was where I went for vacations as a kid. It never really felt like home. I don't feel like *Cosa Nostra* there."

"Do you feel you're part of our family here?"

"Yes. If you were Sicilian and lived there, then I would make my home there. I might consider taking on the role my mother wants me to. But my life is here with you. Olivia will one day be *la madrina* of this family, and I have no interest in usurping that. I'll help her if she wants it since she didn't grow up in this life, but I don't want to lead the women or be the one people turn to if something happens to Luca. That's not my role to have, and I'm more than okay with that. I want to be your wife, have a family with you one day, and run my businesses in that order."

"I'm as Sicilian as a New York Italian can be. I'm one of many *capos* here. If you want to move—"

"Carmine, you aren't just one of many *capos*. You're the don's nephew and have always been a leader. You haven't always led people down the right path, but your family needs you. You can't leave. I would never ask you to, and I don't want you to."

"But—"

"Daddy, you are not listening to me. I want our life here. I don't want what my mother wants."

I study her and recognize the earnest gaze I know so well. She's telling the truth. She doesn't feel like she's sacrificing to be with me, and she won't let me sacrifice my family or my role, either.

"Fina, I'm taking you back to my mom's. I'm going to ask my dad and Uncle Massimo to come over. That means Auntie Nicoletta probably will, too. If Uncle Domenico and Auntie Carlotta are free, then I want them there. Orlando is going back to his place, and I'm going to meet him there. He's going to understand that his time in America is over."

Fina shakes her head. "No. He lives with his fiancée."

"Is she American?"

"Yeah. I don't think she knows anything about *Mala del Brenta.*"

"Do you want them to stay together?"

"I don't care. If she goes with him, fine. If she doesn't, then that's just as fine."

"I'll make sure he can still talk. If they want to go together,

I'll make sure she's on that flight. I'm going to be away for a few days. That's why I'm taking you back to my mom's rather than asking for anyone to come to our place. I don't want you alone or to leave my mom's."

I can tell she wants to ask what's going to happen, but she won't. There are plenty of secrets already, and they will fill our life together with more. I don't want them when we don't have to.

"Fina, I have to deal with the Cartel, who helped your mother. Your father's going to retaliate to defend your mother. He has to, and we both know that. But they need to understand you've made your choice. I won't hurt either of your parents physically. Not unless it's to save your life. But—"

"Why did you only say to save my life?"

"Or any of my men's."

"Daddy." I know what she's getting at.

"Fina, if it's me or your father, I can't do it. I thought I could, but I can't. I won't take him from you, and you'd never be able to live with me if I did."

"I won't be able to fucking live with you if you're fucking dead." There's real anger in her voice. Her gaze darts around, and she sees what I already know. No one but Orlando is watching us, and he can't hear us.

"Daddy, I love my parents. I don't want you to kill my father. I pray to God, Mary, Jesus, all the saints. All of them it doesn't come to that. But you do not let my father or his men kill you because you fear I'll reject you. You come home to me, so we can have our happily ever after. Besides, we haven't had nearly enough kinky sex for me to let go of you."

"Is that why you want me to live? Because of my dick?"

"And what you do with it." She grins at me, and I know she needs to lighten the mood because she's overwhelmed.

"*Piccolina*, I'll tell you what. When I'm done with this, you and I are going to a club we choose together. Not the one you belonged to nor the one I belonged to. We will get there when it opens and stay until it closes. We will scene every fantasy you've ever had."

"Daddy, when you say shit like that, I can't even remember what the word vendetta means." I see the lust in her eyes, and I'm not sure if her accent just got thicker on purpose, but it's enough to distract a saint.

"Fina." She knows what she's doing to me.

"Yes, Daddy."

"You already have a spanking coming your way. I don't think you want my homecoming to start with me edging you. Let's go." I take her hand, but she digs her heels in.

"What spanking?" She more mouths the words than speaks them.

"You didn't stay behind me where I put you to make sure Orlando couldn't get to you. He had a gun, Fina. And I saw the outline of the knife in his pocket."

"He doesn't wear a gun."

"Maybe not when you were together, but I saw the imprint on the back of his chair the moment I walked up. He knew someone was coming for him. He might not consider himself Mafia anymore, but he'll always carry a knife with him."

"That I know. But I didn't notice the imprint."

"Because you didn't know what to look for. That's why I drew my gun. I didn't want to give him the chance to pull his. Fina, I won't force you to be silent while I decide everything. But if I push you behind me or out of the way, it's for your safety. That's the only reason. Otherwise, you stand beside me as my equal. Always."

"Daddy, why do you say things that make me love you even more when we're in such public places? I can't exactly blow you right now, but I would."

"Why do you insist upon saying things that make me hard? Everyone is going to know. Hush, *piccolina*. We need to go."

"Yes, Daddy."

We've lightened the mood to something tolerable for both of us, but that doesn't mean either of us has forgotten the severity of our situation. We walk back to Orlando's desk where Lorenzo, Marco, and Matteo are standing. I wave Gabriele and Luca over too.

"I want you to come to Mama's with me. I'm going to drop Fina off, and we'll wait for our uncles to get there. Uncle Salvatore's probably on the phone with Piero already, but I hope the others can come. Gabe and Luca, can you take Orlando to his place? We'll meet you there once I'm certain Fina and Mama are safe."

The guys nod, and I appreciate they listen to me without reservation these days. It wasn't always like that. So much of my bitterness has slipped away since reconciling with Luca. Now that I'm with Fina, I'm ready to let the last of it go. I don't want to be perpetually angry when she makes me so happy. I choose not to be.

We head out to the street after Marco ensures all the employees left before we started our conversation with Orlando and Allegra. He turns the cameras back on and flips the fuses, so things are back to normal. Lorenzo said he'd already hacked the security system to hide the time the cameras were off. Gabriele, Luca, and our men get into the SUV Fina arrived in. They're headed to Orlando's place with him.

It only takes twenty minutes to get to my mom's. I texted my uncles in a group thread, and they're on their way. They were together playing bocci. Of course, they were. Sometimes they act like they're all retired. A few months ago, they all came on a mission with us to deal with the fuckers messing with Olivia. They're so *not* retired.

"Mama?"

"*Sono nella mia stanza.*" I'm in my room.

Dear God, no.

She sticks her head out, and I see the basket of laundry in her arms. Thank you, Sweet Baby J. Blessedly, I've never walked into either of my parents' home and interrupted anything. I certainly didn't want the first time to be with Fina. Never mind, Lorenzo, Marco, and Matteo being with us.

"Mama, Uncle Massimo, Uncle Domenico, and Papa are coming over. I need them to stay with you, Fina, Auntie Nicoletta, and Auntie Carlotta. I have to take care of some things for a couple days."

My mother darts her gaze between Fina and me before she nods. "Do you want to eat before you go? I made a pot of *pasta con le sarde* for dinner." Pasta with sardines.

It's delicious, and it tempts part of me to take it and make Orlando watch us all eat in front of him while he's hog-tied as his dining room table's centerpiece.

"No thanks, Mama. You have it."

She disappears into her room for a moment, then reappears empty handed. I walk over and kiss her cheek as I give her a hug. I hear my cousins and Matteo grumbling about being hungry and wishing I hadn't said no. Mama does, too.

"Make yourselves dinner you can take with you. Cesare came over earlier with cold cuts from the kosher deli."

"Are you giving away that pastrami I asked for?"

"Carmine, share with your cousins."

She chides me, and she includes Matteo since he's technically our third cousin or second cousin twice removed. Or something. His dad is Mama's second cousin. We've always called him Uncle Domenico because Second Cousin Once Removed Domenico is ridiculous. Matteo calls my mom Auntie Paola and my dad Uncle Cesare. It works both ways.

The guys hurry into the kitchen, not having to be told twice. Fina nudges me. "Go with them. Get something to eat while you can."

I hesitate. I don't want to spend a moment away from Fina that I don't have to. It could be three or four days before I see her again. Mama tsks.

"Sera, go with my son before he leaves hungry."

Fina giggles and tugs my hand. We're all in the kitchen, devouring sandwiches when the aunts and uncles arrive. I watch my parents, and I still marvel how well they get along now. Papa kisses Mama's temple as he walks past. I know they won't reconcile, and we're all fine with that. It's just nice to be in a peaceful home with them. The women leave us while we finish eating. It's so we can talk.

"We're headed to Fina's ex-boyfriend's place. It's been her mom all along. She worked with Alejandro to fuck things up. She got Orlando to steal money from Fina's accounts. We're going to make sure Orlando understands he's not welcome in New York. He's also going to understand that when I tell him to jump, he's going to ask how high. He's going to be our newest informant. This might have been Allegra's doing, but I'm unconvinced Piero didn't know at least some of it. Orlando's going to make sure we know all of it."

Orlando may not know he's about to become a snitch, but that's the only way he'll live. If he refuses, then he won't make any more decisions. I'll kill him. Uncle Domenico speaks as he pours wine for everyone staying at the house.

"Then what?"

I shrug. "Then we move on to Alejandro. I have some ideas. Considering how pissed Joaquin was when Matteo stole his Porsche 911, crashed it, then got it impounded, I can imagine how pissed Alejandro's going to be when I fuck up his favorite toy."

I'm going to do a better job this time than the last time I attempted this kind of revenge. If Orlando doesn't cooperate, I'll kill two birds with one stone. I know everyone in the kitchen understands what I mean. I'll make some calls in the car to get the ball rolling, to make sure my plan really takes off. I chuckle to myself. Poor pun, but funny to me.

We finish our snack—three massive sandwiches each—then head to the living room, so we can say goodbye to our parents. I draw Fina aside after I kiss my mom and dad, giving them each a tight hug.

"Fina, I'll give Orlando the choice. He goes back to Venice and does what I tell him to whenever I tell him to do it. Or it's over. Can you live with that?"

"Yes." We watch each other, and I pray she'll be saying the same thing when this ends. "Carmine, he could have kept his hands clean. He went against the Mancinellis by using me to target you. Even if we weren't together, and you weren't the one leading this, *Zio* Salvatore would do something on my behalf. You'd be just as up to your eyeballs in it as you are now."

"But it's a shit ton different when your uncle-in-law orders a hit on your ex-boyfriend rather than your current boyfriend taking out your old one."

Fina looks back over her shoulder before stepping closer to me and whispering. "Daddy, I understand why you're scared to put me in the middle. Most daughters would probably pick their parents and relatives over a boyfriend. But I know you won't act out of anger. There's too much at stake way beyond just me. If it comes to you killing anyone, I know it's because there's no other choice. Death has surrounded me my entire life. Men have died by my father's and grandfathers' orders for much lesser things. I know the only reason Orlando's still breathing right now is because it frightens you that I won't forgive you. When I saw him, it wasn't like I looked at a man I spent six years with. He could have been a stranger. I didn't have any nostalgia or any feelings of regret. I didn't suddenly miss him. Even when most of my anger calmed. Maybe I am my mother's daughter like she believes. Carmine, kill him if you have to."

She doesn't blink with the last sentence. If she were a don, she would have just ordered Orlando's death. I won't put her on the spot and ask her if that's what she really wants. I won't make her say aloud that she wants him dead. That'll make it too real, and she'll have to live with the guilt if it comes to that. She added the qualifier "if you have to." Her mind needs the justification to live with her endorsement. I get it.

"Only if I must, Fina. It won't be to get rid of a rival or out of jealousy about your past with him."

"I know, Daddy."

"I want to handle Alejandro personally, and depending on how Orlando acts, he might be part of it."

Marco leans forward as he speaks. "What are you going to do to Alejandro?"

"His ass is going to be flying commercial from now on."

Everyone in the car laughs since we all know what a fucking snob the *stronzo*—asshole—has become. The only place he fucking goes is Bogota, so I don't know what there's to be a snob about there. But I guess he likes to travel in comfort before he sweats his balls off there. He bought his own jet. Enrique has one that the entire family uses, just like we have one for everyone. Alejandro claims he travels too often to tie up the family one. Not true. He probably has fucking orgies on there.

The shithead is more of a man whore than I ever was. I just kept up appearances.

"If Orlando doesn't cooperate, then he might wind up just like the plane."

Matteo frowns. "If it comes to that, will you consider that striking back at the *Mala del Brenta?*"

"Hardly. Allegra acted on behalf of her family, but there's no way Piero didn't know. But Allegra is family, even if it's through marriage and not our blood. I have to be careful because I don't want Aunt Sylvia caught in the middle between the family she came from and the family she married into. We need our alliance in Palermo with Aunt Sylvia and Allegra's family. I can justify reacting on Fina's behalf, but the fact that it's any of us doing it will piss people off."

Once we're there, Orlando's apartment soon feels crowded with the five of us standing in the living room. When we arrive, Orlando has his hands zip tied behind his back and a gag in his mouth while kneeling in a corner. He knows we're here, but he doesn't hear me approach. He howls when I grab a handful of hair and slam his face into the wall. I do it three times, hard enough that blood drips from his nose. I yank the gag from his mouth.

"Did you do it to get back at Serafina or because you don't have the balls to tell Allegra no?"

He remains silent, so I pull my knife and flick it open. I put it to the corner of his eye.

"I'd answer if I were you." He remains silent. My laugh has no mirth. "Now you find your balls, *faccia de cazzo?*" Testicle face.

Seems like a fitting name. I know the moment he's about to spit at me as he turns his head. I slam my fist into his right eye, pulling my knife away in time not to impale him with it. He snarls at me.

"*Stanna mabaych.*" Son of a bitch.

"I'd watch how you talk about my mother. I'm overprotective. Did you do this because you're mad that Serafina left you or because Allegra scares you? Or is it both?"

His nostrils flare, causing more blood to flow from his nose.

"So, it's both. You're engaged. Why do you still care that Serafina ended things? Shouldn't that be a blessing since you found the true love of your life?" My tone is nothing short of snide.

"Fuck her."

I lean forward to whisper. "I am, and she loves it. Everything she wanted from you that you couldn't man up and do, she gets from me. Multiple times a day and all fucking night. She would never marry you. Even if you could fuck worth a damn. She was always going to honor that contract. She just gets a way better lover out of it than she expected. The feel of her when I'm balls deep inside her tight little pussy...She's always been mine."

Fina will kill me if she ever finds out what I'm saying.

"You can have her. She's a fat whore now. I wouldn't want her even if she climbed on my dick or sucked me off. She's good at that too."

"Not a good choice, Orlando."

He said it loud enough for the others to hear. Even if he hadn't, I'd still do the same thing. I cut a deep x diagonally from each nostril to his chin. If I let him live, he'll have the scars running across his mouth until he dies. When he returns to his family in Venice, everyone—Mafia and not—will know I've marked him a liar. I lean forward again and whisper to him.

"You sound like a jealous *chooch.*" Jackass. "If you were really over her, you wouldn't care who she's fucking. I saw the photo of your fiancée on the wall. She looks just like Serafina. Her hair, her face, her body. You imagine it's Serafina while you're fucking her. Have you called her Sera? Does she get off when you do?"

He bares his teeth at me like a snarling dog. His nostrils flare yet again, allowing more blood to drip from them, and his lips bleed. I'm almost impressed that he took that without screaming. He's just a bitch, not a little bitch.

"We are going to be your guests until tomorrow morning. If I don't kill you before that, you're going to board a plane to Venice. You're going to stay there. You're going to answer all my calls and texts. You're going to tell me exactly what I want to know. If you don't, I'll kill your mother. Then I'll go after your sister. Then I'll go after your father and brother. Finally, I'll go after the pretty little fiancée you wish was Sera. I will make sure you attend every funeral, and you live with that shame and guilt. They could all stay alive if you cooperate."

"*Ffangul.*" Go fuck yourself.

"Are you refusing?"

"You can have the cunt. You won't touch my family."

I laugh and so do the others. He may know I won't touch the women, but I'll fucking torture the shit out of his brother and father. I'll make him watch too. We continue in Italian, even though his English is perfect.

"Looks like I'm due for a trip to Venice. It's been years. I suppose it's as good a time as any before the city drowns."

"My family will kill you on sight."

"No, they won't. You aren't the don's family. Your grandfather is only the *consigliere*. He can't order a hit on another don's nephew. Definitely not one related to *la madrina*."

Orlando scoffs and looks down his nose at me. "Related. Through her sister's marriage to your uncle. She doesn't consider you related."

"She doesn't have to consider shit. It's what everyone else will think. She used her daughter to go after Don Mancinelli."

"She didn't go after him. She went after you."

"For fuck's sake. Serafina didn't dump you because you suck in bed. You're fucking stupid. An attack on me *is* an attack on Don Mancinelli. You are up to your eyeballs in this shit. If you want to avoid a war, then own what the fuck you did and work for me. Otherwise, not only will I take everything from you, I'll fucking scream from the rooftops who you worked for."

He's not going to cooperate. I can already see it. Fine. I'm over this already. He's going to die. It's the only option because I can't just let him go. I could take everything he loves, but it won't matter if he won't follow my orders. He'll always be a loose end, and I don't like those.

"*Fottiti.*" Screw you.

I'm done going back and forth as he curses at me. I lean forward once more. "No thanks. I have Fina for that. Your time and your choices are up." I turn to my cousins and friends as I pull out my phone. "Fuck up all the shit that's his. Leave his fiancée's crap. She didn't do anything. I have some calls to make."

I put my phone to my ear and listen to it ring. My guy answers on the third ring.

"I have a job for you. Same one as before, but better this time. One passenger again. All off the record. No log of takeoff tonight." The guy on the other end just hums his agreement. "I'll give you all the other details when we're at the airfield."

I give him the address to the private airport where Alejandro keeps his jet. Such a shame he won't be able to file an insurance claim on this.

"Before I forget, wear some warm clothes under your jump suit. Greenland's cold."

I hang up and look around. The guys trashed the place. We need to go before anyone comes to investigate the noise. I nod toward the door. Gabriele and Luca pull Orlando to his feet.

The rest of us watch them walk him to the trash room. Luca and Gabriele will wait until we call up to them from the basement. Then Orlando is coming down the trash shoot. We can't afford anyone seeing him in the elevator or on the stairs. Lorenzo's been jamming the hallway surveillance cameras since we arrived.

As Lorenzo, Marco, Matteo, and I head down to the basement by stairs, I text our regular pilot and tell him to head to the airfield where we keep our family jet. Luca has a couple of houses in the Bronx that he owns as rental properties. One of them is vacant since we often use it as a safe house. We'll head there first because all the supplies I need are already in the basement. The other guys will keep Orlando company while I do a little building. I need to concentrate so nothing goes boom too soon. Once my bomb is ready, Gabriele and I will take Orlando to Alejandro's plane. We hear Orlando scream as he plummets down the trash shoot and winds up in the industrial dumpster. I'm impatient for him to climb out, so I snap at him.

"Get up."

Once we're all in the car, Luca leans forward to speak to Giuseppe, but he looks back at me. "The Bronx?"

"That's what I was hoping. You still have everything I need in the basement, right?"

"Yeah. Livy never noticed. Or if she did, she never asked."

Luca and Olivia had to hide there early in their relationship when the Mexican Culiacán Cartel was after her. We keep a lot of shit in that house when Luca isn't renting it. It's been a while, so I don't think he's going to list it any time soon. It's been too convenient for us. All four of the major syndicates have a presence in all five boroughs, but none of us brag about being in the Bronx or on Staten Island. That makes Luca's place a great stash spot.

"I'll need about an hour to work."

Luca gives Giuseppe instructions, not that our experienced driver really needs it. I sit back as best I can as I run through my head how I'm going to build the bomb. When I took out Liam O'Rourke, I just had the same pilot I'm using today jump. I let aeronautics handle the rest. The plane crashed, but way too much evidence remained despite having our clean-up crew go to the site. This time, there will be nothing left. Gabriele stands next to me when we get to the bottom of the safe house's basement stairs.

"Do you need help with anything?"

"I don't think so. I just need to concentrate. When this is done, will you come with me to drop him off?"

"Of course."

I knew his answer, but I'm trying to get better about asking people rather than just issuing orders. At least get better with the people who matter most to me—my family and Fina. Our men? They'll do what the fuck they're told when the fuck they're told to do it. I watch the others take Orlando into one of two rooms I'm certain Olivia never went into.

Everything the guys need to make Orlando uncomfortable is in one. Gabriele and I go into the other. My best friend watches as I tinker. Majoring in structural engineering came with more than one lesson in demolition. I doubt any of my professors thought they were teaching me to build bombs. Let's see what that Top Tier education got me. Time to make things go kaboom.

Chapter Twenty-Six

Fina

I'm helping Paola and Cesare make dinner while the others are in the backyard playing bocci. I guess the guys were in the middle of a game when Carmine asked them to come over. I can hear their laughter through an open window. It sounds like Nicoletta and Carlotta are trouncing Massimo and Domenico. As I watch my future parents-in-law, I marvel at their relationship. You'd think they were blissfully married from how well they work together.

You'd never guess Cesare doesn't live here, considering his familiarity with Paola's kitchen. They banter and include me in their conversation. Carmine told me they will never reconcile, and they're only like this because they don't have to see each other every day. Whatever the reason, I'm glad these are the parents and dynamic that greet him nowadays.

I feel my phone vibrate in my pocket, so I lower the mixing spoon, propping it against the side of the bowl. I'm making *torta della nonna*—grandmother cake—a cream tart covered with pine nuts and powdered sugar. I've already made the dough; I'm in the middle of making the filling. When I see the name on the screen, I want to groan.

"It's my mother."

Cesare and Paola freeze, then Cesare rushes out of the kitchen. I assume he's going to get Massimo and Domenico. Paola comes to stand beside me.

"Stall until they get back."

I answer it on speakerphone, so my mom doesn't notice any difference in sound when the men come back. I know they'll be silent.

"*Salve, mamma.*" Hello, Mama.

This can't possibly go well. My mom responds in Italian, and I can tell this won't be a short conversation.

"Serafina, where are you?"

I debate how to answer this. Paola nods her head and points downward. "I'm at Paola's."

"With Carmine?"

I watch Paola, and she shakes her head. "No. He's out right now."

"Killing Orlando?"

"I don't know."

"Serafina, you're going to let that bastard kill an innocent man."

I snort. My temper takes little to spike right now. It wasn't a question but a statement, as though it's a foregone conclusion. "He's not innocent. He used his position as the bank manager to steal from me. Something you put him up to."

"For your own good. Carmine's been snooping around your money. He was going to take it."

"Take it? He's richer than me at least ten times over, and that's from his businesses. It has nothing to do with the *Cosa Nostra.*"

"Not because he needs the cash. He needs it to control you. He was going to force you to stay with him, make you completely reliant on him."

"He doesn't need to force me to stay, Mama. I'm where I want to be. He knows that. He has no reason to do anything because I'm not going anywhere."

"He's brainwashed you."

"Do you know how ridiculous you sound? I know why you did it."

"To protect you. To make sure you aren't trapped."

"You're the only one trapping me. You took my money to force me to return to Italy. You don't get it. I could be dirt poor, and Carmine would step in and take care of me. He'd offer, not demand."

It's true. He might be possessive as fuck in the bedroom, and I love it. He might insist upon certain details for my protection. But he won't force me to be with him. That's one thing he's been clear about from the beginning. He's given me so many outs that it pisses me off. I don't want out. I want him to stop fearing I'll reject him and accept that I'm going nowhere. I fucked up more than once, and I get I caused a lot of this. But it goes so much deeper. I want him to understand he's more than good enough for me, and that's why I love him.

"I'm certain he demanded you live together. I'm certain he demanded you stay with Paola."

"You're certain? Are you bugging us?"

There's a second's hesitation, and I know what's coming next is a lie. "I don't have to. I know him. I've known him since you were children, long before Sylvia married Salvatore. You broke his nose because he was the same back then as he is now. Conceited and childish. He's a spoiled only child who's always gotten what he wants."

I watch Paola as my mom rants. She appears completely

unfazed as my mom insults her son and her parenting. The others join us just as my mom finishes speaking. I shift my gaze to Cesare. He doesn't look surprised. No one does. Are they just that stoic? Or are they used to people talking about Carmine like this? Worse, do Domenico, Massimo, Carlotta, and Nicoletta agree?

"How do you know so much, Mama? Are you having him followed? Am I being followed? Are you hacking his emails and phone? Are you digging into Mancinelli business?"

She remains silent, and I'm certain she knows I'm not alone. She won't answer any of those questions. It surprises me when she asks her own as we continue in Italian.

"Paola, Cesare, I'm certain you're there. You screw each other more now than you ever did while you lived together. Are you going to stop your son?"

My eyes widen, and I fear they might land on the island in front of me. I look at each of them, but their faces remain completely neutral. Paola's gaze meets mine. She rolls her eyes and shakes her head, but otherwise, she's expressionless.

My head whips around at the sound of a new voice.

"*Allegra, basta.*" Allegra, enough.

Sylvia's expression tells me everything. She's pissed. Like, super pissed. I've heard and seen my mom and aunt argue before. It's amazing they love each other as much as they do because you'd never guess when they fight. It's gloves off, bareknuckle. They never hit below the belt, but their words cut deep. It's no better this time as they argue in Italian.

"You always like to put yourself in the middle, Sylvia."

"Mama and Papa did that by having me second. You kept me there when you argued with Sophia."

I wince. My dead aunt is still a sore subject for my mom. All three sisters were extremely close, despite how they bickered and how marriage took them to different places. My mom was in the middle of getting her roots done when *Zia* Sophia called for help. My mom sent it to voicemail. She's never forgiven herself. She let herself go gray because she refuses to step inside a hair salon. The guilt overwhelms her.

"This is between my daughter and me."

"No. It's between you and my niece *and* nephew. You stuck me in the middle quite literally since it involves both of my families. Now you're going to hear what I have to say."

"You don't have to get involved. Serafina, take me off speakerphone."

I blow out a breath before continuing in Italian. This is so fucking uncomfortable. "No, Mama. You've dragged the Mancinellis into this. You know their family is just like ours, on your side and Papa's. You go after one, you go after them all. It's better they hear what you say straight from you rather than my version."

"The only version of this is you coming back to Italy then going to Sicily. Salvatore broke the contract, and that opened the door for a new one. There's someone I'd like you to meet."

Like me to meet? Fuck no. I know exactly what that means. "I'm over twenty-one, Mama. You can't force me to marry anyone."

I look around again, and every face now has a tight expression. I rest my gaze on *Zia* Sylvia. I know what I said isn't true. She was in her late twenties when she entered an arranged marriage with *Zio* Salvatore. No one asked her opinion or gave her a choice. She got lucky, though. My *nonno* and *nonna* knew they'd be good together, and they knew *zio* would make her happy. It was obvious my aunt and uncle were halfway in love by the wedding, and they'd only met a couple weeks earlier. I doubt I have the same luck.

"You will do what's best for your family."

I've heard that so many times that it's tattooed on my brain.

I went out with Orlando the first time because my father wanted to strengthen his relationship with his *consigliere*. Never mind, he'd been best friends with the man's son since they were eight. They wanted a second generation to solidify the bond. I fell for Orlando, so it never felt onerous. I still believe I loved him, but it doesn't feel the same as with Carmine. I'm certain my parents will argue I'm merely infatuated, but Carmine fills the gaping holes Orlando never did. He doesn't leave me wondering if I'll find someone who can fill them. He already does.

"For a decade, our family thought me marrying Carmine was what was best. Whether it was to strengthen our alliance or merely to not spend the money to buy us out of the contract. *Zio* Salvatore ended the arrangement, not our family. You would have let it stand."

"We would have paid the penalty when you married Orlando or Elio."

My heart pounds. "Elio Lombardo?"

"Yes."

"No. Absolutely not. I'm not going near that swine." I temper my comment because I'm talking to my mom and because of the others in the room. I have plenty more to say.

"Serafina, we're sending the plane. You will be on it tomorrow morning. The engagement party is a week from now."

"Did you sign a contract already?"

"No, but we—"

"Then end this, Mama. Now. I will not marry Elio, and I will not enter that family. Never."

"Serafina—"

"They ordered the hit on *Zia* Sophia."

Mama and *Zia* Sylvia make identical whimpering sounds. I see the tears well in my aunt's eyes, but there's fire there, too. I close mine because both come from pain that's never healed for my aunt and my mom. I can't look, or I'll burst into tears.

"I have a confession to make. Carmine already knows this. I took out the men who did it. I was in Sicily when it happened. I sneaked out one night. I took from them and their families what they took from ours. I overheard everything at a nightclub. The Randazzos arranged it, but the Lombardos paid for it."

My mom's strangled voice comes through the phone. "Why didn't you tell anyone?"

"Because our family was already at war with the Lombardos, and the focus needed to be on the Randazzos. *Nonno'd* already wiped out most of Elio's family. You know he only spared Elio and Elisabetta because Elio hadn't risen in the ranks yet, and Elisabetta's a woman. *Nonno* thought he could control Elio, and he did. But Elio is as bad as the men who attacked *Zia* Sophia. He learned from *Nonno* and will put all those lessons to use to get back at our family, Mama. I know women he's hurt. Elisabetta's his cousin, and he's assaulted her to manipulate her. He will never touch me and live. I've killed men before. I'll look him straight in the eye when I kill him. Then there really will be a war."

I don't even want to bring up Carmine going berserk over this. There is no way he'll let me marry someone else if I don't want to. This is a dumpster fire waiting to explode. I'm glad he's not here for this conversation. I'm going to tell him everything, but hopefully not for a few days. I need to get my mother to change her mind, and I need to let Carmine finish what he's doing.

"Serafina, the decision's made."

We all turn as the front door bursts open. Cesare, Massimo, and Domenico pull their guns. Paola knocks me to the floor, the island shielding us. Nicoletta and Carlotta scramble beside us. I know the men fire shots because I hear the bullets hitting things. The silencers on the men's guns give nothing else away. I can't tell how close the intruders are, and no one's making a sound. I don't hear screams of pain or orders given.

Movement near me makes me look at the other women. Paola's reaching above her head into a drawer and feeling around for something. I'm unprepared for her to pull out a pistol. She hands it to Nicoletta, who peers around the cabinet she's hiding against. Carlotta crawls to the pantry and opens the door just far enough to reach inside. Next thing I know, she has a rifle. *Zia* Sylvia has a handgun in the purse she carries. There's no doubt all the guns are fully loaded and ready to fire.

I don't know why any of this surprises me. Not the hidden guns in a home where a Mafia woman lives alone. Not in the home of a Mafia don's and *consigliere's* sister. Not in the home of a *capo's* estranged wife. Not in the home of a *capo's* mother.

My purse is upstairs. Otherwise, I'd have a gun too. I didn't always carry it before dating Carmine, but he insists now. This is why.

I grabbed my phone as Paola pushed me out of the line of fire. "Mama, what have you done?"

"What I had to."

"Your sister is here. I'm here. Do you want us both killed?"

"Go with the men, Serafina. You're the one who'll cause their deaths. Refusing means it'll all be on your shoulders."

"*Mama.*" This is a fucking nightmare. It's pure anguish that fills my voice. I raise my hands as I waddle to the end of the island. "*Fermatevi. Vado io.*" Stop. I'll go.

"Sera."

I don't look at *Zia* Sylvia. "Carmine will get me. I know he will. I can wait as long as it takes."

I ease upright until I can look around. Massimo and Domenico stand on opposite sides of the kitchen entrance, using the walls to shield them. Cesare flipped the kitchen table and uses that to protect him.

"Adriano? Nicholas?"

Neither answer, but Nicholas winks. My mind can't process it. I look down at the phone in my hand as my mother speaks again. I'm so stunned to see my bodyguards that I forgot my mom was still on the phone.

"Go with them. They'll take you to a hotel then to the airport."

"Mama, does Papa know about all of this?"

"Of course. He wrote the contract for Elio and is sending the plane. We're already allied with the Mancinellis." I snort. I doubt that's the case anymore. "The Carosis need the alliance with the Lombardos just as much as our family in Sicily does. You will not mess this up, Serafina. You will not waste yourself with a lowlife like Carmine Mancinelli. You will be *la madrina* to two families."

I don't want to be The Godmother to any family.

"Goodbye, Mama."

I hang up. I can't handle hearing her voice anymore. The moment I shove the phone into my back pocket, Adriano and Nicholas lower their guns. I spot Gio and David behind them and off to the side. I can't believe David was in a gunfight with a broken arm. What the motherfucking fuck? Gio raises his hands and steps forward.

"Ms. Carosi, we're taking you to Carmine."

"But my mother—"

"We know Elio. Your father tasked us with protecting you. That means you go nowhere near Elio Lombardo. Besides, Carmine scares the shit out of us way more than your father ever did." Gio grins before he shifts his gaze to my future father-in-law. "Thanks for noticing we weren't actually shooting at you. None of us were sure we'd survive this shitshow."

I swing my gaze to Cesare, then to Domenico, and finally Massimo. They've all holstered their guns, and they nod. None of them are related by blood, but they're in sync. David speaks next, and it makes me smile too.

"Mrs. Mancinelli, are you all right?"

Three voices answer as the women rise. "Yes."

Paola looks around her kitchen. Her lips tighten into a pucker, and her eyes narrow. No Catholic school nun has ever sounded more disapproving than when she speaks. "You couldn't just shoot the same tile in the floor? Look at the mess you boys made."

Despite my men sounding easygoing and no one in my future family attacking them, the tension still runs high. When I walk toward my guards, Cesare steps in front of me.

"Take Ms. Carosi *and* me to my son." He doesn't trust them, and I can't blame him. I realize I no longer trust my guards implicitly.

"Does Carmine know you came here?" I look straight at David, since I know Carmine trusts him the most.

"Yes. You can call him."

Speak of the devil. My phone vibrates, and it's him. "Carmine?"

"*Piccolina*, are you all right?"

"Yes. Shaken, but all right. So's everyone else."

"Go with your men. I'll be there soon."

"Carmine?"

"Yes, little one."

I rush past the men and bolt to the half bathroom. I lock myself in. "Daddy, I'm scared."

"I know. I keep telling you this will end, and I've failed over and over. But this is the last straw."

"Can we go to the courthouse and get married today?"

"Fina, I don't want you to feel rushed just because things are unstable right now."

"Does all of this make it feel more urgent? Of course. But this is what I've wanted since our first night together. I want you and the rest of the world to know I'm not going anywhere without you. I'm yours, Daddy. You told me so, and I agreed."

"You are mine, *piccolina*. Meet me at the courthouse. My family will go with you. I'm already texting them. The guys are with me, and everyone else will meet us there."

"Daddy?"

"Yes, baby."

"I love you."

"I love you, too."

I stare at the phone after we hang up. I'm getting married today. Once my parents find out, will my groom live long enough to go on our honeymoon?

Chapter Twenty-Seven

Carmine

We're at the airfield, and we're watching Alejandro's jet take off. Orlando is aboard. He was bound and gagged when my men prodded him up the stairs, but I made sure the gag was removed. Let him beg. I was tempted to beat him unconscious, but I want to be sure he's awake and coherent for what's about to happen. With Orlando tied to the seat, he can do nothing when the pilot jumps.

It's an almost six-hour flight from New York to Greenland. It'll be a little less than six hours to Nuuk, but they aren't landing there. It's another two hours north to the spot I picked. More than eighty percent of the country is uninhabitable. Between that and the bomb that's set to detonate on impact, there will be nothing left for anyone to find.

One of our pilots is already halfway to Greenland in the Mancinelli jet. I have a team aboard our jet who will snow mobile out to get the pilot from Alejandro's plane. The spot I picked is remote enough that no one lives there, but I ensured it's possible for snow mobiles to reach it. I'm relying on the autopilot to do the work once the pilot is gone. The guy assured me he could set a course that would correct for what'll happen once the door opens. Even if the system doesn't, the plane will explode the moment it hits the mountain face or the ground.

The key is the pilot not waiting too long to jump and doing it over the landing zone I picked. If he fucks around and messes up, he's liable to die in an avalanche. There's still so much that could go wrong, but I have to believe it will go right. I mounted the camera myself, so I'll have a real time feed that I can send to Alejandro when this is done. He'll know the plane is missing before the crash happens, which makes this all the better. I'll let him see his precious toy explode in real time.

"I need to stop at my place to get something."

It's a flawless four-carat diamond with an antique style fila-gree that holds smaller diamonds halfway around the band. There's an eternity wedding band and a thin yellow gold band in the slot behind the engagement ring. Fina told me what style she likes while we were in bed one night. This is likely bigger than she envisioned. I know she won't measure how much I love her by how big the diamond is. And it's not like I need a satellite to see her ring in space to brand her as mine. But I spotted the stone, and I knew it would fit in what I pictured. I recognize neither ring will be practical for her work, so I got the plain gold band for her to wear to the bakery. I hope she approves of all three. Lorenzo joins me in my office.

"Are you nervous, Car?"

"No. It's the only major life event where I've been totally calm going into it. It's more than calm. I actually feel peaceful. I don't know that I've ever felt like this before."

"How'd you know Sera was the one for you?"

"She's the only woman I've ever wanted to know me. I

knew immediately that I couldn't keep my past from her, and as terrifying as it was to tell her, somehow I knew she wouldn't reject me." I shrug. "She fills the holes in my life. The things I want and the things I didn't know I want—she's all of it. I still worry this life will drive her away, but I know she loves me."

"This life is what she's known since she was born."

"And she left it for nine years."

"You heard David when he called to tell you they were bringing Sera to you. Her parents never planned for her to live a normal life in New York. Either she would have married you because the *nonnos* decided it, or she would have married Orlando and gone back to Venice to the *Mala del Brenta*. Allegra believes she'll go to Sicily for Elio and the *Cosa Nostra*. She was never going to escape being a Mafia princess. But she's marrying a man she loves and who loves her. Elio isn't capable of love. And Orlando might have loved her, but she never loved him the way she does you. She's much better off making a life with you than with anyone else. But the Mafia would never let her go. It never lets any of us go."

Lorenzo is right. People get out of the Mafia, or so they say. But they can never undo the things they did, and they can never change what their family was and continues to be. The other syndicates don't recognize time outs or people taking their toys and going home. Once a Made Man or an associate, there's no going back.

It surprised me that Orlando's family allowed him to stay in America for so long, even to marry an American. He must have been truly useless. Piero and Allegra would have agreed to Fina marrying him because of his family connections, but they also would have eventually forced them back to Italy. As the *consigliere's* grandson, he's a Made Man. And that's why he's about to die.

Once I have the ring, we head to the underground parking

garage. Luca ordered another SUV, so there are two to meet us. Much more comfortable. I'd rather have Fina in a car alone with me after the ceremony, but her safety is more important. I don't trust Allegra or Piero not to send men to check that Fina's guards followed orders.

I recognize her immediately, but I don't recognize the dress. She's gorgeous in one of my t-shirts or button downs. She's gorgeous in leggings and a sweater. She steals my breath in the cream-colored knee-length dress. She's wearing her hair down, and I can't wait until I can run my fingers through it, grasp a fistful and kiss her the way we both want. But for now, I settle for a kiss on her cheek as I slide my right arm around her waist.

"I already filled out as much of the paperwork as I can. There are a couple places I need you to add some information and for you to sign."

She doesn't know things like my Social Security Number yet. I fill in the blanks and sign with a flourish. She laughs at me before taking the pen back. We walk up to the counter and hand everything in. Then it's a matter of waiting our turn. I look around, and there's not a private corner in site. But I draw her over to a window, and the sunlight makes her already translucent gray eyes shimmer like cool steel.

"Daddy?" She keeps her voice to a whisper.

"*Piccolina*, I can't think straight right now. You're stunning. You're here."

She grins. "Of course, I'm here. I proposed to you."

"About that." I infuse authority into my voice, even though I'm whispering too. I watch the lust flair in her eyes as she leans toward me. My arm wraps around her again, and I pull her tight against me. "Fina, I'm glad you told me you want to get married. As long as you aren't disappointed by not having a romantic proposal, then I'm not bothered. But we are going out somewhere tonight, and you will absolutely remember who leads."

"In this marriage or in bed, Carmine?"

"Sex. Since when do we limit it to just a bed? There are some things outside of our intimacy where I must lead. It's the only way for us and for our families to survive. But whenever it's possible, you will always be my equal in our marriage. And you know that while I might be the dominant one during sex, you're the one who ultimately holds all the power, Fina. You decide what we do and don't do, and everything I do is for you."

She's pinned in place by my penetrating stare, and I get the sense there's nowhere else she'd rather be.

"I don't hold all the power, Daddy. I don't want to. I enjoy knowing we're equals in everything. Where are we going tonight?"

"That's a surprise. I wish I could whisk you away on a honeymoon as soon as the ceremony is over, but there are a couple more things for me to finish first. However, tonight is ours. We'll still do something special after our wedding Mass, but this is still our wedding day."

"We're getting married again in a church?"

"Absolutely. Fina, this ceremony tells the world you are mine in the eyes of the law. A church ceremony tells the world you are mine in the eyes of God. Your parents can push for an annulment of a civil marriage, but they won't be able to push for us to annul a consummated marriage ordained by a priest."

Her brow crinkles and worry flashes through her eyes. "Daddy, no one is taking me from you. You've already told me how you feel about divorce and children. I feel the same. Whether it's a Justice of the Peace or a priest, the moment we say our vows and sign the register, we're married for good. You will be mine under the law and God."

"And I can't wait, Fina. I am yours. I have been and always will be. There'll be no one else ever. It's you or nothing. I love you."

"I love you, Carmine. Always."

The civil ceremony is over within fifteen minutes, and I savor kissing *my wife*.

"Come on, *piccolina*. Our family would like to congratulate us."

Uncle Salvatore arrived while Fina and I were talking, so I'm thrilled that everyone was there. I notice Olivia standing next to Luca, and I didn't think Maria would join us because I knew she had a shift at the hospital where she's a radiologist. But I beam at her when I turn around and spot her between Marco and Matteo. My cousin's best friend is peering down at her, and she's gazing up at him. I narrow my eyes, and Marco's head swings around. Matteo and Maria look forward, wearing matching scowls directed at me.

"Carmine, duh. Leave them alone."

I glance down at Fina. What the fuck does that mean? My wife reads my mind.

"I'll explain later if I remember. I expect you to make my mind go blank a few times tonight."

"Fear not, wife."

"Mmm, husband. I like that."

I lean over to whisper in her ear. "There are plenty of other things Daddy's going to do that you like. We'll have an early dinner with everyone then go back to our place. I'm going to ask David and Gio to accompany us tonight."

We head to Donatelli's, Uncle Salvatore's favorite restaurant, and we soon have overflowing family-style dishes in front of us. Our peace is shattered a moment later when nine phones ping. All the men look at the text.

MISHA

Since none of you got around to holding up your end of the deal we took care of it. As usual.

Attached is a gruesome photo of Yuri Preobrazhensky, at least what's left of him. It's taken in an empty room with white walls, so no way for us to identify the location. It could be in the U.S. or Russia or Albania for all we know. The body is lying on the floor with all the fingers and toes severed but near their rightful extremity. I zoom in, careful to hold my phone so Fina can't see it.

His nails are missing from every finger and toe. Someone castrated him, but I'm fairly certain that happened years ago. Bruises mottle his naked body, and there are knife wounds that surely gushed when they were fresh. His face is nearly unrecognizable from the battering it took. Despite all of this, what's most noticeable is the gaping hole through his chest. There's a matching one between his eyes.

I can only imagine how many days the Ivankov bratva held Yuri captive while they did this. It actually surprises me how tame this appears compared to what I'm certain each member could do. The four Kutsenko brothers and their four cousins are as fucked up as they come. While *Tres J's* are certifiable, the Kutsenkos are pathological.

They premeditate every move they make. After all, a raving psychopath trained them. The man ensured all of them were as fucked up as he was by the time they each hit twenty. Bogdan's my age, and he started his training at eleven when they arrived in America. It wasn't by choice, but they were quick learners.

MISHA

Besnik is ours from now on. He does business with only us. It's the price you pay for not handling it.

I shove my phone in my pocket and kiss Fina's temple. Right now, all I want to do is finish this meal, take Fina back to our place to get changed, then head out to fulfill every one of my wife's fantasies.

Chapter Twenty-Eight

Fina

"Carmine, I have to call Juliana. I have to tell her we got married. She's going to be so hurt that I didn't include her, especially when she finds out we had a family celebration afterwards. I love my sister, and she was my best friend before I met you. But she's as loyal to my parents as she is to me. She would have tried to talk me out of it, then she would have called Mama. I couldn't let that happen."

Carmine pulls me into his arms as we stand inside our living room. It's been days since we've been here, and it's nice to be back. I don't know if it's just for tonight, so we can have a private wedding night or for good now that we know who's behind all this. He presses a gentle kiss to my lips, not allowing me to take it further when my tongue flicks his lips. Instead, he takes my hand and leads me to the sofa.

Normally, he never sits before I do. But when he does, I always know he's going to pull me onto his lap. I like it when he maneuvers me to where we both want me to be. His hand slides up my skirt but stops before it reaches my pussy. It's reassuring without completely distracting me. I look down at my phone and inhale a fortifying breath before I hit Juliana's contact. I put it on speakerphone. It rings twice.

"Sera, where are you? Mama and Papa are freaking out. They said you planned to spend the night at a hotel then head back to Italy. They can't find you."

I dive in headfirst. "I'm with my husband at our home."

"Husband? What the fuck did you do, Serafina?"

"Carmine and I got married four hours ago."

"Are you safe to talk to me right now? I can get you out."

"Jules, I'm not going anywhere. I asked Carmine to marry me, not the other way around. I suggested we go to the courthouse today and do it. He said yes because he loves me and would do anything for me."

"He's brainwashed you. That's not love."

"Jules, I didn't call to argue with you. I called to tell you I got married. I'm sorry I didn't invite you, but I couldn't."

"Because you know I would have stopped you."

"No, you wouldn't have. We just would have had a massive argument in a very public place. It would have sounded even worse to everyone around us because it would have been in Italian. Did Mama or Papa tell you why they thought I was going back to Italy?"

"They have a husband for you. A real one not some asshole you've hated for twenty years."

"Did they tell you who?"

"No. It doesn't matter. Anyone's better than Carmine Mancinelli."

"Elio Lombardo."

There's silence. I won't be the one to break it. Let that soak in for her. At least a minute passes before she speaks again.

"They wouldn't."

"Yes, they would. They did. They arranged it and would have forced me into it. If I stepped foot onto Italian soil, they would have physically forced me to marry him."

"So, Carmine's your out. You can divorce him once things blow over."

"He is not. Jules, I love Carmine. That won't change. This marriage is for life."

"You got married at a courthouse, not a church. It's not for life."

I've been watching Carmine throughout the conversation. He's appeared concerned, but now there's a smug "I told you so" look on his face. I roll my eyes and nod.

"Jules, did Mama tell you how they were going to force me back to Italy?"

"No. She and Papa called in a panic, looking for you."

"And you didn't call me to check on me?"

"I figure you and Carmine were off—busy."

"We do come up for air, you know. Mama had Orlando drain all my bank accounts. She stole my savings and my livelihood. She stole all the money I use to run my business, including paying my employees. She sent my guards to Paola's home to kidnap me. They shot up the place while Mama and I were on the phone. It wasn't just Paola and me there. Nicoletta, Carlotta, and *Zia* Sylvia were too. Those were very real bullets, Jules."

"Are your men dead?"

"No. They brought me to Carmine. They knew I was on the phone with Mama. They did what they had to, but they could have died. Cesare, Domenico, and Massimo were there. They destroyed Paola's kitchen."

"Good thing the Mancinellis are into construction."

"That's all you have to say? Some smartass quip?"

"Sera, that wouldn't have happened if you hadn't caused all this."

"Caused it? Are you for real? Mama caused this. She sent men to kidnap me. Luckily, they know who Elio is and wouldn't take me anywhere near him. Even if they had, there's not a chance on God's green earth Carmine would have allowed me to marry that swine. Even if I refused to marry Carmine, he would still have saved me. Juliana, we came to America to escape arranged marriages and family politics. We chose that, and Mama and Papa understood. At least they pretended to. I think they always intended to make me come back."

"Why?"

I take another fortifying breath. "Mama wants me to be *la madrina* in Palermo."

"You? I'm older. If she thought one of her daughters would become the matriarch, it would have been her elder daughter."

"Can you kill someone?"

"No. And you can?" She scoffs at me.

"I already have. More than once, Jules. *Zia* Sophia is at peace because of what I did. Could you order someone killed?"

"Sera, this is ridiculous. *La madrina* is just a title. This shit is the men's business. You'd organize parties and make sure they provided for widows. Besides that, you'd have a normal life like you do here."

"And that's why Mama didn't pick you. You never wanted to see what Mama and *Zia* Sylvia do behind the scenes. If anything happened to Papa or *Zio* Salvatore, and their underbosses couldn't step in to lead right away, both of them could. No one would know Papa or *Zio* were gone until Giancola or Luca took over. They would do whatever's necessary to keep our families on top. Do not doubt either of their ruthlessness. Do not doubt mine. Tell Mama and Papa to stay out of my marriage. I chose Carmine, and I'll keep doing that. If they push me, they will lose a daughter and gain an enemy."

Carmine shakes his head furiously. There's warning in his eyes, and I choose to ignore it. He's told me more than once that he never wants me to choose him before my family. That's exactly what the fuck I did today. I'll never question that decision. Carmine's not the one manipulating me.

"Sera, you don't even sound like yourself."

"Do I know every single thing about you? I know I don't. You don't know my thoughts. You don't know everything I've done every moment of my life. I *can* be *la madrina*, but I don't *want* to be *la madrina*. I won't go around in circles with you. I'm sorry you couldn't be there today, but you are the first person I've told."

The sadness I feel comes through my voice. Carmine's embrace tightens until I rest my head against his shoulder. Juliana must hear it, too.

"You really believe Carmine is good enough for you?"

"Absolutely. But don't put it that way. I don't like it. Good enough sounds like he barely reaches the bare minimum. He's amazing. He puts me ahead of everything but the duties he can't avoid. He's thoughtful and generous. He cares about what I think and what I feel. Despite his size and what he does, he's gentle with me." *When I want him to be.* "And he loves me as much as I love him. I know his past—all of it—and I understand his choices and his actions. I can live with it all because I wouldn't change the man he is now for anything in the world."

I mouth, "I love you" before pressing a quick kiss to his lips. I settle back against him, and the world feels a little righter as he kisses my forehead and strokes my hair.

"I hope you're right, Sera. If you're not, come to me. I won't send you to Mama and Papa. I'll do whatever you want. We promised each other that when we moved into your place. I still mean it."

My place. I've barely thought of it since moving in with Carmine. While we stayed at Paola's, men moved my stuff here. I'm going to rent the place, but I think I'll eventually sell it.

"Thank you, Jules."

"Carmine, I know you heard all of this. She's my baby sister, no matter what she's done or that she's married now. I'm not ruthless by nature, but my sister is everything to me. Whatever Sera's done will pale compared to what I'll do to you. That'll be between you, me, and God because no one will find your body."

Carmine grins. "Juliana, I'm glad to hear that. I don't want to be a wedge between you and your sister. Knowing you're that protective means you'll be in Fina's life. I welcome you into mine."

There's a pause. I doubt Juliana expected that. She says as much. "You aren't who I remember."

"I'm not. Life—especially this kind—changes us. For a long, long time, it was for the worse for me. Call it Divine Intervention or what you will, but I'm not that man anymore, and I never want to be him again. Fina is everything to me, too. She's right that there are things that will always come before her, but it's not my choice. The only secrets I'll keep are the ones that keep her and my family alive. All of my decisions will have her and the family we'll make one day in mind. I don't take this duty any lighter than I do my duty to my family. I love Serafina."

He never uses my full name, at least not around me. I don't think he does often anywhere. He wants Juliana and me to know he's serious. I shift to wrap one arm around him and sigh. It would be bliss if we weren't on the phone.

"Sera, what are you going to do about Mama and Papa? They will not accept this."

"I know. I hope in time, they'll see why this is a good thing. I hope they'll watch and see how good Carmine is to me, how happy he makes me. I hope they won't interfere. I don't want the Mancinellis and Carosis at war, but if they keep pushing, that's what it will come to. By involving Carmine in their scheme to get me back to Italy, they made this a family matter. Each family is like the fucking Musketeers. All for one, and one for all."

"You said Mama got Orlando to help her. Carmine, is he alive?"

My husband—God, how I love that idea—looks at his watch.

"For now." What the hell does that mean? He whispers in my ear. "He made his choice, Fina. I had to make mine."

I look at him, then nod. I'd already made my peace with that hours ago. I have a morbid curiosity to know how, but I won't ask. Carmine won't tell me. What's the point of putting him in that position?

"Sera, I have another ultrasound coming up. Do you want to come? Ernesto's coming, but I'd like you to be there, too."

I lean forward and look up at Carmine, my eyebrows raised. I don't know if it's safe enough right now. We're back to an open threat against me. It's Elio I'm worried about now. My parents will make my life miserable. If Elio feels slighted, he'll kill me. But only after I'm tortured. Carmine smiles, and his face is the most handsome sight I've ever beheld. I love this easygoing look. I don't see it often enough, but it makes my heart race. He mouths his answer.

"Go." His lips pucker for a second as he says the word. Suddenly, all I want is to get on with our wedding night.

"Jules, text me the date and time. I have to get going. Carmine and I have plans."

"Ew. I don't need to know about that, Sera."

"It's my wedding night! And you're pregnant. Don't tell me ew. I know how babies are made. Ew to you too."

Juliana chuckles, and it feels like things are back to normal. I'll talk to her in a few days to make sure they really are. But for now, we're leaving this on a better note than I expected. I hang up with her and drop my phone on the sofa. I shift to straddle Carmine.

"*Piccolina*, I think you guessed what I have in mind. Is that what you want for tonight?"

"To go to a dungeon and finally have the kinky sex I've been aching for. That's perfect for us."

"Fina, I have hard limits, though."

I grin. It's funny to hear him say that. "Do you need a safe word, Daddy?"

"With you, no. Fina, you know what goes on there. No one is joining us."

"Daddy! You didn't have to tell me that. I don't want anyone else to touch me. It'll be a fucking bloodbath if anyone comes near you. Part of me wants to be watched, but another part of me doesn't want anyone enjoying the sight of you fucking."

"That's part of my hard limits. Fina, if we do anything in public, I have to stay dressed."

It takes me a second. "Your tattoos. They're too recognizable."

He has a massive outline of Italy across his left pec. The Mancinelli men outside the don's family have it on a forearm.

"Yes. I'm too recognizable, and I don't want anyone to know who you are. You wear the mask you always have, and I wear one too. We only take them off if we're in a room, and no one sees in. I'll gladly be naked with you there."

I unbutton the top two of his shirt and slide my hands beneath the material. The raw yet restrained power beneath my fingertips will always turn me on. He's rough with me, but he'd never forgive himself if he hurt me. Knowing he controls himself just for me is powerful.

"Any other hard limits?"

"I have never and will never use degradation with you. Please don't ask me to call you a slut, a whore, or a bitch. I can't. I will never slap your face. I'll pull your hair, but I won't smother you or hook your mouth. I only want praise kink with you, Fina."

The way he says it tells me he hasn't had this hard limit before. "Thank you, Daddy. I would have accepted it if you wanted it, but I don't want it with you."

Our gazes lock, and he knows I've done it in the past too. It didn't bother me back then.

"Do you have any hard limits, *piccolina?*"

"I don't enjoy caning."

His gaze hardens to shards of glass. His hand fists my hair, and this is the Carmine who truly excites me. I'm certain it would terrify or enrage a woman who isn't into submission. To me, my legs are sticky as I get wetter by the breath.

"When we got together, you just told me you didn't want caning or birching. You didn't say you'd done it. I do not want to know which motherfucker caned you, but I promise if I find out, I will kill him. If you didn't enjoy it, then you gave in because the guy wanted it. He should have known not to ask."

"I tried it twice, Daddy. I wanted to know if I was into it. The first time was—it hurt a lot. But I tried it again to see if it was just my initial shock. It wasn't. I didn't enjoy it."

"Did you ask for it?" I hesitate, and he notices. His hand tightens in my hair.

"The guy suggested it. He was into it."

His jaw tenses, but his hand relaxes.

"Those were your choices before we got together. I respect what you did and what you wanted. But I hate picturing you receiving that kind of pain and the marks it left behind. It makes my heart pound and ears ring."

He nudges my head against his chest, as though he's comforting me, but I think he's the one who needs comforting. It's as though he could take that pain away, but it was years ago.

"Daddy, don't think that."

"Think what? About hating the idea of bruises that likely lasted more than a week?"

"That too. I meant, don't think that if you'd changed sooner, we'd have been together, and I wouldn't have done that. Back then, I wouldn't have considered being in a relationship with anyone. I wouldn't have been receptive, and I would have ruined my chance to have what we do now. It was not long after I left Orlando. I wanted to try all the things, and I didn't want to be accountable to anyone but myself. I was more likely to insist the contract end than look twice in your—or any groom's —direction. It wasn't the right time for us."

"All right. You read my mind, little one. I already told David and Gio what we're doing. There's a club I've never been to, but I know some of its members. Have you been to the Whip and Tail?"

"No. I haven't even heard of that one."

"It's extremely exclusive. No one who hasn't been invited by a member knows about it."

"Someone invited you?"

"Yes."

It's my turn to narrow my eyes and grit my teeth.

"Little one, it was Luca. But you can never tell him you know that about him."

"Is he a Dom?"

"He was. I don't know what he does with Olivia, but my guess is it's pretty much like us."

"Not a real Daddy Dom, or even a regular Dom. Just dominant by nature and protective to his last breath."

"Exactly. Shall we get ready?"

"Yes, Daddy."

We head into our bedroom, and we're soon in darker clothes that'll blend in. It's not the pleather people assume everyone wears in a sex club. We each have a mask in hand. David and Gio are waiting for us in the basement with a town car. I don't recognize the license plate, so it must be a Mancinellis'.

"They're on our payroll now, too. I still don't want you going places without someone from my immediate family, including Gabriele and Matteo. But I trust your men. They put you first, and I respect that. They can get paid into each hand for all I care."

I nod and slide into the car first. Carmine follows me, and Gio closes the door. The privacy glass is up as always. The moment the door closes, Carmine pounces. He lifts me onto his lap and tugs the laces of the vest I'm wearing. In no time, my tits are out, and he's sucking like a starved baby. My miniskirt—which I heard him grumble about—is up to my waist. He's holding my hands at the small of my back with one of his while the other yanks on the button and fly to his pants.

"Tell me right now if fucking in a car bothers you as the first time we're doing this as a married couple. We'll wait until we get to the club if you want."

"If you make me wait another moment, I'll cry or scream. Possibly both."

"Tell me what you want, *piccolina?*"

This isn't a general question. It's an opening for some dirty talk. I lean forward and flick his earlobe with my tongue before I tug it with my teeth. My hips jerk forward and rub his cock when he spanks me.

"That's what I want, Daddy. I'm going to toy with you, and you're going to punish me." I grind my pussy against his cock as I suck on his earlobe again. I receive another spank. "I know how hard you get when you're in control. Make me behave, husband."

"Wife, I'm about to put those lips and that tongue to better use."

"Do you want me to suck you off, Daddy?"

"Oh, no, baby." His lips fuse to mine, and his tongue tangles with mine. I suck softly, earning me three sharp slaps to my ass. "I'll fill your mouth with my cum later. It's going in your pussy, so you walk into the club with it dripping down your leg. You're mine, and you will remember that."

I laugh, but it's as dark as I can make it. "I can never forget I'm yours. Just remember, it's my cream all over your dick when we go inside."

"And it'll be all over my mouth now." He flips us around, so I'm lying on the seat with my legs around his hips. I stopped wearing panties ages ago, so it exposes my bare pussy to him. He slaps it three times before he thrusts his fingers into me. I'm so wet; he slides right in. He withdraws them and licks them.

It's only moments later that I'm brushing sweat from my temples as I watch my husband. He didn't get off after all. He made this entirely about me, as he so often does. I can still feel his tongue inside me. We've pulled up outside the club, so we adjust our clothes and make our way inside. It's far more lavish than my club. A DM—Dungeon Master or Dungeon Monitor

—shows us around until we finally settle on a private room. Neither of us wants an audience.

We can't undress fast enough, and we fling our clothes onto a chair. There's a massive, curved sofa of sorts that I bend over. He connects my ankles to a spreader. He gathers one implement after another, soon torturing me oh so well with a crop against my pussy. Then comes a flogger that whips through the air before landing across my lower back, ass, and upper thighs. I can't stop the sounds coming from deep within my throat as my mind focuses only on what he's doing.

"Pinch your nipples, *piccolina*. Twist until you moan and want to let go, then do it a little harder."

"Yes, Daddy."

His head lowers until his teeth graze my clit. My hips come off the sofa, and he grabs my ass. His grip bites into my more than ample flesh.

"Yes... Yes... Daddy, yes... Harder. I'm so close...Fuuuuck... Fuck me harder, Daddy. Harder... Show me."

He understands what I'm asking for. He pulls out, and suddenly, I'm free of the restraints. I'm on my back, and he's thrusting into me. His hand is in my hair, holding my head in place as his other hand goes around my throat. He pounds into my pussy as his voice fills the room.

"All of you is mine, Fina Mancinelli. It belongs to me. You are all I want. All I'll ever want. I will never get enough of you. I'll never be able to show you how much I love you, desire you. But I will make love to you and fuck you and everything in between. You'll take my cock wherever I put it. You'll take my cum wherever I put it. I will never let you doubt that I'm yours as much as you are mine. You are the only woman I'll ever be inside. You are the only one who will ever get my cum. Only you have me, Fina. Only you have ever had me."

The pressure on my throat has been light, but he tightens

his hold. I instinctively put my hands over my head when he flipped me, but now I run them over every part of him I can reach. I trail my nails along his abs. As my head feels cloudy, and my heart beats in my ears, I grab his chiseled ass and explode. The moment he feels me come, he releases my hair and throat. He smatters my cheeks with kisses.

"Real kiss."

I don't ask. He's happy to oblige. I feel him twitch inside me, then I'm wetter. I do a Kegel, refusing to let him pull out. Refusing to let any of his cum drip from me. I'm twenty-eight. I could probably wait another ten years before having kids. But the thought of making a baby with Carmine is intoxicating. Nothing would make me happier than having a pint-sized model of him running around.

He wraps my legs around his waist and gracefully stands. I cling to him as he shifts to sit on the sofa. His touch is gentle again as he strokes my back and ass. A wave of sleepiness crashes over me. I'm used to this after intense scenes, but never have I wanted to curl up with a partner like I am with my husband.

"Daddy, can I rest for a moment?"

"Of course, sweet girl. I need to hold you."

He needs to hold me. This complex and often violent man craves affection and allows me to offer it. He truly asks so little of me. He asks that I submit to him when we're intimate and defer to him for my safety. That's it. He's always treated me as an equal outside of sex, and even then, my submissive role is just as valuable to him as his dominant one.

"Daddy?"

"Yes, *cuore*."

"I love you."

"I love you, too."

"There's nothing I won't do for you. You're intense. Like

there are no lower gears or low simmers. I get it. You have to be. I hope you feel you can turn off when you're with me. That you feel safe enough with me to do that."

"Fina, you're the only person I feel that way around. You are my refuge from my work and the real world. You bring me peace."

I sit back with his dick still in me, but I feel it softening. I rock my hips and do several more Kegels. I'm not ready to sever the physical connection, but I have a question.

"Do you think you love me more than I love you?"

"No." His brow furrows, and he shifts to sit up straighter as he continues. "Where's this coming from, Fina? I've never thought that. Not once you told me how you feel."

"But you thought that before, and I caused it. I just need you to know that I caught up. You know my past and what I did for my *zia*. I hope to never relive it, but I will if I must. You're bigger than me. You have skills I don't. You have resources I should never ever know about. You're also not the only one who will burn the world down to protect our marriage and our family. You're everything to me too, Carmine. I expect us to grow very, very old together. I'll think you're hot even after you lose all your hair and your teeth."

"Lose my hair and teeth?"

He has gorgeous hair, but he keeps it short. I suppose it's an occupational thing, but I wish it were a little longer. His teeth are perfectly aligned. His parents probably spent a fortune on braces and retainers.

"Even when I have a wrinkle or two, husband."

"*Tesorina*, they won't be wrinkles because your beauty is flawless. They'll be lifelines. Ones that come from laughter, love, and wisdom."

"You are such a romantic, Carmine. You're hardly soft and fluffy, but you really are a massive teddy bear."

I wrap myself around him again and close my eyes. The fatigue hits me once more. We rest together for fifteen minutes before we get dressed and gather our things. Gio and David are at opposite ends of the hall when we step out of the room. We walk toward Gio, and David follows. We reach the bottom of the stairs and look around. It's not crowded, but there are more people than when we arrived. We move toward the lounge, but Carmine suddenly spins me, and we head to the bar.

"Daddy?" I whisper, looking between our shoulders at David and Gio, who shrug. He leads me into a dark nook and watches over my head. I try to look back when I see his chin dip, but he pulls me against his chest.

"Misha and Katerina Andreyev are not who I want to make small talk with on my wedding night."

"Daddy, did they recognize us?"

"Yes, *piccolina*. But neither will say a word because they don't need it getting out that Misha brought his wife here. Shit would really blow up between our syndicates if either of us leaked something that private. Neither of us would turn a blind eye to a man humiliating our wife like that. And neither of us needs that kind of blood all over the streets right now."

"If the *Cosa Nostra* and the bratva weren't arch nemeses, you'd probably all be fucking besties."

Carmine stares down at me for a long moment then smiles. "You don't want to imagine the trouble we'd get into if we got along with the Kutsenkos and Andreyevs. It's a good thing I'm a married man and have settled down."

I look up toward the stairs. "Settled down?"

He turns me, so my back is to the wall, which means his back is to the crowd. I know how much he hates that, but when he squeezes my ass, he doesn't want our men to see him.

"Is settled in a better phrase? Because I'm definitely comfortable inside you."

I glance toward the door and see the back of two blond heads leaving. Then I look toward the sex couches—I can't think of what the benches with the rounded end and contours are called—before I meet Carmine's gaze again.

"I think you need to get settled into my ass, Daddy."

We make our way into the crowd, and I'm certain David and Gio are twitching. But I know Carmine is aware of everything going on down to how many tiles are in the ceiling and any missing screws in a light switch cover. I also know he has his gun holstered at his lower back. It's not long before my skirt is back up around my waist, and I'm bent over the high back of the couch. He promised he would come in all three places, and he does. I'm asleep in the car the moment Carmine lifts me onto his lap. He carries me into the penthouse and helps me undress.

"This has been the perfect wedding night, Carmine. Thank you."

"It has been perfect. Do you want to redecorate a bedroom to suit our tastes?"

"You mean make our own dungeon here?"

"Until we decide if there's somewhere else we want to live, yeah."

"Watch out, Daddy. I'm going to order *all* the things."

"Good thing I'm a very rich man."

"Make a shopping list." I waggle my eyebrows at him. "That way I don't miss anything, husband."

"Come here, wife. All this talk about toys makes me want to bury my cock in your tight little cunt."

"I want to fall asleep with you and your cum in me."

It's a quickie, which is all either of us can manage. I'm sprawled across Carmine's chest with his cock still in me as I drift off. I don't want to think it, but will the honeymoon be over when we wake up?

Chapter Twenty-Nine

Carmine

My wife's sleeping beside me.

I love that it's a fact, and not just a dream or longing. I'm so glad we had a night just for us. Normal couples don't think that about their wedding night. Then again, most newlyweds don't go to a BDSM club after the ceremony. We haven't been much of a conventional couple since the beginning. It works for us, though.

I felt horrible listening to her conversation with Juliana before we went out. It went better than I expected, but I know her sister hurt her several times, and I was the cause. It reminds me of every fuck-up I've made. If I hadn't been spiteful and petty—righteously indignant—then no one in Fina's family would have questioned my suitability. It still wouldn't thrill Allegra that Fina chose a husband based in America rather than Sicily, but at least she wouldn't think I was worthless and beneath her daughter.

I can tell myself only Fina's opinion should matter, but that's bullshit. What her family thinks will inevitably shape our future. If they can't get on board with us, then Fina risks losing her family. That's the last thing I want, but I recognize the hand I have in that possibility.

"Mmm."

"*Buongiorno moglie.*" Good morning, wife.

"*Buongiorno, marito.*" Good morning, husband.

I kiss along her shoulder and up her neck to just behind her ear.

"How long can we hide out here? How long can we avoid my parents and pretend like everything's blissful?"

"I don't know. Fina, I want this done. I keep saying that, and something new keeps happening. I don't enjoy disappointing you."

She jerks back and presses hard against my chest as she sits up. "You do not disappoint me. Don't say that. You're doing everything you can, and I know that. You haven't blown off any of this. You've put us ahead of work I'm sure you were supposed to do. It's not your fault."

I open my mouth, but she shakes her head. Her stare pierces me to the pillow, and I marvel at its intensity. It's fucking hot as hell. It's this determination I see that brought her to a foreign country where she's succeeded in school and in business.

"I know what you're going to say, Car, so don't. Your past is done. So is mine. They are memories, for better and for worse. But I don't want to live there. I want to live in our present and our future. You are the man I want. The one I need. And the only one I will ever love. This isn't on you. If you argue with me, you will discover the true depths of my stubbornness."

"You're so hot."

She stares at me for a moment before she grins and laughs. "That's your takeaway?"

"Not the only one, but it ranks toward the top."

She shakes her head and lies back down. I hold her against me and close my eyes.

"Fina, I don't want a war with your parents. What they've done can't be ignored. You're my wife now, and they need to understand they can't manipulate you with impunity. You're not a little girl, despite what I call you. What they did involves another syndicate. That's not all right. We're supposed to be allies already. If they want our marriage to break that alliance, then they can step forward and say so. By coming after me through you, they made this a Mancinelli issue. My family can't overlook it. Not after Allegra sent men to shoot up my mom's home. I haven't forgotten about that. I just can't handle that rationally yet. It makes me too irate."

"I know all of this. They brought this upon themselves. Whether it was my mom or my dad who started it doesn't matter. They did this together. They had to know there'd be consequences."

"Oh, they did. But they expected to succeed, so they were willing to accept the fallout. I'm certain they were convinced you'd leave me." I tense for only a second, but Fina feels it.

"I didn't marry you to spite them, to prove them wrong. I didn't marry you so I could have my way. Don't think that."

"I'm sorry."

"Remember, the mind reading goes both ways, husband."

"You're quite adept at it. I like it even when I don't."

"That makes no sense, yet I totally get what you mean. Can we promise to only use our powers for good?"

"Of course. How would you handle this if you were me or Uncle Salvatore?"

"I can't answer that. I can't separate them being my parents from this. If I do, I'd obliterate them. There'd be nothing left, and that's not what I want. I just want them to see I'm happy and respect my decision. I want them to mind their own business."

"Obliterate? We don't need to go that far. I thought stealing some money to return the favor might be an option."

"Oh. Well, yeah. I wouldn't mind them knowing how it feels to find their accounts drained."

"Only their personal accounts. I won't take money that's for their people. I won't ignore their responsibility to provide for others like they ignored your need to make payroll. Whatever I take goes into college funds for our future kids. I won't spend it on us, and I won't make it Mancinelli *Cosa Nostra* money either. Uncle Massimo can set up a trust almost immediately with him as the executor or *guardian ad litem* for unnamed children."

"How do you know all that?"

"Luca and Olivia did it already. They moved her savings over and created the trust."

"The old Carmine would have blown it on a car and nights out on the town, wouldn't he?"

"Yes. But you told me we're living in the present and the future. You know I'm wealthy. I have plenty to provide for us and any children we have. I don't need or want their money other than to punish them. I want it to be put to good use, and whether or not they like the idea, they will have grandchildren through us. I see it as their first duty as *Nonno* and *Nonna*."

"Thank you. Is the money all you'll do?"

I hesitate, and she lifts her head. "I don't know yet. It depends on if they've done anything else I haven't discovered yet."

I suspect they have, and Uncle Salvatore promised me as we left Donatelli's that he's looking into it. I look at the bedside table as my phone rings. As though summoned by the gods, it's my uncle. I recognize the ring tone.

"Uncle Salvatore." Fina immediately rolls off me, and I stretch for the phone. "*Ciao, zio.*"

"Good morning. I'm sorry to call you today, but something's come up. We need you."

I look at Fina. She's masking her disappointment, but I know it's there because I feel it, too. Frustration tightens my chest. Maybe we jinxed ourselves by talking about it.

"How soon do you need me?" I know it means his house. If it were the garage, he would have said "we need you *there.*"

"As soon as you can. Bring Sera. She can spend time with the other wives."

"Give us an hour and a half."

"Carmine."

"I got married last night, Uncle Sal. Give me an hour and a half."

"Fine. I really am sorry. Please pass my apologies to Sera."

"I will. Bye."

"*Ciao.*"

"Am I just going there for the day, or should I pack?"

"I don't think you need to pack. But speaking of it, we have a honeymoon to plan. Where would you like to go?"

She tries to roll away to get up, but I pull her against my side. "Carmine, we have to get ready."

"That's why I told him an hour-and-a-half. I'm not rushing this time together. The world will have to wait. It's bad enough that I'm going to be apart from you the day after we get married. I don't need to cut our time any shorter than I have to."

"*Orsacchiotto.*" Teddy bear. "Seriously. I think you're the romantic one in this marriage. You say the sweetest things." She settles back against me.

"Only for you, *piccolina*. You bring it out in me."

"I enjoy having a life-size teddy bear to cuddle with."

"I think I'm more like the Energizer Bunny."

She cups my cock and balls. "You do keep going and going and going."

"Where do you want to go, *cuore mio*?" My heart.

"South Africa." She blurts her answer.

"Really?"

"I've always wanted to see the purple lightning I've heard about. There are breathtaking landscapes and animals to see. I had a calendar a few years ago with animals from South Africa, and I fell in love."

"Then that's where we're going. Decide when you can take three weeks off, and we'll go there and anywhere else you want."

"I can't take three weeks off from my business. I've already been an absentee owner for almost two months." She grins at me. "But I'll make it work."

I inhale and hold a breath for a second. I don't want to explain this part. "Fina, I'm going to ask the guys—well, not Luca—to come with us. I don't feel comfortable going that far from home without them there for your protection."

"What about your protection?"

"They'll see to that too, but you're the priority. Always. I know that's not romantic, but that's how it'll be anytime we go abroad. We'll always stay in private homes."

She looks at me, and I don't know what she's thinking. It sucks. She's slow to nod.

"I get it. A house allows us all to stay in a more controlled environment. I don't love the idea of an entourage, but I don't want you stressed the entire time, either. I know I'll feel safer."

"Thank you for understanding."

She sighs. "It's not like this is new to me."

I give her a quick kiss, and we head into the bathroom. We take less than five minutes to get clean, but at least a half hour to make love. The real world blows. Adulting blows. The only adulting I wanted to do was getting used to being a husband and ensuring I'm available for all my husbandly duties. I love having a demanding wife. She's as lusty as I am. God certainly blessed me with that. Let's see whether I'm blessed with any good fortune dealing with Piero and Allegra.

"I know, Uncle Sal. I won't spend the money. I told you: college funds. But that's not enough. Obviously, I can't touch Piero or Allegra. I wouldn't do that to Fina. His *consigliere* is tempting, but I took the man's grandson. He can live with that for the rest of his life."

We watched the plane crash video when my uncles, cousins, friends, and I came into Uncle Salvatore's office. I mirrored my phone on the TV, so we got the full cinematic experience. Everything went off without a hitch. The pilot started the video just before he adjusted the autopilot course. Because the camera pointed out the window, we could only hear him put on his jumpsuit and parachute. When he left the cockpit, he kept the door open. It's muffled, but we hear Orlando demanding answers. The pilot said one thing.

"You shouldn't have fucked with Carmine Mancinelli."

I know he flicked on his Go-Pro camera then because we watched that footage next. I fast forwarded through the five-minute wait as the plane continued to fly unmanned. But you see it falter as the cabin pressure shifts when the door remains open. Then the snow-covered mountainside appears. The plane barrels straight to it. The moment of impact is when the feed ended.

The pilot's footage showed the explosion in the distance. There's a ton of smoke, but nearly nothing falls from the sky. Only ash. There's no wreckage to examine. I wired the plane with so many explosives that they basically incinerated the entire thing. It's truly a miracle that it didn't cause a major avalanche—only a medium-sized one. It buried under yards of snow anything that might have fallen to the ground.

So fucking satisfying killing two birds with one stone. Orlando's gone, and Alejandro is devastated. I didn't check my messages until I got here. He started blowing up my phone last night and texts kept coming this morning. I haven't responded.

Uncle Massimo brings me back to the present. "What do you propose?"

"Uncle Sal, you said Aunt Sylvia told you her family wasn't involved. This was just Allegra. She'd never lie to you, so I have no reason to believe anyone else helped Allegra. This was her plan, not the Catalanos'. To be honest, the rift she's caused with Fina is punishment enough. We don't go after women and children. I fucked that up before. I'm not repeating my sins. I don't think there's anything I could do besides targeting Juliana that will hurt Allegra as much as what she's done to her relationship with Fina."

Uncle Salvatore sits back in his chair, resting on an elbow on the armrest. He's deep in thought, staring at his desk. He nods slowly a couple times. "Lorenzo, can you make the bank transfers happen?"

"Yeah. I've been poking around in their accounts. How much do you want me to move, Carmine?"

"At the rate university fees are going, I'd say four hundred K for each kid, and let's estimate on the high side. So, four hundred K four times."

"Four kids?" My dad blurts out his question. I shrug.

"I don't know. We haven't talked about an exact number,

but I wouldn't plan for one, anyway. At least not until we see how the first pregnancy goes. But Uncle Massi had four, so maybe."

Uncle Massimo and Auntie Nicoletta are like teenagers when they think they're alone. It surprises me they stopped at four. Thank God Catholics can accept birth control these days, or we'd have twenty Lucas or Marcos or Lorenzos running around. Twenty Marias wouldn't be so bad, but Lord, that would be a lot of unsolicited wisdom coming my way. I should thank her, though. She insisted we try the bakery, and she sat me next to Fina at Easter. It was premeditated.

Uncle Salvatore nods again. "Fine. Lorenzo work on it. Massi, when can you file the trust documents?"

"I can draft them today. As long as one of you is a trustee, then we can make it legal. There's no requirement to file or report in the State of New York. We're not the only ones who like to keep our money private. I'd say while Enzo figures out what he needs to, to get into their accounts, I draft the papers. One of you signs them, then Enzo creates an offshore account. The money goes in there under the trust's name, and we call it a day."

It's not exactly a traditional college fund. I don't even know what those are, but I'm certain Uncle Salvatore does. I know he's set them up for his daughters, but he used his legally earned money to fund them. I don't want anyone tracing this. Uncle Massimo's sitting on a couch with his laptop. He flips it open and gets to work. He and Lorenzo are sitting across from each other, and it's one of the rare times when they're almost identical. Lorenzo looks more like Auntie Nicoletta.

I look around the room, and I can't believe this is done. Unless Piero wants that war, they'll accept the retaliation as their due. It almost feels anticlimactic. No covert mission. No vindication of watching my enemy die—besides the video. I know it's basically resolved, but it doesn't feel like it. Things usually end with a boom. This is more like a splutter. My dad's sitting next to me, and he claps his hand on my thigh just above my knee.

"Be glad it was nothing bigger. Sera doesn't need the worry, and neither does your mother. It's better this way. Prying eyes and ears know nothing, and we don't have to cover any messes. This is the outcome we hope for."

"I know. It just feels too easy."

"Take the win, Carmine. Go on your honeymoon with your wife. Start your life together for real. There's enough shit that will happen. It's inevitable. We've put this to bed. Don't wake it. I'm proud of the way you've handled all of this and the partner you are for Sera."

"Thanks, Papa. That means a lot."

"Go find your bride."

My dad and uncles stay in the office. Uncle Salvatore pulled out his domino set. I swear, sometimes they're like old men. Then I remember them going on the recent mission, and you'd never guess they had adult children. All of them have worked and fought hard to reach their fifties. If they want to play dominos or bocci, then let them.

"Fina, are you ready to go?" I slide my arms around her when she walks to meet me at the entrance to the living room.

"Yeah. Everything okay?"

"Yup. What needs to happen will."

"Good."

I'm glad she understands, so I don't have to spin any lies.

"Did you make your list?"

"I did. We might need a month for everything I came up with. Can we add Victoria Falls in Zimbabwe and a safari in Kenya?"

"We can do whatever you want. We'll make it all work."

"Always."

She tightens her arms around me and rests her head on my chest. She whispers since there are others around us.

"*Ti amo*, Daddy." I love you, Daddy.

"*Ti amo, piccolina*." I love you, little girl.

Epilogue

Fina

I finally don't feel jetlagged. Not wanting to fall asleep until it's nearly three in the morning was rough because we've been up with the roosters. Literally. The house in Cape Town is extraordinary. Luxury is the only word. But there's a rooster somewhere within a mile. The damn thing has a fucking microphone and speaker.

"Are you ready, Fina?"

"Yeah. I'm coming."

It's winter down here, so I grab my coat. The air's been brisk, but there have been a few days in the past two-and-a-half weeks where it's been freezing. I doubt most people think anywhere in Africa has winter, but this country does.

Carmine slips his hand into mine as Gabriele and Matteo lead the way. Marco and Lorenzo follow. Luca offered to come, but neither Carmine nor I would hear of it. In our minds, he's still a newlywed too. He belongs with Olivia. He's gone out of town since they got married, but an international trip for a month is entirely different.

We had to wait a month before we could travel. Whatever loose ends Carmine had to tie up took longer than we hoped. I don't know the details, and I keep telling myself I don't want to. Whatever he did worked, though. Elio hasn't caused any problem. It's been patchy, but my parents apologized last week. They gave us their blessing. I'm certain Carmine's retaliation spurred them to it, but I know my parents. What they said is genuine.

The afternoon after we got married, we went for a walk. Within a minute, Carmine pointed out a man following us. He was pretty inconspicuous, but I recognized him immediately. He was a man who worked for my family in Sicily. Since then, he'd been our shadow in New York. Carmine felt no threat from him, so I haven't worried. We believe he was reporting to my parents about us. Whatever he said and whatever photos he sent convinced them we're for real and in this for good.

We're soon in the van with the chauffeur Carmine hired while we're in South Africa. We started in Kenya and did a two-week-long safari. Then we spent two days in Zimbabwe, so we could see the falls. Now we've been in South Africa for three days. We arrived in Johannesburg and spent two days there before coming to Cape Town.

"Look." I point out the window to our destination, Cape Point. We're pulling into a parking lot, and I can see a set up for a wedding on the promontory. What a spectacular place to get married.

"That's cool."

I glance at Carmine. He's interested, but he's not as intrigued as me. I wonder who's getting married there. It's fucking cold for a wedding dress. He helps me out of the van, and we walk around for half an hour. I take about a zillion photos. I never take photos because I never remember to. But I want to capture every moment of this trip and my time with Carmine. We're almost back to the parking lot when I spot a group of people in tuxedos and elegant gowns. I squint.

"Carmine, is that—"

"Yes, *piccolina*."

I swallow the lump in my throat as I hurry toward the group. Juliana rushes to meet me, holding her rounded belly. We collide and almost knock each other over. My parents are slower to join us. I don't know how I feel about seeing them, but the clothes gave away why my family's here. I spot *Zio* Salvatore and *Zia* Sylvia, along with my parents-in-law. I've grown super close to Paola. Domenico and Carlotta, Massimo and Nicoletta, Luca and Olivia, and Maria are there, too. Ernesto stands off to the side where he'd been with Juliana, Mama, and Papa. He shoots me a warm smile. Turns out, he's been rooting for Carmine and me all along. My sister doesn't appreciate his frequent I told you so's.

I hug my parents, and it's awkward but not horrible. It's going to take a long ass time before we're totally okay. I don't trust them, and the hurt's still there. But I understand them. We exist in a world most people believe is morally black— morally bereft. To us, we live in a world where loyalty, duty, and honor are everything. Duty to family comes first because we have a duty to the people who depend on us. My mom went about it in a completely shitty way, but I get she tried to protect me as much as do her duty to her family in Sicily. I can forgive because of the latter, but the former still makes me sad.

"*Mama, Papa, sono felice che tu sia qui.*" I'm glad you're here.

My mom kisses my cheek as she strokes the hair down my back. Still awkward, but so familiar. It doesn't soothe me like it did when I was a kid, but it feels as close to normal as it's been since I discovered her role in everything.

"*Siamo grati a Carmine per averci invitato.*" We're grateful Carmine invited us.

I look back at my husband, and my heart nearly bursts. He walks over and greets my family. It's hardly effusive, but we're not standing on a polar ice cap either.

"We need to get you dressed."

Maria announces it as she steps forward with a garment bag. I recognize the name of the bridal shop. It's where I picked out a dress the day before we left. I planned to invite my parents to the church ceremony, but I didn't know if they would come. Juliana chilled out sooner than they did.

"Come on."

My sister takes my hand, and I glance back at Carmine again. His grin lights up his face. He looks like a little boy on Christmas. Juliana, Maria, Olivia, and I duck into the bathroom. They help me get into the gown and veil, so they never touch the floor. They even brought the shoes I picked out and a faux fur coat to go over the gown.

"How did you get it ready so fast?"

Maria waggles her eyebrows. "You have a fairy godmother."

"Let me guess. Her initials are MM."

"Maybe."

"Thank you for bringing Carmine to my bakery. And thanks for seating us together at Easter."

"I know we never hung out before you started dating Carmine, but I always asked Aunt Sylvia about you. I might have stalked you a little on social media. From what I could tell, once Carmine got his shit together, you seemed perfect for each other. You have similar interests and practically the same sense of humor. Aunt Sylvia agreed when I asked what she thought. I decided it was time to meddle, so I did."

"I'm glad you did. Thank you a million times over."

We head back outside, and I'm glad for the lined coat. As we walk to join everyone, I slip off my engagement ring and put it on my right ring finger. I hand the two bands to Juliana, who'll stand up with me as my matron of honor. Maria and Olivia will be my bridesmaids.

I spot Carmine and the guys who accompanied us. They've all changed into tuxes too. Carmine is standing next to a priest. Beside him is Gabriele as his best man. His cousins and Matteo are there as his groomsmen. The photos won't be balanced, but that's not a big deal to me like it is to some brides. My family, the people I love most in this world, are here. More than that, they're supporting us.

Mama stands with *Zia* Sylvia, *Zio* Salvatore, and the others. My dad's waiting for me. I stop in front of him while Juliana, Olivia, and Maria head toward the decorated archway. My dad reaches out his hands and speaks in Italian as I place mine in his.

"I know Mama and I hurt you. We know we didn't do any of this right. We won't make excuses, and I think you understand the explanation. I suspect you know Andrea-Diego followed you. We're still your parents, and we love you. We've wanted you safe and happy. We just went about it all wrong. A blind man can see you're happy. Carmine is perfect for you. We should have listened to you and trusted you like we always have. If we believed you had the sound mind to become *la madrina*, then we should have accepted that you were wise enough to marry the right man. I'm so sorry."

"Thank you, Papa. I appreciate it. I understand it all, but it still hurts. Never do anything like this again. I can't be that forgiving twice. Carmine is my husband. He'll come first, especially if we have kids one day. I want you and Mama to be part of our lives. Please don't ruin that."

"We won't. Mama and I want to add to the trust Carmine started."

"Oh?" I give nothing away that I knew Carmine's plan. My dad's gaze darts to where Carmine's growing anxious.

"He decided we should pay reparations. He started a college fund for your future children."

"Reparations? You paid him?"

That's one way to put it, considering Carmine *took* the money. My father just looks at me. He's already said way too much, but he knows I know the truth. I'm glad he believes Carmine's honest and open with me, though I fight not to smile when he makes it sound like he had any choice to begin with. I know if I asked my husband, he'd tell me the truth about how he did it. Maybe not what else he did, and I've gotten the sense it was something violent.

I nod. Papa offers me his arm, and I wrap mine around it. The rest of the world melts away as I approach my husband. I barely notice when my dad lets go and gives me a kiss on my cheek. My eyes are only for Carmine, and his gaze hasn't left mine since they locked while I walked down the aisle of sorts. We recite our vows, and despite being outside and nowhere near a church, the priest performs the full Mass. Tourists watch us, but I don't care. The women have hats and sunglasses on. The men have sunglasses too. My veil covers my face and hair. We're as incognito as a public wedding gets.

"Mr. Mancinelli, you may kiss your bride."

Those words are even better a second time. Carmine opens his arms to me, and I step forward. He moves my veil back, then lowers his lips to mine, but he pauses.

"You've always been mine. We just didn't know it. Now God and the law confirm it. There's nothing in this world I won't do for you, *piccolina*. I love you."

"I got so mad when you pushed me because I had a crush

on you when we were twelve. I thought you were hot when we were eighteen, and I thought maybe I could have been the one slipping off with you. I should have known then what I do now. Destiny has always meant for us to be together. I love you, Daddy."

Our lips fuse, and I know my husband is just the right combo of sinner and saint.

Preorder Mafia Beauty and have your copy on June 27th.

She's the one woman I can't have.

I shouldn't want her.

I shouldn't touch her.

I shouldn't make a move.

But she wants it too.

The moment she lets me know, there's no going back.

No one will keep us apart.
There'll be nothing left of anyone who tries.
We've watched each other for years, and now I will show her it's been worth the wait.
I'll give her pleasure beyond her wildest dreams until she can think of nothing but
us...
Nothing but me.

Preorder Mafia Beauty now

Thank you for reading Mafia Sinner

Sabine Barclay, a nom de plume also writing Historical Romance as Celeste Barclay, lives near the Southern California coast with her husband and sons. She loves her days at the beach soaking up way too much sun, a good Netflix binge, and a strong hot chai. Her heroines are independent women who can defend themselves but love their Alpha heroes who want nothing more than to protect their soulmates in her Mafia Romances. She's Gen Y/Oregon Trail and loves creating engrossing contemporary romances that will make your toes curl and your granny blush.

Subscribe to Sabine's bimonthly newsletter to receive exclusive insider perks.
Sabine's Freebie

www.sabinebarclay.com

Join the fun and get exclusive insider giveaways, sneak peeks, and new release announcements in
Sabine Barclay's Facebook Dubious Dames Group

Do you also enjoy steamy Historical Romance? Discover Sabine's books written as Celeste Barclay.

The Mancinelli Brotherhood

Mafia Heir **BOOK ONE SNEAK PEEK**

Luca

This asshole is pissing me off. We've been going around in circles for five minutes, and the longer we stand out here, the greater the likelihood someone will spot us. I have a sixth sense about these things. It's why I'm still alive at the ripe old age of thirty-one.

"Espinoza, enough already. Either sell to us or don't, but we set the price. Your tequila is good, but it isn't nectar from the gods."

I'm watching Carlos Espinoza, some lackey for the Mexican Culiacán Cartel, try to maneuver me into paying more than the agreed upon price. I know it's so he can skim off the top.

"It's as close as you're going to get. You've upped the order, so the price per case goes up."

My uncle, Salvatore Mancinelli, is the New York don. He negotiated this deal, and I warned him it was a bad idea. But what do I know as his underboss and heir? I'm not backing down.

"Haven't you ever heard of a bulk discount? The more I order the better the price should be. No one else around here is buying from you. You know we're your only choice in three out of five boroughs. You aren't going to the Bronx because you won't get more than pennies there. You aren't going to Queens because you don't want to run into the Colombians. You aren't going to Manhattan because then you face the bratva along with us. And what are you going to do in Staten Island? Sell to us anyway? We control Staten Island and Brooklyn when it comes to liquor stores, so take the money and go."

"Luca, there are plenty of liquor stores in Brooklyn that aren't owned by Italians. I'll go there."

We aren't friends. He's patronizing me by using my first name. Fuck him and the horse he rode in on. I have other solutions for this shit.

"And I'll just take what I want from them for free. That's not a half bad idea. The deal's over. Take your shit with the worm in it and go."

"Motherfucking racist. Not all tequila has a worm in it."

"You're selling Mezcal. It's known for the fucking worm. I wouldn't start calling me names, you *penche hijo de puta*." Fucking son of a bitch.

He has twenty-five crates of stolen tequila that he's trying to offload because he knows he can't sell it at his own liquor store.

"What did you call me?"

Carlos takes what he thinks is a menacing step forward, and his two bodyguards do the same. Not smart. Neither of my two bodyguards nor I react, but the three men in each of my cars open their doors. They won't do more than that. It's just a reminder that the Culiacán can try, but the *Cosa Nostra* still run New York City.

"This is the third and final time I say this. Sell or leave."

Every head turns toward the liquor store's back door as it opens. A gorgeous blonde steps out, and I wish I had the time to appreciate her beauty, but she's about to die. Carlos and his men draw their guns and pivot toward her. My men pull their weapons too, but we keep them pointed at the Mexicans. The woman stands like a deer in the headlights for a second before ducking behind the industrial garbage dumpster like a frightened rabbit. Three shots hit the metal almost at the same moment. That's all it takes for my men and me. The two bodyguards standing with me aim for a guard each, and I set my sights on Carlos. We squeeze our triggers, and the men fall.

Screeching tires tell me Carlos's driver takes off. I hear more gunshots as at least one soldier in my cars tries to shoot the escaping vehicle. Glass shatters, but the sedan keeps going. I hear more tires squeal as one of my SUVs takes off and chases the guy. I holster my gun and wave my men to do the same.

I inch forward toward the trash can, but I see the shadow shift. The woman bolts from the other side. She's still the frightened rabbit, but I'm the fox pursuing her. She's fast, I'll give her that. But she has to be at least a foot shorter than me. My legs are a lot longer and cover a lot more ground with each stride.

She weaves among the cars, most likely believing it's harder to hit a moving object. She isn't wrong, but I have no intention of shooting her. I push myself harder and pounce as she darts out and tries to cross the last stretch of parking lot to reach a better lit area near a bus stop. I lunge.

"Stop running, *piccolina*. I won't hurt you."

I wrap my arms around her and pull her back against my chest, but I'm quick to spin her around and put space between us as I grasp her arms. Of course, she fights me.

"If I wanted you dead, I would have shot at you, too."

"It doesn't mean you won't kill me after."

She's breathless as she continues to struggle. I almost let go to take a step back, insulted at what she implied. But I can't blame her. If I were a woman, I'd be terrified of the same thing.

"I'm not going to rape you. I'm going to talk to you."

"Talk? You are not a man who talks if you just killed a guy."

"To keep him and his men from killing you. I told you, if I wanted you dead, I would have shot at you too. And I wouldn't have missed."

She stops struggling against me, but her eyes continue to dart from one place to another, trying to find somewhere to flee. I know I can keep her in place with only one hand, so I release her left arm. I still have a firm hold on her right one, but I haven't held it nearly as tightly as I could.

"I'm Luca. I know you figured out you interrupted something you shouldn't have. Did that man know who you are?"

"Yes."

"What about his driver? Would he know you?"

"Yes."

"Do you have a name?"

"Yes."

"*Piccolina*, we won't get very far if yes is all you can say. Are you willing to answer me with more than one word?"

"No."

I knew that was coming, and I grin. I can't help it. I wasn't wrong about her being gorgeous, but I doubt she wants to know that's what I think. At least, not if I want her to know I won't assault her.

"Fine. I have more than twenty questions I can ask that you can answer with one word. Do you work at the store?"

"Sometimes."

Ah, an improvement.

"Did Carlos know you were still working?"

"No."

"Do you have a car, or do you take the subway or bus?"

She raises her chin and remains silent. Smart but counterproductive.

"The subway or the bus will get you killed. You're too easy to find and follow. Do you have a car?"

"Yes."

"Can you stay with someone instead of going home?"

She refuses to answer.

"If that man knew you and you sometimes work in the store, then he knew where you live. If he found that out, so will someone in his cartel."

"I know. Let me go. The longer I stand here, the more likely someone is to come back for me."

"No one will touch you while I'm here."

"Arrogant. If he shot at me, he would have shot at you."

"And he would have died, anyway. What's your name?"

"Jane."

"Look, I know you won't get in one of my cars and let me drive you somewhere. In most cases, I would say that's a smart move. But you did nothing wrong tonight except for leave work at the wrong time. I know that, and you know that. But the Culiacán won't see it that way, *piccolina*."

She freezes for no more than five seconds before she trembles so much that I can see it. I don't know what drives me next, but it's the same instinct that's made me call her little girl three times. I pull her to my chest and tuck her head against it. I stroke her hair down to her shoulders, rubbing my hand up and down her back. This is the most inopportune moment to notice she isn't wearing a bra. I will my body not to react.

"What does that mean?"

Her voice is barely more than a whisper, but I know what she's asking.

"It means little girl."

"I should be insulted, but the way you say it..."

"It has nothing to do with your height. I know you're not a child."

God, do I know she's not. She feels amazing. Her tits are soft as they press against me, and I can see she has the most delectable ass. I'd love nothing more than to cup it and squeeze until she goes up on her toes and begs for me to wrap her legs around my waist and fuck her. For fuck's sake. Stop, you disgusting asshole. That is not what you need to be thinking about.

"Why didn't you shoot me? Whatever you were talking about, if it was with a Cartel member, then it wasn't completely legal. Carlos didn't want me alive to talk about seeing you together. Why are you letting me live?"

"I told you. You did nothing wrong but try to leave work. He should have checked the building before starting the meeting. That was on him. The only thing I take issue with is you leaving by yourself and walking into a dimly lit parking lot. I suspect you do that often, and that's too dangerous. Jane Doe, I don't hurt women."

Mafia Sinner

Mafia Beauty (6.27.23)

Mafia Angel (8.22.23)

Mafia Redeemer (10.17.23)

Mafia Star (12.12.23)

The Ivankov Brotherhood

Bratva Darling

BOOK ONE SNEAK PEEK

LAURA

As I sit across from the four Kutsenko brothers, I press my lips together to keep from drooling. No four men should be so strikingly handsome. Not all from the same family, anyway. I fight a valiant battle against letting my gaze drift toward the eldest, Maksim, whose ice-blue eyes bore into me. After years of negotiating billion-dollar investment contracts while facing countless ruthless businessmen, I've learned to keep my expression studiously blank. But it's a true struggle today. Instead, I focus my attention on the squirrelly lawyer sitting across the conference table. While he's disingenuous with each comment, he's a good negotiator. But I'm better. How cliché am I?

While I feel Maksim watching me, I focus on Dmitry Yakovitch as he continues to argue the merits of the venture capitalist company I represent, RK Capital Group, merging with Kutsenko Partners. What he means is the merits of Kutsenko Partners acquiring RK Capital Group, then stripping it and making it another money-laundering shell corporation. While most people in New York have little awareness of the Russian mafia, I do. The Kutsenko brothers' names appear on no titles or deeds anywhere in New York City, but it wasn't difficult to determine which shell companies likely belong to them. Their assumption that I'm unfamiliar with them is proving beneficial to me as they continue to whisper amongst themselves in Russian. I think they may even believe they're convincing me that they don't speak much English.

The senior partners of RK Capital Group know who I'm negotiating with, though they may not know I'm aware of these Russians' more nefarious operations. They've given me the go-ahead to agree to a merger with an eventual acquisition, but only for the right price. A price to the tune of twenty billion dollars. Considering an investment firm like Goldman Sachs is worth nearly one-hundred-and-twenty billion dollars, my clients' asking price appears reasonable.

"Mr. Yakovitch, I shall stop you now." I raise my left hand, pen caught between my index and middle fingers. When I have his attention, I lean back in my chair and casually twirl the pen over my index finger and thumb. "Fifty billion is my clients' asking price. You know that. Your clients know that. RK doesn't oppose the merger. What they oppose is the insulting offer you've made. It's nearly noon, and I'm hungry, Mr. Yakovitch. I have a delicious ham sandwich waiting for me. I even have three chocolate chip cookies waiting for me. If we aren't going to make any progress, I shall let you go, so I can move onto my eagerly anticipated lunch."

I cant my head just enough for me to appear as though my gaze rests solely on the opposing attorney's face, but I can see each Kutsenko brothers' reaction. My face battles yet again against showing my emotions as I fight not to smirk. Their muted but surprised expressions confirm what I already know.

"Please tell your clients to make a reasonable counteroffer, or I will conclude this meeting and enjoy my ham sandwich and cookies."

Dmitry glares at me before turning to Maksim and his three brothers. In rapid Russian, he doesn't interpret my suggestion. Oh no. There's no need for that. I can't catch every word because his voice is too low. But I catch something along the lines of "The bitch refuses to budge. What now? A fucking ham sandwich. More like a stick up her ass."

Maksim swivels his chair to look at his brothers. In Russian, he says, "Fifty billion is ridiculous. She's not so stupid or naïve not to know that. My guess is they'll settle for twenty billion. We offer fifteen."

"That's barely better than what we already offered," Aleksei, the second-oldest brother, argues. "She'll be eating the fucking sandwich and dipping her cookies in milk before we walk out the door. We need the buildings."

"We offer twenty, Maks," Bogdan, the youngest, insists.

As I watch the brothers discuss, their voices barely lowered, I pull my lunch sack from the black leather satchel by my feet and set it beside my laptop. It's a ridiculously pink floral bag with an embroidered monogram, the L and D overlapping. It's an empty prop, but they don't know that. I watch as five sets of eyes narrow. I offer a smile that would appear innocent in any setting other than this meeting. It's patronizing, and I know it.

Bratva Sweetheart

Bratva Treasure

Bratva Beauty

Bratva Angel

Bratva Jewel